The
Stephen Kendall
Mysteries

by

Chris Randall

Short stories
set in the police station
in the fictional village of
Ricton

Contents

Story One – The Longbow Murders
Part One

Detective Inspector Stephen Kendall did not always work in the country village of Ricton, even though he lived there. A high-profile case in the small Berkshire village now engaged his attention. But we will get to that later.

Steve, and his partner, Susan had first lived in London for convenience. They preferred the slower pace of the countryside over the hustle and bustle of the city. Susan suggested they move to Ricton after a short holiday with Steve's long-time friends, Debbie and Mike.

With Steve's long and unpredictable working hours, and Susan's time away, living in the country and commuting to work made sense. So, they decided to relocate and were now happy living near Ricton. Steve spent most of his time in London, travelling back to Ricton when his schedule permitted. Susan, a representative for a fashion house, usually stayed home, her work taking her away when necessary. On the whole, it worked out well.

That Sunday morning, while Mike was on duty, Steve, Susan, and Debbie were out walking along the James Farm track. Debbie's two children, Timmy and Lori, ran ahead along the path bordered on one side by woodlands, and the other, by cornfields.

The adults were casually chatting as you do when out walking, while Timmy and Lori ran off along the farm track, sometimes disappearing into the woods, or hiding in the cornfield. Debbie wasn't bothered. Giggling and shouting in the distance told her the kids were having great fun, as they always did. Suddenly, all three stopped to listen for the children's voices that had been silent for too long. When laughter and shouting started up again, the two tiny visions of enjoyment came running along the path.

Getting back his breath, Timmy said, "Uncle Steve?"

Of course, Steve wasn't his uncle. Just in the time-long tradition of old friends, the children regarded him as such. Steve was chatting with Debbie, so he didn't immediately answer.

"Uncle Steve?" Timmy persisted, tugging at Steve's trousers.

"Yes, Timmy, what is it?" he replied.

"You know when you was round at our house, and my grandad was there?"

"Yes, I remember that," said Steve.

"Well," Timmy continued, "you know he said when he was a boy, they played cowboys and Indians."

"Yes, that's right, he did say that. And it's true. My dad did the same."

"Well, Uncle Steve," said Timmy, looking agitated and shuffling his feet, "when they grew up, did they still play cowboys and Indians?" he asked.

"I don't think so, Timmy," Steve replied. "I used to play marbles when I was your age, but I don't play it anymore." Steve looked at the two women. "That's probably because I don't have any marbles," he laughed. "I might still play with them if I did."

The girls laughed.

"I'll buy you some for your birthday," Susan offered, "but you will have to forget the new laptop."

They all chuckled together, except Timmy and Lori.

"So, young Timmy," said Steve, "why are you asking?"

6

"There's a man in the cornfield, and I think he's been playing cowboys and Indians," said Timmy.

"Yes," Lori agreed. She was a couple of years younger than Timmy, only just turned five. "We're sure that's what he's bin doing."

"Really," said Debbie, "and what makes you so sure?"

Lori didn't answer. "You tell her, Timmy," she said to her brother.

Timmy said nothing.

"Come on, Timmy," Steve urged. "Don't keep us in suspense. Why do you think he's been playing cowboys and Indians?"

Timmy looked at the ground. "He's got an arrow in him," he said quietly.

There was a deathly silence. After a while, Steve said, "Look, you girls stay here with the kids. I'll take a look."

They nodded in agreement as Steve set off along the track where the kids had been playing. After a distance, he came across an area of trampled corn. Someone had been in there. Of course, the children, he had seen them in the distance doing just that. He stepped off the track into the corn and followed the newly trampled path. It only extended a few yards before turning right and ending abruptly where the body of a man lay. He was lying on his front. Projecting from his back was a professional arrow with a green and yellow flight. The man was dead.

* * *

Steve bent down to confirm the man wasn't breathing. There was little chance of that as rigor mortis had already set in. He guessed he'd been dead for at least twenty-four hours. He took out his mobile phone and rang Mike.

7

"Hi, Steve, how is the walk? Get as much of that country air as you can before you return to the big smoke."

"Yeah, will do," said Steve, "but there's something a bit more pressing to deal with at the moment."

"Are the children alright?"

"Yeah, they're having a great time. Look, I'll get to the point. You need to get out here immediately. There's a dead body in the cornfield along the James Farm track, and I would say it's a murder."

"Bloody hell, you bringing your London work back here with you now?"

"Well, he don't look like a Londoner, so I guess he is one of yours," Steve quipped.

"OK, Steve, I'll have to organise a few things first. Can you hold the fort until I get there?"

Mike Compton was not a detective, just a sergeant, but with cutbacks of police budgets, he was the only police presence in Ricton and the surrounding area. When a major crime occurred, it was necessary to bring in aid from another area.

"Sure. What do you propose? This crime is out of my jurisdiction, but I'm here if you need my help." Steve offered.

"If you could just keep people away, I have to get an ambulance out there. Also, a forensic doctor. We'll need a constable on duty there permanently until we've checked and cleared everything, and I don't have anyone here to do that." Mike explained.

"Right," said Steve. "Bring out a crime scene canopy. Do you have one? We don't want people gathering here for an exhibition."

"I have one, and I'll put it in the car now."

"OK. I need to go back to the girls and tell them to make their way home. They're only a hundred yards down the track. See you later."

Steve went back to the women.

"Look," he said in a whisper, out of earshot of the kids, "I'll talk to you later, but for now, it's better that you go home. There's a crime scene along the track. Mike and others will be here shortly, so it's going to get a little busy."

"What is it?" asked Debbie.

"I'll explain later. Not here in front of the kids."

"Yes, of course," said Debbie. Collecting the kids, she said goodbye, and they all walked off. Steve returned to the crime scene.

Out of 'force of habit' from dealing with crimes, Steve had a pair of gloves in his pocket. He bent down beside the body and lifted one side a fraction. It was enough to expose a second arrow that had entered the front. The man had fallen on the arrow, and it had snapped off. The fall would have pushed the shaft deeper into him. It looked like he had bled out. He let the body drop back and waited for someone to arrive.

Once Mike arrived with the canopy, they could cover the scene and put a barrier around the area. Damn, he thought, he should have reminded Mike to bring stakes and crime scene tape with him. This would be a little out of Mike's experience. On the other hand, such incidents were common to Steve, not always deaths, but many disastrous accidents and incidents with knives.

Mike arrived first. He drove his car along the uneven track, then pulled over where there was a clearing in the woodlands.

"OK, Steve, what have we got?" he said as he stepped into the cornfield.

"One very dead casualty of Custer's Last Stand," said Steve.

"Yeah," said Mike looking at the protruding arrow, "not the usual method of killing someone these days. I wonder why they used a bow and arrow?"

"It might have been a crossbow," said Steve.

"No, I don't think so," Mike disagreed. "This kind of arrow requires a longbow."

"Yeah," said Steve, "I think you're right. It's a pretty long arrow."

"It's a bit of a conspicuous weapon to carry about," said Mike. "I'll put some feelers out and see if anyone around here has seen someone with a longbow in the area."

"Good idea, Mike. You could get lucky and tie this one up quickly."

"I won't hold my breath," said Mike. "I have a feeling this one's going to be difficult, and I'm the only guy here at the moment."

"They'll send someone to help you, of course. You'll need an inspector in charge of this."

"Well, I've got one here now, haven't I?" said Mike. "Would you be up for taking this on?"

"Of course, but we'll have to get it approved by the Met."

"Look, I've got to call this in, anyway. I'll have a word to see if we can't get things moving. It would certainly save a lot of time, and it was you who discovered the body, so that's a plus too."

Steve didn't mention that it was the children who discovered it first.

Mike rang his superior, about eighty miles away in another town. They contacted the Met, and after some discussion, confirmed that Steve could take over the investigation. Then, he went to his car and brought back a canopy. The two of them started to erect it.

"Now, where's that bloody doctor?" said Mike, his eyes searching down the track for any vehicles.

As if on cue, an ambulance entered the track and drew slowly towards them. When it came alongside, two men with a stretcher got out. Behind the ambulance, a private car drew up, and a middle-aged guy got out carrying a doctor's bag.

"You'll have to wait with that stretcher," Steve said. "The doctor will need to examine after the sergeant has taken photographs."

"Hello, doctor, this is Detective Inspector Stephen Kendall," Mike greeted him. "Sorry to get you out on a Sunday morning, but we have an unusual situation here. Come look."

"Hmm, this will be a first, Mike," said the doctor. "I've never seen anyone killed with a bow and arrow before. It used to be pretty common five hundred years ago."

He ducked inside the canopy. After Mike had photographed the scene, he got on his knees beside the body, and lifted the corpse slowly, just as Steve had done. Then he rolled it over so that the man was on his back. The first arrow had penetrated the man's chest.

"I think he was still alive when the arrow in his back hit him," said the doctor. "Looks like the other arrow penetrated his heart when he fell onto his front. He would have died very quickly after he fell." He paused. "Damned long arrows, aren't they," he said.

"Mike says it's a longbow," said Steve. "I don't know much about them."

"No, neither do I," the doctor confirmed. "Rigor has set in, and by the look of the blood pool, I'd say he had been here a while. Maybe since Friday evening."

Steve stooped down and searched through the man's pockets. He found a wallet and took out a credit card.

"Bag this," he said to Mike, handing him the card. "Looks like his name is Walter Robson. Good Northern name that, Robson. It wouldn't surprise me to find he's from op north. Get it checked out."

"Will do," said Mike and at once phoned through the details.

"I don't think we are going to uncover any evidence here," said Steve. "It doesn't look as though the culprit came onto the crime scene. Probably just shot him from a distance and cleared off."

"I think you're right," Mike agreed. "Longbows have quite a range. Olympic target distances are seventy metres."

"How do you know this stuff?" asked Steve.

"They have archery competitions about twenty miles from here. I've been to a few of them. Just as a spectator, that is." Mike explained.

"I'll take your word for it and cross you off my list of suspects," Steve joked.

The doctor got up from the body.

"I don't think there's anything more I can do here," he said. "We'll get this body taken back to the morgue, and I'll make out my report for you." He called the paramedics over who put the body on their stretcher and took it to the ambulance.

"Well," said Mike, "I'll get some tape put up around the area. Want to give me a hand, Steve?"

They took the metal poles out of Mike's car, set them up, and taped off the area.

"Look, Mike, if you want to get off and see Debbie and the kids, I'll hang on here until your constable arrives. Is that OK?"

"Oh, thanks, Steve," said Mike gratefully. "I'll keep in touch. I'll also contact James, the farmer, and let him know what is going on here. It's his land, after all."

The Longbow Murders
Part Two

When Mike arrived back home, Susan and Debbie sat in the kitchen chatting over a cup of coffee. The kids were playing in the yard out back.

"Hi, Mike, can I get you a cup of coffee," Susan asked. "Where's Steve?"

"He's staying behind until support arrives from another branch."

"OK. So, what's going on?" asked Debbie.

"There's been a murder in the cornfield. A guy, shot with two arrows."

"My God, that's the man the kids saw. Don't tell them he's dead. They thought he'd been playing cowboys and Indians."

"Some game," Mike replied. "Anyway, it's arranged that Steve will stay on and take over the case."

"Oh, no," said Susan, "not Steve. He's so damned good."

"Well, that's what we want, isn't it?" said Mike, a little confused by Susan's reaction.

"That's what I mean," said Susan hesitantly. "He will clear up the case too soon and have to return to London."

"Oh, I see," said Mike, but he was still a little puzzled.

"How long has the guy been dead?" Debbie wanted to know.

"Probably a couple of days," Susan replied.

"What makes you say that?" asked Mike.

"I don't know. If it had been longer, surely someone would have discovered the body before now." Susan replied.

"Well, let's leave it for now," said Mike. "We don't usually talk shop at home. Especially crimes of this nature."

He remained puzzled by Susan's reaction and comments though, but then he didn't know her as well as he knew Steve. That must be the way she is, he thought, and promptly forgot about it.

Steve had met Susan in London, and they had got on well right from the start. Within a month, they moved in together. Susan was a beautiful, charismatic woman with a considerable talent for selling a fashion range. They sent her everywhere, Japan, Italy, the USA; there were few places she hadn't visited. They left her entirely to her own devices, and she always produced results. That is, except when she suffered one of her occasional bouts of depression. She never took any medication or even visited a doctor and usually she'd get over it within a couple of days. Apparently, Steve had no idea what brought on these short bouts, and Susan never spoke to him about it. Right now, though, she was very upbeat, probably down to the fact they had moved to Ricton.

At that moment, the phone interrupted Mike's thoughts. It was Steve.

"Two constables have arrived. As soon as I've settled them in, I'd like to return home. Any chance you might pick me up? I've no transport here."

"Sure. See you soon."

* * *

The two constables got out of the police car and introduced themselves to Steve. He'd been getting bored, so seeing them lifted his flagging spirits. A few people had stopped by to investigate, and Steve had moved them on without explanation. James, the farmer, had driven up in his tractor and left again. Another

15

person he'd seen was Shirley Kane, a journalist for the local rag. Her disappointment showed when Steve gave her almost nothing to report.

"Don't you think that the local people have a right to know what is going on in their area?" she asked. "What am I going to tell them?"

"Look, Miss Kane," said Steve, who was quite accustomed to dealing with journalists, "this is a police investigation. At this moment, the more information that gets out there, the more it is likely to harm our efforts to get to the truth."

"OK," said Shirly, "but isn't there anything you can tell me? This bloody tent isn't exactly invisible. You can see it from the main road a couple of miles away."

"Of course, you're right. All I can say is this, the death of a man found here this morning, looks suspicious. We don't know yet where he is from but are working on it. As soon as we have some positive information to report, we will have a press meeting to advise you. How about that?"

"What's your name? I've never seen you before."

"No," said Steve. "I live locally but work for the London Met. They've asked me to head up the investigation because I happened to be here. Right place, right time."

"That's convenient. And your name is… for my report?"

"Detective Inspector Stephen Kendall. I shall remain on this case until solved. It might look like a mystery now, but that is what I do, solve mysteries."

She seemed happy enough and went away to write up her column. Naturally, she would write about three times as much as Steve had told her. But right now, the two constables were introducing themselves. They were

16

Johnny and Keith, and neither of them looked very happy with an assignment to watch a crime scene in the middle of a cornfield.

"We don't know much about this," said Keith, "except there's some guy's been shot with a bow and arrow. That's it."

"You know almost as much as I do then," Steve replied. "It's early days. He was only discovered a few hours ago."

"Getting to be a habit, this is," said Johnny.

"What sort of habit?" Steve asked.

"We were on a stakeout only two or three weeks ago," Keith explained.

"Oh, I see," said Steve. "You two are the stakeout experts. Looks like I got lucky then."

"You might have, sir, but we didn't," said Johnny. "Who'd have thought there would be two similar cases in just a few weeks?"

"You're lucky down here," said Steve, "I get them every damned week."

"I don't believe it," said Keith. "Every week?"

"Of course," Steve wondered what planet Keith was on. "I work for the London Met. This is run-of-the-mill."

"What, people shot with arrows?" said Keith.

"No," said Steve with irritation. "Is your partner having a brainstorm?" he asked Johnny.

"I think you got it wrong, sir," Johnny responded. "The stakeout three weeks ago was just the same. The guy had an arrow in him."

"What!" Steve exclaimed. "Say that again."

"The guy three weeks ago. Killed with a bow and arrow. That's unusual, isn't it?"

"No, Constable, it isn't unusual. It's bloody-well unheard of. How is it I am only just hearing about this?"

"I wouldn't know, sir," said Johnny. "I'm just a common stakeout expert."

"Huh," Steve grunted. "Well, thanks for that information. I'll have to investigate it. Do you have a number for the detective in charge of the case?"

"I think so." Johnny took out his phone and wrote a number down for Steve. "His name is Warren Dennis. You can get him at this number."

"Thanks, Constable."

Steve looked up. Mike's car was making its way along the track toward them. He pulled into the clearing, turned the car around, and Steve hopped in and they rode off. He related to Mike what he had just learned. Mike couldn't believe that the Willington police hadn't mentioned the similarities. He'd give them hell when he got back to the station.

* * *

Steve entered the station with Mike and rang Warren Dennis before going into the house.

"Hi, Detective Dennis here," came the response.

"Hello, Warren, I'm Detective Inspector Stephen Kendall at Ricton. I'm working on a new case where the victim died by two arrows, one through the heart. I understand you had a case like that a few weeks ago."

"Well, that's odd, isn't it?" said Dennis. "Yes, I'm still working on it. No way this is a coincidence."

"No," Steve agreed. "I think we need to meet and work some things out together, don't you?"

"Yes, do you want me to come over there or will you come here?" Dennis enquired.

"I've barely begun on this case, so I have a lot to do in the next twenty-four hours. I guess it would help

18

me if you were to come over, unless you have some evidence that I ought to see."

"No, I'll come over. Shall we say tomorrow morning at about ten."

"Yes, that'll be fine. See you here tomorrow." Steve rang off. "Right, Mike, what have you got on the victim, Robson?"

"I've got an address. He lives in a village called North Stainley, just off the M1 near Thirsk."

"Ah, I thought he'd be from op-north," said Steve. "Have you contacted the local force yet?"

"Yes, done that. They're sending someone to check out the address and speak to the neighbours," said Mike. "They'll get back to me when they have something."

"Good. Well done," Steve said, pleased that his right-hand man was on the ball. "And what about the credit card? Do we know where he's used it in the past few days?"

"He used it in the village store buying a newspaper, and he also used it to buy a bus ticket to Willington. That's Dennis's village where the other murder was."

"Right, my guess is he knew the other guy. He either didn't know he's dead, or he had heard about it and went to check it out."

"Yeah," Mike agreed. "You'll probably get some info on that tomorrow."

"We don't know yet where he was staying, then?" said Steve

"Not yet."

"OK," said Steve. "There's not much more we can do today. Let's go and get some dinner. I'm starving."

Mike laughed. "You probably are if you haven't eaten today. Debbie's got a good meal prepared. Let's go eat."

Story One – The Longbow Murders
Part Three

The following day, Steve breakfasted with Susan at their home.

"You're looking upbeat this past couple of weeks," said Steve. "I guess moving to the country has been good for you."

"It's helped, that's for sure," Susan replied.

"Helped with what?"

"A few weeks ago, I made a decision, and since then, things have started looking up, and now; I'm feeling energised."

That's great," said Steve. "What decision did you make? Did it have to do with me?"

"No," said Susan.

Steve waited, wanting to know more, but nothing came. "Well, are you going to tell me what it is?" he asked.

"No," Susan replied.

"I see," said Steve, "Well, actually, I don't."

Susan said nothing.

"You may feel upbeat, Susan, but I'm curious about this. I guess you like to give me puzzles to solve."

"That's what you are good at, solving problems. I'll leave it with you," she smiled and kissed him on the cheek. "You have a busy day today, I imagine."

"That's right," he said, "and I could do without you adding further mysteries to my day. Maybe we'll chat about it tonight."

"Hmm, and maybe we won't."

Steve didn't push her any further. She will tell me when she's ready, he thought. Right now, he had to get to the station and meet with Warren Dennis. He hoped that between the two of them, they might shed some light on the unknown archer. He also hoped there might be some new information from Yorkshire. Who was this guy Robson, and what was he doing down here in Berkshire?

* * *

"Morning, Mike," Steve greeted as he walked into the station office. "What's new?"

"Yorkshire police got back to us earlier on. Nothing apart from that," said Mike.

"What did they say?"

"Seems as though Robson lives on his own. He's got a brother who moved to America with a friend about six months ago. Not a lot more they could tell us at this stage, though."

"That's a pity," said Steve. "It probably means I'll have to go up there myself. It's the only way to get useful information."

"I guess so," Mike agreed. "Maybe your meeting with Dennis might render some results. He should be here soon."

"I hope so. Have you made any progress with the arrows we brought back?

"Like what," Mike asked.

"A check for fingerprints would be a good start," said Steve.

"Oh, yes, I got them away at once. No, no prints on them, so that's a dead end. I'm also looking into the manufacturers."

"When Dennis gets here, we might go out to the crime scene. I need to check around a bit more. The constables need a break too."

"I'll pick up some grub for them," said Mike. "They probably brought some with them, but a hot burger would likely be well received after a night out there."

"Yeah. A cooked breakfast would be more welcome. Is there a place in the village we might get one?"

"There's the hotel down the road. I need to check that place out anyway. Just in case Robson had been staying there."

"Good thinking," Steve agreed. "He had to stay somewhere. I just wish we had more people on the ground here."

"How long are you going to need the constables at the crime scene?"

"If we check out the area this morning, we can pull them off and bring them back here to help," said Steve.

"Yeah, OK."

A car pulled up outside. Detective Inspector Warren Dennis had arrived. He entered the office.

"Good morning, Mike," he greeted.

"Hello, Warren. This is Detective Inspector Stephen Kendall. He's overseeing the investigation."

"Hi, Stephen, pleased to meet you. Weird business this one."

"Yes, it is," said Steve offering his hand. "Please, call me Steve." After a pause, he added, "Don't get too settled; we'll be going out in a moment."

"Yeah," said Mike. "There's a couple of things we have to do, and then we'll be off to the crime scene."

"What can you tell me about your victim? Does he have a name?" asked Steve.

"Yes, it's Ricky Armstrong," said Warren.

"Another northern name," said Steve.

23

"You're right. Comes from Ripon in North Yorkshire."

"That's quite near to Stainley," said Steve. "That's where our guy, Robson is from. Only a few miles from Ripon, so these two probably knew each other."

"Armstrong, was a bit of a loner - moved down here a couple of years ago. Did odd jobs in the area, carpentry, gardening, and the like."

"So, it's likely that Robson, was visiting the area to see him," said Steve. "At least we now know for sure we can connect these two murders. Now we must bring them together with a common motive. We might get somewhere then. What else you can tell us, Warren?"

"Not a lot. The arrow had no prints. Bloody good shot - he was in his garden when the arrow pierced him, and we believe the killer was about seventy-five meters away. Got him in the chest with one shot. Didn't even come near him to leave any evidence."

"Yeah," said Steve. "Most murderers leave something. So far, we've got little from this one."

"Not exactly," said Warren.

"Why? What have you got?" Steve, eagerly asked.

"Well, we haven't got anything, except this," said Warren. "For someone to be as good an archer as this killer, they would have to practice somewhere, and that means archery clubs."

"Very good," said Steve. "That's a start. But I'm sure there's a lot of work to do before we get anywhere with that. Anyway, let's get off, shall we, Mike? Whose car are we taking?"

"I'll follow you two in mine. I'll probably need to get away after we've been to the crime scene," said Warren.

They set off with the first stop at the hotel. Mike asked if they could put two breakfasts together for the constables, in a container for travelling to the site. Then he asked about Robson.

The manager looked at the register.

"Yes, officer, he was staying here, but he checked out on Friday. If I remember right, he asked the directions to James Farm before he left."

"Did he have transport," asked Steve.

"No. I thought it strange at the time because he was going on foot. It's quite a walk to the farm. It's not far to the track, but it's one hell of a long way to the farm."

"OK, thanks. That was helpful. Just one other thing, before he asked for directions, did he get a phone call?"

"Yes, on his mobile."

Steve nodded. They picked up the breakfasts and left.

"What was that about?" asked Mike.

"It seemed to me as though the killer lured him to the place he killed him. Pity we don't have his mobile. We didn't find one at the crime scene," said Steve.

"There's another thing we didn't find," said Mike. "He didn't have any luggage. If he went there straight after leaving the hotel, he must have had some bags."

"You're right, Mike. I didn't think of that. We will have to broaden the search. I'll get the constables onto it."

* * *

They arrived at the crime scene, and Mike gave a delighted Keith and Johnny their breakfast. Steve explained to Warren what they'd been discussing in the car.

"Interesting," said Warren. "How about this. The killer shot the first arrow, which struck the victim's back but didn't kill him. He dropped or threw his luggage so as not to slow him down, and then ran. He turned around to see where the killer was and got hit by the second arrow in the chest."

"Well, that's speculation, but it sounds possible. At least we're getting a different picture now, and it changes the whole scene. Up to now, we thought we could limit the crime scene to the small area where we found the body. We've got to look further afield."

Steve brought the constables up to date with the latest thinking, and after they had finished eating, the group spread out down the track, searching on both sides. About two hundred metres down the path, Johnny spotted a depression in the cornfield about three or four metres in. Steve joined him, and they made their way carefully to the spot. Bingo. It was a small bag on wheels.

"Pity he hadn't used a rucksack on his back," said Mike as he joined them. "It might have saved his life."

Steve retrieved the bag and opened it. There was little of any interest in it apart from odds and ends of clothing, a local map, a pack of playing cards, and an envelope. Steve opened it. The photographs were not family snaps or similar. But they were puzzling - the photographer had taken four of them in a field. A crowd of several hundred spectators stood watching an archery competition. Another photo showed the competitors - all children of about ten to twelve years old.

"Well, I'm damned," said Warren, "You couldn't make this up. It appears the victim has an interest in archery."

"Bet he was sorry he took an interest when that arrow hit him," said Keith. Steve just scowled at him, and he shut up before he could add to his dark humour.

26

"OK," said Steve, "I could be wrong, but I doubt whether we will find much else along here. But keep looking. Do a thorough job now we've started."

They continued along the track until they reached the tented crime scene, looking both in the cornfield and the woodlands on the right. They found nothing further until Warren called out. He was quite near the crime scene and had found an item just on the edge of the track where the ploughed earth dropped to the level of the cornfield. Steve and Mike joined him. Lodged against the side of the track, and the cornfield, was a mobile phone. They hadn't spotted it earlier because its colour blended with the earth.

Steve gently retrieved it with his handkerchief. He turned it on and checked the incoming calls. The last call was on Friday at two thirty-four, the number withheld. Oddly, there was an outgoing call at four fifty-two.

"That's odd," said Steve. "He got the call at the hotel and was killed two hours and twenty minutes later. Where was he for two hours? The walk from the hotel would only have taken about twenty minutes."

"We have to rethink this," said Warren. "There's something we are missing here."

"You're right," Steve agreed. "If you guys don't mind, I'd like to check. Can we all retrace our steps back down the track but concentrate only in the woodlands. We'll spread out about ten yards apart and go through the woods parallel to the track."

"Yes," said Warren, "I think that's a good idea. I think I know what's on your mind."

"OK, let's spread out."

The group organised themselves and moved slowly down through the woods. No one knew what exactly they wanted to find as they searched. They had covered about three hundred metres before Johnny called out. "Got something here."

"Stay at your positions," Steve instructed the others. "I'll see what he's got."

When Steve approached, the sight he saw left him speechless.

"OK, guys, This is it." But nothing could have prepared them for what they saw.

Johnny stood beside a huge tree, an oak, into which were about a dozen arrows. They were well embedded and almost impossible to extract. But it wasn't just the arrows that made the scene diabolical. It was the pattern the arrows had made. They followed the outline of a human form - like the knives thrown in a circus by a professional knife thrower.

"This accounts for the lost time," said Steve. "The killer scared the shit out of his victim by using him as target practice."

"Yet there were no other arrow marks on the body apart from those in his back and chest," said Mike. "I guess after scaring the bejesus out of the poor bugger; the killer let him go and then fired as he ran away."

"This killer is a marksman," said Steve, stating the obvious. "He could go on stage with an act like this."

"Maybe he does," said Warren. "That's another avenue of inquiry we will have to consider."

"Yes, you're right. You could do that from your station. We don't have the resources here to cover every inquiry."

"OK," Warren agreed, "leave that with me, and I'll get some people onto it."

"Let's take a good look around this location before we finish," said Steve. "We need to be thorough, so mark e everything that looks suspicious or of interest."

They spread out around the tree, thoroughly searched for half an hour, but found nothing further.

"This guy is very diligent," Warren commented. "It looks like he might even have cleaned up the area. There are no footprints, and absolutely nothing here."

"Yes," Steve agreed. "I don't think we'll get anything else from here, so we'll call time on it. I'll take some pictures, and Johnny, Keith, can you extract those arrows from the tree. Try not to break them, and only handle them near the head so as not to obliterate any fingerprints we might find.

"This is certainly an odd case," said Warren. "Definitely the strangest case I've ever been on."

"It's odd, alright," said Steve. "Let's call it a day here. Johnny, can you and your buddy get that tent dismantled."

"Will do."

Mike, look at the phone number he was calling. See if you recognise it as local."

"Sure thing," said Mike, then after looking at the number. "Yeah, I would say it is local. It's the number of the police station."

The Longbow Murders
Part Four

The following morning, while Steve put a couple of clothing items and some toiletries into a small bag, Susan prepared breakfast. It was a beautiful day and a pity they had to work. Prospective clients kept Susan busy on the telephone. Steve, on the other hand, needing to get a first-hand feel for the victim, Walter Robson, in his local environment, had a train trip to North Yorkshire. He finished packing the few things he needed, and the two of them sat down for breakfast.

"I don't expect to stay up there long," he said to Susan. "Maybe just one night."

"I agree," said Susan. "There's not much to see in North Stainley."

"How do you know that?" It surprised Steve that she knew about anywhere in Yorkshire, much less a small place like North Stainley.

"I looked it up on the internet," Susan replied. "It's not rocket science."

"Ah, very enterprising," said Steve. "I'll have to give you a job on this case. I need a general run around," he joked.

"Yes, you would like that," Susan replied. "With all these contacts I have to make, I might just make you my general gofer."

Steve grunted.

"I can't quite collate fashion with catching a cold-hearted killer," he said.

"How do you know they are cold-hearted?" Susan asked. "They might be the loveliest person you will ever meet, and the victim probably deserved all he got."

"It's a possibility, but I doubt it," said Steve. "You're not developing an admiration for this killer, are you?"

"How could I? I don't know the person, and that's my point. Neither do you."

"You are right, as usual. However, I think I'll continue to keep a negative attitude about this guy. I might live longer."

Susan smiled. She always created a smile that told Steve nothing. This was one of the mysterious things about her that he loved. She never ceased to keep him guessing. Susan was undoubtedly the most intriguing woman he'd ever met.

He got up, finished his coffee, and put on his jacket.

"I'll take my car and leave it at the station," he said.

"Would that be the Police Station or the Railway Station?" Susan inquired.

Steve smiled. "Yes, I think I could do worse than to take you on as my assistant," he said.

"Maybe," Susan responded, "but not on this case."

"Why is that?" asked Steve.

"You said it yourself. I have too much admiration for this person." The smile on her face was too much for Steve. He took her in his arms and kissed her on the lips.

"I've got to go," he said. "I'll leave the car at the railway station, but I do have to check in at the police station first. I'll call you tonight."

* * *

"Morning, Steve," Mike greeted him as he came into the office.

"Morning Mike, any developments?"

"There are no fingerprints on the arrows, but I didn't expect there would be. What else? Oh yes, Warren called about half an hour ago. They did some checks of stage shows with archery and turned up three or four. Only one of them was interesting - a guy in North Yorkshire. I've got an address here. As you are travelling up there today, it seems a good opportunity to check him out."

Mike passed a slip of paper to Steve with the name and address on it.

"Thanks," said Steve. "Anything else?"

"Not right now," Mike replied, "but I have got the constables looking into all the local competitions and archery clubs."

"Terrific."

"I'll make a list when they've finished. Probably have it for when you return. Any idea when that might be?" asked Mike.

"I'll do my best to get back by tomorrow evening or the next day at the latest. Can't afford to be away for too long."

"OK. Do you want a lift to the station?"

"No, thanks, Mike. I'll take my car and leave it in the station car-park - not likely to get nicked, is it?"

"Not with that Met Police sign on the side," Mike replied pointedly.

"OK. I'll see you when I see you. I'll check in by phone if I get anything you should know about."

Steve drove to the railway station, showed his credentials at the ticket office, and got a ticket to Ripon. Changing at Leeds, the journey took about four and a half hours, so he didn't arrive until mid-afternoon. He hated the waste of time that travelling created and headed straight to the Ripon Police Station. After locating the person who had visited Robson's home, he was able to enlist her services to drive him out there. She was a bright young police constable named Tricia, very keen, and determined to get information from Steve about the case.

"So, when wur Robson killed?" she asked.

"Killed? Who said?" Steve asked, surprised at her direct question.

"Reet, ar don't think a DI from t'Met would come reet up 'ere if he ony swiped a bunch o' bananas," she said, in her North of England accent combined with a dose of good old Yorkshire comic relief.

"Last Friday, but do you know something I don't?" Steve humoured her.

"Don't think so. War d'ya think ar might know?

"Not sure," said Steve, "but we didn't find any bananas."

Tricia laughed. "Nah mate, e's prob'ly moved on frum thar."

Steve liked this girl. It wasn't often a constable called him mate. He simply found it funny.

"Ar wur 'e killed then?" Tricia persisted, "shot, stabbed, strangled ah shagged t'death?"

It was Steve's turn to laugh. "You don't mince your words, do you?"

"Waste o'tarm innit," said Tricia. "Well, ar thee garnt tell us, ah not."

"Probably not," said Steve, still smiling. "But I might tell you tomorrow - depends on what I uncover in Stainley."

"Bloody 'ell. Thought ower guvnor 'ad a tight arse. Least, that's whart lads say anywar."

"Work with a bunch of comedians, do you?"

"We're arl comedians op North. Didn't thee knah?"

"I'm finding out pretty fast," Steve responded.

"Reet. Next turning on t'left 'n we're there," said Tricia, waving her hand toward the row of run-down terraced houses. "Luvli part o' t'world innit."

"I've seen worse," said Steve.

"Reet, thee would 'ave comin' frum down South," said Tricia. The comedic patter seemed to run through her veins. She pulled into the curb and turned off the engine.

Steve walked up the path, shaded his eyes, and looked through the window. There wasn't much to see. A TV opposite a worn settee, coffee table, a couple of dining chairs against the wall, and that was about it. It seemed like a long way to come just to see that.

As he stepped back onto the path, the curtains of the next house moved, but not quickly enough to obscure the face of an elderly lady doing what old ladies do. He stepped over the low fence between the properties and knocked on her door. She opened it about six inches.

"Wacha want?" she said and then turned her gaze toward Tricia, who stood behind Steve.

"Sorry to trouble you," said Steve politely. "It must be getting near TV time. I was wondering what you could tell me about the gentleman who lives next door."

"Ah already told 'er," she nodded toward Tricia. "An' 'e ain't no gentleman," said the old lady.

"What makes you say that?" asked Steve conversationally.

"Always spits on t'pairvmunt outside ower ouse, dirty buggah," she said with disgust.

"Does he have any other bad habits?" asked Steve.

"That's arl e be, one shite 'abbit." It was obvious that she didn't like Mr Robson.

"Why? What else does he do?"

"Always makin' a bloody racket ont shed," she said vehemently.

"You mean carpentry and that sort of thing," said Steve trying to ease more information out of her.

"Nah. It's that bloody target. Ah it every weekend. Drives us nuts."

"Oh, I see," said Steve knowingly. "What does he do then?"

"E 'angs it on t'shed doah 'n fires arrah after arrah a' it. Thud, thud, thud. All t'bloody tarm. Pity 'e don't let us 'av a gur. I'd put one up 'is arse."

It was all Steve could do to stop himself from laughing. Tricia didn't try. "Ar knah a guy lark that," she said, "needs one up 'is arse."

That was enough. Steve couldn't control himself any longer and burst out laughing. "You've been very helpful, Mrs…"

"Cornhill," said the old lady. "It's Mrs Cornhill. 'Ope you're garn ter lock t'bugger up."

"When did you last see him?" asked Steve.

"Can't remember," said Mrs Cornhill. "All ah knah be 'e ain't bin buggering about we um arras fer a coupla weeks, and thaa ain't bin nah gob on t'pairvmunt either."

"Well, thank you very much, Mrs Cornhill. How can I get around the back?"

"I'll shah yah," said Tricia, "Follah me."

"I'm struggling to understand what you Northerners are saying," said Steve. "I came up here to make sense of this case. If I manage it, they should give me a medal."

"Oh, I can speak proper if I want to," said Tricia in a posh unnatural voice.

"Now, you're going to extremes."

"Arl reet, sir. Arl try t' talk Londonish."

Steve laughed, followed Tricia to the end of the block, through a passage, and to the left down a long corridor running behind the properties. Finding the gate to the rear of Robson's house, they entered. It wasn't a long garden, hardly enough to set up an archery target. The shed, with a door riddled with holes, and just a clean circular area where Robson had hung his target, stood next to the gate.

"Not much of an archer, was he?" said Tricia. "Looks like 'e barely hit the shed."

"Blimey, where did you come from?" said Steve in response to her understandable accent.

"This is me, undercover. If I 'ad me clobber on, you'd think I were a bystander an' tell me ter bugger off."

"Careful, I might do that anyway," was Steve's retort.

Steve walked up the path withdrawing a key from his pocket that he'd retrieved from Robson's body. He put it in the lock and turned it. The back door creaked open revealing an untidy kitchen. There were two kitchen cabinets to which Steve opened the cupboards and drawers. There wasn't much, apart from the usual cutlery, pots, and pans.

"Looking fer anything specific," asked Tricia.

"I'm not sure," said Steve, donning his gloves, and opening a drawer. "Ah, what do we have here?" he said and pulled out a pile of paper, receipts, statements, and such. He looked through the pile until he found a small notebook. When he opened it, his eyes lit upon a name and address. It was that of Ricky Armstrong from Willington. He looked at others until he came to Peter

Robson, whose address was in Virginia, USA. He put the notebook in his breast pocket.

Then he picked out a folded newspaper at the bottom of the drawer. He looked to see what might have been of interest to Robson. There was a photograph of a young boy about eight years old. Also, pictures of five men. He at once recognised Walter Robson. The names were beneath the photos. Peter Robson, Ricky Armstrong, David Gill, and Darius Deveaux. Steve folded the paper and put it in his inside pocket, deciding to read it later.

"They said Walter Robson's brother went to the USA with a friend," Steve said to Tricia. "Where did that information come from?"

"The landlord of the pub at the end of the road," said Tricia. "I spoke to him meself."

"Good," said Steve. "Let's go and have a word with him."

Steve locked the back door, and they made their exit out the front. It was a short drive to the end of the road, and they pulled up outside the Miller's Arms. Inside, Tricia found the landlord.

"Hello, Constable," he greeted her. "You back again. See yer got your boyfriend with you."

"This is DI Stephen Kendall," she answered, "and 'e ain't me boyfriend, so give 'im t' respect 'e deserves."

"I understand you knew Peter Robson," said Steve.

"Yep. Used to come in 'ere regular."

"OK. You told the constable he'd gone away with a friend."

"That's right."

"Does this friend have a name?" Steve pursued.

"Probably," said the landlord, "most people do."

"And would you like to tell me what it is, or do I have to set my constable on you."

"Hey, you want me to rough 'im up Guv," said the cheeky constable.

Steve smiled. He just loved how these Northerners were. "I don't think that is going to be necessary," said Steve. "I believe the landlord is about to give up the information."

"I might 'ang on to it a bit longer just to 'ave 'er put me in an armlock," said the landlord. "It's Darius someone or other - can't remember his last name. Coupla jerks the pair of them. I'd kick them out, but you got to make a living, even from idiots."

"Thanks," said Steve. "If you remember his surname, give me a ring." He handed a card to the landlord and turned to leave. "Don't forget to take your Rottweiler," said the landlord, and gave Tricia a bold wink.

Tricia gnashed her teeth at him, then returned his wink with her own.

"Well, that's a start, I suppose," said Steve when they got back into the car. Then, "What time does your shift end today?" he asked Tricia.

"Why? You going to take me out to dinner?" said Tricia. "I'm on until eight o'clock. I know a nice little place not far from here."

"Are you always this crazy?" asked Steve, but without waiting for her answer, said, "Do you know a place called Kirby Whiske? It doesn't sound real to me, but that's what I've got here." He handed her a slip of paper with an address on it.

"Yes, sir, it's about ten miles from here, on the other side of the M1."

"Ah, some respect at last," said Steve, noting her use of the title 'sir.' "Is that because you think there

38

might be a free dinner later? I'll tell you what, we'll whisk off to this Kirby place, interview a man there, and then maybe we'll have some well-earned food. Off you go."

The young constable put the car into gear and headed off to Kirby Whiske. They had to ask directions to the man's house but eventually found it. The only name Steve had for him was Robin the Hood, his stage name. Coincidentally, his name was Robin. He came to the door, and after introductions, let them in.

"I'm informed that you have a stage act using a bow and arrows," Steve started. "Are you any good?"

"Used to be," said Robin. "I'm retired now. Had an accident that buggered up my hand. I could no longer grip the arrows properly and had to give it up." He held out his right hand to show two crushed fingers.

"Sorry to hear that," said Steve. "The only reason I'm here is that I was in the area, and you are simply a long shot. Excuse the pun."

"I used to be a really good long shot," Robin sighed. "Still, no good dwelling on the past, is there?"

"No, quite true. Look, as you are a professional, it's very likely that you know other archers who were as good as you. Would that be right?"

"One or two," said Robin. "Not as good as me, though. I was the best."

"Yes, well, who would be second best, in your opinion?"

"There was a fellow - a Scotsman. But he's a lot older than me and retired years ago.

"Any others?" Steve persisted.

"Not really," said Robin, "but there was this female. Very odd, she was."

"Why? What was odd about her?"

"I used to go to this archery gallery over at Kirkby Stephen…"

"That's about forty miles from here," Tricia interjected.

"That's where I saw her," said Robin.

"Yes?" Steve prompted.

"She used to come in wearing a Muslim Niqab and veil - couldn't see her face, only her eyes. Most of us weren't sure whether she was even female. We thought she could be a man dressed like that as a disguise. No-one said anything to her because they'd get accused of being racist or something."

"Apart from the face covering, what was special about her?" asked Steve.

"Special? Hell, she was the best bloody archer I ever saw. I've got a picture somewhere." Robin went to a cupboard and took out a folder. "These are some photos of my act when I was at the top of my game. Ah, here it is." He handed a photo to Steve.

"This isn't a photo of a woman," said Steve. "It's just the picture of a target."

"Yes, I know, but look at it."

Steve studied the picture, then handed it to Tricia.

"I see what you mean," he said, "and that was by the woman?"

"Yes," said Robin, "or a man in disguise."

The picture showed a target with six arrows in it. All of them were in the centre of the bullseye. But one of them, right in the middle, had hit the centre arrow between its flights and split it down its length before burying itself in the target.

"Bloody 'ell," said Tricia. "She's a bit better'n t' Robson guy."

"So, where is she now?" Steve asked Robin.

"No idea," he replied. "I only saw her a couple of times and never spoke to her. She didn't even bother with a photo of this. It was like it was nothing to her, just ordinary everyday archery."

"Well, Robin, thank you. I have to say you have been very helpful. I have a feeling that this might be the person I am looking for. Pity we don't know whether she's male or female. Can I borrow this photo? I'll get it back to you, I promise. One other thing Robin, what is the name of the archery club in Kirkby?"

"It's called The Bullseye Archery Centre," said Robin.

Story One – The Longbow Murders
Part Five

Back in the car, Steve said to Tricia, "Right, Constable, how long would it take to drive to Kirkby Stephen? Could you do it in an hour?"

"Easy," Tricia replied.

"Good. If you can do that without getting pulled over by the cops, we might be able to call it a day, and have some dinner."

"Yes, sir, I'll do it, sir," said Tricia.

"Do all your senior officers have to offer you dinner before you give them respect?" Steve asked playfully.

"They do, but they 'ave t' get on t' knees. Then I think about it."

"Well, thanks for letting me off that chore," Steve replied. "Now, let's get to Kirkby Stephen within the hour."

"Might 'ave some luck, sir, it being your namesake."

"It hadn't gone unnoticed," Steve replied. "There are certainly some strange place names around here."

"Not like you ain't gottem down South. Pratts Bottom, Little Fiddling, there's few stranger than that," Tricia said.

"Touché," Steve replied. "I guess we have them all over the country."

"I've been thinking," said Tricia. "I reckon an arrer killed your guy, Robson. Right?"

"You are, Constable. I guess it has become a little obvious, hasn't it?"

"Do you think this man in drag is the killer?"

"Who knows?" said Steve. "There's no point in speculating, but she fits the profile. Whoever it was, they are a good archer. Time and facts will tell. Those are the two main ingredients of any case you investigate. Always remember it takes time, so don't be impatient. And never avoid the facts. Facts are everything. Spend enough time and gather enough facts, and you will solve your case nine times out of ten."

"It would be fun working on cases with you, sir. I think I'd like to become a detective."

"If you ever decide on a transfer, let me know. I'll see what I can do."

"That's reet good of you, sir. I won't forget that. Expect a call sometime." Tricia seemed genuine, and Steve would undoubtedly do all he could for her. She was quite the proverbial breath of fresh air.

They pulled into the Bullseye Archery Centre. Steve went to reception and asked for the manager. When he came, Steve pulled out the photo Robin had loaned him.

"Do you remember this?" asked Steve.

"I'd have a job to forget it," said the Manager. "Blown-up copies of it are all over this centre. It reminds people what they're striving for. That picture is archery perfection."

"Yes, I'd worked that one out myself," said Steve. "Can you tell me anything about the person who shot those arrows?"

"Speculation around here says it's a man in a disguise, but I don't think so," said the Manager.

"Why's that?"

"Because I spoke to her on two occasions, and she certainly sounded like a woman to me. I think the guys are just too jealous. They find it hard to believe that a woman could be that good."

43

"Yes," said Steve. "It's difficult to believe that anyone could be that good. What did she sound like? Did she have a Northern accent, for example?"

"Not really. I'd find it difficult to place any dialect on her. Pretty straight middle-of-the-road accent, I'd say."

"When people come to practice here, do you take any references or names and addresses," Steve enquired.

"No, is the short answer," said the Manager. "We wouldn't get many people to come here if we placed that kind of pressure on them."

"OK, so you don't have a name or an address for her. It seems odd that she is so damned good at archery, yet no-one knows anything about her. Not even if she is male or female."

"Yes, it is odd," the manager agreed. "But if she had been a regular, instead of just paying us a couple of visits, I think we would have discovered who she is."

"So, you don't think there is anyone here who might have some idea," Steve persisted.

"No."

"Do you know how she got here? I mean, did she drive herself, was she dropped off, or did she come by public transport or taxi?"

"She came by car - can't tell you what it was, though. It was new, as I recall."

"Was she as good a driver as she was an archer?" Steve wondered.

"Her driving was OK. She got in and out of the car park without hitting any of the other vehicles," the manager joked. "Sorry, I can't tell you anything substantial about her. Believe me, I wish I could. She's one hell of an archer. Probably the best in the country, if not the world."

"Now there's a thought," said Tricia, who had been listening in.

"What's that?" asked the manager and Steve in unison.

"If she's that good, maybe she has entered competitions. Maybe she is t' reigning champion somewhere."

"That's an excellent thought, constable," said the Manager, "but if she had, I would know about it. No. Nice try though. I wonder why she keeps such a low profile when she has such a talent. What's she done anyway? You people seem very interested in her."

"Can't tell you that at this moment," said Steve. "Anyway, thanks for all your help. If you think of anything, get in touch with me." He handed the manager his card and they left.

"Well, Constable Tricia," Steve addressed her when they were back in the car, "where is this wonderful eating place you had in mind?"

"I were only joking," said Tricia, "but if you're serious, I'm sure we'll find somewhere on t' way back."

"Yes, I'm serious. We will find somewhere." Steve put his hand in his inside pocket and took out the newspaper he'd found at Robson's house. "I'll take a look at this while you drive," he said.

He looked at the photo of the young eight-year-old boy. The name under the picture said Jake Whittingshaw, and the article was related to a court case. He read it out loud.

"The five men involved in the killing of eight-year-old Jake Whittingshaw in the Chatfield Woods back in May of this year received sentences today. Their court hearing has taken six months during which time the court heard how the five men, Walter Robson, Peter Robson, Ricky Armstrong, David Gill, and Darius

Devereaux had been taking drugs and alcohol after attending archery practice. They later went to Chatfield Woods to 'do some hunting,' as Gill put it. They met two boys playing. One was Jake Whittingshaw, and the other Chris Benton. Chris Benton ran away, but unfortunately, they chased Jake Whittingshaw through the woods armed with bows and arrows."

"Do you remember this case, Tricia?" Steve asked.

"No, it was before my time, but I heard a bit about it. Of course, I was quite young then and still at school."

Steve continued reading.

"The five men cornered Jake and began teasing him. Eventually, Gill ordered him to stand against a tree for target practice. The other men tried to dissuade him, but he fired anyway. The arrow hit Jake and killed him....

"They charged four of the men with manslaughter, and Gill, with murder under diminished responsibility. The four received three-year prison sentences and Gill, nine years. The leniency incensed the boy's mother, who caused something of an uproar in the courtroom when she said, if the court would not do its job properly, then she would. They removed her from the courtroom and cautioned her, which did nothing to calm her down. The five men have started their sentences."

"Well, I guess we have the motive right here," said Steve, "and probably the identity of the killer too."

"You know what I think," said Constable Tricia. "The woman who practiced at Kirkby Stephen was that boy's mother in disguise. She wore that Muslim gear to avoid identification. Now she's getting her revenge."

"Well done, Constable," said Steve, "We'll make a detective of you yet."

"It's times like these that I don't want to be in the police," said Tricia.

"Why's that?"

"These idiots killed her son, and the law was not up to the job to put things right. We should leave her alone and just let her get on with it."

"Surprisingly, there are a lot of officers who think like you," Steve informed her, "but it doesn't make it right."

"Why not, if someone killed my son, I'd want revenge too."

"I know, so would I, but that doesn't make it right. Look at it rationally. They were all idiots, but four of those men tried to stop Gill from shooting. They did their time, but already two of them are dead."

"Two of them?" said Tricia. "I thought it was just Robson."

"No," said Steve. "Armstrong died the same way. And I believe the others are also at risk."

"Well damn, she's some girl. You think she's going to kill 'em all?"

"I'm quite sure of it. My next point of call is going to be America, as that is where two of them are."

"Bloody 'ell," Tricia expounded. "I'd like to meet her."

"So, my argument didn't have much effect on you then, Tricia," said Steve with disappointment in his voice.

"Not totally. I know what you are saying, but those idiots started chasing the boys with bows 'n arrers. That ain't right. I'd like to put an arrer up their arse. Bloody fools."

"Where this case has gone wrong," Steve explained, "is not with the course of action, but the ineffectual sentences handed down. If the judge had been more in line with public feelings, these men would have received much more substantial sentences. If the four had got ten years each, and Gill twenty years, I don't think these murders would have happened."

"Sorry, sir, you're right. I realise that. But there is something else you haven't considered."

"What is that, Constable?"

"The fact that it didn't happen, and so the mother has every right to be angry. And being angry don't fry no eggs."

Steve burst into laughter. "So, you've reduced this case to frying eggs," he said. "I'll have to remember that. Ha ha. I do understand what you are saying though."

"You do? So, you agree with me. She should go out and get the bastards and good luck to her."

"Ha ha. Tricia, you're a gem. If you were on my team it would be a pleasure to go to work each day. Oh, and just to clarify, no, I don't think she should go out and murder the bastards. They deserved the longer sentences I suggested. But the death sentence? No. We don't have the death sentence in this country. But I can fully understand why she is doing it. The poor woman cannot get past the fact they murdered her lovely son and got off lightly."

"OK," said Tricia. "You are more mature than me. I'm only twenty-three, what do I know?"

"You know a lot more than many other twenty-three-year-olds I've met," said Steve. "Constable, you are a credit to the force. Let's concentrate on finding somewhere to eat."

* * *

Steve decided to spend the night at the Police Station and return to Ricton in the morning. He rang Susan to tell her what was happening.

"Hello, Steve," she answered, "are you still up in North Yorkshire?"

"Yes, I'll be back sometime tomorrow."

"How did you get on up there?"

"Quite well - better than expected. I might even have discovered the identity of the killer."

"Really? Who is it?"

"I can't tell you that; I haven't even discussed it with Mike yet. Besides, I could be wrong." Steve admitted, but he didn't think he was. "What have you been up to today?"

"Just chatting with some contacts. I might have to go to France soon - back to America as well. But not yet."

"OK," said Steve, "but I will have to go to America. Probably the day after tomorrow."

"Why's that?" Susan asked.

"There are a couple of guys out there who could be in danger. I need to warn them and speak to them to round this thing off."

"What does that mean?"

"It means I want to get the full picture. It's facts that get results. The more I have, the better I will feel about this case." Steve explained.

"Yes, of course. Let's hope you get the full facts then. But, you know, sometimes they are not always available," said Susan.

"That's an odd thing to say. What do you mean by that?

"Nothing."

"Susan, you are the most mysterious woman I have ever met," said Steve.

"Wow, you're a lucky guy then."

"Why is that?" Steve asked.

"There are not many men who have a mysterious woman."

Steve laughed. "Ha ha. There probably aren't many men who would want one."

"Well then, that makes you unique as well, doesn't it?"

"Hey, you're a mystery wrapped in an enigma. I'll see you tomorrow. By then, I'll have fathomed you out," said Steve.

"You're a very clever guy, Steve, but you're not that clever," she said. "Just as well, I guess. See you tomorrow." They rang off.

Why was it every time he chatted with Susan, she became just that little bit more unfathomable? Would he ever have the answer? He doubted it, but he loved her more than anything in the world and wouldn't have her any other way. Yes, he thought, he was unique in having a woman so incredibly mysterious.

The following morning, he thanked the guys at the police station and sought out Constable Tricia to give her a special thank you.

"Don't forget," he said as she dropped him off at the railway station. "If you ever want a transfer, ring me first. I promise I'll do what I can."

"I will," she said. Then, as an afterthought, she said, "Oh, but remember, sir."

"Remember what?"

"Promises don't fry no eggs."

Story One – The Longbow Murders
Part Six

It was mid-afternoon when Steve picked up his car at the Railway Station and drove to Mike's.

"Hello, Steve, how did you get on yesterday? Successful trip?"

"Yes, very productive," said Steve, and proceeded to give an update on what he had learnt.

"So, tomorrow, you'll be off to America," Mike surmised.

"Yes. I'll get in touch with their local police today and let them know I'm coming. What about here? Any additional information I should have?"

"The constables have been digging around but haven't come up with anything substantial. I had a woman come into the Station reporting that on the day of the murder she had seen a red car just inside the woods at the beginning of the track, but didn't note the make. I went up there to see if I could find any tyre tracks but found nothing. That's about it."

"Thanks."

"Oh, by the way," Mike added. "Susan was here this morning to see Debbie; she popped in here before she left, just to say goodbye. That was when the woman rang about the car in the woods. I took the caller's name and address, and Susan wrote it down for me on that pad." He picked up the pad and showed it to Steve. I didn't mean to get her involved in this. Sorry about that."

"Alright, Mike, I'm going home as I'm on an early flight to New York tomorrow. In the meantime, if you could carry out some investigations into the whereabouts of Jake Whittingshaw's mother, that might be the best lead we have to this mystery. They are also checking into that up in Yorkshire for me, so you might want to liaise with them."

"Good," said Mike. "I'll get onto it straight away. Have a good trip; I'll see you when you get back."

When Steve went home, Susan's car was missing. She hadn't said she was going out anywhere, so he wondered where she was. Soon Susan returned and came into the lounge, dropping her coat on the settee next to Steve.

Steve greeted her. "Why did you have a coat with you on a sizzling summer day like this?"

"Oh, it was in the car; I just brought it in. How are things?" She planted a kiss on his cheek and went into the kitchen.

"Where have you been? Anywhere interesting?" he inquired.

"No, just had to pop out to see someone. Nothing important. How was your trip?"

"It was pretty good. Think I picked up some useful information," said Steve. "But I'm off to America early tomorrow. I hope that's as productive, but I doubt it."

"What's in America?" she asked.

"Just a couple of people I have to check on. I think they might be in danger."

"It's a long way to go just to give someone a warning," said Susan.

"It is, but you know me; I always try to find a new angle. There might just be one in the states."

Susan called from the kitchen, "Steve, I can't find my phone. Have you seen it?"

"No," Steve replied. "I'll locate it with mine."

He rang Susan's number, and surprisingly, he heard a phone ring next to him. He checked the coat pocket on the settee. Sure enough, there was her phone with a slip of paper. Steve looked at it. It was a name and address. He thought nothing of it and returned it to the coat pocket.

"Here's your phone," he said, walking into the kitchen.

Susan had made them a coffee, and they went back into the lounge to drink it over a chat. Later, they watched some television before Steve turned in early, having to get up at the crack of dawn to get to Heathrow. It was while he was waiting in Departures that his mind wandered onto the address in Susan's coat pocket. That was when he realised he'd seen it before.

It was the address of the witness who had seen the car in the woods. How strange that Susan would have it in her coat pocket. Perhaps she knew the woman? Maybe she had something to do with her business? Maybe... Maybe... There was no future in maybes. He would need to talk to her about it when he got back. Even so, it was another oddity to add to Susan's list of peculiarities.

* * *

Steve touched down in New York the next day and transferred flights to Richmond, Virginia. After checking into the police station to register what he was doing there, he took a taxi to a place just outside of Montrose. He studied his notebook to verify he had the correct address for Darius Deveaux. Peter Robson's address was the same, so he assumed they were living together. He was correct. There were two properties next to each other but within the same grounds.

He went up to one and knocked on the door. There was no answer, even after several knocks, so he went to the next. No luck there either. These places were expensive, and Steve wondered where they got the money to buy them. Or had they just rented them? He looked around the grounds. At the rear were some stables. As he walked around, he could hear horses moving inside, so he looked in.

"Who are you, and what do you want," said a man around sixty-years-old hanging up some livery.

Steve introduced himself and showed his identification.

"A cop from England, eh," said the old guy. "Is that because of the killing? Didn't think you'd have any jurisdiction here, even though he was from England."

"Sorry," said Steve, "I don't follow you. Are you saying someone died here?"

"Oh, you didn't know. Well, what are you doing here, then?" asked the stable guy.

"I'm looking for Darius Deveaux and Peter Robson. Have you seen either of them?" Steve asked.

"Who ain't looking for him?" said Stable Guy. "Robson is dead, and Deveaux disappeared two days ago. Think he's making his way back to England."

"Wow," said Steve with genuine surprise. "How did Robson die?" he asked.

"Shot with an arrow," Stable guy responded. "Ain't been no-one killed with an arrow in Virginia for the last hundred an' fifty years," he said pointedly.

"No, I don't suppose there has. Is Deveaux a suspect?" Steve asked.

"No," said Stable Guy. "Robson died in Deveaux's arms with two witnesses."

"I see," said Steve. "So, does anyone have any idea who killed him?"

"Not really," Stable Guy shook his head, "He was out riding, as he did every day. Deveaux was chatting to Al and Shirley when up comes Robson's horse across the fields," Stable guy waved his hand toward the fields beyond. "When the horse stopped at the stable, Robson fell off. He had an arrow in him, and he was taking his last breaths."

"Interesting," said Steve. "Did Robson say anything with those last breaths?"

"Hey, you ask a lot of questions. I don't think I should be telling you any of this," said Stable guy, suddenly concerned.

"Asking questions is what I do," Steve explained. "I'm a detective with the London Metropolitan Police. This killing ties in with a case I am working on in the UK."

"Oh, I see," said Stable Guy. "How's it tie in?"

"The case I am working on is the murder of Robson's brother." Steve didn't see any point in not telling him this, even though he usually wouldn't.

"Hell," exclaimed Stable Guy, "He weren't shot with an arrow, was he?"

Steve didn't answer the question. "Who is handling this case locally," he asked. "Any idea?"

"Yeah, the Sheriff's Office. You passed it about two miles down the road. Don't think he's getting far with it, though."

"What makes you say that?" Steve asked.

"He's been working on it for nearly three weeks, and I ain't heard of any arrests."

"Oh, so this happened three weeks ago, did it? said Steve.

"Yeah."

"So, what made Deveaux suddenly take off?" asked Steve.

"Dunno, better ask the Sheriff." Stable Guy didn't appear to have anything further of interest to add, so Steve decided to go and see the Sheriff.

"Can I get a taxi anywhere around here?" he asked. Steve had arrived by taxi, and it had left when it dropped him off.

"No," said Stable guy, "but if you want to see the Sheriff, I'll give you a lift," he offered.

"Thanks," said Steve. "That's good of you."

They got into Stable Guy's car and he dropped Steve off at the Sheriff's office. It was just a small building on the side of the road with four rooms, a kitchen, and a toilet. Steve entered. The sheriff was sitting behind his desk.

"Hi," greeted Steve. "I'm Detective Inspector Stephen Kendall from The Metropolitan Police in London."

The Sheriff got to his feet. He was a large man both in height and girth. The stomach, hanging precariously over his belt, had probably seen an extended period housing large steaks and quantities of beer. Steve wondered what happened to it when the Sheriff removed his belt. The visual was too much for him, so he concentrated on the Sheriff's face which was jovial and kindly.

"Hello, Detective," he said. "I'm Dan, what brings you to my county."

"I was here to see two Brits who live in the area," Steve informed him.

"That wouldn't be Robson and Deveaux, would it?" said the Sheriff.

"Yes, unfortunately. I've just come from the house and learned about the killing."

"Yeah, bad business. We haven't had a killing by an arrow for…"

"One-hundred and fifty years," Steve completed the sentence.

"I was going to say, 'for a long time'," said the Sheriff, "but you could be right. So, why do you want to see these two people?"

"I came partly to get some information, but also to warn them. Seems like I'm too late for that," said Steve.

"What did you want to warn them about?" asked the Sheriff.

"Exactly that," said Steve. "The fact that they might get shot with an arrow."

"Now you've got my interest," said the Sheriff. "How would you know that?"

"I'm investigating a similar case in the UK."

"So, how do these guys fit into the picture?" the sheriff asked.

Steve pulled up a chair and sat down to go through all the information he had to date.

"And that's it," he concluded. "I think this killer is out for revenge, and these two poor buggers are in the picture. Tell me, why do you think Deveaux disappeared. No one has warned him of anything, have they?"

"Not exactly, but I guess he put two and two together," said Dan.

"I don't know," Steve was sceptical, "I can't see how he would connect this killing with the one ten years ago. There's the coincidence factor, but it's a bit shaky."

"All I know is that I went to the Archery Club, heard a few odd things, and when I mentioned it to Deveaux he got agitated and left. Haven't seen him since. Willy, he's my deputy, said he'd seen him in the travel office in town."

"Right," said Steve. "That's interesting. Could be a lead. Can we contact that travel office?"

"Sure. Sally will get you the number."

"So, Dan, what did you learn at the Archery Club that got Deveaux agitated?"

"I don't know. They said there had been a woman practicing there for a couple of days about three or four weeks ago, and she was very good."

"How good?" asked Steve.

"They said she was the best they'd ever seen, but she was a Muslim. She wore a Niqab thing on her face."

"Damn," Steve exploded, "she's been here."

"You know her?" asked Dan.

"No. I mean, I've never seen her. That's the problem, no one's seen her without her niqab on."

"But you know who she is?" said Dan.

"Not really, but I have a strong suspicion, and she isn't a Muslim."

"Who do you think she is then," asked Dan.

"I suspect she's the boy's mother I told you about, but apparently there are no photos of her, and she disappeared from her area about eight years ago," Steve explained.

"Ha, I'm getting the picture," said Dan. "This woman has got it in the bag. No one knows who she is, no one has seen her or knows what she looks like, and she's a bloody archery expert. Poor prick, don't stand much chance, does he?"

"Well, put it like this," said Steve, "I wouldn't like to be wearing his shoes."

"You couldn't say you wouldn't be seen dead in them 'cause you probably would be," said Dan.

Sally came up with a phone number. Dan picked up the phone and rang the Travel Office. After chatting for a while, he put the phone down and spoke to Steve.

58

"Apparently, Deveaux booked a flight to Heathrow, London. It's a late flight and will be arriving early tomorrow morning at 6.30. Looks like he's done the sensible thing and got out quickly."

"Maybe," said Steve. "Maybe not."

"I'm about to knock off," said the Sheriff, "do you want to get something to eat?"

"Sounds like a good idea," said Steve.

"Come on then. Where are you staying tonight?"

"I haven't looked for anywhere yet," Steve admitted. "Is there anywhere around here?"

"Don't worry about it," said Dan, "I've got a spare room. You can stay with me, and we can catch up on the finer details."

"Sounds good," said Steve.

Story One – The Longbow Murders
Part Seven

After eating and settling in at the Sheriff's place, Steve rang Susan as he always did when he was away.

"Hi, Susan. How has your day been?"

"Hi Darling. Rather good, actually. I must go off to Cornwall on Monday for three days. How is the US?"

"Very interesting," he replied. "This case gets more intriguing. It wasn't what I expected to find when I got here."

"Really?" said Susan, her interest piqued. "What did you find?"

"As you know, I came here to speak with two people. Now I find one is dead, and the other has left the country."

"Really? Where has he gone?" Susan asked.

It wasn't the most obvious response Steve was expecting, but then Susan always surprised him like that.

"I'm told he's getting a late plane back to London and will arrive at Heathrow at about 6.30," he said.

"OK, I'm guessing the other one died when he couldn't dodge an arrow," Susan said.

"Yes, you're right," Steve replied. "This archery-style killing spree is getting to be like the Battle of Hastings."

"Or perhaps Robin Hood is still alive and well," Susan joked.

"Whatever it is, this guy Deveaux is still at risk. I'll have to get someone to warn him," said Steve, "otherwise, that will be another killing to investigate."

"If you solve one, you solve them all, don't you?" said Susan.

"Yes," Steve agreed, "but I'm starting to get a feeling that I won't solve any of them."

"Oh, why is that?"

"Because the killer is very elusive. No one knows where she or he is or what they look like."

"Ah, so they have the upper hand. Maybe they'll keep it that way, and you'll never find them."

"That's what I'm afraid of. Won't do my reputation a lot of good, will it?"

"I wouldn't worry about that, Steve. You have a good record of solving crime. This one might get away, but you can't win them all. Looks like she has the better of you."

"Sounds like you admire her," Steve observed.

"Maybe I do, don't you?"

Steve laughed. "Perhaps a little. I certainly admire her archery skill."

"She put a lot of work in to get that good," said Susan. "I think she deserves some admiration."

"Could be," said Steve. "Anyway, I'm staying at the Sheriff's house tonight and will probably get a late flight home tomorrow."

"OK, take care, darling. You better start practicing."

"Practising what?" Steve asked, perplexed.

"Dodging arrows," Susan laughed. "If you get that mastered, I'll see you back here soon."

"And if I don't, you had better get your black dress out."

"You mean the sexy one? I'll get that out anyway, just for you."

He loved this quirky woman. She was always very mysterious, and that is what had attracted him to her. Kept him on his toes, and he loved a challenge.

"I love you," he said.

"I know," she replied in her quiet voice.

They rang off, and Steve chuckled at her sense of humour. What a girl Susan was.

Before turning in, he rang Mike to update him.

* * *

The following day, Steve caught the red-eye, and arrived at Heathrow at 6.30 in the morning, the same as Deveaux's flight the previous day. The major surprise was that Susan had turned up to collect him. She drove him back to Ricton. Steve asked her to drop him off at the Police Station, and as it was a little after nine in the morning, Mike was in the office.

"Hi, Mike," Steve greeted him as he came in, "did you manage to get someone out to Heathrow to warn Deveaux?" he asked.

"I got someone out there, but he didn't find him. He checked the passenger list, and it included Deveaux's name. Somehow, he must have missed him. So, no, he wasn't warned," said Mike, "and that's a great pity."

"Yeah," said Steve, "I guess it is."

"No, Steve, you miss the point."

"What's that?"

"Last night, we got a message that someone found a body in Richmond Park. The body had an arrow in it. It was Deveaux. The poor bugger is dead."

"Bloody Hell," said Steve. "Susan joked the other night that maybe Robin Hood is still around. It's more like all his merry men. This woman is everywhere."

"How does she know where to be, at the right time, and the right place?" said Mike. "You know what this means, don't you?"

"I know it means four out of the five guys are now dead," said Steve.

"It also means we've got to protect David Gill," said Mike.

"I guess he might be in some danger," said Steve, "but I don't think she is going to get into prison with a longbow, do you?"

"No chance," Mike agreed, "but then she won't have to."

"Why not?"

"Because David Gill is being released on Sunday," Mike revealed.

"I didn't know that," said Steve. "We are going to have to put him into protection, I guess."

"I already started the process last night," said Mike. "Got the wheels rolling anyway."

"What have you got planned?"

"We have a safe house arranged. Someone will pick him up at the prison and bring him here. We'll keep him in the station until the evening when you and I will deliver him to the security team. After that, it's out of our hands and into those of the protection unit."

"That's good," said Steve. "Well done, Mike. We must keep him safe. The other four are all dead, and it's assured that she will be after him. Gill was the one who had killed her boy. She wouldn't let him get away."

"It's quite incredible how she has managed to eliminate the other four and leave no trace," said Mike. "I have to admit that I have a certain admiration for her. Do you think that is wrong?"

"No. I have some admiration for her too. I can understand her anger at the lean sentences given to these guys. I would feel angry too."

"Yes, but would we be angry enough to take revenge as she has?" Mike pondered. "I guess it's something we'll never know unless we find ourselves in the same circumstances."

"Anyway," said Steve, "this reflection on an experience we know nothing about will get us nowhere. So, I am off to spend what remains of my Sunday at home with Susan. What time do you want me back here?"

"It will probably be around seven or eight," said Mike. "I'll give you a ring."

"OK. See you later."

* * *

Susan greeted Steve with a kiss when he arrived home.

"Hello, darling. Are you finished for the day?" she asked.

"More or less," Steve replied.

"What does that mean? Are you finished or not?"

"I'm finished until I get a call from Mike around seven or eight. Then I have to go out again."

"What for this time?" asked Susan. "I thought you might at least have had the Sunday off."

Steve explained the latest development so that Susan understood, which she did.

"So, this man Gill is being released today? How is it you didn't know that?"

"I think if I'd had another day, I would have. It's the murder of Deveaux that has brought things to a head."

"Technically, it is murder, but morally I don't think it is," said Susan. "They didn't get proper punishment for a crime that resulted in the boy's death. I think she is just setting things right."

64

"I guess that's one way of looking at it," said Steve.

"It's the way she sees it. You have to put yourself in her shoes."

"Mike and I were kinda talking about that before I left the station," Steve explained. "Anyway, it's our job to protect this Gill fellow, and that is why I have to go out again tonight. What will you be doing?"

"Don't worry about me. I have a nice book, and I'll sit here in comfort, relaxing with it and a few glasses of wine. I guess you will be back late then?"

"Probably," said Steve. "Don't wait up as I've no idea when I'll be back."

At seven-thirty, the phone rang. Steve answered it, put on his coat, and left. He drew up outside the station and went in. It was a good half-hour later before he appeared with Mike. Gill came out afterward with the constables on either side of him. Steve spoke to Gill. "You will sit in the back seat with these two constables on either side of you. We will be up the front. It's about two and…"

Steve didn't complete his sentence. He sensed rather than saw what happened. Gill dropped to the ground like a stone in front of him. Steve put his hand up to where something had brushed past his right ear. Gill lay on the ground, an arrow with a blue and white flight had entered his left eye and buried itself in his brain. Gill died instantly.

Everyone was so surprised that they didn't immediately realise what had happened, much less know what to do. Then Steve turned around to see where the arrow had come from. As it had come over his shoulder, it had to be from a height.

On the other side of the road was a two-story car park. Following the trajectory, it was clear that the arrow came from the upper level over the parapet.

He and Mike went across the road and into the quick access entrance, where a staircase led to the top-level parking. There was no-one there. The car park was empty. Beside the front parapet, was a discarded longbow. Steve went to it and looked over the parapet to the street below.

At that moment, a red car crashed through the barrier. It turned right and sped up the road to weave in and out of the sparse traffic. He knew that by the time they returned to the street and into their vehicles, the red car would be long gone. There would be no point in trying to chase it.

"Damn," said Mike, "we'll never catch it now. I don't have any staff for a traffic patrol. That car is well gone."

"Yeah," Steve sighed, "this would have been our best chance of getting the killer, but she has eluded us yet again. There'll be no evidence on the longbow; you can be sure of that."

They went back inside the station while the two constables guarded the body until a coroner arrived. After that, there wasn't much more to do apart from reporting the incident to the higher authority and making out their written reports.

* * *

Steve arrived home at around ten-thirty. It had been one hell of a week, and his exhausted body felt drained of all energy. He parked up alongside Susan's car and dragged himself out. As he made his way to the front door, he leaned on the bonnet of Susan's car for support.

He made his way around the front of the car, his hand on the bonnet. He felt a groove and stopped to examine it. There was a dent. He slowly put his key in the front door, his mind working overtime on the sudden thoughts that were congregating. It didn't bear thinking about, so he tried not to.

Steve entered the lounge and poured himself a drink. Susan's book was lying on the settee. He poured a second drink, and then a third before climbing the stairs to the bedroom.

Susan was fast asleep. Her beautiful innocent face lay peacefully on the pillow. Gently, he got into bed so as not to disturb her as she'd need to be up early to go to Cornwall. Thoughts racing through his mind kept him awake, and it was about four o'clock before he finally dropped off to sleep.

When he awoke Susan had already left for Cornwall and would not return for three days. He didn't mention his suspicions to Mike, nor did he talk about the case to Susan when she phoned in each day.

At six pm on Wednesday, he heard her car pull up in the drive. He looked out. The bonnet was like new. Had he dreamed about that dent, or had she had it repaired while she was away?

Susan came in and planted a kiss on his cheek.

"That's just what I could do with," she said as she sat down to the dinner Steve had prepared for them.

They chatted about her trip to Cornwall and the new contacts she had made. She told him about the several new contracts signed and the extent of the orders she'd obtained. She related her frustration at the terrible traffic she had to contend with on the M3 motorway and many other things.

Neither of them mentioned the case, nor the dent in her car that had mysteriously disappeared. In fact, neither of these things were ever discussed again; it was as though they had never happened.

On rare occasions, Steve found himself wondering if indeed they had.

Story Two – Kidnapped Justice
Part One

It had been several months since the Longbow Murders, and it was now the end of March with spring starting to show its face in Ricton. The powers that be decided that Detective Stephen Kendall would stay at his post in Ricton until further notice. Despite his inability, or was it his unwillingness, to solve the Longbow Murders, he had solved several other minor crimes over the dark winter months. For now, his position in Ricton was secure.

Once determined, his thoughts turned to Constable Tricia Mason of the Ripon Police in North Yorkshire. He had been impressed with her when he visited the North to investigate the Longbow Murders. She had shown some interest in becoming a detective, and Steve promised to help her if she decided to do that.

When Tricia phoned him to say she was going on a course to become a detective, he put in a good word for her. When the course was over, he managed to employ her at Ricton so he could keep an eye on her progress. Unexpectedly, Tricia became very friendly with Susan, and the two of them got on very well together.

Susan, Steve's live-in partner, had been very busy in her job travelling afield every week. She was an excellent salesperson bringing her company a great deal of new business. So much, in fact, they were having to set up extra facilities, and rewarded Susan by promoting her to Head of Mobile Sales. This meant she organized and met with all the sales teams throughout the country.

Since the death of the released prisoner, David Gill outside the Police Station back in the summer of the previous year, Steve had made the conscious decision to no longer discuss his work with Susan. The whole inconclusive episode stayed in the background of his mind constantly and he had to fight with himself to keep it from surfacing.

Yet despite this, and his grave suspicions, his love, and respect for Susan simply increased. A woman who could achieve what he suspected she had, and in such a remarkably efficient and successful manner, deserved anyone's respect. If it had been Susan, her motives were human, understandable, and in a way, noble.

But that was last year. Today, was the last day of March, another year, and the circumstances completely different.

The phone at the Station rang and Mike answered. Steve was sitting at his desk carrying out paperwork. He looked up when Mike spoke on the telephone.

"Hello, Mr Johnson, Yes, I do know your boy. He's about eight and goes to school with my son, Timmy," Mike was saying. "Yes… I see… And it has been six hours you say… Yes, I know it is difficult with kids to know where they are and what they are doing… OK, I'll get someone to come over. Yes, I'll either come myself or ask Detective Kendall to come… Yes, Mr Johnson, we'll get straight onto it. If you have a recent photo it would be helpful… Thank you. See you soon."

"I take it that was Mr Johnson?" said Steve.

"Yes," Mike replied, "his son has been missing for around six hours and they've searched widely."

"Johnson. He's the guy with the huge country house and about two thousand acres, isn't he?" said Steve.

"Yeah," Mike agreed. "Great Ricton Hall. Can't say that I like the guy much, but his son is missing, and

70

we need to get onto it quickly. These things can get away from us if we're not careful."

"Yes, you're right. I'll cover this. I don't mind. I'm only doing paperwork and that can wait."

"OK, Steve, if you're all right with it. You know where it is, I suppose?"

"Yes, I know it," said Steve. "I'll go right away."

Steve left the station and took the back road out to Great Ricton Hall. It stood on a hill proudly overlooking the Ricton Valley. Beautifully maintained fields sloped down to the river that bordered the front of the grounds, while woodlands occupied the rear. It was a huge place, and with only six people living in it, there were about two dozen vacant bedrooms and other rooms.

Steve drove right past the picturesque scene to gain access via a long drive that wound its way up the hill on the right of the property. As the landscape levelled off, the road entered through a huge gate, guarded on either side by enormous bronze lions mounted on stone pillars.

The name, 'Great Ricton Hall,' painted in gold and black, stretched across the road from pillar to pillar. It was an imposing entrance, as was the house beyond, with its circular towers on each corner and crenellated parapet above.

Steve drove up to the house and rang the doorbell. A maid, dressed in black with a white pinafore apron opened the door. Mr and Mrs Johnson hovered in the hall and came forward when they saw who it was.

"Thank goodness you've come," said Mr Johnson. "My wife's worried out of her mind. We haven't seen James for more than six hours."

"Hello," Steve greeted the couple, "I'm Detective Inspector Stephen Kendall. Now, where does he usually go during these hours?"

"He goes all over," said Mr Johnson. "As you can see, we have a lot of ground here. But he usually doesn't stay out on his own for more than an hour or so. He will usually come back by then."

"He has never been out for this amount of time before," said Mrs Johnson.

"Right then," said Steve. "Is there anywhere in particular he likes to go?"

"Yes, he does like to go down to the river," said Mrs Johnson.

"And can he swim?" asked Steve.

"He's a very good swimmer," Mr Johnson replied. "He is so good there has been talk of him training when he gets older."

"So, you think if he fell into the river, he would be OK?" Steve enquired.

"No problem," said Johnson. "He swims in the river all the time."

"But if he intends to go swimming, he will take his swimming things with him," Mrs Johnson interjected.

"Right," said Steve, "so we can rule out the river. That's a big plus for us. Cuts down the areas to spend time on."

"We have plenty of fields here and they are well maintained, so he would be easily visible. That leaves the woodland," Johnson explained.

"Except, he never goes into the woods on his own," said Mrs Johnson. "He is a little afraid to."

"Is there any reason for that fear other than normal childish fear of such places?" asked Steve.

"I don't think so," the Johnsons responded in unison.

"I gave James a whistle," said Johnson, "so that he could use it if he was afraid, but we haven't heard it today. That's surprising because he tends to blow it without any excuse."

"I think we need to just concentrate on the woods, for now," Steve said, taking control of the situation. "I'll get who I can to help with that, but we are short on staff. Do you have any local friends who could help?"

"Yes," said Johnson. "I'll start ringing around and get as many as I can."

"OK," said Steve. "If he has been missing for six hours, he must have gone out early. It's twelve-thirty now. I'd like you to arrange for them to be here at two o'clock so that we can organize it. Can't have people wandering aimlessly everywhere."

"We'll get onto it right away," said Johnson. "Thank you, Detective."

Steve drove back to the Station and discussed everything with Mike. Mike agreed to get constable Johnny involved with the search operation. Johnny had come from a neighbouring station to help with the Longbow Murders and had been kept on at Ricton. Steve took Tricia to help him, an if this turned into something more sinister, which it could, he wanted Tricia involved in the case.

Both Johnny and Tricia had built up a circle of friends in the Ricton area and they set about recruiting as many as they could to go on the search. Steve had made a point since the Longbow Murders case not to include Susan in any of his day-to-day cases, but this policy had become very difficult to keep now that Susan and Tricia were so friendly. It was with a little concern that he learned Susan would help in the search operation. So, he gave up. What was the point?

They all congregated in the drive of Great Ricton Hall. In all, there were about thirty people. Steve instructed them to make their way to the top left corner of the estate where the woodlands started. The group spread out in a line from the edge of the trees, back into the woods and up to the boundary fence.

Tricia decided to test whether James might be in the woods by taking out her issued police whistle and blowing it loudly several times. There was no responding whistle in return.

Steve noted that the fences were all quite high, and very substantial, so young James could not have got out that way. Besides, being afraid of the woods, he would not have contemplated going in them on his own.

The group of helpers made their way slowly through the trees examining everything. Many had brought walking sticks, so they could disturb the ground. It took them about one hour to cover the full length of the boundary, but they found nothing. Despondent, they made their way back to the house. Mrs Johnson made tea for those who wanted it before they made their way home.

Steve decided to look along the riverbank and took Johnny and Tricia with him. They examined the area minutely without finding anything. It surprised Steve to see that the boundary fence did not go right down to the river but stopped short by several metres. Tricia went through the gap and studied the ground on the other side.

When she was several metres inside the adjoining field, Tricia bent down to investigate something.

"Got summat 'ere," she said, and Steve came to see what she had found.

The ground was damp and something shiny showed in the wet grass. Steve took out his penknife and carefully levered it out of the ground. Although caked in mud, none-the-less it was clear what the object was.

"That's James's whistle," said Tricia, stating the obvious.

"OK," said Steve, "so we know James has been past this boundary fence and we know it was today. Johnson said he always carried the whistle with him."

"It looks like someone stamped it into the ground," said Tricia. "Was that accidental, or was it deliberate," she mused.

"Right, you two," said Steve, "be very careful not to trample on that spot. I'll get a mould-pack out here and we'll see if we can get a footprint."

"Can't see any sign of one," said Johnny.

"Don't mean there ain't one," said Tricia, proving to Steve that he had made the right decision when he helped her into this job. "I might have a pack in t' boot of me car," she said enthusiastically. "Shall I run back and get it, sir?"

"Yes, Detective Constable. That would save a lot of time if you do have a pack," said Steve, using her title deliberately to give her a boost.

Tricia smiled at him and ran back up the grassy hill to the car park. It was thirty minutes before she returned carrying a pack of Dental Stone compound, a litre bottle of water, a large plastic bag, and various implements. She gave them to Steve.

"Here, sir," she said. "I've ain't done this before. I think you oughta do it."

"Yes, I think you're right," said Steve, "Not because I think you aren't capable, but this isn't a very deep impression, so we'll need an experienced hand."

While Tricia had been gone, Steve had taken two battens off the perimeter fence. He had snapped them in two, and with the four pieces, had formed a square shutter around the footprint area.

"I've done this to give it some depth," Steve explained to the two constables. "Without that, the mould could quite easily break in two."

"Yes," said Tricia, "I understand that. I would have done t' same."

"I'm sure you would have," said an admiring Steve.

He opened the packet of Dental Stone compound and poured it into the plastic bag. Then he added the water carefully so as not to overdo it. All the while he was kneading the mixture in the bag to get it to a good creamy consistency without any air in it. When it was ready, he transferred the paste to the footprint area.

With a wooden spatula, he worked the paste until it had a smooth finish. After that, it was a matter of waiting for the mixture to set. This took about ten minutes.

When it was hard, he gently lifted the block of plaster by releasing the edges using the spatula. He turned it over and the three of them inspected it.

"Don't see nothing on it," said the uninspired constable Johnny.

"No, Johnny," said Tricia. "We'll 'av' t' take it back t' station an' examine it in detail," she said with some authority.

"You're right, Detective Constable," Steve agreed. "I'm sure we will get something from it with a little patience."

They made their way back up the hill to the house. Steve spoke to Johnson, explaining what they had found and done.

"Don't worry, Mr Johnson," said Tricia, "We 'ave a lead now an' you can be sure we'll do everything we can t' get yer son back."

"Mr Johnson," Steve added, "please have someone here at the house at all times keeping an eye on the telephone. Also, make sure your mobiles are fully charged. If you get any calls, contact me immediately."

"Thank you, I will Detective Inspector," replied Johnson.

"I'll be leaving the constable here with you," said Steve, nodding toward Johnny, "Don't forget, if anything out of the ordinary happens at all, don't let it pass. Report it."

Steve and Tricia left in their respective cars.

"Meet me back at the Station," said Steve.

Steve brought the mould into the Interview Room and placed it on the table, smooth face down, and Mike joined them. They all examined it carefully. After a while, Steve said,

"You see these two very faint ridges," using a pencil as a pointer, he indicated the marks. "You will notice they are not exactly straight but have a very slight curve."

Steve took a ruler as a straightedge and placed it along the line to prove his point.

"They are the edges of the shoe that made this imprint," he continued. "Also, you will notice that the right line is a little less curved than the left line." Again, he placed the ruler along both lines to show the difference in the curve. "It is only slightly different, maybe two millimetres. That indicates the shoe is from the left foot, rather than the right."

"That's interesting," said Tricia. "So, even though this mould is not very good, and t' details are faint, we can still identify which foot created t' imprint."

"Yes, correct," said Steve, "but can we get even more from this imprint. For example, if the owner of this shoe deliberately stamped on the whistle, it's almost certain that he's left-footed."

"Does that mean that he is also lefthanded?" asked Tricia.

"I wish it did," Steve laughed. "That would be some useful information to have. Unfortunately, statistics do not support that. Ninety-five percent of right-handed people are also right-footed, but not the other way around."

"That's disappointing," said Tricia.

"However, there's a good chance that they are also left-handed. If we were comparing handedness with footedness, it would be a lot easier."

"Is there anything else we can get from this?" asked Tricia. She was really into this detective business, which made Steve smile.

"Actually, there is," Steve assured her. "Do you see that very faint line there?" he said indicating again with his pencil. "It's not very clear, but it does follow an elliptical route, albeit broken."

"Yes," said Tricia excitedly, "I think that might be a hole in t' sole."

"And I think you would probably be right," said Steve. "It's certainly wearing of the sole. So, what does that tell us?"

"Sir," said Tricia. "I think it tells us that the wearer was not rich. Otherwise, he would have some decent shoes on."

"Well done," Steve congratulated her. "It indicates he is either not rich or not very clothes conscious, or both. Another thing is, there are no patterns, so this shoe is unlikely to be a trainer or similar. It's more likely to be a traditional shoe with a plain leather or rubber sole."

"Amazing," said Tricia. She was really enjoying this lesson in investigational work. "Just one other thing," said Steve. "If this shoe stamped on the ground, it would almost certainly have left a heel print, but there isn't one."

"What does that mean?" asked Tricia.

"It more than likely means that the shoe was either very flat without a heel, or it has what is commonly referred to as a wedge heel," said Steve. "If it was a wedge heel that would indicate the wearer might have been fashion-conscious with money at some time but had fallen on hard times."

"Bloody 'ell," said Tricia, "if we keep on like this, we'll soon know his name an' address."

Everyone laughed. Yes, Detective Constable Tricia Mason was just the person to brighten up a dull day.

"We are getting there," said Steve. "Is there anything else you think we might learn about its wearer?"

"Apart from what he had for breakfast, I can't see what else there is," Tricia replied.

"Well now," said Steve, "we don't know what he had for breakfast, but we do know that it isn't usually very much. This guy, and by the way, it is a man, not a woman - this is not a woman's shoe - is either not very tall or he doesn't weigh very much. If he had been heavier, the footprint would have been deeper than this."

"Is that all you've got, sir?" said Tricia with her usual humour."

"Yes, that's about it," said Steve. "I think we might call it a day. We'll meet here in the morning unless something turns up overnight."

That evening Steve sat with Susan. The discussion soon got onto the missing boy. Steve told her they hadn't found the boy, but they had got a footprint that might bring some results.

"I hate these crimes against children," Susan revealed. "Not that any crime is good but when it involves children, it's so much worse. You cannot begin to imagine the fear they must go through. Young James must be so scared right now."

This was the first time either of them had opened up about crime since the Longbow Murders, and of course, that related to a child murder too. Steve's suspicions that Susan knew more about the killing of the five perpetrators had remained securely hidden away from discussion for many months. Steve was not about to mention it now.

"Yes," Steve agreed, "I'm sure he must be, but never mind, we will find him."

"You really think so, Steve?" Susan asked.

"Yes, I do. We don't always get any clues but this time we have a footprint that I'm sure the kidnapper didn't intend to leave."

"You can't get very much from a footprint though, can you?" said Susan.

"It would surprise you," said Steve, "just as it did Tricia when we examined it this afternoon."

"Oh, Tricia has seen it, has she?" asked Susan with just a little too much interest and enthusiasm.

"Yes, so don't you go pumping her for information about this case," Steve warned.

"As if I would," Susan smiled. Steve let out a big sigh, realising he had just given Susan an unintended invitation to do just that.

"I give up," he said.

"Oh, don't give up Steve," said Susan mockingly. "Did I tell you I am having lunch with Tricia tomorrow, darling?"

"You have now," he said in resignation.

Story Two – Kidnapped Justice
Part Two

The following morning, Steve and Tricia went to Great Ricton Hall and Johnny was still there. Steve sent him back to the station. After updating Mr Johnson on the evidence, Steve asked if he knew anyone who might fit the description, as slender as it was.

"I know most people around here, and none of them would have done this," said Johnson. "There are a couple of empty houses and farms in the area, though, so maybe you might check them."

"I'll look into it," Steve assured him.

"How about people who might have got into financial difficulties?" Tricia asked.

"I couldn't tell you," Johnson admitted. "I'm not privy to people's financial details."

"No," said Tricia. "I wasn't suggesting that. I wondered if there might be anyone you know who was fine but might be showing some signs that things are not quite as usual."

"Oh, I see," said Johnson.

"There's Harry Bordon," Mrs Johnson suggested. "He had to sell-off half of his land last year."

"That's right," said Johnson. "He only has about two-hundred and forty acres now. It used to be much bigger."

"Yes, that's t' sorta thing," said Tricia. "Does 'e fit t' profile?"

"Not really, not if you're looking for a small or slim guy. Harry is a giant of a bloke, and I don't think he's lost any weight lately."

"OK," said Steve, "but think about it, will you? Any help in identifying the guy will be useful."

Around midmorning, as they chatted, Johnson's telephone rang. He answered it quickly.

"It's him," he said. "Wants me and Mrs Johnson to meet him in the village park in one hour."

"Ah, now we're getting somewhere," said Steve.

"No police - that's what the kidnapper said."

"Of course," said Steve, "but we will be nearby in our cars, out of sight."

"We've got to go to the bench under the tree in the centre of the park to be there in an hour. We should get ready."

The Johnsons got ready to leave, and the two detectives went to their cars.

"Mine's a bit obvious, Detective Constable," said Steve to Tricia. "We'll go back to the station, leave my car there, and go to our point of observation in yours."

Soon afterward, they left for Ricton. Tricia drew into the kerb about three hundred behind the johnson's.

The Johnson's walked down the main path through the park until they got to the tree with the park bench beneath it. They sat down and waited. After a short while, Johnson's phone rang.

"Johnson," said a man's voice. "Listen carefully. Under the seat, there is a CD taped to the underside of the wooden struts. Locate it and tell me when you have it."

Johnson slid his hand under the seat until he found the CD.

"I've got it."

"Good," said the voice and rang off.

The Johnsons waited a while to see if the man would ring back, but he didn't.

Johnson opened the CD case. There was a disc inside with the word 'PLAY' written on it in felt tip pen.

They quickly made their way back to their car and put the CD into the car player. The voice of young James came through the speakers.

"James, are you OK," said Mrs Johnson.

"Be quiet, woman," said Johnson. "This is a CD. James can't hear you."

"Dad, I've got to tell you to go to the bank and get one-hundred thousand pounds. You must put fifty in a plastic supermarket bag and take it down to the river where the white stake is and the wooden seat you made. Do it this afternoon at three o'clock."

That was it; there was nothing more on the CD. Johnson played it back twice. It was during the third time that Tricia drove up behind him. Steve got out and came to the car window as Johnson wound it down.

"Listen to this," he said to Steve and played it back one more time.

Steve sighed. "That's pretty straightforward. Can you get one hundred thousand?"

"Yes, that's not a problem," said Johnson.

"It isn't very much if you'll excuse me saying so," said Steve. "I would have expected it to be much more than that."

"Yes, me too," said Johnson. "Hardly worth the effort for a hundred grand, but I'm pleased we can sort this out quickly. I'll go to the bank right now. It's only a little way down the road."

"OK," said Steve. "We'll have some lunch and meet up at your place at two o'clock."

"Yes," Johnson agreed. "We'll see you later." Then he drove off.

"Detective Constable," said Steve to Tricia. "Do you have a pair of binoculars in the vehicle?"

"Yes, sir," she replied.

"Bring them with you this afternoon? I'll bring mine also. We don't want to miss anything on this exchange, so we'll view them from the house."

They went back to the station, and Tricia set off to the restaurant in Ricton to have lunch with Susan. When she entered, Susan has already arrived.

"Here, Tricia," said Susan, handing her the menu. "Choose your order; this one is on me."

"Thanks, Susan. I s'pose this is a bribe ta pump me fer infermation."

"I can see why you're a detective," Susan grinned. "You're pretty astute. About what do you think I want information?"

"Now, let me guess." A look of mock concentration spread across Tricia's face. "No. My detective skills 'ave deserted me; I've no idea."

They both laughed like a couple of schoolgirls, even though Susan was about fifteen years older than Tricia. They had become good friends since Tricia came to Ricton, and with Steve's high recommendation of her, Tricia had found a place in Susan's life that was otherwise vacant. Of course, Susan was also a good friend of Debbie, Mike's wife, but Debbie had two children, which made casual meetings difficult.

"Have you been busy this morning?" Susan asked.

"Yes, quite busy. There's been contact."

"You mean by the kidnapper?"

"I shouldn't be chatting about these things, and I hope you don't think I do with anyone else, 'cause I don't. But you being Steve's partner, well..."

"Tricia, darling, I know that you wouldn't. You are much too professional. If you don't want to tell me anything, I'll understand."

It was the kind of comment that made Tricia feel unique to Susan, and as she was new to the area, she wanted to feel special.

"That's arlright, Susan. Ah know you're as professional as me." Tricia occasionally slipped back into her Yorkshire brogue.

"Thank you," Susan responded.

"Yes. He's made contact. He's asking fer money an' there might be a 'andover later t' day."

"Really? How much is he asking for?"

"That's the surprising thing. He only wants a hundred thousand pounds and only fifty of it t' day."

"Fifty thousand?" Susan couldn't believe it was such a low sum. "It hardly seems worth all the effort, does it? Johnson is a very wealthy man."

"Yes, it's hard to believe," said Tricia. "We'll be going back t' 'ouse 'safternoon."

"So, where will the exchange take place?"

"I don't know, but it might be on t' riverbank."

"What makes you say that?"

"Johnson has to go down t' river with t' money 'safternoon."

"That's crazy," Susan exclaimed. "The guy could get caught easily on the river. I reckon he must be a nut case."

Tricia nodded. "It's possible, unless there's something we ain't aware of. I've been trying 't think about what it could be, but I've got nothing. Steve has arranged for Mike to be hidden somewhere along the river in a motor launch."

Susan started thinking. "Look, Tricia, I know this is asking a lot, and I don't want you to put your job on the line, but would you do something."

"That sounds ominous. Depends on whatcha asking."

"Of course. When the exchange or whatever has happened, would you send me a text saying how?"

"That's asking a lot. I don't know. It's one thing chatting privately like this, but sending texts - Why do you want that?"

"There's something on my mind that I want to check. Would you please, please, Tricia."

"OK," Tricia agreed. "I'll try, but I don't promise anything. You should give up yer fashion job an' become a detective. Then ah wouldn't 'ave ter risk me job."

"Don't worry, Trish. I won't be jeopardising your job."

They finished their lunch, and Tricia made her way back to the station. After checking to make sure her binoculars were in the car, she and Steve separately made their way to great Ricton Hall.

Mr Johnson was preparing to meet the kidnapper by the river. It was a solid fifteen-minute walk down through the fields, and he set off at one thirty carrying a supermarket bag containing fifty-thousand pounds, as instructed. The money was in fifty-pound notes, so there were one thousand of them. The bag wasn't heavy, but it did weigh more than two and a half pounds.

On a seat in Great Ricton Hall car park at the top of the hill, Steve and Tricia sat watching through their binoculars.

"Keep your wits about you, Detective Constable," said Steve. "Try to catch as much of what goes on as you can. It's a good way away, but I can pick out the white post quite clearly."

"Yes, me too," replied Tricia, "I'm scanning up an' down t' riverbank but don't see nothing 'appening yet."

Soon Johnson arrived at the seat by the white post. He looked around but found nothing, then scoured up and down the river. All was quiet, so he sat down on the seat and waited. Eventually, his phone rang.

"Hello," he said.

A man's voice responded.

"Wait quietly. Soon, something will arrive and you will hear it coming."

Johnson said nothing and waited. Gradually, a sound became louder and louder. At first, he thought it was a motorboat coming up the river, but he saw no-one. Then he realized the sound came from overhead. He looked up instantly, and there it was.

Arriving from across the river was a drone. As it got nearer and descended, Johnson saw that a hook hung beneath it. Eventually, it hovered about six feet above the ground behind the seat.

The voice on the phone said, "OK, hook on the bag. Do it gently and don't unbalance the drone."

Johnson did as asked. When the bag was secure on the hook, the voice spoke again,

"Be here the same time tomorrow with the other fifty in a bag." He rang off.

The drone took off gaining height as it flew across the river and over the hill. All returned to quiet. Johnson looked a lonely figure as he made his way back up the hill.

Steve and Tricia had seen this in their binoculars. At first, they had no idea what was happening until Tricia caught sight of the drone.

"Well, bugger me," she exclaimed in her Northern accent, "this has got t' be a first. This guy might be a poor man, but he ain't stupid. Who'd 'ave thoughta that?"

"Quite brilliant," Steve agreed. "That's why he only wanted fifty-thousand in a supermarket bag. Any more would be too heavy, and the bag's handles are ideal for hanging below the drone."

"I could do my shopping like that," joked Tricia, "but it would take all week with one can of beans at a time."

"It's not the right time for joking. I wonder if he's got any news of the kid?"

"Let's hope so. Poor little sod must be out of 'is mind."

Johnson arrived back at the house and reported what had happened.

"I've got to repeat this at the same time tomorrow. Is there anything we can do to catch this bastard?" he asked.

"We will certainly give it our best shot," said Steve, "but we'll have to be careful until we have your boy back safely." Steve turned to Tricia.

"Detective Constable, thanks for your help. I think you can return to the station while I talk discuss our options with Mr and Mrs Johnson. I'll catch up with you later."

Tricia got into her car and left, but not before sending a short and to the point text to Susan.

'Collected by drone. Same again tomorrow.' Was all it said. Tricia wondered why Susan had asked for that information but could think of no good reason.

She returned to the station, reported to Mike, and about one hour later, Steve returned. He gathered them together in Mike's office.

"Right, we have to make some plans for tomorrow if we are going to catch this guy," he started. "First,

Detective Constable, I would like you to be at the Johnsons tomorrow and keep a lookout like you did today. We might have missed something, so you will need to look uniquely. Concentrate on the surrounding area rather than on the point of action."

"Yes, sir," said Tricia. "Maybe I could get a little nearer. There're a couple of trees about a third of the way down the field. If I get there early, I could get t' them and look out from there."

"Yes, good thinking. There are some bushes beneath those trees that might give you some cover."

"Yes, sir, "Tricia said with excitement. This kidnapping was a new case for her, and she loved it.

"OK, then, Mike," Steve turned his attention to the sergeant. "I see you have a map of the area. Let's look."

Together, they studied the map. There was a narrow road running along the top of the hill on the other side of the river up which they concentrated.

"Here is a turning," said Mike pointing a little way along the road from Ricton. "I think I should stay in that vicinity. I know from driving there many times there's a farm gate to the field opposite the junction. I would be able to see the action from there."

"Yes, and if the drone seems to be going in the direction of that side road, you could follow it. Have you ever driven along there?"

"Yes, quite a few times. It's quite winding but otherwise heads generally in one direction."

Steve studied the map again. His eyes headed further along the top road until he found another junction.

"How about this road? What is that one like?" It looked straight, but then so did the other one on the map.

"It's very similar," said Mike, "but there isn't a gate at that junction. It's a pity because that is on the other side of the action."

"Never mind about that. I will be able to get through or over any fences in that vicinity. I'll find a spot near there, and we'll watch what happens from both perspectives. Will it be as elevated there as it is at the first junction?"

"I think so. The top road is quite level, I'm sure."

"OK, that's the plan," Steve wrapped it up. "With Tricia, we will be watching the action from three points. If we see the drone heading off between our points, Mike, we'll follow it from the side roads."

"OK. I think we'll call it a day and convene here tomorrow morning."

They cleared away. Steve and Mike went off to do some paperwork, while Tricia went to the lady's room and phoned Susan.

"Where are you, Susan? Are you busy?" Tricia enquired.

"I'm in Septon," Susan replied.

"What are you doing there?" Tricia was surprised that Susan would be in that town. "Doing some shopping?"

"Sort of," said Susan non-committedly.

"How can you be sort of shopping, Susan?" Tricia was unhappy with the answer. "What shop are you in?"

"Ah! I can hear Detective Tricia speaking," said Susan, "I'd recognise that voice anywhere."

Tricia laughed, but she felt that Susan was simply fobbing her off and wasn't having any of it. "So, are you going to tell Detective Tricia where you are, or am I going to have to get my team onto it?" she joked.

"No, please, Detective, don't set them on me. I'll come quietly," joked Susan, then said, "If you must know, I am in a Joytoys, the large toy shop here."

"Oh, I see," said Tricia, satisfied with the answer. "You are buying a present. Timmy has a birthday soon, doesn't he?"

"Yes, he does," Susan agreed without further commitment on the matter. "Thanks for the message. That was very useful."

"Really, in what way," asked Tricia, quite unable to see what use it would be to Susan.

"It satisfied my curiosity," Susan explained. "You see, I suspected they might use a drone."

"You did?" Tricia couldn't believe it. Neither Steve nor herself had considered it. Not Mike, either for that matter. "Susan, you are incredible. Why didn't you say so? We could have checked it out today instead of waiting for tomorrow."

"You forget, Tricia," said Susan patiently, "I am not supposed to know anything about this case."

"Oh, yes, I'd forgotten that." It was only later that the thought occurred to her that Susan could have shared her suspicions with her, and she could have mentioned it as her idea. She guessed that Susan, like herself, had not thought of it at the time.

Meanwhile, Susan was thankful for Tricia's acceptance.

"You are so clever, Susan," said Tricia with great admiration. "How on Earth did you think of that, a drone?"

"I guess it must be my criminal mind. What else could it be?"

"Criminal, or not, it certainly found the answer to this one. How did you become such a criminal mastermind?" Tricia laughed.

"I don't know," said Susan, "but I assure you I only use it for good."

"Well, that's a relief. I'd hate to go up against your mind." The two women laughed together before concluding their conversation.

* * *.

At the office the next day Steve spoke to Mike.

"We'll have to be careful while on the lookout. Our guy will probably have his own car somewhere there, and we don't want to draw attention."

"Right," Mike agreed. "We'll get our cars off the road somewhere, so we don't stand out."

"We'll soon have to be off," said Steve. "Please all stay in constant telephone communication and report everything suspicious or pertinent."

The two men took their cars out onto the top road. Tricia left for Great Ricton Hall. One there, she explained to Johnson that she was going to get closer. He had already got his cash prepared and placed it inside another plastic supermarket bag. Eventually, he set off down the hill, and Tricia hid in the bushes near the trees. Her binoculars waited around her neck. Before handover time arrived, she browsed the area looking for anything amiss.

Johnson arrived at the seat by the white post and waited. Soon, he heard the drone as it approached. Tricia picked it out with the binoculars. She noticed something she hadn't seen before. It was a camera attached to the drone. Of course. How would the kidnapper be able to direct it so easily without a camera? She spoke into the live telephone connection.

"Sir, I didn't notice it yesterday, but there is a camera attached to the drone."

"I didn't notice it either, but there must have been one," Steve replied.

Tricia returned to her observations. Although she was very alert and scouring the landscape, she never noticed a second drone that had appeared off the side from the Ricton direction.

The same as the day before, Johnson secured the money to the drone, and it took to the sky in the direction of the hill opposite. Steve and Mike had picked up the action as they waited patiently for the drone to reach the top road and pass over it. So, it surprised them when it stopped advancing halfway up the hill.

Gradually, the drone decreased its height and carefully sunk to the ground where it lay motionless. Steve and Mike waited for it to continue its journey.

"What's he playing at?" said Mike.

"Probably cat and mouse," said Steve.

They waited. It was now ten minutes since the drone had landed and there had been no movement. They continued to wait. Fifteen, twenty, thirty minutes.

"Do you think it has actually conked out," said Mike, "Maybe its battery has failed."

"It's possible," said Steve. "We'll give it another ten minutes and if it still hasn't moved, we'll have to go and retrieve it. There are fifty thousand pounds in that bag."

On the other side of the river, Johnson had retreated to the bushes where Tricia was watching.

"What are they playing at," he said, "They should be going down there and rescuing the money."

"Don't worry, Mr Johnson," said Tricia. "All the while it is in sight it is safe enough. We all have our eyes on it."

After forty minutes of no action, Steve and Mike decided they had best look. They both walked down the hill from their various positions towards the drone.

They'd each gone about one-hundred yards when Tricia's voice came over the connection.

"It's just a thought, sir, but don't you think it might be better if one of you stayed up on the road?"

"Why's that?" Mike asked over the radio. At that moment the drone got into action and started to rise from its stationary position.

"That's why, Sargent," she said, vindicated.

"Damn," said Steve. "Why do I never listen to you when you are always one step ahead."

The drone rose into the air and continued its way as it had the day before. Steve and Mike struggled back up the hill, but the drone was not in sight any longer. As they strolled back to their cars and Tricia walked up the hill with Johnson, none of them noticed the second drone following the first one over the horizon.

About ten minutes later Steve drove into the Great Ricton Hall carpark.

"Well, so much for that cock-up," he said as he got out of his car.

"Yes, he's a clever bugger," said Johnson, "but all I want is my boy back safely. I hope he will have some good news for me in the morning."

"Why," asked Steve, "What is happening tomorrow?"

"That's it, I don't know," said Johnson. "I spoke to him when he called me down by the river and all he said was 'be by your phone early tomorrow'. I don't know why or what he is going to say. He might even be going to ask for more money."

"Damn," was all Steve could say. He was so disappointed that they had screwed up. "Got any ideas, Detective Constable?" he asked.

"Huh, what would I know," she said but avoided saying, "I'm just a lowly constable," which was what was going through her mind.

Susan will have some ideas she thought. She would wait and see what happened in the morning and then speak to Susan. She was so keen to know what the kidnapper was going to do next that she didn't call in at the Station the following morning but went straight out to Great Ricton Hall about an hour before she was due to start her working day.

It was quiet when she got there, but Mrs Johnson was up and about, and seeing Tricia in the carpark, she invited her in for a cup of coffee

"Mr Johnson is in his study waiting for the phone to ring," she explained.

"So, the call hasn't come in yet?" said Tricia. "I do hope it is good news for you."

"Yes, it's very worrying. James is a sensitive boy, and this must be terrifying for him."

"It would be terrifying for any of us," said Tricia, "but I think he is a brave boy. He did try to blow his whistle down by the river."

"Yes, he did, didn't he," said Mrs Johnson upon reflection.

Mr Johnson came rushing into the room.

"Mary, the call came."

"Yes, well what was it. Are you going to tell us?"

"I have to go to the old barn," said Johnson.

"You mean the old disused wreck over on the west boundary?" said Mrs Johnson.

Tricia had seen this barn and examined it the first day before all the searchers had arrived. It was just a very old barn in much need of repair. There was nothing special about it. The three of them went outside and

96

walked to the barn on the west boundary. It's large door, closed shut, wasn't locked. Johnson pushed it open and they all looked inside.

"James was standing on a chair in the middle of the floor space, his hands tied behind his back with a cable tie, and his mouth taped with duct tape. A blindfold was around his eyes. Around his neck was a noose at the end of a rope, thrown over the high beam of a roof truss, and pulled tight.

But what was most disconcerting was that the chair wasn't positioned directly under the rope's support but about three feet to one side. This meant the pressure applied, could unbalance the boy from the chair. Had that happened he would have hanged.

Mr Johnson rushed to the boy and lifted him. Tricia went to the far side and undid the other end of the rope tied to a hook on the wall. When he was safe, they removed the blindfold and tape, and Tricia set about releasing his hands. As for Mrs Johnson, she could not stop cuddling and kissing the boy as they all made their way back to the house.

When Steve arrived, he thanked Tricia for coming to the Johnsons early and taking part in the release of young James. There was no doubt that Steve was very pleased with the participation of Tricia on this, her first real case. She was certainly an asset. He told her she could go back to the Station but to take an hour off for breakfast before doing so.

Tricia wanted to let Susan know that young James was safe and sound, so she phoned her first. They decided to have breakfast together. Tricia told her about the way the poor lad was precariously standing on a chair afraid to move an inch in case he slipped and tumbled to his death.

"What an animal," said Susan, incensed at the unnecessary cruelty of the act.

"I'd like to put a rope around his neck and leave him," said Tricia.

"Don't worry," Susan replied, "this guy is going to get what he deserves."

"Not until we catch him," Tricia pointed out.

"Oh, you'll catch him," said Susan with conviction. "I guarantee it."

"I hope you are right. I wish I could be so certain."

Susan smiled with a knowing look. "I am," she said quietly.

They finished their breakfast and Tricia returned to work. Steve and Mike were discussing their next move and had decided that in the afternoon they should all go up above the top road and scour the countryside for clues. They had to find this guy before he did something similar again.

The ransom money was comparatively insignificant compared to what it might have been. It seemed that the only restriction was down to the load capability of the drone he was using. Two payment collections had worked for him. Any added attempts would prove too risky. He was no fool and had calculated his moves very carefully.

That afternoon, the team was preparing to go up to the top road when the telephone rang. The muffled voice made it difficult to tell whether it was a man or a woman speaking. They recorded calls for obvious reasons, and this call was no different. Mike played it back over the amplified speaker.

"Please, listen carefully. I shall say this only once. You will find the kidnapper of James Johnson at this address." The voice then read out the address and rang off.

Mike played it back several times, but they were unable to read into it any more than the voice had said.

"Do you know where this is Mike?" asked Steve.

"Yes," Mike confirmed. "I don't know the exact property, but I do know roughly where they are indicating.

"OK," said Steve, "what are we waiting for?"

The three of them set off in their separate vehicles following Mike onto the top road. Mike turned at the third junction left. About two miles along the road he turned right and headed toward a woodland. A track went off to the left and they all followed Mike into the woodland.

Eventually, they came to a driveway on the left. An old car stood in front of a dilapidated old farmhouse. A disused barn was to its left and a cowshed beyond that.

They stopped in the drive and Steve knocked on the front door. There was no answer, so he knocked again. Meanwhile, Tricia went around to the rear of the house and knocked on the back door. Still no answer. She tried the door and found it to be open.

Tricia went inside and made her way to the front where she opened the front door for Steve and Mike. They came inside and between them made a search of the house. Finding nothing Mike led them outside and on to the disused barn. Closed but not locked was a large wide door to the barn. Mike took hold of the edge of the door to open it, but it was stuck, held back by something.

Steve joined Mike and together they pulled the door open. Muffled sounds came from the centre of the floor where a chair lay on its side. From the roofbeam hung a rope with a noose. The noose was around the neck of a man who was struggling and groaning as he fought for his life at the end of the rope. A second rope tied to his left leg stretched back to the entrance door where it was firmly secured.

The man, his hands tied behind his back, his mouth taped with duct tape, wore a blindfold around his eyes.

Steve rushed forward and grabbed the man by his legs lifting him to release the tension on the rope around his neck. Mike came forward to help him as Tricia went to the far side and released the end of the rope from a batten on the sidewall.

The man dropped to the floor.

Steve undid his hands, mouth, and blindfold as the man gasped to get his breath. Tricia, however, was more interested in the man's feet. She inspected his left shoe. It was a well-worn shoe with a platform heel and a hole in its sole.

"This is our guy," she said to Steve showing the shoe. "I'll bet that's 'n exact match t' cast we 'ave back at t' station."

"No doubt about it," Steve agreed, dragging the man to his feet.

Mike handcuffed him, read him his rights, and bundled him off to his car. When they returned to the station, they were very surprised to find two supermarket bags containing fifty-pound notes hanging on the door handle.

After they had the man locked away, Steve said, "What puzzles me is how this good Samaritan knew so much."

"How do you mean?" asked Mike.

"Well, Mike, this guy was set up exactly, and in every detail, the same as the boy, James. Except, of course, for the rope tying his leg to the entrance door. Everything was identical yet the only people who know about this, apart from the kidnapper, are we three plus the Johnsons."

"True," said Mike.

"And I'll bet," Steve continued, "that the Johnsons haven't been anywhere near. I was with them for quite some time. Young James had no information he could give us and we three have been together for the past few hours."

Mike shook his head in bewilderment.

Steve let out a long, exasperated sigh.

Tricia, on the other hand, said nothing, nor would she. Not only did she value her job, but she also valued the closeness she had with her best friend. When she turned away, she had a large grin on her face and a degree of admiration she could not, nor would ever express.

Story Three
The Girl With Persuasion

The kidnap of young James Johnson had occurred a couple of months ago. After an anonymous tip, they apprehended the culprit, and no-one was any the wiser about the secret mastermind behind it. Except, maybe, Detective Constable Tricia Mason, who might have had an inkling, but was keeping it to herself. So close to her chest was this suspicion that even the person she suspected knew nothing about it.

As for the famous Longbow Murders, that case now a year past, remained unsolved. Detective Inspector Stephen Kendall had overseen the case, and while he had not located the perpetrator, he had suspicions. Again, he was keeping them to himself, as revealing them would be a disaster. Just like Detective Constable Tricia, Steve held a very close secret.

One might wonder if others at the police station also had secrets too wild and inflammatory for exposure. Sergeant Mike Compton, and his wife Debbie, had been there for many years. There was also Constable Johnny Parsons, a relatively new addition to the understaffed village police operation. It was unlikely that Johnny had any wild secrets. He had a job to keep his hands out of his pockets, much less keep a secret.

So, it was extraordinary that a small group of law enforcers managed to get along and develop a successful local operation without wrapping up their cases. The station thrived like a family business, all forgetting their place in the pecking order.

On one beautiful summer Saturday, Mike, Debbie, and the kids hosted a bar-b-que for Tricia, Johnny, Steve, and his loving partner, Susan. They sat around in the early evening, drinking and laughing. It wasn't surprising given the company that conversation would sometimes drift to police work.

Mike said how odd it was that they had never picked up any clues as to the identity of the Longbow murderer. They set to wondering whether the culprit was still living in the vicinity and whether he or she would be a danger to other people if never apprehended. Steve remained strangely quiet on the subject, but his partner Susan was not so hesitant.

"I don't think there's any danger at all," she said.

Steve glanced at her beneath his brow, disapprovingly.

"No," Susan continued, "by all appearances, this episode was the mother's work. She balanced the law on the matter until satisfied. That's what she set out to do. Nothing more nor less - job done."

"Well, that has answered that then," said Mike. "It's a good thing that Steve brought his legal expert along."

"Your clear-thinking mind, Susan, is just what we need," said Tricia. "I agree with you, one-hundred percent."

"Me, too," said Debbie.

"Looks like we blokes are surplus to requirements on this matter," said Mike. "What do you think Steve?"

"I've learned never to question the logic of a woman. I think that's something you're still working on, Mike."

Everyone laughed, and Tricia pumped the air, shouting, "Woman power."

"The one that has me beat is how the person who got the kidnapper knew about it," said Johnny. "That's one mystery that keeps me awake at night."

"And you didn't yet find the answer?" asked Tricia.

"No," said Johnny abruptly.

"Then I reckon you would do better getting a good night's sleep," said Tricia bringing everyone to more laughter.

Debbie spoke up, "Do you remember that case when we first came here, Mike?"

"Which one was that? Not the whore in the bag?" said Mike.

"God, that sounds gruesome," said Tricia. "Was there really a whore in a bag?"

"Certainly was. That's what they called it," said Debbie. "Tell them about it, Mike."

"Yeah, it was quite gruesome, but strangely, it eventually became more of a light-hearted matter. I think that's because we remembered the woman rather than her corpse."

"What was she like?" asked Susan. "Come on, Mike, tell us about it."

"Well," said Mike, "if the rumours are true, she was the woman who screwed every man in the Ricton area, probably more than once."

"Blimey," exclaimed Tricia. "She really was the local whore."

"Apparently," said Mike, "although she wasn't born a local. Her name was Marietta Duvalier. She spoke with a strong French accent, and no one exactly knows when she moved here."

"And no one figured out who killed her?" asked Steve.

"No. Marietta's body turned up in a plastic bag discarded on the refuse tip. Such a waste. She was the most remarkable looking woman you ever saw."

"But you say the case was when you first came here," said Steve. "Did you meet her."

"Unfortunately, not," Mike replied, to which Debbie quickly retorted, "And that's just as well from what everyone says about her. He's not that strong, my Mike. He was putty in my hands. God knows what he would have been in the hands of an expert."

Steve and the others laughed.

"So, you are making your assessment of her from photos, then?"

"God, no," Mike responded, "there's a video film on record. The guy before me must have been a bit taken with her too. He tried to record her prostituting and had her followed by a camera-toting constable. The thing is, he never caught her doing any soliciting. He did catch her chatting up a lot of men, though."

"So, who keeps this film?" asked Tricia.

"We do," Mike replied. "It's kept in the files with her case notes."

"Well, what are we waiting for," Susan interjected. "Aren't you going to show us. We all want to see what the fuss was all about, don't we?" she looked at everyone.

There was general agreement causing Mike to give up and go to the station next door to find the film. It was on standard cinecamera, so Debbie set up the mobile screen and projector while Mike was gone. When he returned, everyone was waiting in great anticipation of the sight of this remarkable woman.

Mike put the reel on the projector, turned out the lights, and started the film rolling.

There were various shots of Marietta, usually eyeing up her target before pouncing on the defenceless individual. And from the way she looked and spoke, the poor bloke never stood a chance.

Marietta was of average height. She wore extremely high black heels, dark stockings that reached to the hem of a short, black, pencil skirt, open from the hem to the waist, on one side. The tops of her nylons were visible as she sauntered up to her selected victim. Miss Duvalier wore a tight, not very secure, white blouse, her ample breasts spilling out over the top. Her skin was very pale, accentuated by her long jet-black hair that hung down in waves that almost reached her waist.

Marietta did not look real, more like a character in a dark mystery thriller from a nineteen-forties movie. But what brought her to life on the screen was her voice, that of the stereotypical French seductress.

"Ello, you luvly man. I bin lukin atchu an I bin tinkin 'bout us. Do you vant cum viz me so ve tink 'bout us togedder?"

The poor man looked like he might have had a knife in his ribs from the expression on his face. It was just like an arrest where the man had to come quietly. He didn't answer, just looked dazed as she took hold of his shirt front and led him away to a dark passage between the buildings.

"Bloody 'ell," said Tricia, "so that's how to do it. I'm getting some good tips from this."

Everyone laughed.

"Ha ha," Johnny chuckled, "does that mean you are coming to work on Monday in six-inch heels and a pencil skirt."

"You'd like that Johnny," said Tricia, "but then you'd get even less work done than you do now."

With everyone in high spirits and still watching the captured events of Marietta on the prowl, Debbie took Susan's hand and whispered to her, "Come with me, Susan. I want to show you something."

Debbie took her into her bedroom and opened her wardrobe. She took out a hanger containing a short black pencil skirt with a slit, a pair of black high-heeled shoes, and a white blouse. Then she reached up to the top shelf and took out a box. Inside was the most beautiful long black wig.

"A couple of years ago, I went to a fancy-dress party in the village. I wanted to go as something special rather than the usual old costumes people wear."

"So, you went as Marietta Duvalier," said Susan.

"I did, and I got second prize," said Debbie. "And to be honest, I didn't look much like her. I don't have the legs nor the tits for it."

Susan laughed.

"But you, Susan, are a natural for her. Why not put this gear on and we'll go next door and frighten them all?" Debbie begged.

"OK, I'll give it a go. It should be a laugh."

Susan got herself dressed in Debbie's clothes and looked so real; she even amazed Debbie.

Debbie returned to the lounge. "OK, everyone," she said, "we have a visitor."

"I wondered where you'd gone," said Mike. "Who is it?"

A long leg, clad in a black stocking and wearing a very high-heeled black stiletto, draped itself around the doorframe. Everyone looked with anticipation. Then the woman slid around the frame into the doorway. Stepping into the room was Marietta Duvalier.

"Ello, boys," said Marietta in a French accent, "are you 'avin some fun 'ere. Vould you like 'ave more fun? You mistere Steve. You vant touch me," she said sidling up to him and placing one of his hands on her breast that the tight blouse could not contain.

Everyone in the room burst into hysterical laughter.

Susan continued with her act. "Why you laugh? I will go find udder man," she said, and they just fell apart laughing.

Susan disappeared into the bedroom to change out of her fancy dress. When she returned, they all applauded enthusiastically.

"Susan," said Steve, "I had no idea you were such a great actress. The eroticism I did have a little knowledge of."

Johnny and Tricia whistled loudly, and they all laughed together again.

When all the hilarity had died down, Steve was keen to learn more details about the case.

"Mike, what can you tell us about the case? If this is still unsolved, well, one never knows, we might be able to put something in place that wasn't there before."

"There's not much I can tell you, Steve," said Mike thinking about the details. "As I said, just about everyone in the village had intimate knowledge of Miss Duvalier. And when I say everyone, I mean a lot of the women as well."

"Really?" said Susan. "Please tell us more."

"There was this married man, Jeffrey Cant. His mother also lived in the village; still does, as far as I know. It was well known that he had turned Miss Duvalier down several times. He used to get teased about it, what with his name being Cant as well. But he put up with it until it became known that Marietta also seduced his wife."

"What!" exclaimed Tricia. "What kind of village have I moved to?"

That got the usual laugh out of everyone before Mike continued.

"Before then, people used to tease him with the words, *Jeffrey can't*. But now it changed to, *Jeffrey can't, but his wife can*. Jeffrey didn't like that and got into a couple of fights over it. We thought he was the most likely candidate for Marietta's murder and brought him in for questioning."

"His alibi was that he was at home watching a big match on the TV. His wife confirmed it, saying she had been with him. Later, when questioning his mother, she also claimed to have been there watching the match with the Cants. No one believed her, even though she is a very strict churchgoer, but there was no evidence one way or another. We suspected she knew something about it, but what could we do? We had to drop it, and no-one has ever been able to shed further light on the matter since."

"So, where are these people now?" asked Susan.

"The Cants have moved away, but the mother, Mrs Cant, still lives in the cottage where she has always lived," said Mike. "And that is the case for Marietta Duvalier's murder. It's an unsolved crime, and I doubt we will ever find the truth."

The group mulled it over between them, and, finally, the party ended, everyone had a very good time.

* * *

Mrs Cant, the elder, was a stickler for routine. Every day at eleven in the morning, if the weather was fine with no rain forecast, she would make sandwiches. With a slice of her favourite Madeira cake, and a couple of extra slices of plain bread, she would place them in a plastic box, put it in her bag, and wait until twelve. At midday precisely, she would go out for her daily walk along the path beside the river.

Mrs Cant would walk this path until she came to a particular bench donated by an anonymous village member. The bench portrayed a small brass plaque, which simply said, Marietta Duvalier. There, Mrs Cant would sit, eating her lunch, and feeding the ducks that waited near the bench for her each day. This particular day was no different.

As she sat contemplating when she had met Marietta near that very spot and throwing bread to the community of ducks in front of her, she heard a voice.

"Ello Dority, are you joy your lunch," said the voice in a French accent.

Mrs Cant froze in her seat, not daring to look up to see whose voice it was. She slowly, turned her head to look at the beautiful woman in a black pencil skirt whose luxuriant black hair hung down just as she had always remembered it.

"Marietta, what do you want?" she asked, her voice quivering from her lack of understanding.

"Vy I vant anyting?" asked Marietta. "Question is, vat do you vant?"

Marietta reached out her hand and stroked Mrs Cant's cheek.

"Dority, you know vat you 'ave to do," said Marietta.

"No, Marietta, I don't know. You must tell me."

"Dority, jus tell truth. You vill feel much better."

Mrs Cant closed her eyes and took in a deep breath. When eventually, she opened them, Marietta was gone. Mrs Cant didn't bother to look for her. She knew it was a message from God telling her to do the right thing - to tell the truth, the secret she had kept for the past ten years.

Mrs Cant got slowly to her feet. At first, her steps were slow and laboured. But gradually, she stepped forward with more confidence as she hurried back to her home.

Two days after her encounter with the deceased Marietta Duvalier, Mrs Cant walked into the Ricton Police Station and gave Detective Constable Tricia Mason a letter. The detective passed it on to Sergeant Mike Compton. Mike opened the letter and read it.

To whom it may concern,

My name is Mrs Dorothy Cant, mother of Jeffrey Cant, accused of the murder of Marietta Duvalier. When questioned, I said I was at my son's house watching a football match with him. That is not true. I was not at Jeffrey's house when Marietta died.

Sometime before that date, Marietta propositioned Jeffrey three times, and each time he had turned her down. About two weeks before her death, Marietta had propositioned Jeffrey's wife, and she had taken Marietta home, and the two of them had engaged in a sexual liaison. I know this because Marietta told me.

The day Marietta died, I met her by chance along the footpath by the river. She stopped to talk to me. I had seen her before but never met her. She was the most strikingly beautiful lovely woman I have ever seen; she mesmerised me. Before I realised what was happening, we were kissing.

Marietta took me to her home, and we engaged in a sexual liaison in her bedroom. It wasn't until after that I felt a deep sense of shame and guilt. I looked at her and no longer saw a beautiful woman, but someone who was the devil's instrument. I knew then it was my duty.

I took a paperknife from her dressing table and killed her, stabbing her several times to make sure the devil inside her was dead.

Although that was the purest act I ever made, I know it is my duty, to tell the truth, and take my punishment.

Finally, I feel free.

Signed

Mrs Dorothy Cant

Story Four – Disadvantaged Friends
Part One

Mrs Cant's confession to the murder of Marietta Duvalier turned up unexpected by the Ricton Police personnel. As a plus, it did give them a positive result for a case hitherto unexplained and unresolved. This was pleasing to Mike Compton who took little time in reporting it to the higher powers.

Detective Inspector Steve Kendall thought it both strange and extraordinary that Mrs Cant's confession came only a little more than a week after they'd been discussing the case in detail. He was also suspicious of his partner Susan who had portrayed a credible likeness to Marietta at the Bar-B-Q party that evening.

As for Mike's wife Debbie, she had wondered why Susan had been so keen to borrow her Marietta costume that week and why she wanted to keep it secret from everyone. All this seemed very strange to everyone except to Tricia, the Detective Constable, who began forming an opinion of Susan.

As Susan was her best friend, Tricia never voiced her suspicions, but she was certainly growing in respect for this beautiful, mysterious, and clever woman. She realised that friendship with the lovely Susan might be advantageous, so continued to cultivate the secrecy of their meetings.

Right now, things were quiet in the village and surrounding area covered by the team. In fact, the oddball constable, Johnny went as far as to say, "I wish someone would get strangled, so this place livens up."

It was an unusual thing for him to say, seeing as how Johnny was the one member of the team who did the least work and didn't get bored too easily. Perhaps it was merely a measure of how quiet everything was right now.

So, when the call came through to Mike's phone reporting a man sitting on a bench in the park who hadn't appeared to move in the past twenty-four hours, it was something of a relief. The caller went on to say, "Do you think he might be dead?"

"It's a possibility," said Mike. "I'll send someone over. Please stay there. What's your name?"

"Jessie. I'm out jogging with my friend, Tizzy."

"OK," said Mike, "just wait there, and someone will be with you very soon."

Tricia, overhearing the conversation, volunteered to go, and some six minutes later, she was at the park. Jessie and Tizzy were standing under a tree, waiting. The man they referred to sat on a bench about thirty yards away.

"That's him there." Jessie pointed. "He still hasn't moved."

Tricia went over to the bench and studied the man before placing her hand on his. It was stone cold. She knew he was dead, but she checked his pulse anyway. She quickly rang Mike.

"Hi, Sarge," she said when he answered. "We've got a stiff here. Been dead a while, I would say."

"OK, Detective Constable, don't touch anything. I'll get the doctor to come out with an ambulance."

"Will the Detective Inspector come out?" asked Tricia.

"Yes," answered Mike. "I'll have a word with him now. Hold tight there, and don't let anyone near. Are the girls who phoned this in still there?"

"Yes, they're nearby."

"Good," said Mike. "Keep them there and take down their particulars."

"OK, Sarge, I'll do that. Thanks."

She walked over to the girls, and after asking them to stay until the Detective Inspector arrived, she wrote down their names and addresses in her notebook.

"When did you first notice him?" she asked.

"We come out jogging every morning," said Jessie - Tizzy was not so talkative - "and yesterday he was there just like he is now. Then we saw him again last night. When he was still there this morning, we thought we had better report it."

"Well, thanks for that," said Tricia. "Pity you didn't report it last night though."

"If he's dead, it won't make much difference, will it?" It seemed that Tizzy had a voice after all.

"Not to him, no," said Tricia wondering how these girls had so little imagination. "I think it might make a difference to his relatives though if he has any."

"Never thought of that," said Tizzy.

"Also," said Tricia, demonstrating the difference between her mind and that of these girls, "it could be the result of foul play, and we have lost a day of our investigation. The most important day too."

"Wow, you're on the ball," said Jessie. "I wish I was a detective."

"Nothing's stopping you, is there?" Tricia asked. "I wished the same, and now I am one."

At that moment, Steve arrived.

"Hello, Detective Constable, what have we got here?" he said

"Just waiting for the doctor and an ambulance," said Tricia. "These girls phoned it in. The guy on the bench is dead, and according to them, he's been there since yesterday morning. I've got their details, sir."

"Well done," Steve turned to the girls, "Anything else you would like to report?" he asked them.

"Like what?" said Jessie.

"When you saw him yesterday, were there any other people near him, for example?"

"No, nothing," said Jessie. "Didn't pay much attention to him yesterday."

"OK," Steve continued. "He doesn't appear to have any bags or such with him. Do you remember if there were any yesterday?"

"Don't know," said Jessie. "Don't think so."

"OK," said Steve. "We have your details, so if we need anything else, we'll get in contact. If you think of something that you haven't mentioned, give me a ring."

Steve handed her his card.

The girls wandered off. As they went, Tricia heard Tizzy say, "Handsome bugger, ain't he? At least you've got his number. She ain't bad either." Jessie giggled.

Tricia smiled and followed Steve to the bench. An ambulance pulled into the park, followed by the doctor in his car.

"Hello, Doctor," said Steve. "I don't think I've seen you since the Longbow Murder case."

"I think you're right, Detective Inspector. Funny business that; did you find out who did it?"

"We did," Steve replied. "Just haven't been able to locate her."

"It was a woman, was it?"

"Yes," said Steve, "but let's not dig up that case. Take a look at this one."

"Right, what have we got here?" The doctor moved to the bench.

"Apparently, he's been here for at least thirty hours. I'm surprised only two joggers spotted him," said Steve.

"Not exactly invisible, is he?" replied the doctor taking a closer look.

Steve went through the man's pockets and took out a wallet, some small change, and a set of keys, which he handed to Tricia. He kept the mobile phone.

"Check out who he is and then bag the rest," said Steve. Tricia looked in the wallet and took out a couple of cards.

"His name is Phillip Collins," she said, and according to this business card, he lives at Winston Street."

"What's that?" said the doctor taking a closer look at the man. "Dammit, yes. I know this man. He used to be a patient of mine some years ago now. If I remember correctly, he used to be in the pump business."

"Sounds about right." Tricia held up a card. "It says Jackson Pumping Systems on the back of this."

"That's the one," the doctor agreed. "Well now, time of death? If he was here yesterday morning, that's a little over twenty-four hours ago. There's also some lingering rigor mortis, so it's less than thirty-six hours. I'd say thirty hours or thereabouts."

"Thanks." Steve checked the body over and found no marks that might indicate the cause of death.

"I'll get back to you on the cause," said the doctor. "I'll get the post-mortem started."

"Let me know to me as soon as you have something, please," Steve requested.

"Just got to wait," said Steve to Tricia. "Meanwhile, we'll check out that address seeing that it's nearby."

* * *

They found the address in Winston Street and knocked on the door. Getting no reply, Tricia offered up the keys, and they let themselves in. It was a tidy home and had the appearance of just Collins living there. There were no family photos, so they guessed he might be single.

However, there was a framed photo showing a group of eight friends together, smiling. Then Tricia found another similar photo with seven of the same people. She continued looking around while Steve checked the mobile. There were a number of contacts, so Steve checked the recent messages. The most frequent contact was with someone called Alan. Steve rang the number.

"Hello, Alan," he said. "I believe you know a man called Phillip Collins."

"Yeah, he's my brother. Who is this?" asked Alan.

"This is Detective Superintendent Stephen Kendall. Are you anywhere near Alan's house?" Steve asked.

"Yeah, just around the corner. "What's this about?"

Steve obtained the address details, and he and Tricia drove round to see Alan. Upon arrival, they immediately recognised him as one of the people in the group photos. Steve broke the news to him, and after the initial shock, Alan said, "I'm not completely surprised. He had been ill recently. Never told me what it was, but I suspected cancer. It took my dad and my older sister."

"Sorry to hear that," said Steve. "It's a bugger when it runs in the family."

"Yeah, sure is," said Alan. "Life can be shit. I feel sorry for those idiots across the road."

Steve and Tricia looked out of the window to the opposite side of the road. There was a church.

"See what I mean?" said Alan. "Bloody God-botherers are afraid of life. Got to make up stuff to make them feel good. Well, there ain't too much good about this life, and if their God ever pops across to see me, I'll tell him to piss off."

Steve guessed losing his dad and sister, and now his brother, all to cancer, had made him bitter. Yes, it could make one lose faith too.

"Right," said Steve, pulling out the two group photos from his pocket. "We don't have a cause as yet but could you put some names to these faces."

Alan looked at the photo and smiled.

"Right, let's take a look. Those are the best friends a guy ever had," he boasted. "I've been friends with them ever since school days."

He studied the photos.

"This one is the latest," he explained. It was the one with only seven people. "Gary died last year."

"Sorry to hear that. What did he die of?" asked Steve.

"Don't know exactly. I know he had been ill but the coroner never found the exact cause of death."

Alan went back to the photo.

"This is Janet. I got engaged to her for a short time, but we mutually decided to call it off. She's a lovely person, and we are still great friends. Next to her is Simon. Good mate. We play golf together every week. Of course, that's my brother. Unfortunately, he won't now be in next year's photo, will he?"

Alan was a little sad as he looked at his brother's picture.

"Then it's Stef. She is Simon's partner. They've been living together so long now I can't remember when they were not. In the front row are Brian, me, and

Gorgeous Georgie. She gets called Gorgeous more than Georgie for obvious reasons."

"She certainly is a looker," said Steve, and Tricia leaned over to see who the woman was.

"Have you written those names down, Detective Constable?" Steve asked.

He looked at her notebook. Silly question: Tricia had done that in her usual efficient manner.

"Now, Alan, let's take a look at your brother's phone. Can you identify these people on it?"

Alan went through the directory of contacts.

"Yes, I think he has every one of them there. You'll be able to identify them quite easily if you are going to contact them," said Alan. "You don't think there is any foul play here, do you?"

"No, Alan, not really. But we won't be able to rule it out until after the autopsy. Was your brother married or did he have a partner who we should contact?"

"No, a bit of a loner was Phillip when it came to women."

"Was he gay?" It was the first time Tricia had spoken, and a typical question from her. Possibly one Steve would not have thought of asking.

"Nothing I know about," said Alan, a broad smile showing on his face.

"Why does that make you smile?" Steve enquired.

"I just remembered a guy who was gay who fancied Phillip. I never saw Phillip so embarrassed in all my life. He got teased terribly after that. But no, Inspector, he wasn't gay."

"Just one other thing," said Tricia seeing that they were about to finish with Alan. Could you write down the occupations of these people against my list of names." She handed her notes to Alan, who did as she requested.

"Don't know what that's for," said Alan.

"Neither do I," said Steve, "but she is often one step ahead of me," he smiled.

"Is that it?" asked Alan.

"No, sir," said Tricia, and Steve looked at her, wondering what she might next ask him.

"You didn't give me your occupation, sir," she said.

"I'm a consultant at the hospital," Alan informed her. "You are lucky to find me at home as I have a day off today. That is unusual."

"Does that mean you are a doctor?" asked Tricia.

"It could do." A rather odd reply, Tricia thought.

"Well, thank you for your help," said Steve. "I'm sorry for your loss. We will contact you if we need to talk to you again."

As they went out the door, Tricia turned around. "Sir, one last question. You said your brother had been ill, but you didn't know what it was. Is there a reason for that?"

"I'm not his doctor," said Alan simply.

Tricia frowned while making a mental note of Alan's obscure answer.

* * *

Later that day, as was her habit, Tricia met up with Susan, and they went for a drink and a chat.

"So, Tricia, anything interesting happened today?" she asked.

"Depends on what you call interesting," Tricia responded. "We did have a guy found dead on a seat in the park today. Been dead thirty hours. Crazy how people can walk past someone sitting on a park bench and not realise they are dead."

"That does sound unusual. What did the man die of?"

"Don't know 'til 't post-mortem's done," said Tricia.

"I see."

"We've got a list of his friends and their occupations. His brother said he had been ill lately."

"What occupations are his friends in?" asked Susan.

Tricia took out her notebook and handed it to Susan to look for herself. Susan read them out.

"Janet, Nurse; Simon, Banker; Stef, Housewife; Brian, Sales Rep, and Georgie is a Model."

After checking the list, Susan asked, "What is his brother's occupation?"

"He's a consultant. Why?"

"No reason. I just wanted to complete the picture," said Susan in her usual offhand manner.

"You are a strange one, Susan," said Tricia, "but that's what I like about you. You always keep me guessing."

"That's good, isn't it?" Susan said with a smile. "What more could a detective wish for?"

"Not much."

Story Four – Disadvantaged Friends
Part Two

At the station the following day, Steve was looking through the post-mortem paperwork when Tricia arrived.

"Morning, sir, any developments?" she said gaily.

"My god, you're bright this morning," said Steve, "why is that?"

"That's just me, sir. I'm ready for anything today."

"Well, I hope you're ready for this. The autopsy report is back, and our friend Phillip Collins didn't die from cancer as his brother suggested."

"What was the cause?" asked Tricia.

"That's our problem," said Steve. "The autopsy didn't reveal the answer, so we have an unexplained death on our hands. That probably means a lot of telephone calls and footwork to see if we can shed some light on it."

"Oh, good, I enjoy detective work."

"Hmm," Steve murmured. "Have you got that list of people from the photograph?"

"Yes, sir." Tricia pulled out her notebook.

"We'll start contacting them today," said Steve.

"What about the other photo, sir," Tricia enquired.

"What about it?"

"His brother said the extra guy died, and they didn't have a cause of death," Tricia pondered. "Maybe we should check that one first."

"You are getting the hang of this, aren't you Detective Constable?" Steve said with some admiration. "OK, do we have any details?"

Tricia looked through her notes.

"All we know is his name was Gary. Nothing else," said Tricia.

"OK, ring Allan Collins and see if he has anything we can use."

When Tricia called, Alan was in a meeting at the hospital. The receptionist checked, so it was a few minutes before Collins came on the phone.

"Sorry to interrupt your meeting, Mr Collins. Yesterday, you said the absent person in the second photo was Gary. Does he have a surname?"

"Yes, it's Benson. Why?"

Tricia ignored his question.

"And an address?" she asked.

He gave her the address. "Why are you asking about him?" Collins wanted to know.

"Just routine," said Tricia. She had learned that any time you wanted to end someone's curiosity, you just had to say it was routine questioning. That was usually enough, but not this time.

"How does Gary have anything to do with my brother's death?" he asked.

"He probably doesn't, Mr Collins, but we have to carry out all our routine procedures," Tricia explained. "When did Gary die?" she asked.

"About four months ago," said Collins. "Is that all?"

"I think so, Mr Collins." Tricia heard the receptionist in the background.

"I'm sorry to interrupt doctor," she said, *"but they need you back in the meeting."*

"OK, I'm coming," he said. *"If the young lady has finished asking questions."*

"That will be all, sir," said Tricia. "Thank you for your time."

"Well, well, well," she said to Steve. "That's the strangest thing."

"What is?" asked Steve.

"Did you realise that our dead man's brother is a doctor?"

"I guessed he must be something like that," said Steve.

"He hadn't been forthcoming though, had he?" said Tricia. "And here's another thing. He never asked if there was any information from the post-mortem. If it was my brother, I think I'd want to know."

"Yes, that is strange, unless being a doctor in the same hospital as the coroner, he had already found out."

"Gary Benson. That's the name of the missing guy in the photo. He's from the next town. Maybe you'll have to speak to your friend there who was investigating the Longbow Murders." Tricia was nothing if not thorough, and also pretty much on top of everything required in an investigation. "Can I leave that with you, sir?"

"OK, I'll deal with that. You start contacting some of the others."

"Yes, sir."

Tricia went through the list contacting Collins' friends. She had spoken to two or three when Steve came to her desk. "This is beginning to look interesting," he said.

"Oh, good." Tricia liked nothing better than to be in the thick of an exciting investigation. "What's happening?" she asked.

"It seems that the dead Gary Benton had no known cause to. However, he did have the early stages of bowel cancer, but the doctors thought it was much too early to contribute to his death. So, they looked for other signs. They couldn't find anything except that he had an injection mark on his arm."

"Wouldn't he be taking drugs for his bowel cancer, sir?"

"That's what I thought," Steve agreed, "but the medical records show his treatment was in tablet form, not injections."

"So, it could have been foul play after all," said Tricia.

"Yes. Another thing is that he was particularly friendly with Brian from your list. The investigating team also checked all of these people you are checking. When they spoke to Brian, he said he couldn't remember where he was when Gary died. Also, they discovered that Brian took drugs by injection. He was their prime suspect, but they had no evidence."

"I haven't spoken to Brian yet," said Tricia. "It's good to know this information before I do. Something up the sleeve in addition to your arm is always useful."

Steve agreed.

"I'll get back onto the coroner. Get them to check for needle marks on Phillip Collins," said Steve. "You carry on with what you're doing."

* * *

Tricia continued with her phone calls. This guy Brian is intriguing, she thought and decided to leave him until last. Eventually, she got to him and rang his number.

"Hello, Brian, this is Detective Constable Mason from Ricton Police. Have you got a moment?"

"Er, yes, how can I help you, Miss."

Tricia tried to detect anything that might reveal nervousness, pausing, hesitation, quivering in his voice.

"I have some unfortunate news for you. Your friend Phillip Collins is dead, and we are contacting his friends and associates, as a matter of routine, you understand."

"I see. Poor Phillip," Brian replied.

Tricia paused for Brian to say something more, but he didn't.

"Can you tell me where you were three nights ago? That would be the seventeenth."

Brian didn't answer. Perhaps he was thinking about it.

"Brian?" Tricia prompted him.

"Er, sorry," said Brian. "Er, I can't remember," he said.

"Do you have a bad memory, Brian? It was only three days ago, after all."

"Um, no. Sometimes. Yeah. Sometimes I do. I can't remember where I was."

"Might you have been with Phillip Collins?" Tricia prompted.

"Er. Er, maybe. Yeah, maybe, I don't know."

"Do you remember your friend Gary, Brian?"

"Gary? Er, yeah, I remember Gary."

"You remember he died, and when the police asked you where you were, you didn't remember?"

"No, I don't remember where I was when Gary died."

"OK, Brian. We will probably want to talk to you again. You might want to give some more thought to where you were when Phillip died."

"OK," said Brian.

Very strange, she thought. Brian wasn't a bit curious as to how Phillip had died. Tricia decided to have a chat about all this with Steve.

"I've spoken to everyone on the list, sir," she said, "and that now includes Brian. Just like before, Brian doesn't remember where he was, and that was only three days ago. Now the others, they sort of remember, but none of them have a concrete alibi, which is strange in itself. However, the odd thing is that none of them asked me how Phillip died."

"Really?" said Steve. "Now, that is strange. You would have thought at least one would have had an alibi, and several might have wondered how he died."

"You know what I think?" said Tricia. "I think they all know how he died."

"Hmm," Steve grunted, not fully convinced. "It's not completely beyond the realm of possibility, but I'll need more than your hunch to go with that one."

They broke off for lunch, and Tricia met up with Susan at their favourite restaurant. There she related what had transpired.

* * *

"Do you have a suspicion about who the killer is?" asked Susan after they had been mulling over everything.

"The only person I think it could have been, is Brian," said Tricia. "Who do you think it was, Susan? Was it Brian?"

"I don't think so," Susan disagreed.

"So, who do you think it was?"

"Will you do something for me, Tricia?" Susan asked. "It isn't anything that will get you into trouble."

"OK, what do you want?" Tricia asked trying not to show the excitement in her voice. "You've got something, haven't you?"

"We'll see," said Susan with her usual mystique. "First, I'd like you to check out each of those people and find out how their close relatives died."

"What on Earth for," Tricia stared at her in surprise. "You don't think… no, not murdered?"

Susan laughed. "No, Tricia, they weren't murdered. Check it out and get back to me when you have some information."

They concluded their lunch and Tricia returned to work.

Tricia spent some time looking into the family history. As most were local, it didn't prove too difficult.

Steve came in and told her that he was zeroing in on Brian as the prime suspect and would be visiting Brian later. Tricia would accompany him.

They arrived at Brian's shortly after four p.m. Steve hadn't informed him they were coming, and Brian was quite surprised when he let them in. Tricia looked around as Steve made the introductions, and her eyes soon alighted on replicas of the group photos. However, she noticed a third group photo.

She turned all the photos over. Written on the back was, 'DC in Cornwall,' 'DC in the Lake District,' 'DC on the Isle of Wight.'

Steve was asking Brian about the reason for his terrible memory.

"So, why is your memory so bad," he asked. "After all, most people could tell you what they were doing three days ago."

"I take drugs," said Brian.

"What type of drugs? Medication or illegal drugs?"

"Illegal," said Brian. A nervous twitch developed on the side of his right eye.

"It's OK; I'm not here to tackle you about your drug habit. That's the domain of the drug squad. Mine is homicide."

Strangely again, Brian never questioned that it might be a murder. It was as though Brian already knew, which upped the stakes somewhat for him to be the culprit. Tricia, listening to this, felt the same. Solving this crime would be the quickest she had ever been on if they were correct. She picked up the extra photo. "Brian, this photo has an extra person in it. Can you tell me who it is and why he is not in the other photos?"

"That's Trev, said Brian, "he died."

"Damn," said Steve, "all your friends seem to be dying at a young age. How old was he?"

"About forty-five," said Brian.

"And how and when did he die?"

"Not too sure," said Brian.

"Not another memory gap, is it?" said Tricia.

"It was about three years ago, and they think it was cancer."

"Why do you say they only think it was cancer?" said Steve. "I'm sure the autopsy would have revealed that clearly, wouldn't it?"

"No," said Brian mumbled.

"Why not?"

"I don't know," said Brian with some irritation, "they weren't sure."

Tricia interrupted. "Brian, what does DC stand for?" she asked.

"Don't know," said Brian.

"Well, it's written on the back of all these photos. It must mean something."

"Can't say," said Brian stubbornly.

"OK," said Steve. "We need to discuss this further. Come down to the station at ten a.m. tomorrow."

130

They wound up the interview, returned to the station, and Tricia sent a text message to Susan telling her what she had discovered about the relatives of this group. Steve said that they might be charging Brian tomorrow.

'Gee, this was a quick result,' thought Tricia. It was nice to have something positive on her record. That would go down well for her future in the job.

* * *

Brian came in for his interview at ten the following day. After about two hours of interrogation, Steve decided to charge him, even though his evidence was only circumstantial. He had a sneaking suspicion that his action might create something better to work with among these tight-knit friends. Tricia was so delighted she immediately phoned Susan to tell her the good news. Susan did not share her delight.

"You've got the wrong man," she told Tricia. "You should be looking at either the doctor or the nurse. My guess is it's the doctor."

"Why do you think that?" asked Tricia, a little disappointed by Susan's lack of support.

"I'll tell you later," she said. "I have a feeling that things are going to take an unusual turn on this one."

* * *

By, the afternoon, news had got out about the arrest and charging of Brian. *'No, thought Tricia, it's done now, and I believe Susan is wrong.'* She continued to think that until a little after four-thirty. That was when Stef came in.

"I have something to report," she announced to the room. "The dead man, Phillip Collins, I killed him."

There was no alternative. They had to record Stef's confession. Steve and Tricia were halfway through when Simon came in with something to report.

"Phillip Collins," he said abruptly. "I killed him."

"What is this," said an angry Steve." You're Stef's husband, I believe. Are you merely saying this to protect her?"

Before Simon could respond, Janet came in and made the same claim.

"Phil Collins, poor man. It was me who killed him."

And within the next fifteen minutes, both Dr Alan Collins and Gorgeous Georgia came in with the same confession. With five different people now confessing to the murder of Phillip Collins, Steve was in a quandary, not sure what to do. He rang one of his former superiors at the Met in London and put the problem to him.

"Sorry, Steve," he said, "but since your arrest was only on circumstantial evidence, a confession usually takes precedence. With five confessions, I think you'll have to let Brian go."

And so, it was. Steve released Brian along with all the others, and they were back to square one. Tricia could not understand why all these friends were confessing to a murder that possibly only one person carried out.

Susan had told her they had the wrong person. Tricia rang Susan as soon she could and told her what had transpired. Oddly the mysterious Susan was not in the least surprised.

"Tricia, do you want to sort this out and take the credit?" she asked.

"If only," Tricia replied, "but I don't see that happening."

"That is because you are not looking at all the evidence you have."

"Are you telling me you have the solution to this fiasco," asked Tricia.

"No, Tricia. You have the answer. Tomorrow, you will tell them at the station that you have the solution, and we will be out tomorrow night celebrating your success."

"How is that possible?"

"You have the facts, and I know you can put them together. You told me earlier how their relatives died. I know you will align everything to solve this case. Just one other tip, Tricia. Do a little research on drugs."

* * *

Tricia thought long and hard about Susan's words and then did her research. The following day she approached Steve and Mike.

"I think I have the answer to this case," she said, and promptly explained all the facts that she had discussed with Susan. She then added the result of her research.

"These people died from a drug that shows no trace. Any chemical that will get broken down into by-products normal to the body, might be enough to kill a human without leaving a trace. For example, the drug potassium chloride, when injected, is simply metabolized into potassium and chloride ions, both normally found in the body."

"Well," said Mike, "tell us something we don't already know. Obviously, this is the way they died, but who was the killer and the motive?"

"Hold on, Mike," said Steve. "Do you have anything else, Detective Constable?"

"Yes, sir," said Tricia. "It's my opinion that all these people, knowing they were going to die in pain, formed a club. They knew that because I researched the deaths of their relatives. Most died painfully from

133

cancer. Cancer runs in the families of all these people. As euthanasia is illegal in this country, they conspired to escape their fate.

"When the time came for the euthanisation of any individual, someone used this drug or one similar. Anyone, several, or even all of the group, could administer it. And if we charged one of them, they had this plan where they all confessed, and it's quite possible they are all guilty. I don't think we will ever know."

"Did you find out what DC on the back of the photos stands for?" asked Steve.

"Yes, sir," Tricia replied with a smile. "Death Club."

Mike stood with his mouth open.

Steve smiled with pride.

And that evening, Susan and an elated Tricia were celebrating at their favourite water hole.

Story Five
A Day On The River

It was early on a Monday afternoon, and everything was quiet. Johnny, the Police Constable, had a day off. Detective Inspector Steve Kendall, and Sargent Mike Compton, were catching up on paperwork that never seemed to reach completion, while Detective Constable Tricia Mason merely twiddled her thumbs, as the saying goes. Actually, she was manicuring her hands as is the practice of most twenty-four-year-old women.

So, it was with some relief when the telephone rang, and Mike picked it up. As it was a call from a member of the public, he automatically switched it to audio, redirecting it through the speakers.

"Hello, Ricton Police, Sargent Compton speaking."

"I want to report something strange," said the female voice on the line. "There is a rowboat on the river. There seems to be someone slumped in the boat, and it's just drifting downstream."

"Have you tried to make contact?" asked Mike.

"Yes, Sargent. I have called out, but there is no response, and the boat keeps on drifting down the river," said the woman.

"Where is the boat now?" Mike inquired.

"It is just coming up to Tanner's Bend," she said.

"OK. Thank you. We'll get someone down to Tanner's Bend straight away."

Steve and Tricia agreed to go and take a look. Mike said he would get Simpson, a local boatyard owner, and boat-hirer to meet them at Tanner's Bend.

Their vehicles pulled into the car park near the bend at a picnic area. They got out of their cars and looked up and down the river, just catching sight of the boat as it drifted around the bend. A few minutes later, Simpson arrived in a small motorboat and drew alongside them.

"What's going on," he asked as they both got into the boat.

"There's a lonesome boat drifting down the river," said Steve. "It's just gone around the bend. Can you get us alongside it?"

"Sure," said Simpson as he pulled away from the bank. Within minutes he was beside the loose rowboat, and it was apparent something terrible had occurred.

Looking down into the boat, they saw a man slumped over. The entire floor of the boat was awash with blood, as was the man. It looked like a cut throat, and he had bled out into the boat.

"Bloody Hell, looks like his throat's cut. That's a sight I don't want to see every day," said Tricia.

"Ah," said Simpson. "I didn't want to see it today."

"Can you try to manoeuvre it into the bank?" said Steve.

"I can try," said Simpson, and steered his motorboat against the rowboat until it wedged into the riverbank.

Steve leaped out of the motorboat onto the grassy bank and straightened up the rowboat.

He looked around.

"This is private property," he observed. "Mr Simpson, can we tie a rope onto this boat and tow it back to the car park at Tanners Bend?"

Simpson threw a rope that Steve secured to the bow. Then Steve got back aboard the motorboat, and they made their way back to Tanners Bend. Meanwhile, Steve phoned Mike back at the station and asked him to get the doctor and an ambulance down to the car park.

"What have you got there, Steve," he asked.

"We've got a dead body," Steve replied. "I'll explain later."

Steve and Tricia jumped ashore and pulled the rowboat close to the bank.

"It would be good to get this out of the water," said Steve. "We'll wait for the ambulance and get the medics to give us a hand."

Soon after that, the ambulance and the doctor pulled up in the car park. The doctor strolled over to them.

"We are going to have to stop meeting like this," said Steve. "You know something; I don't even know your name."

"It's Richard," said the doctor. "Dr Richard Handsworthy. What have we got this time?"

"I don't think we'll know for certain until we get this boat out of the water and the body out of the boat," said Steve with an awkward look on his face.

"Ugh, yes it's going to be quite messy," said Richard. "I'll get the drivers to give us a hand." He called them over.

The two drivers, plus Steve and Tricia, took up the task and, after a struggle, got the boat onto the grass. Then, very carefully, they set about getting the body out of the boat which was soaked with the man's blood.

"It's quite clear from all this blood that he's bled out," said Richard, "but I can't figure out what made that ghastly wound in his throat."

"Me neither," Steve agreed. "Usually, a throat is cut with a sharp blade. This looks more like a blunt butcher's knife."

"Looks more like t'was dun by pit bull," Tricia gave her opinion which, as always, she put into words that others only dared to think.

"Yeah," said Steve. "I guess it's an option we will have to consider." Tricia's face lit up.

"Don't get too excited, Detective Constable," said Steve. "I don't think that is what killed him."

"Well," said the doctor, "at least we can say that he hasn't been dead for very long. There's no rigor-mortise, and the blood in the boat hasn't even started to coagulate."

"Hmm, I suppose we will have to take the boat away. Can't leave it here," said Steve.

"No," Tricia added, "it's not t' best sight to see when yer eating yer picnic sarnies." Despite the gruesome situation, the group couldn't help but laugh at the cheeky Northerner.

Tricia noticed there was a card in the deceased shirt breast pocket. She put on her thin protective plastic gloves and gently retrieved the card.

"His name is Michael Leeson," she said, looking at the card bearing his photograph.

Mr Simpson, who had got out of his motorboat, said, "Leeson, I know him. Lives about half a mile up-stream. His property goes right down to the river, and he has a boathouse there."

"That's good," said Steve, "at least we now know who we are dealing with."

"I can take you up there if you want," Simpson offered, but Steve declined.

"No, thanks, Mr Simpson. We have our cars. What you could do for me, if you don't mind, is to tow the rowboat up there and leave it in the boathouse. We will go around in our cars and meet you there."

"All right," Simpson agreed. They got the boat back into the water and tied the rope to the bow.

"See you there," said Steve, He and Tricia got into their cars and drove off up the road, over the river bridge, and down on to the Leeson property. After pulling up in the drive, Tricia knocked on the front door. There was no response. Steve was going around to the back when he bumped into the gardener.

"Hi," he said. "I'm guessing you don't live here. Is there anyone at home?"

"No," the gardener replied. "Mr Leeson is out on the river, and Mrs Leeson is away until tomorrow."

"Oh, I see," said Steve. "I'm Detective Superintendent Kendall, and this is Detective Constable Mason. We are just going down to the boathouse."

"What's this about?" asked the gardener.

"Can't tell you right now," Steve apologised. "By the way, do they have any dogs here?"

"Yeah, they have two," said the gardener. "They're in the house."

"Do you have a key, so we can take a look?" Steve asked.

The gardener took a key from his pocket and unlocked the door. In the hall stood two dogs wagging their tails. Although they appeared friendly enough, they were pitbull terriers.

"There, I said so. Those buggers are the culprits?" said Tricia.

"We'll see," said Steve. "Let's go down to the boathouse."

They strolled down the long, lawned garden, and the gardener followed behind them.

"You can remain here?" Steve instructed him. "We won't be long."

Simpson was waiting at the boathouse. They unhooked the rowboat and secured it. Tricia looked all around the area.

"There's no sign of any trouble been happening here," she said. "No blood or nothing."

"You're right, Detective Constable," Steve agreed. "Not a lot we can do here."

"This is very puzzling," Tricia mused. "There's no sign of a problem here. The guy got in his boat and rowed downstream, and somehow someone was able to get into his boat, hack is throat out, and disappear."

"Yes, Tricia," said Steve using her name rather than her title. "I've been trying to come up with a scenario where that might happen, but nothing fits, unless there was someone with him when he got into the boat."

"Maybe…" said Tricia, "just maybe the dogs were in the boat with him, or perhaps swimming in the river."

"Yeah," said Steve, "and maybe it was a spy in a diving suit like in a James Bond film. No, I don't think that is the answer. There would have been water in the boat, but there isn't any, and the dogs aren't wet." They walked back up to the house in conversation, meeting the gardener on the way.

"Was there anyone with Mr Leeson when he left in the boat," Steve asked.

"No sir. I watched him leave. He was alone. He usually is when he takes his morning rowing exercise."

"Oh," said Tricia. "He does that every day, does he?"

"Most days, Miss."

"Look," said Steve, "there's been some trouble with Mr Leeson. He won't be returning. Do you know where his wife is?"

"No, sir," said the gardener. "Not got a clue. All I know is that she is away until tomorrow."

"Are there any relatives nearby that you are aware of?"

"No, sir, afraid not."

"Can you keep an eye on those dogs until Mrs Leeson returns? When she does, please ring me on this number," said Steve handing the gardener his card.

"Yes, sir. I'll do that, sir," said the obliging gardener.

"Right, Detective Constable, it's getting late, and we had better be off. I'll report back to the station. You can finish now and go home if you want. I'll see you tomorrow morning."

"Yes, sir," said Tricia, and they each drove away in their cars.

* * *

The following morning, at the station, Tricia had served them tea when Constable Johnny arrived, surprisingly late considering he had been away the previous day.

"Hello, Johnny," Tricia greeted him. "How was your day in bed yesterday?"

"I wasn't in bed," Johnny replied indignantly. "I was in the park with my mate Dave."

"I wouldn't have put you down as someone who spends much time in the park," said Steve.

"I don't, but Dave was going to let me try out his drone. He's a bloody genius. You should see what he can do with it."

"After the recent fiasco we had with drones with that kidnapped boy recently," said Mike, "I wouldn't have thought drones were that popular around these parts now."

"So, how did you get on with it?" asked Tricia.

"Not good, "Johnny replied. "I lost the bloody thing."

"How on earth did you manage to do that, and in the park too?" said Tricia in disbelief.

"It wasn't my fault," Johnny protested like a little boy. "There was something wrong with the controls. I took it up high and then started moving it along, and it suddenly lost height. The controls didn't work, and it kept coming down until it disappeared behind the row of trees along the riverbank. Dave said it had probably gone into the river."

Steve swung around, spilling his tea down his jacket. "Bloody hell," he exclaimed.

Mike dropped his cup, which shattered across the floor, and Tricia looked at Johnny with her mouth open wide. "Jesus Christ, Johnny," she exclaimed.

Johnny just looked confused.

"Crikey," he said, "there's no need to get so serious. It's only a bloody drone. Ok. Ok. For fuck's sake, I'll buy him a new one."

Story Six
The Scarecrow

For about a month something had changed in the village of Ricton. There was the air of the carnival about it. Not that there was a carnival. There weren't even plans for a carnival. No, what had changed was the arrival of the stranger, now nicknamed, 'the Scarecrow.' Going by his other attributes, a more appropriate title might have been 'the entertainer,' as it was that which gave the village it's festive atmosphere. However, someone called him the Scarecrow, and the name seemed to stick.

The Scarecrow had a rather narrow, scrawny face with a larger-than-usual hooked nose, a long, pointed chin, and unusually bushy eyebrows that hung above his bright, sparkling eyes. On his head, he wore a strange hat. It was like a fez with a small brim and had red and green stripes that run from the top down.

His baggy trousers terminated about six inches above his shoes. He wore a bright yellow jacket that had seen better days, and over everything, a large black cape fluttered like the wings of a bat as he moved in swift, jerky movements, one step to the next.

The Scarecrow never spoke in sentences or proper words, but rather imperfect phrases uttered melodically. He visited all the shops in the main street, wafting in like a demented dragonfly, singing things like 'Mornish syrup,' 'Watchamis duzzit,' and 'Howzim yussup.' None of this made sense, but the villagers eventually worked out what he meant was 'Morning Sir,' 'What are you doing?' and 'How are you?'

Soon, the managers of the post office, the grocery store, the butcher, and Miss Irlene Candish, the owner of the fashion shop, got used to him and looked forward to his visits. He entertained them by changing his umbrella into a bunch of flowers right under their noses or revealing the cute little white bunny under his hat, only to make it disappear without a trace until he pulled it out of his pocket.

All these characteristics went down particularly well with the children he entertained endlessly in the village square every afternoon. He even whizzed around the police station rooms each day before swirling back onto the street, his cape fluttering behind him like the accessory of a superhero.

Yes, this had been going on for more than a month during the summer. It was long enough for the Scarecrow to have become a permanent character of Ricton so that the villagers could no longer remember what it had been like without his eccentric presence in their community.

It was a Tuesday morning, and the Scarecrow covered his usual rounds, leaving each of his contacts laughing and happy, set up for the day. He visited the butcher, where he pulled a stream of coloured handkerchiefs from the mouth of the pigs head on the serving counter. In the grocery store, the cashier opened the till to find three white mice that the Scarecrow took and put into his pocket. Then on to Miss Irlene Candish, in the fashion shop. He would go to see her daily on the upper floor of her two-story establishment.

At the top of the stairs, he would weave through the rails of dresses and skirts, to find Miss Candish's small kitchen area, a sink unit with a cupboard above, where she kept her cups for tea. The Scarecrow would entertain her with card tricks, disappearances, and the production of his white rabbit. Afterward he would sweep down the stairs and out into the street.

These premises bordered the village square. When the children were not at school, they gathered there laughing and giggling at the loveable Scarecrow's antics, with his endless programme of magic tricks. To the children, he had become Uncle Scarecrow.

As had become his habit, Johnny, the Constable from the Police Station further along the road, strolled into the square to keep an eye on things. He would check with the owners and managers of the shop premises to ensure that the Scarecrow had not bothered them, but no-one ever complained.

On this particular day, the Scarecrow had made his usual visits and had fluttered into Miss Irlene's fashion shop, bounded the stairs two at a time with his long ungainly legs, and ended in her kitchen area where she was making herself a cup of tea. She was not surprised. He did this every day.

Johnny, who was doing the rounds, had seen the Scarecrow go into the fashion shop. He had even given Johnny a wave as he disappeared. Johnny entered the butcher's shop, had a brief chat and a joke with the butcher, then went into the grocery store. As usual, he spent a little more time in this shop on account of the pretty little assistant he had been chatting up now for a couple of weeks.

Eventually, Johnny departed from the store at the same time that a tall upright gentleman with short grey hair and a striped suit strode out of the fashion shop. The man was carrying a bag in one hand and a walking stick in the other. He smiled as he walked past the young constable. Johnny had never seen him before. He was certainly not a local; Johnny was sure of that.

Johnny entered the shop. There was no one on the ground floor. Unaccustomed to taking the liberty of climbing the stairs to the upper level, he went to the counter where he saw a newspaper. It was a very old issue, dated some twelve years earlier, and from someplace he'd never heard. The heading read,

"Computer company director's nightmare." With nothing better to do, Johnny leaned on the counter and started to read the article.

Robert Ashton started his computer company many years ago before desktop computers were an everyday thing. In those days, the main company business was always held on a mainframe computer with operating stations all linked to it. Mr Ashton gradually converted to modern computers, but, as old habits die hard, he still used individual workstations connected to a central operating system.

Last month, his many years of work building up his customer base fell apart. His secretary and accounts manager, Miss Daphne Desmond, absconded with all his money, some three-hundred and forty-six thousand pounds, and disappeared without a trace. But what she did before leaving was an act of pure evil. She took a hammer and destroyed his mainframe computer which contained all his clients' work. She also destroyed his collection of backup discs.

Mr Ashton is now bankrupt and forced to sell his house and his car, along with his wife's car. Mrs Ashton was so distressed, that yesterday she committed suicide by cutting her wrists in the bath.

"Nasty bitch, that Desmond woman," said Johnny but didn't read any further. He took one last look around the ground floor before leaving to continue his round. On his way back, a little after closing time for most village shops, it was his habit to check the doors, ensuring they were locked securely. He'd been checking doors for several months and never found one open. It was, therefore, a surprise to him that Miss Irlene Candish had left the door of her fashion shop unlocked. He entered, calling her name, but received no answer.

'That's odd,' he thought, making his way up the stairs to the next level. When he reached the top, he stopped abruptly. Unhooking his mobile phone from his jacket, he phoned the Station. Tricia answered.

"I think you and the Super should come to the fashion shop right away."

When Tricia and Steve turned up at Miss Irlene Candish's fashion and surveyed the scene, Tricia almost threw up. She had a pretty strong constitution, but this was something she hadn't expected.

As the two detectives tried to get to grips with the spectacle, Johnny picked up the newspaper and continued to read where he had left it.

Mr Ashton was a magician and says that when he has recovered from this nightmare, he might have to take up his old profession again. We wish him luck.

Johnny's thoughts went to his memory of seeing the Scarecrow enter the shop, and later, seeing an elderly, well-dressed man leave.

* * *

The Scarecrow waved at the police constable as he drifted into the fashion shop, bounded up the stairs, and presented himself to Miss Irlene. She had just made herself a cup of tea. He made his usual musical non-introduction and then proceeded to remove his flowing cape. With a few deft movements, he converted it into a bag that he placed on the vacant chair in the room.

Miss Irlene watched this with interest. She hadn't seen this trick before.

The Scarecrow took his umbrella, and detached the canopy, leaving a smart gentleman's walking stick.

Miss Irlene watched, mesmerized. Then the Scarecrow gripped the top of his trousers very tightly, and with one deft movement, swept them aside where they detached from the Velcro holding them together, revealing a smart pair of striped trousers. Miss Irlene continued to watch.

He then removed his yellow jacket, turned it inside out, and put it back on. The coat now matched his striped trousers. The Scarecrow removed his peculiar hat and put it into the bag. When he took off his long hair wig, it surprised Irlene to see he had short grey hair. This was becoming very strange, she thought.

Looking less like a scarecrow, he observed her intently as he removed the large fake bushy eyebrows. Then he peeled off the accentuated false hooked nose, and finally, the long, pointed chin. Miss Irlene looked at him with fear in her eyes.

"Robert Ashton," she whispered.

"That's right, Miss Irlene," said Robert, "or should I more accurately call you Daphne Desmond?"

* * *

Tricia and Steve looked up from the paper report Johnny had shown them. Miss Irlene was hanging from one of her fashion rails, her hands tied firmly to the rail, and her mouth gagged with an exquisitely patterned high-value headscarf. Her cut wrists had bled out, soaking the dresses with blood.

It didn't take a genius to realise that this death, combined with the newspaper article, imitated that of Mr Robert Ashton's wife. Whether they would ever find Ashton to answer for his crime was another matter. The reason for Mrs Ashton's demise was down to the actions of Daphne Desmond, and it looked as though the evil Daphne had now paid the price.

Everyone realised the Scarecrow was responsible, so Steve let out a deep sigh, "Another crime solved without closure," he said. "This is getting to be a habit."

Story Seven
Dog Rescue

The usual morning routine had settled in at the Ricton Police Station. Sargent Mike Compton was manning the phones as he worked on some sketches for a new poster for the village weekly, Ricton News. Steve was talking on the phone to an associate at the London Met, and Detective Constable Tricia was reading a procedures manual, one of many at the station.

Meanwhile, Johnny was strolling through the village, keeping an eye on things and chatting to people, mainly young ladies, and particularly, Lisa, the blonde who worked in the grocery store.

No one noticed the first dog that came into the station. The Welsh Border Collie trotted along the corridor, sniffing everything. Fortunately, it didn't cock its leg anywhere. Neither did the second border collie that followed it. It was only when the third dog entered the police station that anyone noticed them.

"What the fuck," Tricia exclaimed when she saw them, "whose bloody dogs are these. This place is looking more like a doggy day-care centre than a police station."

Mike got up from his desk.

"How did they get in here?" he asked.

No one had entered who might have been their owner. Mike crouched down and stroked the nearest animal, as did Tricia.

"OK, boy, where did you come from?" said Mike in a friendly voice. Unfortunately, the dog did not answer, so no one was any wiser.

"None of them has a collar on," said Tricia, "so they've got no names either."

Tricia went to the front door and looked up and down the street. There was no sign of anyone who might have left them there.

"You know what I think," said Steve when he had finished telling his London friend what was going on and put down his phone.

"We never know what you think, sir," said Tricia. "Bit of a mystery is what you are. Are you going to let us into your mind and tell us?"

"I think these dogs have got out from somewhere, someone has found them and aren't bothered to do the proper thing, so they've shoved them in our door."

"And what is the proper thing?" asked Mike.

"The proper thing is to take them to the RSPCA who can sort out these matters," said Steve. "I guess we'll have to do it instead."

"Anyone volunteering?" asked Mike.

"I'll do it," said Tricia gathering the three dogs together, "but I think I'll go to the vets first."

"What for? They look in good enough condition to me," said Steve.

"Yeah," Tricia agreed, "but the vet is just around the corner, and they have microchip detectors there. I might find out their names and addresses before I go out to the RSPCA."

"Alright constable," said Mike, "you never know. They might be quite local, and you can return them yourself."

"OK, Sargent," said Tricia, "I'll get onto it. Come on, you little buggers," she said as she guided them out to her car.

* * *

As the vet was, as Tricia had said, located around the corner, she only put the dogs in her car to keep them

150

together. It would have been quite a job managing all three of them without leads. She entered the vet alone and spoke to the receptionist.

"Hello, Marsha." Marsha was a friend who sometimes joined her for a drink with Susan. "Have you got a microchip scanner here?"

"Hello, Tricia. Yes, why do you ask?"

"I've got three mutts in the car outside. Either abandoned or lost, and I want to find out if they' have chips."

"OK, bring them in."

Tricia returned to her car and collected the first of the dogs. It was all over her, licking and jumping up. Any passer-by would have thought it was her dog.

"Seems like dogs love you, Tricia," Marsha observed as Tricia struggled in with just one dog who could not leave her alone.

"Ar, yer reete," said Tricia falling back into her broad Northern accent. "I bin oot with som reete dogs in ma time. Cud na keep their hands off me."

Marsha laughed. "You shouldn't be such a pretty Northern lass," she said. "Bring it through to the back room, and I'll have him checked out."

They took him to the vet who scanned the dog's neck to find if there was a chip.

"Yes, there it is through, and," he said. "Lives at Buckle Farm." He wrote down the address. "Hang on," he looked at the address. "We only chipped this dog this morning. We did two others at the same time. They had silly names."

"Really," said a surprised Tricia. "What's his name?"

"Do you want to write this down," asked the vet. "So that you remember it."

Tricia took out her notebook, "Go on," she nodded to the vet.

"Alaferme," he said, spelling it out for her.

"That's French, isn't it?" said Tricia, "What does it mean?"

"Haven't a clue," said the vet.

"Neither do I," said Marsha, "I never learned French.

"Alaferme, Alaferme," Tricia called, but there was no response. "Don't know his own name," she said. "What were the other dog's names?"

"Hang on," said the vet. "I wrote them down somewhere, so I didn't misspell them."

He looked on the desk until he found the paper.

"Here we are. Write these down."

Tricia jotted the names in her notebook.

"So, who brought them in?" she asked the vet.

"It was a young lad of about eighteen. He was a foreigner."

"Well, I guessed that much," said Tricia. "French, yeah?"

"No," the vet corrected her. "He was either Polish or Hungarian or from somewhere like that. He certainly wasn't French."

"Well, bugger me," said Tricia, "this gets stranger by the minute."

Marsha took Tricia back out to the reception area. "You don't have a dog, do you?" she asked Tricia.

"No," Tricia confirmed, "it wouldn't be fair on the dog. I would have to leave it at home all day alone. I couldn't do that."

"No, I understand. It's just that we have an old lady who has a dog and she can't look after it anymore. We have it out the back in the animal waiting cages."

"Oh, can I see it?" asked Tricia. Marsha took her out to the back rooms, and there was the cutest little dog Tricia had ever seen. The dog wagged its tail incessantly when Tricia bent down to say hello.

"Hello, beautiful," Tricia scratched it behind its ear. "What's its name?" she asked.

"His name is Tricky," said Marsha. "He is beautiful and deserves a good home. The RSPCA will be collecting him later today."

"I hope they find him a good home," said Tricia as she gathered up the Welsh Border Collie and went back to her car. Leaving them in the vehicle when she went back to the Police Station, she spoke to Mike.

"I've got an address here," she explained. "Do you know where that farm is?"

Mike looked at the address. "That is quite a long drive out," he calculated. "I reckon it must be thirty miles or more. That's where the dogs are from, is it?"

"Yes," Tricia confirmed. "They were only chipped this morning. I reckon they must have escaped from the lad's vehicle. How they got in here though, is still a mystery."

"So, what are you going to do?" Mike inquired.

"I think I'll take them to the RSPCA and let them return them," said Tricia. "They probably know exactly where this farm is."

"Good idea," said Mike.

* * *

At the RSPCA, Tricia dropped the dogs off together with their address.

"We'll get James to drop them off," said the duty officer. "He'll be back shortly. He's just gone to collect a dog from the vet."

"Oh, that will be little Tricky," said Tricia.

153

"What's tricky about it?" the officer wondered.

"No, it's not tricky. Tricky is the dog's name."

"Oh, you know this dog, then?"

"I've just seen him at the vet's," Tricia explained. "Lovely little dog. I wish I was able to have him, but I am out all day."

"Don't you spend a lot of time at the Police Station?" asked the officer.

"Yes, of course."

"Couldn't you take him to work with you? Brighten up the station, wouldn't he?"

"Well, that's an idea. I never thought of that," said Tricia encouraged by the suggestion. That would be great to have Tricky there every day, and she would take him home at night and on her days off.

"I'll have a word with the Sargent," she said.

At that moment, James arrived, and there was little Tricky with him. He jumped all over Tricia when she greeted him.

"I'll tell you what," said the officer. "You take him with you, and if it's a problem you can just bring him back here. If not, then he is yours."

"Really," exclaimed an excited Tricia.

* * *

When she arrived back at the Police Station, she explained what had transpired, and after begging the Sargent, almost on her knees, he gave up and agreed that she could keep it to see if it would be a problem.

So, Tricia had spent the day with dogs and was now the satisfied owner of little Tricky. Meanwhile, the RSPCA delivered the three Welsh Border Collies to Buckle Farm.

Tricia called in at the RSPCA the following morning to thank them and say that it was OK for

Tricky to stay with her. James was there when she entered, and he related something to her that just sounded odd.

The lad who had taken the collies to the vet was from Bosnia and worked there at the farm, which produced vegetables. James had stood at the beginning of a long driveway up to the farm, speaking to the farm owner, Henry Buckle. A lad was painting a fence further along the drive. Buckle had his back to the lad who was constantly pointing to a shed while placing his finger on his lips, indicating quiet.

He kept on doing this but stopped when the farmer turned to look in his direction. Something told James not to mention this strange behaviour to Buckle as he was of the impression the lad did not want Buckle to see him.

"Yes, James, that is very strange," said Tricia. "I wonder what he meant by it."

"I thought he was trying to say the farmer was doing something illegal." James was puzzled by the incident.

When Tricia arrived at the Police Station that morning, she related this strange behaviour to the Sargent, but he decided there was too little to go on to investigate it. Especially as the farm was some thirty miles away. and so, they let it pass.

Tricia was very keen to show off her little dog to Susan, and as they had arranged to have lunch together, they decided to go to the park. Tricia took Tricky with her on a new lead she had bought that morning. They found a bench in the park and settled down to eat their lunch. She let Tricky off the lead, and he ran around investigating his new environment.

"So, Tricia, what's been happening at the Station," she asked. "Steve never talks about work, but he did tell me you have a dog now. How did that come about? I didn't even know you were looking for one."

"I wasn't," Tricia replied, and she related the story.

"Well, Tricia, I don't know whether he's tricky, but he is certainly a lucky dog."

"He is beautiful, isn't he," said Tricia tickling him under the chin when he came back to the bench."

"Now," Susan put on her serious face that she always had when she was trying to work something out, "let's see if I have got this right. Three dogs just suddenly appeared inside the Police Station. Someone must have opened the door for them. I know Welsh Border Collies are intelligent, but they have their limits."

"I think someone found them, and just pushed them in to get them off their hands," said Tricia.

"And you don't think the young lad from Bosnia was the one who let them in?"

"Why would he do that?" asked Tricia. "It doesn't make sense."

"That's what we have to find out," Susan explained. "Now you say those Collies had strange names, probably in French. What sort of names?"

"I've got them written down in my notebook," said Tricia, getting it out and showing it to Susan. Susan looked at the names.

"You don't speak French, Tricia, do you?"

"No," Tricia admitted.

"If you did, you wouldn't have dismissed this so readily. Look at these names. Alaferme, Aidezmoi, and Jesuisemprisonne."

"Yeah, weird, aren't they," Tricia frowned.

"They are not so weird when you apply two things," said Susan. "First, they are in the wrong order."

"How can you write names down in the wrong order," Tricia laughed. "That's ridiculous."

"If you don't understand French, it won't," said Susan. "Look at this. I'll rearrange them and split the names into their proper parts. Aidez moi, je suis emprisonne a la ferme."

"Hey, that sounds proper French," said Tricia.

"That's because it is," Susan explained.

"What does it mean then?"

"It means, my darling, Tricia, *Help me, I am imprisoned at the farm.*"

"Shit, it doesn't."

"It most certainly does, Tricia. Someone is in trouble, and this is a message. He chipped the dogs for one reason, to send that message. And they even delivered it to the Police Station. You have here a case dropped into your lap."

"Bloody hell," Tricia used her favourite expression. "But the Bosnian lad who works at the farm is not imprisoned."

"So, it has to be someone else," said Susan. "Someone else is being held prisoner at the farm and probably held with a threat so that the Bosnian lad doesn't try to get away."

"Susan, I've got to go," said Tricia gathering up her things and putting Tricky back on the lead. Susan smiled. "Meet me again when you have solved this case," she said as Tricia rushed off to the station.

* * *

After explaining everything to Sargent Mike and the Superintendent, Mike decided that all four of them, including Johnny, should drive out to the Buckle Farm.

"I think we should get a search warrant first, though," said Steve. "I'll sort it out."

Thirty minutes later, they had the search warrant and drove out to Buckle Farm. They drove up the long entrance track and into the farmyard. The owner, Buckle, came out on hearing the vehicles.

"What's going on?" he asked.

"We would like to take a look around," said Steve showing the search warrant to Buckle.

"Why? What the fuck is this about?" he said, getting angry.

"We have reason to believe that you are holding someone here against their will so we shall take a comprehensive look around your premises. You will stay here out in the open where we can see you, and the Constable will stay with you. Don't give him any trouble, sir, or we will have to put you in our vehicle."

Buckle protested, but Johnny took his arm and pulled him aside.

"Sir," said Tricia, "the Bosnian lad was pointing to that shed, I think. That's what the RSPCA guy, James told me."

"Where is the Bosnian lad?" Mike asked Buckle.

"He's in the field working," Buckle grudgingly replied.

"OK, Steve. I'll leave you and Tricia here to check out the buildings. I'll go and find the boy."

He wandered off up the track to the fields beyond as Steve and Tricia went over to the shed. There was a lock on the door.

"What's in here?" asked Tricia.

"Nothing," Buckle replied.

Steve knocked on the door and said, "Is anyone in there? This is the police." There was a muffled sound.

158

"Don't bother with the key, Buckle," he said and stepped back before launching himself against the door. It broke open. It was dark inside, so he took a torch from his pocket and looked around. He thought he would find one person but was unprepared for the sight that met his eyes.

Gagged and blindfolded were eight people all tied to a rail along the wall.

"Fuck me," said Tricia in her expressive language. "Who are these people?"

"I think you will find they are what is commonly known as trafficked workers. They probably get no pay and the barest of food and water." Steve and Tricia stepped into the shed to remove the blindfolds and untie the people. There were three men and five women. They looked unsure of what was happening.

Tricia put her arm around a particularly vulnerable looking girl of about sixteen to comfort her. The girl clung on to her and would not let go. One by one, they led the people out into the sunshine. Meanwhile, Mike was coming back down the track with the Bosnian lad.

"What the hell is all this?" Mike said to Buckle, grabbing him by the neck. "Constable put the cuffs on him and put him in the car."

"There are six more people out in the fields," he said, and I'm guessing they are all prisoners here too. Is that right?" he directed his question to the Bosnian boy.

"Yes," said the lad.

"Johnny," go and bring them in," Mike instructed.

Tricia had extricated herself from the girl and had gone into the house. She came out with a woman in handcuffs who was more than likely Buckle's wife, and the three Welsh Border Collies followed her. Mike got on the phone and ordered a minibus to collect all the people they had found.

Mike was talking to the young Bosnian lad. "You did very well sending your message yesterday," he said. "I'm sorry it took us so long to get here."

"The person we have to thank for this is the Detective Constable," said Steve. "Without her incredible detective work, we would never have caught this criminal. Tricia, you are an absolute asset to this police force. More than that here is finally a crime that we have solved properly. And not before time too."

Tricia had a radiant look of satisfaction on her face as she bundled the three Collies into the back of her car and then got into the driving seat. Only Tricia knew it was Susan who had put things together. Susan didn't know it, but in her mind, Tricia was already planning their celebration party for that evening.

Story Eight
A Tricky Problem

It didn't take Tricia's new little dog, Tricky, long to become the centre of attention at the Ricton Police Station. Suddenly, the station seemed oddly quiet and empty when he was not there. So, Tricia was frequently disciplined for her lateness, while before Tricky came along, no-one noticed her timekeeping. Now, it was Tricky who was being admonished - by Tricia.

"You little bugger. Why are you so bloody cute? You're getting me into trouble. It's cuteness overload, and I get the stick for it."

"Quite right too," said Johnny, the permanent constable. "You've got him all night. Why deprive us just because you can't get to work on time?"

"Ha, that's good coming from you, Johnny. Not exactly the epitome of good timekeeping, are you? At least I do get here eventually."

"Well, I'm on time, aren't I?" said Johnny, pointedly.

"Only since I got Tricky," Tricia replied. "You should be thanking me for improving your time-keeping."

Steve laughed out loud. "Can you two hear yourselves? Arguing about a dog that has changed your attendance records."

"Anyway, Johnny," said Tricia, "it was nice of you to give Tricky that fluffy toy rabbit to play with."

"I didn't give it to him," Johnny replied.

"Was it you, sir?" Tricia directed her question to Steve.

"No, it wasn't me either."

"Must have been you then, Sargent," said Tricia.

"It wasn't me either. For goodness sake, can you guys talk about something other than that bloody dog?" Mike remonstrated. "Constable, haven't you got to go into the village for your morning checks? And Detective Constable, go over the road to the car park and see the ticket attendant. He says he's got something that might interest us regarding the longbow killing last year. See what it is."

When Steve glanced up, there was a strange look in his eyes. He remembered the night that the last of the five men involved in killing the Yorkshire boy received an arrow right through the eye as Steve talked to him. The shot came from the roof of the car park across the road and the killer escaped in a red car into the night. Steve didn't like to think about it.

"Yes, Sargent, I'll go and see him. I wonder what he's got. It would be nice to clear that case up, wouldn't it, sir?" she said to Steve.

"Yes, Constable, it would," he replied.

Tricia went out to the car park across the road. As she was entering, she met Marsha, the vet's receptionist.

"Hi, Tricia, how are you? And how are you getting on with Tricky?" she asked.

"Tricky is great, and everyone in the station loves him," she replied.

"Mrs Chalfont says he has been in to see her. How come?" Marsha showed surprise.

"Who is Mrs Chalfont?" asked Tricia, not knowing to whom Marsha referred.

"Mrs Chalfont is Tricky's previous owner," Marsha explained. "She lives next door to the vet. But you must know that."

"No," said Tricia. "You didn't tell me. Why do you say he has been in to see Mrs Chalfont?"

"I saw her yesterday, and she said Tricky had been to see her."

"She is an old lady, and I guess she gets confused," said Tricia.

"Yes, I suppose that must be it," said Marsha. "Anyway, it's nice to see you. We'll have to have lunch sometime."

"Yeah, I'll give you a ring," said Tricia as she entered the car park ticket office.

"Hi," she greeted the ticket collector, "I think you have something for us. What is it?"

"This has been lingering under my desk for months," said the ticket collector holding up a piece of wood, painted white, and about three feet long with ragged ends.

"What makes you think we might want that?" asked Tricia.

"Well, I'm no expert, but from what I've seen on the telly, you detectives like to examine such things. Look, there is some red paint on it left by the car that broke through the barrier."

"Oh, I see," said Tricia, suddenly interested in the piece of wood, "and you've been sitting on this for months?"

"No one asked for it," said the ticket collector.

"OK, sir, thanks. I'll take it to the Super. Maybe he can get it analysed at forensics."

* * *

"What are you up to constable, collecting firewood," said Mike when Tricia re-entered the station.

"No, Sargent," she said proudly, "this firewood might just solve our Longbow murder case."

"Why? What have you got?" asked Steve suddenly interested.

163

"Here, sir, look at this red paint. This wood is from the damaged barrier. Can we get anything from it? Like what make of car it was?"

"I think it was a Vauxhall," said Steve. "OK, we'll get it analysed. Can you cut a piece off with the paint on it, and I'll have it sent away?"

"Sure," said Tricia taking a penknife out of her pocket and carving a strip from the edge of the barrier. Steve put it in an envelope and wrote the forensics address on it. Then he placed it in the out tray.

"So," said Tricia, looking around, "Where is the little bugger?"

"He's outside in the garden," said Mike.

Tricia went to get him. When she came back, she looked anxious.

"He's not there," she said. "Where has he gone?"

"I let him out myself," said Mike, "he must be out there." Mike went to look for himself. When he opened the door, Tricky came bounding in. In his mouth, he had another toy. This one was a stuffed pig.

"Hey, where are you getting these toys?" asked Tricia. "Have you got a stash somewhere?" She turned to Mike. "Are these your kid's toys Sargent?"

"No, never seen them before."

"I'd better go and take a look," said Tricia and went out to the back garden. She looked all around, finding nothing until she examined the space behind a small shed. There was a gap in the chain-link fencing. She put two and two together.

Returning to Mike, she explained how Marsha had said Tricky had visited his previous owner around the corner, next to the vet. It seems like Tricky had been getting out through the gap in the fence and visiting Mrs Chalfont.

"He's got the right name," said Mike. "He certainly is a tricky little bugger."

"I'll use that plank from across the road and block the hole with it. We won't need it now, will we, sir?" she asked Steve.

"No, carry on, use it," Steve responded.

Things settled down, and they got on with their work. Later, Tricia phoned Marsha to ask her to lunch, and Steve rang forensics to tell them something was on its way.

Two days later, Steve received a call from forensics, telling him the make of vehicle they had identified from the paint sample.

"Are you sure?" asked Steve. "OK, if that is a definite, I'll enter it into the file. Send me the report when it's ready," he requested.

"That's odd," he said to Mike. "I was sure it was a red Vauxhall, but they tell me there's no chance of that. It was a Peugeot using a special new colour of red. I can't believe it."

"You know why you think that?" said Mike. "It's because Susan drives a red Vauxhall. So, you have that fixed in your mind."

"Maybe," said Steve, but he was confused.

Mike changed the subject.

"What is that on the floor?" he asked, pointing to some white powder that littered the tiled floor.

Tricky was playing with his newly obtained toy, shaking it vigorously. A white powder spread everywhere. Tricia went over and took the toy from him. It was filled with powder.

"This isn't normal, is it?" she said, "They use something else, not powder."

"Better sweep it up," said Mike. "It's a damned mess all over the floor."

Tricia got the broom and started sweeping it up. Just out of interest, she took some from the toy and tasted it on the tip of her tongue.

"Bloody Hell," she shouted. "This powder is bleeding cocaine."

"Are you sure?" Steve wasn't so convinced. "Let me have that toy."

He wet his finger and tried a little of the powder. "Damn," he said excitedly. "Well done, Constable. You are right on. That is cocaine. Where did Tricky get this toy?"

Tricia explained that Tricky had been getting out and going to his previous owner's house, which was just around the corner.

"We had better look into this, Tricia," he said, and the two of them went around to the vet. Marsha was at her reception desk.

"Hello," she greeted them. "Not after another dog, are you?" she grinned. "Isn't Tricky handful enough for you?"

"He is more than enough," Tricia answered. "We would just like to check on the previous owner. She lives next door, doesn't she?"

"Yes, why?"

"Does she live alone?" asked Steve.

"Yes," Marsha confirmed, "but she has a grandson who drops in from time to time."

"What's he like? Have you ever met him?" asked Steve.

"No, but Mrs Chalfont doesn't think too much of him. There's another lad who drops in sometimes too. I don't know who he is. Haven't seen him."

"I see," said Steve. "Anything else you can tell us?"

"Well, the other lad is a friend of her grandson, but the odd thing about him is he only goes in for about two minutes before he leaves. She doesn't like him either."

"Thank you, Marsha. You've been very helpful."

"What's this all about?" Marsha asked.

"I'll tell you when we have lunch," said Tricia. Then they left to go and see Mrs Chalfont.

Tricia knocked on the door and pushed it open.

"Hello, Mrs Chalfont," she called out, "it's Tricia. I took on your dog, Tricky." Mrs Chalfont came to the door.

"Hello, Tricia. That was so nice of you to look after him. I can't manage him any longer. He's quite a little scamp."

"Yes, he is," Tricia agreed.

"He came to see me this morning, you know. It surprised me he was running around off the lead."

"I'm sorry about that," said Tricia. "There was a gap in the fence, and he was getting out. I've fixed it now."

"It's nice of you two to come and visit me," said Mrs Chalfont. "I don't see many people these days. Only my waste-of-space grandson and his useless friend."

"That's why we are here," said Steve. "I'm Detective Superintendent Stephen Kendall. What can you tell us about your grandson and his friend?"

"Oh, no, they're not in trouble, are they?"

"How old are they?" asked Tricia.

"My grandson, Billy, is about twenty now. Never had a job since he left school, lazy little bugger. The other one, I don't even know his name. He never stays long enough for me to find out. He's older. Maybe twenty-six."

"Where does Billy live?" asked Tricia.

Mrs Chalfont went to the sideboard and picked up an old envelope. It had Billy's address on it. She handed it to Tricia.

"Oh," she said as she passed it over to Steve. "It's in the village. I know where that is."

"Mrs Chalfont," Steve asked of her, "does Billy ever bring anything with him when he comes to see you?"

"Yes, he is always bringing toys for Tricky. He's still bringing them even now Tricky isn't here. The funny thing is, they all disappear. I think his friend steals them when I'm not looking. I used to think that was the only reason he came here. He's just a bloody thief."

"Where does he live, Mrs Chalfont? Do you know?" asked Tricia.

"No, he don't live in Ricton, though."

"OK, Mrs Chalfont, we have to be off now. You have been very helpful. And your little dog is brightening up the Police Station," said Steve.

Outside, Tricia said, "I guess we'll have to go and visit Billy Boy. We'll get my car. I know exactly where he lives."

They went around the corner to the Police Station. Steve told Mike where they were going, and they drove off in Tricia's car.

Of course, Billy wasn't expecting them.

"Your name is Billy Chalfont?" asked Tricia, taking the lead. Steve hung back and observed Billy's reactions. Neither were wearing uniforms, so Billy had no idea who they were.

168

"If you are Jehovah's Witnesses, I'm not interested," he said.

"That's good then," said Tricia, "because we are not Jehovah's Witnesses. However, we have witnessed something this morning that concerns you. I am Detective Constable Mason, and this is my boss, Detective Superintendent Kendall. We would like to step inside to ask you a few questions."

"What about?" asked a very nervous Billy.

"Look, Billy, people are walking past here who can hear everything we say. Do you want that? Or maybe you would prefer to come down to the Police Station." Tricia looked at Billy with a raised eyebrow.

Billy shuffled on his feet and let them pass him into his sitting-room. He fiddled with his hands and looked as though he was going to be sick.

"You are very nervous, Billy," said Tricia in a comforting voice. "Have you been in trouble with the police before?"

"No," Billy replied. "Why are you here? Am I in some kind of trouble?"

"I think you might be, Billy," said Tricia.

"If you are in the trouble we believe," Steve spoke for the first time, "it might even mean a long prison sentence."

"I haven't done anything," Billy protested.

"Then it wasn't you who took toys to your gran's house for her dog, Tricky? Was your gran mistaken?"

Billy suddenly realised what this was about and the look in his eyes gave him away.

"Yes, Billy," said Steve, "we are fully aware that you often take toys to your gran's house. And we also know that your friend picks them up when he visits a day or two later."

"There's nothing wrong with toys for the dog," said Billy, trying unsuccessfully to minimise the importance of the toys.

"Yes, you are right Billy," Tricia agreed. "I own that dog now and we just love watching him play with his toys. But when those toys start to leak cocaine powder all over the Police Station floor... Well, Billy, I'm sure you can see how that might be a problem."

Billy shuffled his feet again and looked at the floor.

"So, Billy, "Tricia continued, "this is what we have. You get a toy for the dog, fill it with cocaine, and deliver it to your gran's house. Later your friend arrives, picks up the toy, and sneaks it out of the house. What we don't have yet, and what you are going to tell us to keep your police record at a manageable level, is one: Where do you get the cocaine, two: What is the name and address of your friend, and three: What does your friend do with the cocaine after he has picked it up?"

Billy said nothing.

"OK, Detective Constable, that's enough," Steve intervened. "I think it's time to take Billy to the Police Station. You do realise this is not going too well for you, don't you, Billy?"

"Alright, I'll tell you," said Billy, giving in to the pressure. "I get the toy from the pet shop."

"Yes," Tricia urged him, "and then?"

"Then nothing. That's it. I get the toy from the pet shop and take it to my gran's house."

"Are you trying to tell us that the pet shop sells toys full of cocaine?" Tricia laughed. "And I suppose you buy bags of pot from the grocer and packets of joints from the newsagents too?"

"No," said Billy, "there's this guy who delivers to the pet shop once a week, and I see him when he arrives before he takes his stuff in."

"Ah, I see," said Tricia, "so there is another guy involved. And where does this guy get the cocaine from."

"I don't know," said Billy. "I met him in a pub, and he asked me if I would like to make some extra cash. It's an easy job. Who wouldn't do it?"

"Unfortunately, not many these days," said Steve. "And your friend who collects it from your gran, who is he?"

"He's not my friend." Billy was adamant.

"OK, who is he?" Tricia urged.

"His name is Jeff. He can never fix a definite time for me to meet him, so he picks up the toy at my gran's when he is in the area. I don't know what he does with it. I didn't even know they had cocaine in them until recently."

"OK, Billy, we'll take it from here. When is the next pet shop delivery, and what is the name of the driver?"

They collected as much information about the operation as possible and left after warning Billy to stay in the area and be available when needed. Billy was only too willing to co-operate.

"Constable," said Steve in the car back to the station, "I think you handled that like a seasoned professional. Well done."

"Thank you, sir," she responded with a broad smile on her face. That smile got even brighter when Steve said, "When this is over, and I think it will be quite easy to sort out, I'll put in a good report about you at head office."

Over the next few days, they put operations in place. The first person they picked up was the delivery driver who brought the toys to the pet shop. They visited Mrs Chalfont to explain what had been going on, and put a lookout in place in the form of Johnny, who kept an eye on Mrs Chalfont's house. When Jeff turned up, Johnny quickly contacted the station, at which point Steve, Mike, and Tricia arrived in less than two minutes to arrest him.

This operation led to extended arrests further afield in London, and the Ricton Police got much of the credit for it. It was time for a proper celebration, so Mike invited everyone to his home where Debbie put on a great spread, and they celebrated with champagne.

The conversation was heavily concentrated on their surprising success in not only solving local crime but also starting investigations elsewhere.

"Who'd have thought it," said Tricia, "when I came here after working with Steve on the Longbow murders, that we would be celebrating such great success? You know, if it wasn't for Tricky, this case would never have come to light."

"True," said Johnny, "but what I don't understand is why Jeff picked up the cocaine from Billy's gran. Why didn't he get it direct from the pet shop delivery driver?"

"It was to break the chain," Tricia explained. "The police knew both were involved in drug peddling. But by using Billy, and then his gran, neither of whom were connected to drugs, the involved police operations were unable to tie the two together. That's why Ricton came out on top. And it's all thanks to Tricky."

"Huh!" Johnny exclaimed. "You'll be giving him a title next."

"Good idea. CIA. Cute Investigation Associate." Tricia offered, causing all to laugh.

"Yes," said Susan, it's good to know that you are all doing such a great job. You know, Steve never really talks about his work. It's only at times like these, when we get together, that I know about anything."

Steve grunted.

"You know what," Susan continued, now that she had their attention, "I never even found out how the Longbow murder case turned out. Did you ever arrest anyone for that?"

"I'm afraid not," said Tricia, "but we did find out that the killer was driving a red Peugeot and not a red Vauxhall like yours, which Steve thought originally."

Susan smiled and looked knowingly at Steve. "I know he got hooked on that idea for a long time. I can't think why. Why was that Steve?" she asked innocently.

"I don't want to talk about that case," he said, "shall we move on."

Susan couldn't help herself. Her laughter spilled out into the room.

"Poor darling," she said as she kissed him on the cheek, causing Steve to blush visibly.

This reaction confused everyone except for Susan, the only person who knew the answer.

Story Nine – A Visit to the Doctor
Part One

Detective Constable Tricia Mason took a five-day break. Her good friend, Susan, joined her for a short trip to Devon. The two of them lay on the beach, getting a last-minute top-up tan before returning home to the village of Ricton. A shadow fell across Tricia's sun towel. Tricia opened her eyes behind her sunglasses and looked up to see a young man looking down at her.

"Would you mind moving about a foot to your left?" she said.

The man did as asked.

"That's better," said Tricia, pushing her shades up onto her head. "I can see you now that you're blocking the sun."

"I wonder if your view is as good as mine," said the cheeky young fellow. Tricia turned to face her friend.

"What do you think, Susan?" she asked.

Susan studied the man. "I don't know. Pretty boy, isn't he?"

Tricia turned her attention back to the man. "Pretty boy? Yeah. But I prefer rugged and virile."

"I agree," said Susan. "Might as well have a girl," she leaned over Tricia and kissed her on the lips.

Tricia, shocked but she not disturbed by the intimacy, thought it quite pleasant. The young man looked deflated.

"Huh, a couple of dykes," he said.

Tricia pushed her glasses back down over her eyes. "Would you mind moving to the right again?" she said, "You're blocking my sun."

The lad moved on to find someone else to pester.

Susan laughed playfully, and Tricia joined in. "That's how to get rid of unwanted attention," she said.

"It worked," Tricia agreed.

"Usually does."

"Do you publicly kiss girls often, then?"

"Not as often as I might," said Susan giving Tricia a wink. Tricia smiled to herself and wondered about Susan. The most engaging thing about her was the way she always surprised her. She always had her work cut out (beyond her detective abilities), simply trying to fathom Susan. But that was Susan, the original enigma. And so beautiful too. To her surprise, Tricia realised she hadn't minded about that kiss and wondered what it would be like to do it at a time when Susan was not merely joking. *What strange thoughts. Better get off this pattern before it takes a turn in the wrong direction.*

Tricia looked at her watch. "I guess it will soon be time for us to make a move," she said. "Shall we have some lunch and then get on the road home?"

Susan sighed reluctantly and agreed.

They had their lunch in the hotel restaurant before checking out and were soon on the M3 heading back to Ricton in Susan's car.

* * *

The following morning Tricia was back at work.

"Good morning, Sarge," she greeted as she breezed into the office. "Is everyone OK?"

"We certainly are, Detective Constable. How was your time off?"

"It was pretty good, Sarge." Tricky was jumping all over Tricia, so pleased to see her. "Thanks for looking after Tricky. I hope he was no trouble."

"None more than usual. So, you enjoyed your break."

"Yeah, but it would have been better if I hadn't been worrying so much."

"Worrying? What have you been worrying about?"

"Why, all of you, of course. I know how you depend on me, so how you manage when I'm not here… well, I get very concerned. I'm glad you're all OK. I won't worry so much in the future."

"What has Constable Tricia been worrying about?" asked Detective Inspector Kendall as he walked into the office, having caught the end of Tricia's banter.

"Oh, she worries at how indispensable she is, Stephen. What were you saying yesterday about getting a replacement for her?"

"Oh, yes, Mike, she's out in the car. She'll be in here in a moment."

Tricia couldn't contain her shock. Her mouth dropped open, and Mike put out his hand to assist her in closing it. As if on cue, the door opened and in came Susan. She walked over to Tricia.

"Here, honey," she said, "you left this bag in my car yesterday. I hope you didn't need it."

"Thanks," said Tricia.

"Got to go," said Susan, and left.

Steve and Mike burst out laughing.

"The look on your face, Tricia, was pure magic," Mike grinned.

"Well, that's the last time I worry about your arses. From now, you're on your own. Anything in, sir?" she asked of Steve.

"Nothing much I'm afraid, just that hotel business, but I suppose we'll have to look into it."

"What's that, sir?"

"Come on. The hotel is nearby. I'll tell you about it on the way."

As they strolled down the street, the Detective Inspector filled her in.

"We had a call from the manager, a Shirley Dennet. A guy staying there who checked out yesterday had a problem with his bill. Said it was about four times what he had been expecting. When management looked into it, the extra amount was for the completely used up mini."

"Hell, he must have been on some binge," said Tricia.

"Well, that's the point. He says he only had two drinks, and that seemed to check out by the two empty bottles found in the room."

"So, you're saying the other drinks were gone, including their bottles."

"That's right."

"Did they check his luggage?"

"No, they don't have the authority to do that, but they say his luggage was not large enough to have held all the bottles."

"Ah, so it's a mystery."

"Yes, but I'm sure you will be able to solve it. I'm afraid it's not much of a challenge."

"Don't you mean 'we,' sir?"

"No, Constable. I'm leaving this one to you. I'll introduce you and be off. Just do your thing. It usually gets results."

"Well, thanks for your confidence."

They turned into the hotel foyer and asked for Miss Dennet. When she arrived at the reception desk, Stephen made the introductions and left.

"Right," Tricia started, "this is what I know." She related what Steve had told her about the problem. "Is that correct, Miss Dennet?"

"Yes, more or less, except there's more to it than I told the Inspector.'"

Tricia wondered, 'Did this customer steal more than just booze?'

"And that would be?" she asked.

"This problem happened two days ago. However, it also happened with two other customers, one last week and another the week before. It's getting so we are expecting problems every week now."

"I see. So, from what you say, it's unlikely the customers themselves are responsible for the disappearance of the bar contents?"

"That's right."

"What about your staff? How many work in the hotel?"

"There are four of us. Then there are the day and night porters. That leaves the cleaning and restaurant staff."

"How many cleaners are there?"

"Just two for the rooms and one for the general areas."

"And do you trust all your personnel?"

"Yes, they are very trustworthy. They have worked for us for a long time."

"How about the catering staff? Do they have access to the rooms?"

"No. Of course, they may gain access one way or another, but I don't think they are responsible."

Tricia thought it over. Then she said,

"That only leaves one other set of people."

"Does it? Who do you mean?"

"I'm referring to the customer's guests."

"Well, I did ask each of these customers if they'd had anyone in their rooms. They all said they hadn't."

'Huh,' Tricia thought, 'That seems unlikely.' If the occupants were men, would they admit to taking girls into their rooms? There was more to this than appeared. She engaged Miss Dennet again.

"Tell me, Miss Dennet, these customers, were they male or female?"

"They were all male."

"And how old, roughly?"

Miss Dennet thought about the question before answering.

"I would say they were all about forty plus. One of them was probably fifty-five or sixty."

"So, if they had a girl in their room, it is unlikely they would admit to it."

"I guess not."

"Right. Just one other question. This hotel is on two levels. The rooms in question, were they on the ground floor or the first floor?"

"They were rooms 17, 25, and 31. All of those are on the ground floor."

"Can I take a look at them, Miss Dennet?"

"Of course. I'll get someone to show you, but number 25 has a guest at the moment."

She called to the porter.

"Stanley, can you take the Detective Constable to these rooms," she said, handing him the keys. Tricia followed him along the ground floor corridor. Stanley opened the door and let her into number 17.

It was a double room with an en-suite bathroom. The so-called bar was a refrigerator in the corner with a table next to it, bearing a tray and two glasses. Tricia opened the fridge. Inside were several bottles. Four were full-size bottles of whiskey, gin, vodka, and rum. Additionally, there were some two dozen smaller bottles of various drinks.

"I wonder why the hotel supplies their customers with so much booze. Half a dozen people could get drunk on this lot."

"Yeah," Stanley agreed. "It does seem like a lot of drinks for one or two people. I guess it's just the hotel policy, providing variety to keep the customers satisfied."

Tricia went to the window and looked out. Below was shrubbery.

"Does this window open?" she asked.

Stanley came to the window, slipped the lock, and opened it.

"I guess it does," said Tricia and looked out to the ground. It was dry, and she saw no footprints. She closed the window.

"Is the other room the same as this?" she asked. Stanley confirmed that it was identical.

"OK, Stanley, thank you. I'll just go and have another chat with Miss Dennet."

She found her attending the reception desk with another younger woman.

"Miss Dennet, do you have any single rooms here?"

"Of course."

Why would you book a double room if you were alone? Several conclusions passed through Tricia's mind. One in particular lingered.

"Is it normal that your male customers book a double room?"

"No. Not always. It's usually the travelling reps who take a double room. Probably paid for on expenses."

"Yes, you are probably right. Now, you say all stated they hadn't had any guests in their rooms. Is there any evidence to confirm that?"

"How do you mean?"

"Do you have any closed circuit tv covering the corridor areas."

"Yes, we do, but I'll have to get Alan to show you. I don't know much about it."

She took Tricia to see Alan, and he went through the video.

"I'm afraid I only have it for the past week. After that, we record over it for the next week. What are you looking for?"

Tricia explained, and they ran through the pertinent periods.

"There you are Alan. There's our guy with a young girl. They've gone in at about eleven pm. What time did she leave?"

Alan ran through the video. Surprisingly, the girl left before midnight. If they were getting up to the naughties, they must have been pretty quick. Unfortunately, nothing on the video gave a facial shot of the girl, so they could not identify her. She didn't have any bags with her, though, so she could not carry out any bottles. Tricia returned to the desk.

"Miss Dennet, are your room cleaners here at the moment?"

"Probably. They start soon for the morning cleaning."

Miss Dennet located them, and they came to the reception desk. Tricia asked them a few questions which didn't produce any useful information.

"So, there was nothing unusual about the rooms on those days."

"No, constable, nothing at all," said one of the cleaners.

"There was just one thing," said the other cleaner. "There was a pillowcase missing in one of the rooms, but I can't remember which room it was now. Probably wasn't any of those you are talking about."

"OK," says Tricia. "Everyone has been very helpful."

"Do you have any ideas?" asked Miss Dennet.

"It's too early to say yet, but I do have something on my mind. I suppose you wouldn't have any telephone contacts for these three people?"

"Only Mr Carter from number seventeen. Nothing for the others."

"Alright, Miss Dennet, I'll jot that number down," said Tricia, taking out her notebook. "I'll get back to you when I have something," she said and left.

* * *

Later, back at the station, Tricia sat at her desk. Little Tricky had finished greeting her as though she's been away again for days, instead of an hour or so. He sat curled up at her feet. She phoned the number Shirley Dennet had given her. A man answered the call.

"Hello, Carter, here."

"Hello, Mr Carter, this is Detective Constable Tricia Mason from Ricton police."

"Detective. How can I help you?"

"I'm looking into the losses claimed by the hotel where you stayed. Would you mind answering a couple of questions."

"What do you want to know?"

Tricia paused for a moment and then asked,

"Tell me, Mr Carter, are you married?"

"Yes. What has that got to do with it?"

As if he didn't know. What a jerk. Well, she wasn't about to let him off the hook. Time to have a little fun to break up a tedious investigation.

"Okay, I thought as much. Look, I'm not here to get you into any trouble with your partner, but I do need you to be honest with me."

"What makes you think I am not honest?"

"The fact that you show up clearly on video taking a girl into your room at eleven o'clock, yet you said you didn't have any guests."

There was no response from Mr Carter. Tricia waited, while she visualised the man squirming as he worked out how he would get out of the hole he had dug. When the pause became ridiculous, she said, "Well, Mr Carter, would you like to revise your earlier comment?"

"Okay, okay, I had a girl in my room."

"That wasn't so difficult, was it?"

When they act like kids you have to treat them as such.

"Now, Mr Carter, what time did she leave?"

Again, Carter paused.

"Let me help you, sir," said Tricia. "You don't know, do you?"

"No, I don't."

It was time to teach this guy a few things.

"Let me tell you what I think happened. You took her to your room at eleven. Either you or she poured drinks from the bar. When you weren't watching, she poured some sleeping drug into your glass. You had a chat and finished your drinks, by which time you were sound asleep. The girl removes one of the pillowcases,

183

fills it with the bar's contents, opens the window, and gently lowers it onto the ground. She then fastens the window and leaves. The time, for your information, Mr Carter, was a little before midnight."

She let that sink in before continuing.

"Having left, she goes around to the back of the hotel and retrieves her cache of booze, expecting you to pay for it. Since the hotel did not make you pay for it, even though it was your fault that the bar contents disappeared, I suggest that you ring the hotel and offer them your thanks. And if you intend staying there again in the future, you might tell them it will never happen again."

"I see, Detective, yes, thank you. I'll do that."

"Please be sure that you do, sir."

"Don't worry. I'll phone them right away."

Tricia smiled to herself. Poor bugger, she thought, no way of training the bastards. He's probably got some girl lined up for tonight already. Maybe he'll think twice, but she didn't hold her breath. Mr Carter had a question.

"Detective, are you close to finding this girl, and if you are, will you charge her?"

"At this moment, we have no idea who she is. If we do identify her, then yes, we'll charge her. After that, it's out of my hands and up to the courts."

"So, they could call me as a witness?"

"It's possible. I'm afraid how you handle that will be up to you, though."

"Huh, so I'll be on my own then. Left in the lurch."

Tricia released a heavy sigh of frustration.

"Mr Carter, the lurch, as you call it, is a situation. I think you know very well who caused that situation,

184

so no one but yourself has put you there. They usually call that 'taking responsibility for one's actions.' Sound familiar?"

"Jesus," said Mr Carter.

"Yes, he might help you," said Tricia, "but I wouldn't hold out too much faith in that. I've never seen him in court yet. Goodbye, Mr Carter. I'll be in touch if I need you again."

Tricia rang off and heaved a sigh. What next? The afternoon was pushing on, so she tidied up her paperwork and checked with Detective Inspector Kendall.

"How are you getting to grips with that hotel problem," he asked.

"Got it pretty much sorted out, sir. Can't do anymore unless we can locate the perpetrator."

"Good, Detective Constable. I think you can call it a day today."

"I'm afraid I won't be in tomorrow morning, sir. I've got a doctor's appointment."

"Nothing serious, I hope."

"No, sir. Just routine female things."

"Really? I'm trying to work out what routine male things are at the doctor's but can't think of anything."

"That's cos you guys have got it easy. Whoever determined the sexes must have been a man. Bloody favouritism, that's what it is."

Stephen laughed. "You've got a point there, Tricia. I'll see you when you get finished with your female things."

"Never gets finished - bloody lifetime marathon," she said as she left the station.

Story Nine – A Visit to the Doctor
Part Two

The next morning, Tricia turned up at the doctor's office for her routine check-up at nine forty-five for her ten o'clock appointment. She couldn't stand people who were late, so she went out of her way to be early. Tricia checked in at reception and went to the waiting room for her call. There were several people in the waiting room. She motioned to a young woman sitting alone.

"Morning," she greeted, "do you mind if I sit here?"

"No, please do," said the girl. Her voice was more mature than one might expect from a young lady with blond ringlets framing her face.

"What time is your appointment?" Tricia asked.

"I don't have one. I'm just waiting for my mother."

"Oh, it's your mother's appointment. I see."

"I'm afraid you don't," said the woman. "My mother is a consultant, and she has a patient at this surgery this morning. She goes to several surgeries, depending on who needs her."

"Is your mother a specialist?

"Yes," the woman replied, without offering any further information.

Tricia smiled. "I like your hair," she said. "Very pretty."

"Thank you. I like your face," said the woman, "very sexy looking."

Tricia thought the observation was a little forward. Maybe she is a lesbian and is trying to see if I am interested.

"Yeah," she replied, "but then, everyone is sexy in their way, don't you think?"

"Oh, what a lovely thing to say. Do you think that?"

"Of course, if that weren't the case, no-one would ever find a partner, would they?"

"No, of course, you are right. My name is Georgina."

"Tricia. Bit boring, actually."

"No. It's a beautiful name, and memorable too."

I think I'm right, Tricia thought. *She is a lesbian. Pretty though, in an unusual way.* Just then, the nurse's door opened.

"Miss Mason, the doctor will see you now."

Tricia got up and went into the doctor's surgery. She found it difficult to concentrate on anything with her legs spread apart, and knees raised. It felt even more troublesome when someone she barely knew was fiddling around under her gown, in places where few had ever dared. She had to distract herself. Tricia thought about Georgina and, for some unfathomable reason, let her mind wander to the kiss from Susan on the Devon beach, and how pleasant it had been. It wasn't the most appropriate thing to occupy her thoughts while the doctor touched her nether regions. She quickly recoiled.

"I'm sorry," said Doctor Rosemary Ramsey. "Did I hurt you?"

"No," said Tricia. "Sorry."

"That's okay; I'm finished. There are no problems to worry you. If you'd like to get dressed, you can check with the reception desk, and they will give you a date for your next appointment. I won't need to see you again until next year."

"Thank god for that," said Tricia. "It's bad enough having someone under my skirt when I've invited them, but…" she left the sentence hanging, and the doctor smiled at her.

Tricia left the doctor's office and stopped at reception. While she waited, a young boy of about twelve years came out of a consulting room and joined his mother. They left together. Tricia hung on for the details she had to collect. Then a woman came out of the same consulting room, leaned over the desk, spoke to the receptionist, and left. Georgina got up from her seat, waved to Tricia, and left with the woman.

"My god," said the receptionist when the woman left the building. "Stinks of booze every time she comes here."

"Who is she?" asked Tricia.

"That's Doctor Francesca. I don't know how she keeps her license."

"And that's her daughter, Georgina, is it?" asks Tricia.

"Huh," said the receptionist with a jerk of her chin, "Georgina. Yes, that's her daughter."

There was something strange in the receptionist's response that Tricia couldn't put her finger on.

"So, she is always the worse for drink, is she?" Tricia asked.

"It's not for me to judge," said the receptionist. "They," she used the all-embracing term that covered everyone whoever employed someone, "seem to tolerate her, so who am I to say anything?"

So why did you?

Tricia left and returned to the station.

* * *

That afternoon, Tricia carried out a few checks on the police system. She entered the name, Doctor Francesca, amazed at what came up. She went to see Stephen Kendall immediately.

"Excuse me, sir, but I've something I'd like to look into if that's okay?" She explained what it was and got his permission.

Tricia made a call, and eventually, a Miss Daphne Peacock answered.

"Hello, Miss Peacock. Detective Constable Mason from Ricton police station here. I wonder if I could meet you to discuss the details of a rape case in which you gave evidence. I know it was a long time ago, but I'd like to ask you some questions that no one asked at the time."

"I suppose so," said Miss Peacock, with very little enthusiasm.

"Are you still at the same address?"

"Jeez, no, I've moved several times since then."

She gave Tricia her current address, fifty miles away. Tricia agreed to drive and meet her that afternoon. It was about three-fifteen when Tricia arrived and knocked at the door.

Miss Peacock, an attractive woman of about forty-five years, dressed in an outfit more suited to a twenty-year-old, let her in. She made Tricia a cup of tea, and they sat to talk.

"Are you still in contact with Doctor Francesca?" Tricia asked to break into the subject gently.

"No, I'm afraid not. We've both moved on since those days."

"Is she married? I haven't discovered any husband."

"You don't know very much about her, do you?" said Miss Peacock.

"I have to be honest with you; I didn't even know she existed until a few hours ago."

"So, why the sudden interest?"

"I'm a detective. It's what I do. Let's just call it a gut feeling."

"Oh, gut feelings. If they were of any value, you would have known that Doctor Francesca is a lesbian and doesn't have a husband."

"I couldn't be sure, but that's what I suspected."

"Oh, did you?" Miss Peacock didn't look convinced. "Did you suspect that I am also a lesbian, Detective?"

"I did," said Tricia with a smile. Miss Peacock's look indicated she was still unconvinced.

"Lucia and I were in a relationship when the rape occurred. It eventually tore us apart."

"So, she didn't get over it?"

"Get over it? It changed her entire personality."

"In which way?"

"In every way. Lucia used to be a lovely, outgoing person, bubbly, and great fun. I loved her the first moment we met. We were perfect together. After the rape, she was a different person. First, she developed an intense hatred of men."

"Interesting, but not surprising."

"Yes, she gradually fell apart. The only time I saw her smile after that was the day she heard the news her rapist had committed suicide."

"And that, Miss Peacock, is what interests me," said Tricia. "What can you tell me about it?"

"Not a lot. I just read in the paper that he had cut his wrists in the bath and died."

"You didn't think anything prompted it, then?"

"Prompted? In what way?" asked Miss Peacock.

"I guess you don't know any other details about his death, then?"

"No, like what?"

"I suppose there's no reason for me to not tell you as it is on the public record. You don't know that the rapist had a sex change, Miss Peacock?"

"You're kidding. Must be the only case ever of a male rapist having a sex reassignment. Why would he rape a woman if he was transgender?"

"Good question. I believe he felt very much like a male when he carried out the rape."

"Well, damn it, that's the oddest thing I've ever heard."

"Yes," Tricia agreed, "and his suicide was no more than four years after the rape. What else can you tell me about Doctor Francesca during those four years?"

Miss Peacock breathed deeply, and examined her hands lying in her lap.

"We lived together at my house. I took care of her during her pregnancy." She looked up suddenly. Her eyes flared. "You know the bastard got her pregnant?"

"Yes, I do."

"After he was born, she would disappear for days at a time. When she returned, she always seemed happy, so she went off again for a few more days. That went on for about eight or nine months. I was usually left looking after the baby. Eventually, things got so bad I'd had enough, and we split up."

"That's it?"

"Yes. Lucia had started drinking and was always half pissed. I couldn't put up with it any longer. There's nothing much more to tell you. She became a pain in the ass, and there was no more fun with it. I told her she would have to leave as I had a new job and was selling the house."

"Was that true?"

"Yes. I haven't seen Lucia since, although I've followed her career. She seems to be good at her job, but I don't know what her specialty might be."

"Really?"

"No. I just know it's kids and usually boys."

"So, you don't know she's a specialist in transgender - boys to girls?"

"Hell, no," said Miss Peacock. "No, I didn't know that."

"Okay, Miss Peacock, that might give you something to ponder. I have a feeling we might need to talk again in the future. Before I go, I've just one other question for you."

"What is it, Detective?"

"Earlier, you spoke about her pregnancy, and said, 'After he was born'. Does that mean her child was a boy?"

"Yes, cute little chap he was too. Had curly blond hair."

"Thank you, Miss Peacock. I'll be in touch if I need to speak to you again."

Tricia left and headed back to Ricton. Her mind was full of questions. As yet, she had no answers. It was getting late when she left the countryside and village houses engulfed her, so she went straight home. Fortunately, her enquiring mind might get some relaxation later, as she had a date to meet up with Susan at their favourite watering hole.

She put the key in her door, glided over to the drink's cabinet, and poured herself a stiff one.

"Whew!" *Here's to a good evening out.*

Thankful that the day's work was over, she swigged it back in one gulp.

* * *

Tricia sat at the restaurant table, sipping her customary beverage. She never did anything by halves. As usual, it was a double tequila. She closed her eyes and let the stresses of the day slip silently from her shoulders. A peace descended, and a calm drifted over her such that she had to jerk her eyes open lest she drop off to sleep. She had been waiting for Susan for time enough to be on her second drink. Her mobile rang. It was Susan apologising, saying something had come up, a large fashion-order needing her attention.

"Okay, Susan, that's alright. Don't work too late. I'll have a bite to eat here and then have an early night. Perhaps we can do this later in the week?"

"Yes, sure we can. I'll give you a call."

Tricia rang off and called the waiter over. After she ordered, she discovered someone observing her. To her great surprise, it was Georgina. She gave her a nod of acknowledgment and carried on drinking.

The waiter, who was new, delivered her meal and commanded an extra few moments of examination. *Not bad.* Tricia didn't have a boyfriend and had to take her opportunities as they presented themselves. This waiter was a presentation she might have to unwrap sometime. Smiling, she tucked into her meal. She hadn't realised just how hungry she was. The business of eating so engaged her concentration that she didn't notice Georgina coming over until she'd pulled a chair out and sat down.

"You don't mind if I join you, do you, Tricia?"

Should have asked that before you plonked yourself down.

"There, I said you had a memorable name, and I remembered it. I've got this special thing. If a woman is gorgeous, and sexy, then I write her name down in my diary. I wrote your name down but didn't need to check on it, did I?"

"Obviously, not," said Tricia, slightly irritated by the unwanted attention.

She looked at Georgina's dress. She had to admit it was beautiful. Not the dress she'd wore in the doctor's waiting room. Yet she was sure she had seen a dress like it but couldn't remember where.

"Look, Georgina, you are a very forthright and outspoken person," she said. "Can I be forthright too?"

"Of course, you can, darling."

"Right, then. I think, from the way you speak to women like me, that you are a lesbian, and that's okay; you can sit and chat with me so long as you don't interrupt my eating. You can even chat me up if you want. But you might find it a bit of a challenge, so consider yourself forewarned. As for me, listening to you will broaden my experience."

"You put that very nicely," said Georgina. "It makes me want to take up the challenge in all earnestness."

Admiring the fork full of juicy steak that she was about to consume, Tricia rolled her eyes and continued with her meal.

"You're not going to stop me eating. I'm starving, and when I'm this hungry, nothing will slow me down."

"I know exactly how you feel," said Georgina, "I'm ravenous too, and nothing is going to put me off."

"I don't think we are talking about the same hunger here, are we?" said Tricia, her words semi-coherent due to a mouthful of food.

194

"Of course not. There's more to be hungry about than the taste of food. There are other tastes, you know?"

"So, I've heard."

"Never tempted?"

"Not yet."

"Ah, there's hope for me then."

"You are persistent, I'll give you that," said Tricia, then she changed the subject. "How is your mother?" she asked.

Georgina showed surprise at the sudden change.

"My mother? I don't think you've met my mother."

"I didn't say I had. I simply asked how your mother is."

"Oh." Georgina paused, "She'll be okay this evening. I have to take care of her," she said.

That was an odd thing to say, thought Tricia. *Why does she have to take care of her?* And so, she asked.

"Well, I say, 'take care of her.' What I mean is, keep her under control. She's an alcoholic, you see."

"Oh. How do you keep her under control?"

"If she brings any drink into the house, I confiscate it. I keep her in any alcohol she needs to get through the day without her overdoing it and getting drunk. And she would if I didn't intervene."

"Ah, so you are her Off-License?"

"Something like that."

"Must cost you a fortune?"

"No. I have other ways of supplying her, but let's not talk about my mother. It's you I want to talk about."

They continued chatting throughout Tricia's dinner, one innuendo following another. Then, quite suddenly, from the far reaches of her consciousness, Tricia's lights came on, and her mind lit up like a room full of people at a surprise party. Her detective mind became alert again, the earlier stresses forgotten. She had remembered where she'd seen that dress before. Okay, she thought, time to play a new game.

Tricia finished her dinner and her drink and said, "Georgina, why don't we go somewhere, not so public, where we can have a little privacy."

Georgina looked like she could not believe her ears. "Where shall we go?" she asked, hardly able to control her excitement.

"Why don't we go to the hotel across the road?"

"Okay, lead on." Georgina was up out of her chair much faster than when she had occupied it.

Story Nine – A Visit to the Doctor
Part Three

Georgina followed Tricia to the corridor leading to the rooms.

"Wait here," Tricia instructed and went across to the reception desk.

"Is Miss Dennet here?" she whispered.

"I'll just go and get her," said the receptionist.

As Miss Dennet approached, Tricia placed her finger to her lips, indicating privacy.

"Could I have one of the three rooms," she asked.

Miss Dennet took the key to room 17 off the hook and gave it to her. Quietly, she said,

"I see you are getting somewhere," nodding towards Georgina who stood near the corridor.

Tricia nodded and took the key. "Thank you."

With Georgina, they went to room 17.

Once inside, she said, "Georgina, why don't you pour us a drink from the bar. I'll have the same as you. I've just got to do something. I won't be more than one minute."

Tricia left Georgina in the room and went back to the reception desk.

"Miss Dennet," she said, "what did you mean when you said, 'I see you are getting somewhere'?"

"I recognised the girl. I've seen her before in here, although I can't remember where or when. Is she the one?"

"We will see," said Tricia, and she went back to the room. Georgina was pouring the drinks.

"What's the bathroom like?" asked Tricia.

"I haven't looked, but I think it's okay."

"Never make assumptions, go and take a look," she instructed and picked up her drink.

It seemed like Georgina enjoyed the dominant Tricia and went into the bathroom. As soon as she was out of sight, Tricia opened Georgina's handbag. Apart from the usual things, there were two medication bottles. One was Valeriana, which Tricia recalled were strong sleeping pills, and the other contained Ova-Glan capsules. A little earlier research revealed these were for female hormone treatment, especially for transgender male to female changes. She quickly replaced the bag and sat on the bed.

"Looks alright to me," said Georgina as she returned to the bedroom and flopped down onto the bed. "You are full of surprises, Tricia. What made you decide to sleep with me?"

Tricia smiled. "Sleep with you? I guess that would be a nice surprise. But no, I have several different surprises for you, Georgina. Do you often hook up with people about whom you know nothing?"

"Life's too short to waste time on those things."

"You think so?"

"Of course. I'd never make any connections if I spent all my time checking someone's background. Never had one backfire on me yet."

"I see. It's a bit dangerous, though, isn't it?"

"Maybe, but it's worth the risk."

"What do you know about me?" Tricia asked.

"That you are a lovely girl and I can't wait to get it on with you."

Tricia smiled before asking, "Do you know what my job is?"

"No, you didn't say."

"Can you make a guess?"

"Let me think. You are such a beautiful girl; you must be a dancer in a nightclub."

"Not exactly," Tricia responded, "but I've danced a few rings around some people."

Georgina giggled.

"I bet. You are getting to be quite a tease, Tricia." She leaned over the bed to kiss Tricia, but Tricia turned her head. Instead, she opened her handbag and took out her badge and a pair of handcuffs, stood up, and walked around the bed to Georgina.

Georgina looked at the handcuffs, probably thinking she was in for an exciting evening. "Wow, no one's ever seduced me in handcuffs before."

Georgina looked so excited; Tricia was almost loath to continue. But she clamped the handcuffs on her.

"Georgina Francesca," said Tricia "I am arresting you on suspicion of theft from this hotel on several occasions. You have a right to remain silent, but anything you do say may be used in evidence against you. Do you understand?"

Georgina was too shocked to say much of anything; it took her completely by surprise.

"Damn, you are good," was all she could say. Then, "What a line. Have you used that before?"

"Many times."

"Is this for real, or are we going to do the naughties?" Georgina lay flat on the bed, ready.

"Sorry to disappoint you, Georgina, but you are under arrest. I am Detective Constable Tricia Mason of the Ricton Police. I believe the last time you visited this room; you emptied the mini-bar of all its contents."

Georgina looked flabbergasted. "I guess I was right the first time. You are good."

"As a habitual predator and thief, you will probably get a custodial sentence for this. However, subject to a certain amount of help from you, I might be able to get the hotel to drop the charges. What do you say?"

"I don't know. What do you mean?"

"I'm talking about your mother, Georgina. Whether you help me or not, it isn't going to go well for her, but you could clarify a few points and save me a lot of time and trouble."

Georgina's face took on a startled expression. Then a look of fear inhabited her eyes.

"What about my mother?"

"I don't know, Georgina. I think you must assist me there. Let's start with you. What would you like to tell me?"

"Nothing. What can I tell you?"

"Are you sure you can't get this thing started? It would help you a lot."

"No," said Georgina adamantly.

Tricia picked up her phone, turned the sound to audible, and rang a number.

"Hello, this is Miss Peacock," came the voice at the other end.

"Oh, hi there, it's Detective Tricia Mason. Earlier, we spoke about Doctor Francesca, and you said she had a child. Can you tell me the child's name?"

"Yes, it was George."

"Thank you."

Tricia turned to Georgina, looked at her sympathetically, and in a soft voice, asked,

"Georgina, when did you go from being a boy to a girl?"

Tricia noticed tears forming in Georgina's eyes. She put her arm around Georgina to provide some comfort and compassion. She could only imagine what the girl, or boy, had gone through in her life.

"It's alright, Georgina, you don't need to cry. I'm not judging you. I would like to know how old you were and whether it was yours or your mother's decision."

Georgina got herself together, and they sat talking. Tricia knew it wasn't the correct procedure, and that she ought to conduct the questioning at the police station, but she realised how traumatic this must be for Georgina. She wanted to give her as much support as possible, and that would be easier to do there in the privacy of the hotel bedroom.

Georgina had been George up to seven or eight when her mother introduced her to the tablets. She had no idea whether she had felt feminine at any time. She just became a female. To Georgina, it was the natural thing to be. She didn't even know whether she felt like a female or a male. In short, her entire life was just one confusion caused by her mother.

Tricia suspected that Georgina was not naturally transgender, but her mother distorted her life after hers changed following her rape experience.

Tricia assumed the rape trauma repelled Doctor Francesca so much she had kidnapped her rapist and drugged him. Then she had carried out the transgender operation on him, castrating him and turning his manhood into womanhood, while feeding him transgender drugs. When satisfied, she had set him loose. Unable to live with his new self, he had taken his own life.

This was her revenge.

What should Tricia do now? She knew what she would like to do but thought it better to leave such decisions up to the Detective Inspector. In any event, an investigation needed to get started on Doctor Francesca. And pretty soon, as she would probably take action after hearing of Georgina's arrest.

Tricia took the girl back to the Station. Sargeant Mike booked her in for the night, and the following day she laid out the case to Steve.

"Damn it, Detective Constable, I give you one case to wrap up, and you solve two. Any more criminals sitting handcuffed in your car?"

"Not unless they are giving themselves up, sir."

"Huh. Might be better for them if they did."

She set out her suggestions, but Steve disagreed with her. It would go against the laws of justice they employed him to uphold.

Tricia thought Georgina had had a very rough deal, first being born of rape, and then forced into a situation over which she had no control. Her mother was a rape victim, and the perpetrator remained unpunished. In the mother's contorted mind, she did what she thought was an appropriate punishment for the man who had brutally raped her and changed her entire life.

No, thought Tricia, neither of these two people deserved anything, but sympathy, but not she nor Steven, could do that. Perhaps the courts would look on their misdemeanours more favourably.

All Tricia could do was have a word with Miss Dennet. If she knew the truth, she might drop the charges against Georgina. She could only try.

Story Ten – The Sat Nav Murders
Part One

"Tricia did very well on her own the last couple of days," Stephen Kendall said to his partner Susan.

"So, I heard," Susan replied, "but do you know the strangest part about her evening activity?"

"No, I can't say that I do."

"I had arranged to meet Tricia for dinner at our favourite restaurant, but I couldn't make it. You remember how that large order came in and I had to work on it."

"Oh, so otherwise, you would have been out with her?"

"Yes. Because I wasn't there, she met up with the girl, Georgina. Odd how things work out, isn't it?"

"Yeah, it certainly is."

"I'll tell you another thing I also think is odd."

"OK, go on." Stephen put his paper down to pay attention to Susan.

"I think it's more than odd that so many of your cases are one-offs."

"What do you mean, one-offs? Every case is a one-off."

"Well, in one way, yes, they are. But I'm not referring to them like that. They are one-offs in a very different way. I mean, the method of the crime. They are not just one-offs, but in many cases, unique."

"I don't follow you, Susan. What are you talking about?" asked a confused Stephen.

"Take that first case you were on at the start of working here in Ricton - The Longbow Murders."

"What about it?"

"Have you considered that there has probably never been another murder investigation in this country where the weapon was a longbow and that there were four separate killings by the same person, using that weapon?"

"That's probably true, but you said so many of my cases are one-offs."

"It's true, I did, and I meant it. What about the kidnapping of Mr Johnson's son? That was also unique."

"How so?"

"How was the ransom collected? By a drone. Don't you think that was probably the first time a kidnapper used a drone to collect ransom money?"

"Damn it, Susan. I think you are right. Go on."

"Whilst we are talking about drones, what about the man in the boat with his throat cut. What cut it? The blades of a drone."

"Wow, Susan. Soon you will be claiming that Ricton is a unique place for one-off crimes."

"Maybe it is, Stephen. Now you have these two crimes solved by Tricia. One, a robbery of bar drinks by a picked-up sex-worker, and two, a woman who converted her rapist from a man into a woman. Women raped would like to see their rapist castrated, but that is taking it to a whole other form of punishment. Don't tell me that's a commonplace crime."

Stephen laughed. "Before you drag up any more unique crimes here at Ricton, perhaps I should mention the new one that has recently come in."

"Only mention it if it is unique," said Susan. "I can't be dealing with any common or garden-type crimes anymore."

"How about 'the Sat Nav murder'? Does that satisfy your lust for the unusual?"

"What's the Sat Nav murder?" asked an incredulous Susan.

"We have just learned of a murder where the perpetrator led his victim to his place of execution by Satnav."

"Get away. I don't believe a word of it."

"I've got to go now to look into it," said Stephen. "Maybe you can add this one to your list of conspiratorial one-offs."

Steve kissed Susan goodbye and drove off to the station.

* * *

"Hi, Mike, what's all this about a Satnav murder," asked Steve as he walked in.

"That's how it looks. Tricia has already gone out there to look at the scene and get some notes ready for you. I sent Johnny out there with her. He can tape off the area and keep the spectators away.

"Good thinking, Mike. Where is it?" Steve enquired.

"It's about twelve miles away on the enterprise park. No need to give you directions. Enter this the Post Code that was flashing on the dashboard, and it will take you there."

"Thanks, Mike."

"I've contacted the doctor, and he said he would be out there in about an hour after he has concluded something."

Steve headed back to his car. He entered the code and set off. Then he contacted Tricia to tell her he was on his way. Fifteen minutes later, the Sat Nav said, *'Turn left here, then turn right, and you will have reached your destination.'* He pulled in and stopped next to Tricia's car. Johnny had taped off the

206

surrounding area and was on duty to keep the public away.

"Hi, Detective Constable, what have we got here?" he asked.

"Hello, sir. Two dead buggers. Came here by Satnav."

"Yeah, explain that to me."

"The engine was still running. I eventually turned it off, but the Satnav was repeating over and over, *'You have reached your destination.'* "

"I see. So, it is pretty clear that these guys didn't know exactly where they were heading and needed the Sat Nav help."

"Yes, sir. There are two of them - both shot dead. One is lying beside the car, and the other in the driver's seat."

"Let's take a look."

The man on the ground lay on his stomach, head towards the rear of the car, shot in the back of the head.

"It looks as though he had got out of the car and was walking toward the rear when the bullet killed him," said Tricia.

"Yes. I'd agree with that. The other one didn't even leave the car but remained in the driver's seat."

"Yes, sir. The bullet entered through the front windscreen and hit him between the eyes - didn't stand a chance, did he?"

"No," said Steve, and opened the door to the driver's seat. The bullet had not merely come through the windscreen and entered his head. It had gone right through, lodged in the back seat somewhere. Steve flipped the lock to the car boot and walked around to open it. He examined the back seat and saw where the bullet had passed through. It lay on the floor of the boot.

"That's some power behind that shot," said Tricia. "What do you think fired it?"

"Well, looking at the bullet, it's probably a high-powered sniper rifle."

"Bloody Hell, a sniper," said Tricia, "None of us are safe if that's who is firing around here."

"Don't worry, Detective Constable, he won't be around here now."

"How d'you know that, sir?"

"If these people received a Sat Nav destination to follow, then their killer lured them here for this execution."

"Could be," said Tricia, not thoroughly convinced. Steve smiled. "Come on," he said, "let's calculate where the bullet originated."

Tricia followed him back to the driver's door. Steve opened it and looked through the windscreen.

"I'll tell you what," he said to Tricia. "This is the car park to a builder's supplies. Why don't you go in and ask if they have a length of half-inch wooden dowel?"

"This is no time for DIY, sir, if you don't mind me saying," she said in her usual comedic manner. "Whatcha want it for?"

"You'll see. Go and fetch it."

Tricia walked off toward the builder's supplies entrance. Steve heard her muttering as she left.

"Bloody hell, playing fetch with bits of wood now. Tricky will be jealous."

Tricky was her little dog that spent most of its time at the station and kept everyone amused when Tricia wasn't doing so. She picked up a six-foot length of half-inch dowel from the supplies shop and brought it back to Steve.

208

"Could make a nice couple of arrows out of that," she said, "if you wanted to start up another longbow mystery."

Steve took the dowel from her and went around to the front of the car. He inserted the dowel into the bullet hole.

"Tricia," he said, "take hold of the end of this dowel. I'll go in the car and line it up with the hole in the driver's head. Then, if you could hold it as straight as you can, I'll try to get a bead on where the sniper might have been."

"OK, sir."

Steve entered the car and took hold of the dowel through the bullet hole. He then pulled on it until it was at the hole in the driver's head. Then he looked along the dowel. After a while, he got out of the car.

"Hang on there, Tricia," he said. "I'm just going to my car to get my binoculars."

When he returned, he stood at the front of the car and directed his view ahead, then passed the binoculars to Tricia.

"Take a look. You see that building about a quarter of a mile away, five storeys high. With the naked eye, you can see a white patch on the fourth floor. That is a towel or something similar hanging on a line on the balcony."

"Yes, I see it. Looks like a shirt."

"Ok. Well, these shots came from the flat next door to the left. That is where the firing point lines up to when you look back along the dowel."

"Right. Got it."

"We'll have to go take a look there pretty soon. I'll get Johnny to take care of things here with the doctor who I see has just turned up."

He called Johnny over.

"Morning, sir," Johnny greeted them.

"Morning," said Steve. "We have to go visit somewhere. Can you look after things here until we get back? We probably won't be too long."

"Yes, sir, no problem."

"Check the dead men's pockets for wallets and mobile before you let the doctor take them away."

"Already done that, sir," said Tricia. "Got them here in my pocket. Haven't had time to look at them yet."

"Oh, great. Well done, Detective Constable. OK, let's go."

Five minutes later, Steve and Tricia drew up in the carpark of the five-story flats. Steve led the way up to the fourth floor via the covered staircase. The balcony was a continuous passage along the front of the building. They located the flat with a garment hanging on the line and went to the flat to its left. Tricia looked around.

"Got something, sir," she said excitedly. "It's a shell case. Here's another one."

Tricia picked them up with the end of her biro and took a plastic bag out of her pocket. She placed both shell cases in the bag, while Steve examined the veranda wall. There were no visible marks that a rifle might have made. He knocked on the door. After a short wait, the door opened to reveal a woman of about fifty-eight or sixty holding a little boy, probably eighteen months old.

"Sorry to trouble you, but we are from the Ricton Police Station." He and Tricia showed their credentials. "Do you live here alone, or do others occupy this flat?"

"I live here with my granddaughter, who is at work right now. I look after her boy while she's at work."

"What about the boy's father?"

210

"What about him?" said the woman.

"Does he live here?"

"No." answered the woman abruptly.

"Where does he live?" asked Steve.

"Your guess is as good as mine. Ain't seen him since the boy was born."

"I see. Tell me, did you hear anything in the early hours, say two or three o'clock?"

Tricia had been looking at the mobile phones in her pocket.

"Two-thirty, sir," she interrupted. "Says so here."

"What's this all about?" asked the woman. "And no, I ain't heard nothing at two-thirty this morning. That's about the only time we get to sleep with this little man."

"Someone shot a rifle outside your flat at two-thirty this morning," said Steve.

"Couldn't have," said the woman. "That would certainly have woke me."

"Probably had a silencer on it," Tricia suggested.

"No, I ain't heard nothing. How'd you know someone was shooting here anyway?"

Steve ignored the question. "Where does your granddaughter work, and what time does she get home? We will need to speak to her."

The woman gave Steve the information.

"Maybe we'll go see her at work," he said to Tricia. "Can you write down those details. Thank you, Ma'am, I'm sorry to bother you."

"So, you ain't going to tell me what this is about then," she said. "Bloody typical."

"No, I'm sorry, I can't tell you right now as we are still gathering information. But seeing as how the rifleman fired from your veranda, we will let you know as soon as possible."

"Oh, well, thank you, officer, and I hope you find what you're looking for."

Steve and Tricia made their way back to the crime scene, calling in on their way to see the granddaughter who could not, unfortunately, supply any useful evidence, as she had not heard anything either. Tricia took out the phones and wallets from her pocket and studied them.

"Got a couple of names here, sir," she said. "One is Danny Bluton, and the other is Ross Riley. Mean anything to you?"

"Danny Blue, yeah. His name has come up a few times concerning drugs."

"Buying or selling, sir."

"Both, Detective Constable. He buys in bulk and sells to pushers."

"Ha, that makes sense," said Tricia.

"Why is that?"

"These messages on one of the phones, sir. It says, 'Much as you want. Bargain price.' Then the next message says, 'Put this code into your Sat Nav and be there at two-thirty am.' "

"Yes, that does sound like a message for buying drugs."

"It's a scam though, isn't it, sir."

"Is it? Why do you say that?"

"Because the shooting was pre-planned; it was a set-up."

"Well done, Tricia. What else is your detective mind working on."

"I think that's it, sir. They set these buyers up with the idea that they had some drugs to sell, as much as they wanted - no prices mentioned. The buyers decided how much they would spend for as much as they could get. Took the money to the meeting place, and as soon as they got there, they killed them. The sellers took the money. We have no idea of how much it was, though."

"That's excellent. We might have some idea of the amount from the records of these two drug dealers. Once we get things tied up here, we'll go back to the station and check the records. Then we will have to visit the homes of these two villains."

"Yes, sir. We'll need to check out these phones too and see if we can find out who sent the messages."

Returning to the station, Steve looked through the two men's records. They seemed like average buyers, probably spending about fifty thousand at a time on the purchase of cut drugs. As the perpetrator introduced this as a bargain buy, they might have gone up to one hundred. Lives are pretty cheap in the criminal community these days. They would need to go out to their homes but didn't think that would prove anything more than a formality. Meanwhile, Mike was looking into the phones for clues.

Breaking the news of deceased husbands or lovers is never good even when it is a criminal. Often the spouses are simply caught up in the activities of their husbands and seemed to be the case with these two. In the vicinity of the crime, Johnny checked out all the available CCTV tapes in the area. More than that, there didn't appear to be much more to go on. Danny Blue's credit card confirmed a briefcase purchase that day, probably bought solely to take the money in.

They examined the two cartridge cases for fingerprints, but they didn't show any.. Two videotapes showed both the vehicles used, but when taken, the car park lights were off, so very little detail showed. They did, however, identify the make of the vehicle, which was a Ford. That was all they had to go on, which was insufficient to provide any real evidence.

The only action remaining was to carry out a detailed house call on the residents of the block of flats. Perhaps someone had seen something suspicious. Tricia and Johnny spent the following day there speaking to everyone they found at home, and later in the evening, spoke with those who had not been home during the day. There were just two flats where they had been unable to contact anyone. This investigation was getting nowhere and needed a break.

* * *

Three weeks later, they were nowhere nearer to a lead, much less a solution. It was then that the unexpected happened. A report came in that a dead body lay beside a car at a disused quarry not too far away. Steve and Tricia drove out to the crime scene.

They located the car at the top of the quarry. The body lay just outside the driver's open door. Again, with the engine left running, the man who discovered it whilst walking his dog had not touched anything. Tricia checked inside the vehicle. The Sat Nav repeated the phrase, *'you have reached your destination.'*

"This has all the hallmarks of a repeat performance," she said to Steve. Steve looked at the body. As before, the bullet had gone right through the man's skull. He looked up in the direction where the shot would have originated. It could only have come from a large steel structure about five hundred yards away. The structure was a crushing plant used to reduce the quarried rock to the various aggregate sizes.

Steve phoned the station and asked Mike to send Johnny to the quarry and arrange for the doctor to attend with an ambulance. Steve examined the body and searched the pockets for the man's identity. After finding the information, he phoned it into the station.

214

When Johnny arrived, Steve and Tricia walked over to the crushing plant. There was only one point from where the shot could have come, and that was a platform at the top of a steel staircase.

"Let's take a look up there," said Steve.

At the top, there was a steel plate. One shell case had visibly lodged against a gap at the side. Tricia picked it up and bagged it for forensics.

"They don't seem very bothered about leaving evidence," she said.

"That's because they are confident and professional," Steve commented. "They know there are no prints on those cases - extremely meticulous."

"Yeah. This killing has the same MO as the other one, so I don't think we'll get far with it."

"We have even less to go on with this one, so I don't think we'll get as much."

"Yeah, less than bugger all don't add up to diddly-squat," Tricia pointed out.

"Let's wrap this up and get back to the station," said Steve.

Mike had been making inquiries about the dead driver. Again, he found that he was a drug dealer. It was clear these perpetrators were operating a con, luring drug dealer to a prearranged location, immediately shooting them and taking whatever money they had arranged with them. Although carrying out all the usual investigations, they were getting nowhere with these two cases.

Story Ten – The Sat Nav Murders
Part Two

A couple of weeks later, Steve was chatting to his friend at the London Met when the Sat Nav cases came up in the conversation. With extraordinary coincidence, Steve learned these were not isolated cases. There had been similar ones, three in London, two in Manchester, four in Liverpool, and three in Birmingham, plus their two cases. These totalled fourteen, all resulting in the death of drug dealers lured to their death by SatNav.

"So, how are they progressing with these cases, sir?" asked Tricia. "Are they having more luck than us?"

"It doesn't seem so," said Steve. "They appear coordinated in some way, so there has to be a common connection."

"Do you think they are all carried out by the same people?" Tricia wondered.

"No. The date of one of the London crimes is the same as one in Manchester," Steve explained.

"Sir," said Tricia. "I have a gut feeling about this. Could I take a couple of days to follow up?"

"Well, if you think you might have something to get us going forward, then yes, by all means, take a couple of days. What's on your mind?"

"Give me two days, sir, and I'll be able to tell you if I am on the right path or not."

"OK, two days," Steve agreed.

* * *

Tricia had a good feeling about this and was going to do everything she could to get things moving. *'If I get this right,'* she thought but left it hanging. Tricia could have told Steve what she was thinking but it may help her prestige if she came up with something positive independently.

She called the Military Records Office to learn the details of all Army personnel who had left the army in the past six to twelve months. To narrow her search, she asked for only exceptionally expert marksmen. She was particularly keen to know their current addresses as well. It wasn't easy obtaining this information, and she had to pull a few strings to get the answers. But after twenty-four hours, she had the data. Now, to put the names to the locations of the crimes. That was considerably less difficult.

As expected, few experienced army marksmen were demobbed over that period. The Military was keen to retain as many seasoned fighters as possible due to the great expense of recruiting and training new people. After that, they would need to be on active duty situations for some time to gain the necessary experience, and their expertise catalogued.

Tricia discovered something she hoped to find but not been confident she would. Many of these people had served together, mostly in Afghanistan. She spent most of the next day studying the list. At the last moment that she discovered something extraordinary. Many on the list were currently housed in rented accommodation while previously on leaving the army, they'd been homeless.

She needed more time, so Tricia took all the details home to study everything more specifically. At the end of a very long evening that went into the early hours, she had all she needed to present to Steve the next day. Even though she had worked until very late, she couldn't sleep. Tricia arrived at the station the following morning an hour before her shift started, surprising Mike.

"What brings you to work so early?" he asked.

"Couldn't sleep, Sergeant."

"Why is that? Something on your mind?"

"You could say that, Sarge. What time is Detective Inspector Kendall due in?"

"Same time, as usual, Constable. Silly question, isn't it? You arrive pretty much together every day. What's different about today?"

"Nothing, Sarge, except," she didn't finish the sentence but tottered about in agitation.

"Damn it, Tricia, sit down," said Mike. "You're making me fidgety now. What the hell is the matter with you today?" Then he remembered. "Oh, I see. You have worked something out, and it's trying to burst out of you. What is it?"

"I can't tell you, Sarge. I've got to tell Steve first."

Mike laughed, "Oh, I suppose you've solved the biggest case in the country, have you?"

"Yes, Sarge," she said and finally sat down.

Mike looked at her. She was undoubtedly on edge. Tricia was always keen on her job, but he had never seen her this edgy. He didn't laugh at her again. That was Tricia. He had never met anyone as crazy, rude, funny, and hilarious as her. He had never met anyone so dedicated and immersed in her job either. Maybe she had solved the case. He wouldn't put it beyond her ability. But this was some unusual case, and if anyone had anything constructive to bring to the table, it would Tricia. He hoped she would not meet disappointment, and now, he was edgier while waiting for Steve to arrive. Eventually, he could wait no longer and phoned Steve.

"Hi, Steve, are you up and about."

"Yes, Mike, what is it? Has something come in?"

"Yes," said Mike. "Tricia has come in, and she is going to explode if she doesn't speak to you soon. Any

218

chance you might get here early. I don't fancy the job of cleaning up the mess."

Steve laughed.

"OK, Mike, see you in about ten minutes."

Soon after, Steve arrived. "OK, what is this all about?" he inquired as he came into the station office.

Tricia started, but her commentary was so garbled that none of it made sense.

"Hold it, hold it, Constable," said Steve. "I can't understand a word you are saying.

"She's trying to tell you she has completely solved the biggest case in the country," said Mike.

"Well, Tricia, if you have, I'd like to understand how you did it. So, take a deep breath, calm down, and explain sensibly from the beginning."

"Yes, sir," said Tricia pulling herself together.

"I had an idea. If there are so many SatNav murders, fourteen of them, all the same in MO, it must be a coordinated effort, carried out by people who knew their way around sniper rifles. The most obvious and likely was the military. I contacted them, and after bowing and scraping and pulling the right strings that I won't go into now, I have a list of all those demobbed in the past six to twelve months. I also know who sharpshooters with a sniper rifle were.

"I then set about locating the ex-snipers related to the Sat Nav crimes, and bingo, there are matches for all of them. We will just have to set up an operation to keep watch on these people. But then, after solving that part of the story, I discovered something that makes me not want to catch these snipers."

"Really, Tricia, what was that?" asked Mike.

"Many those demobbed had no physical addresses. They were homeless. At least some of them didn't have until fairly recently. Then, suddenly, they had rented apartments. I checked the dates and found these apartments had become available shortly after each of the Satnav incidents in their area.

"I've concluded that their buddies have summed up the situation. They have seen that there are drug dealers all over the country who the Bill know, yet are unable, through our ridiculous system, to do anything about. Simultaneously, their buddies, who have fought for their country, are left in poverty to live on the streets.

"As any intelligent person would, they have realised it's not right. So, I think they have set out to eliminate the drug dealers, and they are doing a pretty good job of it. I believe they are using the money they get to fund the accommodation their buddies so desperately need. Sir, these are not people who like committing crimes. These are acts of compassion and justice, and I, for one, am now sorry I've solved it. Poor buggers will get life for just being human."

"Well, Constable, you have been busy, and I do think you might have the solution to these crimes," said Steve.

"I think you are right, Steve," Mike agreed. "Tricia, you have indeed come up with the goods this time."

"I'll tell you what we'll do," said Steve. "We'll test out your theory on our local crimes first. If we get results, we'll disclose this evidence to the other areas. How does that sound, Constable?"

"I guess so," said Tricia.

Steve and Mike laughed. "A bit different from when you were hopping up and down half an hour ago," said Mike.

"Got her own version of justice has this one," Steve observed.

"Yeah," Tricia agreed. "I need that job."

"What job?" Steve asked.

"Secretary of State. I'd sort the buggers out."

"God, help us if that ever occurred." Mike grimaced. "Just as well, it never will."

The three of them got on with sorting out how they would go about the investigation, and by the end of the day, they had identified prime suspects and planned their actions for the following day. Finally, they went home. All, except Tricia, thought the next day would be one to remember but for all the wrong reasons.

That evening, Tricia took a trip to see a man named Trevor Butcher, who lived about twelve miles outside Ricton. He had only been living in the apartment for a couple of weeks. Before that, he had been sleeping rough in the streets. She had a long discussion with him and then returned home.

The following day, the team set out to raid the home of one Nicky Masters, an ex-army sniper who had served time in Afghanistan. First, they knocked on the door. There was no response, so they broke into the property. No-one was at home, and much of the furniture had gone. Disappointed, they moved on to the next, Will Walters but found very much the same. A neighbour told them there had been a lot of activity during the night, and the family had moved out.

"This is very peculiar," said Steve. "It's almost as though they were tipped off. Let's go over to Trevor Butcher's apartment and see if he can shed any light on matters."

They travelled the twelve miles and knocked on his door. When he answered it, Steve spoke to him.

"I understand Nick Masters and Will Walters are friends of yours," he said.

"Yes, that right. What about it?"

"They seem to have up and moved last night. I don't suppose you have any idea where they went, do you?"

Mr Butcher looked at Tricia.

Tricia straightened up to her full height, which didn't make a lot of difference, and said, "Mr Butcher, I hope you are aware that withholding information in a criminal case is, itself, a crime for which you can go to prison?"

"When did they move?" asked Mr Butcher.

"In the early hours of this morning," Steve replied.

"Then how do you expect me to know where they've gone?"

"OK," said Steve. "If you hear anything, perhaps you will let us know."

"Maybe," said Mr Butcher. "I suppose you realise that Nick saved my life on three separate occasions, and Will had my back constantly in Afghanistan?"

"I didn't know that," said Steve.

"So, Detective Inspector," said Butcher, "just in case you find out where they've gone, I hope you will let me know."

Steve grunted.

"Come, Detective Constable, we had better get back to the office."

Although Tricia's theory remained inconclusive, Steve notified the Met giving the credit to Tricia. Over the next week, the police arrested several ex-servicemen throughout the country.

* * *

Two weeks later, Steve received a large envelope in the post and opened it to find two envelopes inside. One, with the words, Detective Inspector Stephen Kendall, he opened, staggered at what he read.

222

"You're not going to believe this," he said to the other three. "They have only given me a promotion, haven't they? Who would have thought it?"

"Yes, who would?" said Tricia.

"It is on condition that I spend three days a week, when possible, at the Met, and the remaining time here at Ricton."

"Well," said Mike, "they only loaned you to us in the first place, so we can't complain much about that. Congratulations, Steve." Mike led the three of them in a round of applause for him.

"It feels nice to give your working partners a career boost now and then," Tricia said.

"Come on, now Tricia," said Mike, "you don't begrudge Steve his promotion, do you?"

"Of course not, Sarge," she replied, "Whatever gave you that impression?"

"The look on your face was one indicator," said Mike.

"It's a Monday, Sarge," Tricia replied. "I always look sour on Mondays. He should have received the letter on a Friday."

"Oh, I almost forgot," said Steve. "There's another envelope here with your name on it." Steve handed the envelope to Tricia. She put in her handbag to read at home.

"There's another letter for you sent here," said Mike.

"Bloody popular today," said Tricia. "That can't be a good sign. Where is it?"

"I put it in the tray on your desk."

Tricia picked it up and placed it with the other letter in her handbag. Later that evening at home, Tricia took out the two letters, made herself a cup of tea, and

223

sat down to read them. She opened the one Mike had given her first. To her great surprise, it was from Trevor Butcher.

'Dear Trish,

You surprised me when you turned up at my place. It was great to talk over all the wonderful times we had when we were kids. Being a single parent, my mum didn't have very much, and if it hadn't been for you and your mum being so kind, I don't know how we would have survived.

I didn't have the nerve to tell you when I saw you, but I'd hoped, when we grew up, we would become close. I even imagined we'd get married. But then you went off to join the police and was so dedicated to your job; there wasn't any time for me. That's why I joined the army.

As I told you, before I got demobbed, my mum died. I didn't want to put on your mum, so I never told her I had nowhere to stay. I travelled to London, thinking I might get a job there, but it's worse than Yorkshire. I ended up sleeping rough until some army buddies got me a flat. I still haven't been able to get a job, and the rent finishes at the end of this month.

So, I've decided to go and live in Spain with other army buddies. It's worth a try as it can't be any worse than here. If I don't go, I'll end up sleeping rough again, and with winter approaching, I don't look forward to that.

I'm pleased you didn't indicate that we know each other when you came the next day with your boss. I kept schtum as I didn't want to get you into trouble. I never did find out where my mates moved to and often wonder who gave them the wink that you were visiting. They thought it was me. What a laugh. I didn't even know about your investigation. That's how professional you are.

224

Anyway, Trish, I wanted you to know where I've gone. I often think that if I could get my life sorted out and make something of myself, I'd come looking for you. So, don't think you're off the hook yet. If you ever see me again, you'll know what I want. I never stopped loving you since we were kids. I hope you realise that.

Take care, Trish

Your very good friend, Trevor.'

The letter's writing was getting smudged where Tricia's tears fell in a continuous stream onto the page. Susan was always asking her why she had no boyfriend, and she never had an answer. It was because of Trevor, her childhood sweetheart. *Oh, Trevor. Why is life so difficult?*

Putting her melancholy thoughts aside, she brushed away her tears, took a long sip of tea, and opened the other letter. A big smile spread across her face. She punched the air, spilling her tea everywhere. Then she returned the letter to her handbag and got up to make her dinner.

* * *

The team sat at the station looked intently at Johnny holding the letter Tricia had given him to read.

'Detective Constable Mason,

It gives me immense pleasure to hear of the faultless work you have been doing over the past few years at Ricton. The number of successes in fighting crime that has been solely down to your efforts and skills have not gone unnoticed. Your superior, Detective Inspector Kendall, has sent many reports extolling your abilities, and it is not possible to let them go unnoticed.

It is therefore with great pleasure that I am recommending you for promotion to Detective Sargent. It will not take effect immediately, but your name is on record.'

Tricia got up from her chair, went over to Steve, and planted a big kiss on his cheek. "Thank you, sir. Thank you." The tears started to roll down her cheeks. Johnny couldn't bear to see her crying and planted a big kiss on Tricia's cheek.

"Constable Johnny," said Tricia, "you do that again, and Sargent Tricia Mason will arrest you for assault."

Applause arose from all of them.

"Steady, Tricia, you're not there yet," said Mike. "There's just one slight problem, though."

"What's that, Sarge?" Tricia inquired.

"I've no idea how we are all going to live with you if you get three stripes," he joked.

They all laughed and queued up to give Tricia an affectionate hug. Tricia picked up her phone and started dialling.

"Who are you calling, Tricia?" Steve asked.

"I'm calling Susan to book our piss-up," Tricia laughed. "It's about time we had something real to celebrate."

Story Eleven
Tricia Gets Tough

Not all Ricton police cases were homicides. There were also the everyday cases of burglary, car theft, muggings, and the like. Steve and Tricia often dealt with those too, while Mike held the fort. On the whole, Tricia was a relatively easy-going woman. However, as with anyone, there is always one thing that will make a person furious enough to spoil their usual composure. It was a Friday evening when such an incident turned up at the station. A concerned neighbour called about domestic violence in her street getting out of control.

Apparently, a neighbour heard a man abusing his female partner. Nothing incensed Tricia as much as when a man attacked a woman. So, it was predictable that she would volunteer to go to the scene of the assault. She took down the caller's name and address and quickly drove to see the woman who had made the call, taking Johnny as back-up.

"Miss Fullerton? Hello, I'm Detective Constable Tricia Mason. I believe you phoned the station."

"Yes, Detective. It's the house across the street, number forty-two. I came home from a night out with my girlfriends, and there was a hell of a racket going on in that house."

"Do you know the people who live there?" asked Tricia.

"Not by name, no. I know there is a woman and a man. I don't know if they are married or not, but I do know he is always taking it out on her. I've heard them before, and I've seen the bruises on her face."

"OK. And you think he attacked her tonight?"

"Damned sure of it. She was screaming, 'Don't hit me again.' "

"Are they still there?" Tricia wanted to know.

"She is. He left while I was on the phone," said Miss Fullerton.

"OK, so you don't know their names. I'll go and have a chat with her."

Tricia crossed the street and knocked on the door of number forty-two. After a while, she heard the safety chain go on, and the door opened a couple of inches. Tricia introduced herself.

"We have received a call from one of your neighbours saying you were in some trouble tonight with your partner. Can I come in and have a chat with you?"

The woman opened the door. Tricia noted bruises on her face and blood trickling from her lip.

"Are you alright?" asked Tricia with some concern.

The woman nodded but said nothing. A tear escaped from her eye, and quite suddenly, she broke down altogether. Tricia put her arm around her for comfort.

"What's your name, honey?"

"Tracey. Tracey Ash," replied the woman between her sobs.

"Let's sit down, Tracey, and you can tell me what happened."

They sat on the settee, and Tracey said how it was a regular occurrence for her boyfriend to come home after drinking and start a fight.

"This is the last time," she said. "I'm not putting up with it anymore. I'm changing the locks tomorrow."

"What started the argument?" asked Tricia.

"He came home after drinking and tried to smooth it over by offering me a diamond ring. I asked him where he had got it, and he avoided telling me, so I assumed he had stolen it. He's carried out burglary before, and I've made it clear I don't want him doing it. So, he got annoyed and said I didn't appreciate anything he did for me. I told him I didn't appreciate him stealing for me, and that's when he got angry and started punching me. Well, I've had enough. He can clear off and find someone who don't mind accepting stolen property."

"What's his name?" asked Tricia.

"It's Jerry. Jerry Jameson," Tracey replied.

Tricia took out her phone and checked through her numbers.

"Here," she said. "Write this down. It's the number of a locksmith. Phone him first thing tomorrow morning and tell him I gave you the number. He will come straight out and change your lock for you."

"Thank you," said a grateful Tracey.

Tricia gave her a card with her number.

"If Jerry tries to pester you again, ring me straight away, and I'll be here before you can put the phone down. I can't stand bullies, especially men who hit women. You should try kicking him in the balls a few times. Maybe he would think twice then. Bloody coward. I bet he don't fight with men who might hit back."

"Thank you, Detective."

"Call me, Tricia. Us girls have got to stick together, don't we?"

Tracey tried to smile, but her split lip was too painful.

"You had better get that looked at, darling," said Tricia. Would you like me to run you to A and E?"

"No, thank you, Tricia. You have been very understanding. I'll be alright now."

Tricia kissed her on the forehead and said goodbye. "You take care of yourself now."

"I will," Tracey replied.

Back at the station, Tricia reported to Mike. She gave him the name, Jerry Jameson.

"Oh, Jameson, is it? Yes, we have records on him, but it's usually for burglary, not domestic violence," said Mike.

"I reckon that's because people don't report it," Tricia replied. "This one was reported by a neighbour."

It wasn't very often that she was on duty at such late hours, and as it was now past midnight, Mike said she should go home.

"Thanks, Sarge," she said and breezed out the door just as spritely as she had sailed in earlier in the day.

* * *

The following morning, Mike called Tricia informing her that two burglaries had occurred the previous evening, and he wanted her to look into them. He gave her the details, and Tricia noted them in her notebook. Before work, Tricia called on Tracey. The locksmith was already there, changing the locks.

"Hi, Dave," she greeted him. "Is she in?"

"Yes, she's out the back."

Tricia located Tracey and asked how she felt this morning.

"I'm OK," said Tracey. "My face hurts a bit, though."

Tracey's face had swollen, and her eye was deep purple. She looked terrible. Tricia took out her mobile phone and shot two photos of Tracey. In one of them, she asked Tracey to hold the current newspaper with the date and headlines visible.

"That's to record when this took place," said Tricia. "In case you might need it in the future. Let's hope you won't."

"I hope not," said Tracey. "This bloody well hurts."

"Tracey, changing the subject, can you describe the ring Jerry showed you?"

"Yeah, it was gold with a double band, quite unusual. There were three diamonds set in it too."

"Thanks," said Tricia. "I'm afraid I have to go now - got crimes to investigate. If you hear from Jerry or you know where I might find him, give me a call. You have my number."

Tricia left and went on to the first of the burglary addresses. It was Mr and Mrs Johnson. Their son, kidnapped the previous year, found Tricia working on the case. She drove up the long drive to the house.

"Hello, Mr Johnson. It looks like someone is singling you out for crime."

"Yes," Johnson agreed. My garage was broken into, and a lot of my tools stolen."

"Do you know which tools, in particular, are missing?"

"Pretty much. Here, I've written out a list together with a description, where appropriate. I hope it will help in retrieving them."

"That's very thoughtful. It will help when we check out the usual places where such items are sold," said Tricia. "Now, perhaps I might take a look at the garage."

Mr Johnson led Tricia to the garage.

"Not much to see here," she said. "I'll get someone to look for fingerprints we can check with local records."

"OK, thanks. I don't hold much hope in getting them back," said a dejected Johnson.

"We'll do our best, sir."

"Yes, I know you will, Constable. Thanks for coming out so promptly."

Tricia returned to her car and drove to the second burglarised home, that of Nancy Freeman. It was a large house for a widow, Nancy's husband had died in a road accident. Tricia knocked on the door. A woman of about fifty-eight opened the door. She was attractive, and even in the early morning, had dressed as though she was meeting royalty. She invited Tricia inside.

"So, Mrs Freeman, what exactly are you missing?" Tricia asked.

"I had gone to bed early as I usually do when I have nothing special on and a noise awakened me. I went to the landing to check it out, and whilst I was there, the burglar must have slipped into my bedroom. After I looked around, I returned to my bedroom, and this morning found my jewellery box was no longer on my dressing table."

"So, you didn't see the burglar," asked Tricia.

"No, it wasn't until this morning that I noticed the broken window on the French door. That must be how he got inside."

Tricia checked the French door.

"There might be some fingerprints here," she said. "I have someone coming out this morning who will check it out. In the meantime, can you describe the stolen jewellery?"

"I can do better than that," said Mrs Freeman. "I have photos of everything."

She went to a drawer and took out a folder. Selecting those relevant, she handed them to Tricia, who studied them. There were two necklaces, a bracelet, two pairs of earrings, and three rings. The one that stood out was the double-banded gold band with three diamonds.

"This is good," said Tricia. "I don't want to raise your hopes too soon, but we might already have a lead on this."

"Really?" said an astounded Mrs Freeman. "How is that possible?"

"I can't go into that right now. Can I take these photos with me?" asked Tricia.

"Yes, please take them."

"OK, I'll get someone here to check for fingerprints and get back to you as soon as I can," said Tricia. As she was leaving, her mobile phone rang. It was Tracey.

"Hello, Tracey. Has he come back?" she asked.

"No, he hasn't, but I just remembered something. He has a friend called Tommy, who lives on Gerald Street. Number fifty-five. There's a chance he might be there."

"That's good, Tracey. I'm going past there shortly. I'll check it out. Thanks."

But Tricia didn't need to. As she drove along Gerald Street, a man came out of number fifty-five and walked towards a car park between the houses. She stopped her car and followed the man into the car park. As he reached his parked vehicle, Tricia caught up with him.

"Excuse me," she said, "is your name, Jerry Jameson."

As Tricia was in plain clothes, the man didn't realise she was a police officer.

"Hello, sexy," he said, "who wants to know?"

"I do," said Tricia evasively.

"And who are you?"

"I told you. I'm the one who wants to know if you are Jerry Jameson."

"Cheeky little bitch, ain'tcher," the man replied.

"Is that all you think I am? Then you don't know me," says Tricia confidently.

"What if I am?" says the man.

"If you are, then you are going to have to answer for yourself," Tricia replied.

"Yeah, well, I am Jerry Jameson. What you gonna do about it."

If there was one thing that Tricia hated above all others, it was a cocky man who hits women.

"Well, I'm not going to let you hit me like you did Tracey."

"Tracey? She's a lying bitch."

"And quite brave too," said Tricia, taking out her phone and showing it to Jerry. "Is this what a nice brave man does to a lovely woman?"

"Whatcha talking about? I didn't do that, and if I did it was 'cause she asked for it." As he said it, he drew back his fist.

As quick as a flash, Tricia's fist came out of nowhere and hit Jerry squarely in the eye, knocking him back so that he fell against his car and slumped to the ground.

"What the fuck!" says Jerry, struggling to get to his feet. "Why did you do that?"

"I didn't do that," said Tricia, "and if I did, it's only because you were asking for it."

"You fucking bitch," Jerry started, but before he could continue, Tricia's knee swept up between his legs and felled him again so that he ended up on the ground. Tears formed as he held on to his crotch in agony.

"Who the hell are you?" Jerry asked.

Tricia pulled out her ID card. "I am Detective Constable Tricia Mason." Then she took a pair of handcuffs from her waist belt.

"You are under arrest, Jerry Jameson. Now I need to think about this so that I get it right. Don't want to miss anything out. I am arresting you for attempting to strike a police officer, grievous bodily harm to Tracey Ash, suspicion of burglary at the home of Mrs Nancy Freeman, and an all-around coward and bully. Have I left anything out? Oh yes, generally being an arsehole." Tricia looked inside his car, and there, in full view on the back seat, was a box full of tools. "Looks like I still forgot something. Suspicion of the burglary at the home of Mr and Mrs Johnson, too."

"You have the right to remain silent, but if you do say anything…" Tricia finished off her arrest caution while attaching the handcuffs to Jerry's wrists.

By now, Jerry was crying properly. "Don't do this, please. Tracey will never speak to me again, and I love her."

"You love her? Jerry," said Tricia. "Do you want me to punch you again?"

"No, no, please don't."

"Then shut up and get in my car. You're giving me an earache."

When Tricia returned to the station, Steve, Mike, and Johnny were astounded. Having gone to investigate two robberies, Tricia had not only solved the case but also arrested the perpetrator. And it was still morning.

"Jesus, Tricia. What are you doing for the rest of the day?" Mike asked.

"You saying I ain't getting it off?" Tricia responded. "Bloody slavery, this is."

Later, at home when Steve told Susan about Tricia's success, she phoned her.

"Hi, Susan," said Tricia. "You don't usually call me this time of night. What's happening."

"I've heard about your actions this morning and reckon we should re-examine your fancy dress for the party at the weekend."

"Oh, yeah. What you got in mind?"

"As you know, I'll be going as Marietta Duvalier. After your recent success, I think you should go as Wonder Woman."

"Bloody 'Ell, that will put the wind up the village."

"Yes, especially when Debra joins us as Queen Boudica," said Susan.

She chuckled as she put the phone down.

Steve, who had heard the exchange, said, "I suppose me and Mike will have to change our choices now, then."

"Why, who did you have in mind?"

"We had decided on Sherlock Holmes and Dr Watson."

"Perhaps you should go as Batman and Robin," Susan advised.

"Yes, but what about Johnny?"

Susan gave it some thought.

"Goofy?" she suggested.

They were still laughing as they retired for the night.

Story Twelve
The DNA Murders

This particular morning when Stephen arrived, Mike sat, as usual, already at his desk. Johnny attacked his first cup of coffee of the day. Otherwise, quiet prevailed.

When Tricia came in, the Station atmosphere would quickly change, becoming more like a school reunion with her laughter and joking, and often like a doggy day-care centre when Tricia's little dog, Tricky, started his antics. If ever a human and a dog were more suited to each other than Tricia and Tricky, the boys had not yet found them.

So, yes, things remained quite dull before Tricia arrived, and this day she was uncharacteristically late. As it got later, Mike decided to ring her mobile. Tricia's face appeared around the corner of the door.

"Hello, guys, sorry I'm late, hang on a minute, I gotta take this call."

"Go ahead," said Mike.

"'Ello, Detective Constable Mason here," said Tricia authoritatively.

"Good morning, Constable," said Mike into his phone. "You're bloody late this morning. What you got to say for yourself?"

Tricia made a face, snapped her phone shut, and put it into her bag.

"If it's all the same ter you Sarge, it's Detective Constable, soon to be Sergeant, and that's why I'm late."

"Really, how's that?" asked a puzzled Mike.

"Cause I bin doing some detecting. I start early, not like some of you lazy buggers around here."

It seemed that no matter how rude Tricia could be or what she said, Steve generally found her put-downs hilarious and so burst out laughing.

"OK, Detective Constable," he said, placing extra emphasis on the word Detective, "I think we had all better sit back and listen to this. Johnny, get your notebook out."

"Good idea," said Tricia. "Gotta keep him on his toes."

"Go on," said Mike. "Let's hear it."

Tricia made her way to the coffee machine and poured herself a coffee. Then, making herself comfortable in the chair behind her desk, fussed about until Johnny ran out of patience.

"Bloody 'ell, Tricia, you gonna tell us today or 'ave we gotta make an appointment?"

"Calm down, Johnny, I ain't going nowhere," said Tricia calmly. "Crikey, there's more suspense in 'ere than at the Psycho movie. Right, why am I late? I was driving to work this morning, oh, and I would 'ave been 'ere before you lot if I 'adn't got held up when I got to Walter street."

Mike sighed loudly but knew better than to interrupt Tricia again, else they would never get the story out of her.

"Nearly knocked this bugger down. Came running out of a passage right in front of me. 'Ad ter put on me brakes quick. Good job I 'ad 'em sorted out last week. Took the car to Jerry's. He done a good job too. Stopped sharp before the sod went under the car.

"I got out, but he ran away. Well, I say ran. He hobbled away. Thought I'd injured him. He was limping badly, and he also 'ad a dodgy arm. I chased him up the road, and he slipped down a gap in the buildings. I know where it leads to, so I went back to the car and drove

238

around to Jinks Lane. He saw me, but it was too late. I jumped out an' grabbed 'im by the collar."

"So, what had he been up to?" Steve started showing more interest in Tricia's story.

"No idea," Tricia replied. "I asked him what he was running away from, and he didn't give me an answer. That was mainly because the guy struggled with speech. I think he has learning difficulties, but whatever, I didn't get no sense out of him. Couldn't even get his name."

"So, what happened?" Mike chipped in.

"Nothing really. I couldn't get anything out of him, so I let him go."

"And that's what made you late, Tricia?" Johnny asked. "Bit of a waste of time if you ask me. Think I'll be late termorra. I'll say I was trying to catch a stray dog, and it got away."

"Too late fer that one, Johnny. You've already used that excuse. Yer gotta think outside the box, not inside it, in your head," said Tricia cheekily.

"What yer got for me today, Sarge?" asked Johnny.

"Just do your usual beat through the village," said Mike. "You might want to keep a lookout for the guy with the gammy leg, the dodgy arm, and the imprint of Tricia's car on his arse. If you see him, just try to get more sense out of him than Tricia did."

"That shouldn't be difficult, Sarge. Something makes more sense than nuffin'."

"We'll look forward to that, Johnny," said Tricia. "OK, Inspector, whatcha got fer me?"

"Right, Detective Constable, I got a call just before you arrived. A woman heard some odd noises from her neighbour's house and wants us to look into it.

We might as well go together as there's nothing else. At least we'll look as though we are on the ball."

"Yes, sir. Looking on the ball is what I do best. Shall we go in my car?"

"Might as well. We won't need two cars. It's a Mrs Jenkins at number 14 Tennant Way. Do you know it?"

"Yes, sir."

They got into Tricia's car, and she drove them to 14 Tennant Way. It was one of a pair of semis. Tricia knocked on the door, and an elderly woman opened it.

"Good morning, I am Detective Inspector Kendall, and this is Detective Constable Mason," Steve said. "Are you Mrs Jenkins who rang into the station earlier?"

"Yes, that's me. I didn't expect two detectives around here this morning," she said. "Lucky if we ever see a copper these days."

"Not in Ricton," said Tricia. "We are pretty much on the ball here. So what is the problem?"

"I don't know if there actually is a problem, but I heard something this morning that made me phone you."

"What exactly did you hear, Mrs Jenkins?" asked Steve.

"I heard Mrs Jameson. She was saying, 'What have you done? What have you done?' and then she screamed. After that, there was silence. It just didn't sound right."

"OK, Mrs Jenkins, we'll look into it," Steve assured her. "Are there any others living in the house? Any children?"

"There's one boy. I say boy, but he is about twenty-five now. I still think of him as a boy, though.

There's also an adopted son. He doesn't live there. Turned out to be no good."

"In what way?" asked Tricia.

"He got mixed up with gangs and got into crime. He's in prison now for robbery and GBH."

"OK," said Steve, "so there's just the three of them. The parents and the twenty-five-year-old son."

"That's right."

"Do any of them work?"

"Mr Jameson does. Works at the dairy out on the Radcliff Road. She doesn't work though."

"How about the boy?"

"No, he doesn't. He has some problems, so he's never had a job. I know he has been quite friendly with a man in the next street. Spends quite a bit of time with him."

"OK, if we need to speak to you again, I'll get back to you," said Steve, and he and Tricia made their way next door. Tricia knocked on the door but received no reply, so she knocked again. When there was still no response, they walked around to the back of the house. Everything was quiet. Tricia looked in the window, but there didn't appear to be anyone there.

Steve took out his phone and rang Mike.

"Hi, Mike. Could you get the number for the dairy on Radcliff road? I don't know what it's called, do you?"

"Yeah, it's the Brunswick Dairy. Hang on a minute, and I'll get it for you."

Mike looked up the number and Steve rang it.

"Could I speak to Mr Jameson? I believe he works there."

"Sorry," said the Manager, "he hasn't come in today."

"Is that usual?" asked Steve.

"No, it isn't. I can't remember when he last took time off. What's this all about?"

"I can't say right now. I just need to get hold of Mr Jameson. Do you have his telephone number?"

"I'll check," said the Manager.

After finding it, he gave it to Steve.

"It's his mobile number. I would have been calling it myself if he didn't turn up all morning."

"Thank you," said Steve, and rang off.

The mobile number for Mr Jameson did not respond when he phoned it, but oddly, Steve heard it ringing in the house.

"Doesn't sound good, sir," said Tricia. "What are we gonna do now?"

"I think we have no choice but to break in," Steve replied. "We'll break a glass panel on the back door and see if we can get in this way."

Steve broke the pane with his elbow and put his arm through to unlock the door.

"Idiots," he said, "it isn't locked. We should have tried it first."

They entered the house and searched the ground floor. There was no-one there. Tricia made her way up the stairs. Steve followed her.

"Oh, shit," Tricia exclaimed when she walked into a bedroom.

"What is it?" asked Steve as he followed her in.

There on the bed were Mr and Mrs Jameson, both covered in blood. Mrs Jameson had a large carving knife protruding from her chest.

* * *

"This is the first murder we've had since the satnav murders," said Johnny as he attached the police cordon across the front of number sixteen Tennant Way.

"Yes, it is," Doctor Richard Handsworthy agreed. "We don't get too many here but those we do get are normally very unusual."

"Give it time," Tricia interjected. "We'll probably find the cat jumped off the dresser and sent the knives flying, or something like that."

Doctor Handsworthy laughed.

"Shouldn't really be laughing," he said, putting a serious look back onto his face. "After all, these unfortunates are dead just the same. Better go and look at them, I suppose."

Steve was in the bedroom.

"Hello, Doctor," he greeted him, "You know, the only time we have ever meet is at a murder scene. We'll have to see if we have anything else in common."

"Yes, we should," the doctor agreed. "Do you play golf?"

"Unfortunately, no."

"Yes, double unfortunate, because I don't either."

Steve laughed. "Looks like our only common interest is dead bodies then."

"Right," said Doctor Handsworthy, "what have we got here? Two people dead. Looks like the man died first as he is still covered up. The woman is partially covered, but it looks like the killer was too quick for her."

"Hey, Doctor, leave the detective work to me, will you. Just carry out the medical examination."

The doctor smiled. "Just trying to find some common ground," he said. "They haven't been dead very long. Not more than three or four hours, I would say."

"Yeah, sounds about right."

"I'm pretty sure they were both killed with that knife. Nothing much more I can do here. Do you want me to remove the knife?"

If you don't mind," said Steve.

The doctor removed the carving knife, Tricia held out a plastic bag, and the doctor dropped it in.

"I'll get this off to forensics, sir," she said efficiently.

"If you can get Johnny to stay with the Doctor while he takes the bodies away, I am just going next door to have another word with Mrs Jenkins."

"Yes, sir."

Steve went to speak with Mrs Jenkins. Outside, the weather was exceptionally fine, at odds with the gruesome scene in the house. Mrs Jenkins came to the door before Steve had a chance to knock.

"So, Detective Inspector, what has happened next door? You have police cars, an ambulance, and a constable taping up the entrance. It doesn't look good."

"No, Mrs Jenkins, I'm afraid it isn't good. Have you seen the young man today?"

"No, I haven't," Mrs Jenkins confirmed.

"What's his name?" asked Steve.

"It's Phillip. Phillip Jameson. What's going on?"

"It's too early to tell you, Mrs Jenkins. If you hear anything to guide us to the young man, I hope you will let us know immediately."

"Of course. There is the man in the next street I told you about, but I don't know his name or where he lives. Phillip tells me all about his work, though."

"His work? And what exactly is that?"

"Well, I couldn't tell you exactly, but I do know he is into genetics and stuff like that."

"I see. And what is Phillip's interest in that?"

"Oh, he's very interested. It seems his problems are genetic, and they talk about the latest technology. Phillip is always hoping they will find a way to cure him, but I think that is just wishful thinking."

"Just what are his problems, Mrs Jenkins? Do you have any idea?" asked Steve.

"Only what I can see."

"And what can you see?"

"Well, there are three things. First, the most noticeable is his left leg. It's deformed in some way so that he can't walk properly. He often says he'd like to have it amputated and have a false leg fitted. Still, this friend has told him that it wouldn't make any difference because the control of the movement is by the brain, and he would still have the wrong signals operating the leg even if it was artificial."

"I see. He talks a lot about this, does he?"

"Oh, yes. He really hates himself like he is. His arm has similar problems as his leg. And in addition to that, he is kind of autistic and can't communicate unless he knows the person very well."

"It seems like you know him well, Mrs Jenkins."

"Yes, I've known him all his life. He spends half his time around here."

"Doesn't he get on with his parents then?"

"Oh, yes, detective. He loves them to bits. He just feels like he is letting them down all the time. Poor lad."

"So, he wouldn't do anything to harm them?"

"Good God, no. Sounds to me like someone harmed them," said Mrs Jenkins as she looked out of her window. Then she held her hand to her mouth.

"What is it?" asks Steve, but then he saw the reason for her reaction. The bodies of the two neighbours came out covered up on stretchers.

"Oh, no, they're both dead." she said.

"I'm afraid so," said Steve.

"What on earth will Phillip do?" Mrs Jenkins was aghast.

"Thank you, Mrs Jenkins. You have been very helpful." said Steve, and left to returned next door. He caught up with Tricia.

"The lad you were chasing this morning, Constable. How old was he?" Steve asked her.

Tricia thought about it. "I'd say mid-twenties, sir. Why? Do you think he knows something about this?"

"No, I don't. I think he is the son, and I can't see that he has any motive for murdering them. Let's go and take a look inside. They entered the house and climbed the stairs to the bedrooms. Steve looked around the parent's room while Tricia examined Phillip's room. There was a laptop computer on his dressing table. Tricia unplugged it and picked it up.

"I think it's worth looking at this," she said to Steve. "Should we take it with us?"

"Yes, good idea. I can't find anything specific here. I'll get forensics down here. We had better get back to the station."

* * *

The following day Tricia came in early. She set Phillip's computer on her desk, together with a bunch of A4 sheets she had printed out from it.

"What have you got there, Constable," asked Steve.

"Motive, sir."

"Motive? What do you mean?"

"Sir, yesterday you said Phillip had no motive for killing his parents. I think I've found one."

"OK, let's hear it," Mike chipped in. "This had better be good."

"Oh, Sarge, you do me an injustice. Come on, own up. Do I ever bore you?"

"The words boring, and Tricia will never appear in the same sentence," Mike agreed.

"Ok, Constable," said Steve. "What have you found?"

"I think the best way to explain it will be to read out all these relevant emails. That's why I printed them out. They are between Phillip and a guy called Professor Lucus Branston. Phillip calls him Lucus, so they know each other quite well. These emails spread over a few months with the last one received early yesterday morning."

"Dear Lucus, it was very interesting looking at the DNA strands you sent me together with your explanation of what they mean. It is exciting stuff, isn't it."

"Phillip, you are correct. It is very exciting. That is what gets me out of bed in the morning."

"Lucus, if I came around to see you, could you take something to do my DNA read-out?"

"Phillip, of course, I could. Come around today, and it will be a simple job of taking some body fluids from inside your mouth. That is all I will need."

"Lucus, I'll come around tomorrow."

"Phillip, thank you for visiting me last week. I have the analysis of your DNA and am attaching the read-out with this email."

"Lucus, that is terrific. I am so pleased to see my DNA read-out. It's very interesting. What would be even

247

more interesting would be to compare it with my dad's? If I get some samples, can you do it for me?"

"Phillip, of course, bring them around when you have them."

"Phillip, thanks for the samples you brought around. They are very interesting, and you will see why from the attached read-out."

"Lucus, this is so exciting. I didn't realise just how great your job is. You know what I am going to do? I am going to bring around my mother's samples too. They would go crazy if they knew I was looking at these. Just as well that they don't know then."

"Phillip, be careful. This is not ethical. I am only doing it because it is for you, so please don't mention it to anyone."

"Lucus, I won't say anything if you don't?

"Phillip, I received the samples you brought around, and I am attaching the read-out with this email. However, I'm afraid you have made a mistake. The sample you gave me is not from your mother but from your aunt. This read-out is definitely from your father's sister."

"And that's it, sir. There you 'ave it. The motive you said was absent," said Tricia triumphantly.

"Am I missing something here?" said Mike. "How is this a motive."

"Yes, Mike," said Steve, "I think you are missing the point. Well done, Tricia."

Tricia made a comic curtsy and stuck out her tongue at Mike.

Steve continued. "The point you are missing Mike is that Phillip has always been angry about his body and his deformities. Now he suddenly finds out why he has them. He will be well aware of the fact that incest can

248

create such problems, and now he has discovered his father and mother are brother and sister."

The smile on Tricia's face was hilarious, as Johnny was quick to point out.

"Just look at her," he said. "Bloody 'Ell Tricia, I don't know how you do it. It ain't natural."

"Never mind, Johnny," she responded, "at least you can always use that as an excuse."

Everyone laughed.

"I think we have another excuse, too," said Mike.

"What's that?" said Steve.

"It's the excuse to go out tonight for a celebratory drink. What else?"

"Really," said Tricia. "So, I guess I won't be buying tonight."

Story Thirteen
Susan Saves The Day

It was quite common for Susan and Tricia to go out for a meal at their favourite local restaurant at least once a week. This week was no different. Susan looked her usual glamorous self, a picture of pure beauty that attracted everyone's attention. Of course, she was some fifteen years older than Tricia and looked attached to someone already, so although she created admiration, Susan always appeared safe from unwanted attention.

On the other hand, Tricia, a cute modern woman in her twenties, displayed beauty in her unique way. She had an innocent face that did not convey the person she was. Most people mistook her character but when they discovered her true personality, they became even more enamoured. For any man, Tricia would have been a great catch. However, she remained uncompromisingly single and unattached. This puzzled Susan, and she often said as much.

"Tricia, you still don't have a boyfriend. I simply don't understand it. Look at you. You are so beautiful and quirky. All the guys love you. Are you holding out for someone special?"

"I don't know," said Tricia. "Who is special anyway? You can't tell these days. Most men are far from special."

"Maybe," said Susan, "but I found one." She smiled.

"Yes," said Tricia, "just as well he dotes on you, else I'd be all over him."

"I believe you would be too, Tricia. I've seen the way you look at him."

"Really? How do I look at him?"

"I think you know what I mean. It's a good thing we are best friends."

"Yeah," said Tricia, "and that he is about twenty years older than me."

The girls laughed. Then Susan looked at Tricia intently.

"Seriously, Tricia, you should get yourself a guy. Look at that waiter there. He is always looking at you. I think you interest him. Saying that, they are all pretty interested in you, I would think."

"You mean that handsome one with the towel over his arm?"

"Yes, damned good looking, isn't he?"

"Yeah, but he's Italian, ain't he? And me a Yorkshire lass. A bit like chips with tiramisu," said Tricia.

Susan laughed. "What about that one over there?" she said, nodding in another direction.

"What, the 'Ungarian? That's more like Yorkshire pudding and goulash."

Susan laughed again. "Tricia, you are hilarious. So, I suppose that west country lad is more like you?"

"Getting nearer," said Tricia. "Mushy peas with Cornish pasty is quite tasty."

"All right, Tricia, I think I've got the picture now."

"And I don't think it is going to include the Frenchman either, is it?" Tricia replied. "The silly bugger can't keep off his phone."

"I've noticed that," said Susan. "He's constantly speaking to someone."

"Don't like the way he looks at me either," said Tricia. "Greasy little bugger, ain't he?"

Susan couldn't stop laughing. "Greasy, haha. I've never heard a Frenchman called that, but in this case, I think it is perfect. Ha ha."

"Hold on," said Tricia, "the Italian is coming over."

The Italian sidled up to their table.

"Ello laydees. Are you raydee to order, please," he asked in a broad Italian accent.

The two of them could not contain themselves and both burst into laughter.

"Tiramisu," said Susan.

"With chips," Tricia added, and they laughed again.

"Unfortunate, laydees, we no 'ave tiramisu," he stated, "but plaintee cheeps."

It took a little while before the girls stopped laughing. All the while, the waiter stood patiently waiting for them to order. The girls placed their orders with as much decorum as they could manage. They struggled through their meals when it arrived. The whole restaurant seemed filled with their giggles.

"We'll get thrown out of here one day," said Susan. "You know, I shouldn't say this but I honestly look forward to the evenings when Steve is working the late shift. The week wouldn't be the same without our night out."

"This is certainly the best place with four nationalities to keep us amused," said Tricia.

"That Frenchman is still clocking you," said Susan.

"Yeah. Still on his bloody phone, too. I wonder who's on the other end. It ain't me, I've switched me phone off. Can't be having interruptions on our night out."

"You'll never know who he's chatting to," said Susan.

"Not unless I nick him for not doing his job, and nick his phone too," Tricia replied, and that set the two of them off laughing again.

"And I wouldn't put that past you, Tricia. You're cheeky enough."

"Looks like he's left now," said Tricia. "Can't see that he got any work done tonight. The other three have done it all."

Eventually, they finished their meal and decided it was late enough for them to go home. Tricia hadn't brought her car as Susan had picked her up.

"I think I'll walk home, Susan," said Tricia. "I need the exercise and some fresh air after that meal."

"You sure?" Susan asked with a little concern in her voice. "It is late, after all."

"Yeah, I can handle meself, you know that."

"I guess I do. OK, Tricia, take care. Give me a call when you get home."

"Will do."

Susan drove away and Tricia walked off.

Susan had been home for about twenty minutes, and Tricia hadn't phoned, but Steve called.

"Hi, Steve, how are things at the station this evening?"

"Fairly quiet, but tell me, is Tricia there? I can't get her on her phone."

"No, she isn't here. She decided to walk home. Anyway, I do know that she turned her phone off in the restaurant. Why do you want her at this time of night?"

"Look, Susan," said Steve in a quiet voice, "don't get anxious, but we got a call in from a woman who reported that she saw a young lady forced into a blue van on Lendle Street. She counted a driver and two others."

"So, why do you want Tricia?"

"The point is, the description she gave fits Tricia, so we are a bit worried.

"Hell. Did you get a description of what she was wearing?"

"The kidnapped woman had on a pink blouse and a short black skirt."

"Bloody Hell, Steve. That's what Tricia was wearing."

"Don't worry, Susan, we'll get onto this straight away. I've got to go now."

Steve rang off. Susan thought for a moment and then got into her car and drove back to the restaurant. She sought out the Italian waiter.

"Excuse me," she said, "the Frenchman who works here, do you know where he lives?"

"No, Madam, but I can find out if it's important."

"Yes," said Susan, "it's very important."

The Italian went off to the office and returned with the address. Susan read it to be sure she knew how to find the place. It was number twenty-four Valley Way. She thanked the Italian and got into her car. The properties were sparse on Valley Way, so she had to keep alert. Eventually, she arrived at number twenty-four. Amazingly, the blue van was in the drive. Her instincts had been right.

Susan was about to phone Steve when her phone rang. She got the surprise of her life when she answered it.

"Hello, Susan," Tricia's voice came through.

"Tricia," screamed Susan, "you don't know how good it is to hear your voice."

"Don't get excited. Sorry I didn't get straight back to you. Tricky was playing up, and I had to walk him around the block. He's OK now, settled down in his basket, the little bugger."

Susan explained what had transpired.

"So, anyway, I found where they are. I'm outside the house right now."

"Give me the location," said Tricia, "and I'll come straight over."

"OK, I'll phone Steve and get him out here."

They rang off. Very soon, Tricia pulled up behind Susan's car, got out, and came around to Susan's passenger seat.

"Damned good detectiving to find these French buggers," Tricia applauded Susan.

"How do you know we are at the Frenchman's house?" asked Susan.

"Well, darling," said Tricia, "while you're pretty good, I must say, you have to leave the real detective work to me."

"But how do you know?" Susan persisted.

"Well," said Tricia, "while this house is number twenty-four, it also has a name. See there on the wall."

Susan read the name of the house. It was Jolie Violette.

"I think you will find that is French," said Tricia.

"Yes," said Susan, "it means Pretty Violet, but you can't tell just from that."

"No, of course not, but if you look at the back of the van, you'll see an F. That's a France sticker. If it were English, it would have GB."

"Damn, I didn't see that," Susan admitted.

"Elementary, dear Watson," says Tricia. "And then there is that statue in the centre of the lawn."

"Well, I don't see how you can get anything from that. It looks like Boadicea."

"Ah," says Tricia mysteriously, "but it isn't."

"What! Who is it then?"

"It's Joan of Arc, and you can't get more French than that."

"Well, damn it," said an impressed Susan. "Detective Constable? You'll soon be taking over Steve's job."

"Well, I don't wanna boast," Tricia replied in a boastful manner.

"Tricia, it's so good that you are OK. We all thought it was you what with the girl wearing the same clothes."

"Me?" Tricia sounded indignant. "That girl will be local."

"What does that have to do with it?" asked Susan.

"She ain't from op North like me. It would take more than three puny Frenchman to kidnap this girl."

Susan leant over and kissed Tricia on the cheek. "Well, anyway, it's likely they have a kidnapped girl in there."

"Hope she's alright. We gotta get in there before anything serious happens. 'Bout time Steve and Mike got here."

Just then, vehicle lights appeared, and Steve and Mike drew up behind them.

"Tricia," said Steve. "It's damned good to see you. Thought you might be the kidnapped girl."

"Crickey," Tricia exclaimed. "Not another one who don't know me."

"What's she talking about," Steve asked.

Susan laughed. "I'll tell you later."

When they approached the house, they found the Frenchmen were so confident and arrogant that they hadn't even locked the door. The detectives and Sergeant Mike all rushed into the house, taking the occupants by surprise. They found the girl unharmed but tied up. The shock on the Frenchmen's faces was inimitable.

"You ain't too good at this, are you?" said Tricia. "No better than your waitering."

"Oh, he's a waiter, is he?" Steve remarked.

"Yeah. Been on 'is phone all evening, 'stead of serving Susan and me."

"I think you girls had better be more careful where you eat."

"Don't think so, sir. If we 'adn't ate there, Susan wouldn't 'ave brought us here, and these dickheads might 'ave got away with it." Tricia directed her attention to the girl. "You alright, honey? What's your name?" Tricia untied the rope from her hands.

The girl was OK, gave her name, and Tricia took her back to her car. Steve arrested the Frenchmen and put them into the back of Mike's car.

Later, Susan chatted with Steve, explaining how it was time Tricia's promotion came through. She made no mention of her most important part in the arrest.

"After all," she had said to Tricia, "I'm just a woman who sells clothes, right?" To which Tricia had replied, "And I bet you sew identity tags in them."

Susan mentioned Tricia's comment to Steve.

"Sewing identity tags into clothing. Trust Tricia to come up with a comment like that," said Steve.

"She's too clever for her own good," Susan observed. "But that's an idea worth investigating. Don't you agree, Steve?"

Story Fourteen - Tricia Helps Johnny
Part One

The wind howled, the rain lashed down as if it were pouring out of a bucket, and thunderous clouds swept furiously across the skies. It was one hell of a day, and certainly not one for plodding the beat through Ricton or doing anything else outside of the shelter of the Ricton Police Station.

Tricia's dog, Tricky, huddled on a blanket in the corner under a table.

"He's got the right idea today," Johnny said as he sat at his computer. "I wouldn't mind joining him under there."

"Might as well," Tricia replied, "you're usually in the dog-house anyway."

"That's true," Johnny admitted. "I'd probably be now, if anyone knew what I was doing."

"Ah," says Tricia conspiratorially, "up to no good online, are yer?"

"Pretty much," Johnny agreed. "It's boring in here with nothing to do."

"Can't argue with that, Johnny. It's a slow day, and I'd much rather be out catching criminals," said Tricia.

"There are criminals on here," Johnny stated, "but I've no idea how to catch them."

"What? You're communicating with criminals online?"

"Yeah. But they always get away with it. It's bloody frustrating."

"Whatcha talking about Johnny?" asked Tricia. She came over and looked at his computer. "Crikey,

Johnny. When I said you were up to no good, I was only joking. I didn't think you were."

"I'm not," Johnny protested. "There's nothing wrong with this except they are all lying sods."

"Well, that's a sex site, isn't it?"

"No, of course not."

"So, why is there a woman on there showing off everything she's has?" Tricia asked. "I don't believe you."

"She's looking like that to get my attention," said Johnny.

"Well, from what I can see, I think she's succeeded, ain't she? If that ain't a sex site, then what is it?"

"It's a dating site. I'm only trying to get a date."

Tricia laughed. "Johnny, you're a fool. Look at you. You're a fine-looking lad. You don't need to go onto dating sites."

"That's easy for you to say. All the guys are trying to get off with you. Including me. Don't see you trying to chat me up, though."

"Oh," exclaimed Tricia. "Yeah. I s'pose you've got a point. Even so, just 'cause I ain't chatting you up, it don't mean you ain't a good looking lad. So, Johnny, how many dates have you been on."

"None. That's the point. These contacts are all liars and crooks, and if I could get them for it, I would."

"You've lost me, Johnny. I've no idea what you're talking about."

"No, right, I'll show you."

"Whatcha doing?" asked Tricia as Johnny left the page he was on.

"I'm getting up all the profiles of the men on this website."

Tricia watched as the profile pages came up on the screen. Johnny scrolled through them, one after another. There were dozens of pages and hundreds of profiles of men.

"What do you see?" asked Johnny.

"What do I see? I see hundreds of ugly looking buggers trying to get dates. That's what I see. Never seen so many ugly sods all in one place together."

Johnny laughed. "Shut up, Tricia. I'm one of those ugly sods."

"No, Johnny, these guys are something else. Look, about a quarter of them can't even get their photo around the right way. Look at that stupid twat, got his photo upside down. How does he think he'll get a date with that?"

"No, I agree, Tricia. He won't. But then, none of them will ever get a date, no matter what."

"Why not?" asked Tricia.

"Hang on," said Johnny. "Take a look at this. I'll put up all the female profiles."

Johnny pressed a few keys, and eventually, the female profiles came onto the screen. There were dozens of pages with photos, just like with the men.

"Bloody hell," exclaimed Tricia. "What is this, a beauty competition? Every one of them is beautiful. And not a single photo that isn't round the right way either."

"I wish there was," said Johnny. "I'd certainly send her a message."

"Whatcha talking about, Johnny. You are a strange lad to be sure."

"You don't get it, do you?" said an exasperated Johnny.

"Don't get what? That all the men have crap photos and all the women have good photos. What is there to get?"

"Well, Tricia, you do surprise me. That's what you get when you convince yourself that all women are great, and all men are idiots."

"I'm not really like that, am I?"

"Probably not, but I still think you should have seen what is obvious here. I didn't see it until I looked at the male profiles."

"Right, Johnny, let me think," said Tricia, not wanting Johnny to think he had got the better of her. After a while, it clicked.

"Crikey, Johnny. Are you suggesting what I think you are?"

"Afraid so," said Johnny "All the men on here have genuine profiles, while all the women are fakes. Every woman can't look as fabulous as these women."

"So," said Tricia, "you are suggesting that all these beautiful women have gathered their photos from all over, anywhere, and their profiles are made up."

"Exactly," Johnny agreed. "It took me a long time to figure it out, and all the time it is costing money to buy credits and chat with people who don't exist and who will never, ever meet you."

"Blimey. That's an incredible con. They must be making millions from this."

"Yeah, they made a lot just from me before I figured it out. I guess I chatted with about ten or twelve women, all of them very interested in me and wanting to meet me. But what they really wanted me to do was keep chatting and spending money on credits."

"How much do the credits cost."

"A bloody fortune. You use one credit for every message you send. The cheapest you can get is one pound each, but you have to buy about one hundred. If you only buy ten, they'll cost you one pound fifty each. It doesn't take long to spend a fortune."

"And I guess, if these women are fakes, it doesn't cost them anything."

"That's right, Tricia. The other thing is, although I have chatted with about ten or twelve women, I have never had to initiate contact."

Tricia looked across at him. "Why is that, Johnny?"

"Because I'm getting almost one hundred messages every day from them. And naturally, I'm not responding to ninety-nine percent of them, so they message me again saying how disappointed they are that I haven't replied to them. This is one very big con game. I don't know why I didn't twig it sooner."

"So, Johnny, why are you still on this website?"

"I'm trying to figure out how to catch them out and see if there's any way of throwing the book at them."

"Good for you. Can I help? I ain't going nowhere today. Just listen to that wind and rain out there."

Little Tricky, hearing all the conversation, came out from under the table and jumped up onto Tricia's lap. Tricia stroked him for a while before putting him back under the table on his blanket. "There you go, Tricky. You can't sit on my lap when I'm supposed to be working."

"Oh. So you agree this is work now, do you?" said Johnny.

"I guess so."

"If you've got any ideas, I'd be grateful," said Johnny. "You know, I don't usually open up this website when I'm at work, but seeing as I am trying to catch the buggers, I thought it wouldn't matter."

262

Tricia thought about it. If these people did have fake profiles, they certainly needed to be caught. Johnny did the right thing by looking into it. Even so, all he had was suspicion. She considered the matter for a while, then said to Johnny, "Look, apart from all the gut feelings, what actual proof do you have? Anything concrete?"

"Yes, but you will have to be patient while I show you the proof," said Johnny mysteriously.

"What do you mean?" asked Tricia.

"Take this latest one. We've exchanged quite a lot of messages. If we go through them, by the time you catch up with where I am, you will see definite proof that it's a scam."

"OK. Lead on McDuff," said Tricia, using an expression that Johnny had never heard before.

"What?"

"Never mind. Show me what you mean."

"OK. All the messages are on record, so I'll start at the beginning. This is the first message I received from Felicity. I'll read it."

Johnny put the message up on the screen and read it out loud. *"Hello Johnny, my name is Felicity. I have to say I do like the look of you. You're the first guy I've found on here that I think I would like to date. Have you met anyone yet?"*

"See how innocent and inviting that message is? Not only that, just look at her. She's like a model. Way out of my league," said Johnny.

"Yeah, she really is something. So, what did you reply?"

"Here it is. *Hello, Felicity, that's a lovely name and suits you because you are gorgeous. I would certainly be very pleased to have a date with you. I see you are not far from me in Bilston. I'm in Ricton. What do you do for a living in Bilston?* And then she replies. *Thanks for getting back to me, Johnny. I think it's going to be fun getting to know you. I'm a dentist and run my practice from home. Mostly children. What do you do?"*

"Did you tell her you are a policeman?"

"No," said Johnny, "not exactly. This is what I wrote next. *Hello, Felicity. Yes, I think it will be fun knowing you, although my teeth are OK for now, so I won't be making an appointment. I am a civil servant and work for a government security department."*

"Right, Johnny, so you didn't exactly tell a lie. You just didn't explain fully."

"Yeah. Then she wrote back. *That's alright, Johnny, I'm fully booked up now anyway. It keeps me very busy, so I don't get a lot of time to myself.* That's where she lets me know it will be difficult for us to meet. I checked it out in my next message. *Sorry to hear that, Felicity. It's no good working so hard that you can't find time for yourself. That's how you make yourself ill. So what times are you free for us to meet up?"*

"Nicely done, Johnny." Tricia seemed impressed. "What did she say to that?"

"Right now, it's difficult to get any time free. But, of course, we can still get to know each other on here, can't we?"

"Ah! I see what she is doing. She's setting you up to keep spending on credits."

"Yeah. And remember, every message I send costs me about one pound fifty. So, I wrote. *That's surprising. Do parents really send their kids to you throughout the evening?"*

"That's a good question. How did she answer that?"

264

"She used a new tactic, but I'm sure she has used it before. *Johnny, you are not doubting me, are you? That upsets me. No, they don't all send their kids to me in the evening. I have adult patients, too, you know.*"

"Very clever," said Tricia. "She's trying to put you on the back foot to make you feel bad. Of course, she knows her profile is too good to be true and will hook you in. I bet the real person writing these messages is probably as ugly as sin. If they weren't, they wouldn't need to be doing this. I wonder how much they get paid?"

"We don't even know if it is a woman writing these messages. It could be a man for all I know."

"Yeah, I never thought of that, Johnny. Wouldn't you just love to be able to see them?"

"If only. Of course, you're right. I did feel bad and thought I'd better say something to make amends, even though I haven't done anything wrong."

"So what did you say to her... or him?"

"Sorry if I upset you, Felicity. That was not my intention - quite the opposite. I want to make you happy, not sad. You see, while we are only communicating online, I don't see your facial expressions or hear the tone of your voice, so I really can't judge if I have upset you. Is it so difficult for you to take off enough time for us to maybe go for a meal somewhere? Then we can really get to know each other."

"Nice one, Johnny. How did she respond?"

"It's hard to see how you can respond negatively to that, but she managed to do it. *It's nice of you to offer to take me out for a meal, Johnny, but I'm not that much into eating in restaurants and what with my house used as a dentist, it isn't very suitable for inviting you around for a meal. Sorry."*

"Bloody 'Ell. She certainly knows how to work this, doesn't she?" said Tricia. "How on earth did you respond to that?"

"Well, I was a bit pissed off, so I just wrote... *Felicity. You don't make things easy, do you? It's difficult to see how this is going to work.*"

"Crikey, I bet that didn't go down well."

"She handled it like a pro. Listen to this. *No one said it would be easy, Johnny. In my experience, good things happen after some time and effort. So, what we are doing now is just setting up the basis for a wonderful relationship.* I replied. *You could be right, Felicity. Look, it's getting quite late now, and I have to be up early, so we'll chat again tomorrow. Goodnight.* That was the seventh message I'd sent, so I've already spent over ten pounds and not the slightest indication that we might meet up sometime soon."

"Yes, Johnny, I can see how the costs could soon add up," said Tricia.

"Yeah. Now, remember that this is about the twelfth woman I've chatted to, and it's now well over one-hundred pounds spent and no meetings even remotely on the horizon."

"I'm sure some sad guys who haven't sussed it out like you, just keep on spending money and go into the hundreds. What a bleeding racket it is." Tricia was disgusted, and she showed it too. "If it wasn't equally disgusting, I'd spit," she said.

Story Fourteen - Tricia Helps Johnny
Part Two

"Johnny," said Tricia, "seeing the way you've been handling this, I've got to say that my respect for you has increased enormously in the past hour or so."

"Bloody 'Ell," Johnny replied, "you'll be asking me out on a date next."

"Steady on, Johnny. Respect is one thing; dating is something else entirely."

Johnny sighed.

"But don't lose hope, Johnny. I'd still like to receive your awkward attempts at chatting me up once in a while."

"Yeah, yeah, yeah," said Johnny. "Anyway, back to this website. This is when things start to get very odd."

"How so?"

"Look at this message I got the next evening. *Hello, Johnny. How you today? You not much say. Are you work too hard?*"

"What? What the devil was that?" said Tricia, taken aback by the sudden change in the writing.

"That was my reaction, so this is what I wrote. *Felicity, that was a strange message. Have you been drinking?* She replied. *I out with my girlfriend. Just got in home. I can talk now.* And then I wrote back to her. *Yesterday you were saying how difficult it was for you to find time for yourself. How did you find time to go out with your girlfriend. Where did you go?*

267

Anywhere interesting? And next. *We went meal in pizza place. We can go there sometime. No?"*

"Johnny, this is not the same person you were chatting to before. Someone else has taken over the chat, and they can't even speak proper English."

"Is that proof enough that these are just crooks. God, I wish I could get hold of the bastards," said Johnny, getting quite angry.

"I'd like to be with you if you did," said Tricia. "I might only wear size five shoes, but I'd like to lose them up their cheating arses. Is that the last of the messages?"

"No, there are a couple more from last night," said Johnny putting them up on the screen. I thought I'd have a game with her. *The best place in Bilston is definitely Folly Gardens. It has six follies built there. Which is your favourite?* Of course, there's no such place as Folly Gardens. I wondered what she would say. This was her answer. *I no have favourite. I like all."*

"Haha, that's a good one, Johnny. She likes every one of the non-existent follies. She no have favourite. Bloody 'ell, you couldn't make this up, except it's all made up"

Tricia opened her purse, took out a twenty-pound note, and handed it to Johnny.

"Here, Johnny, use this for a few more credits. Can I have a chat with her?"

"Sure, Trish, help yourself."

Tricia settled in a chair, made herself comfortable, and started to type.

"Good morning, Felicity. How are you today? Do you have a hangover? Can't be too good for the poor children having you drill their teeth today."

Reply.

"What do you mean? I don't have a hangover. I don't drink except on special occasions. Are you a drinker?"

Tricia wrote, *"Oh, yes. I like a drink, but I don't get hangovers. At least not if I have less than fourteen pints."*

Johnny laughed as he read Tricia's response.

Felicity responded. *"Do you like reading books, Johnny? I read all the time. What books do you like?"*

"Looks like the original person is back today," said Johnny. "At least she speaks in a language one can understand."

Tricia typed back.

"My favourite is the Daily Mail. I read that every day. I did like reading the Mr Men books when I was a kid."

Felicity replied *"Oh, Johnny, you are funny. I hope you don't read the Mr Men books now. You see how good it is getting to know each other with messages."*

"She's a clever bitch," said Tricia and replied, *"Not really, Felicity. I have to say that we are finding out quite a lot about you, but actually, I don't believe you know very much about us."*

Felicity's response said, *"I don't understand, Johnny. Why are you saying we and us?"*

"Ah! Now you understand the difference between online chat and face to face meeting, don't you? Do you still think online chat is better?"

"Of course, I do. What are you saying? This conversation is getting to be very strange."

"Yes, Felicity, and it all started last night when, for a few messages, you suddenly became a foreigner with a poor understanding of basic English."

"That'll make her think," Johnny said. "It'll be interesting to see how she responds."

"Why is that? What did I say last night?" said Felicity.

"Don't you remember, Felicity? That was when you went out with your girlfriend to a pizza restaurant (something you say you don't like doing) and returned speaking as though you were drunk (strange for someone who doesn't drink). There are only two credits left Johnny." Tricia gave Johnny another twenty pounds for credits, which he purchased. "I'm enjoying this, Johnny. Certainly better than plodding the streets in the rain, ain't it?"

"Yes. Where are you going with this, Tricia?" asked Johnny.

"You'll see," Tricia replied with a cheeky grin. "Hang on, she's replied again. Don't give up easily, does she?"

"I don't understand, Johnny. There must have been some mix up in the messages. I don't know what you are talking about."

"Of course, you don't understand, Felicity. It wasn't you messaging, was it? Did you have a night off, or were you drilling teeth all evening? Oh, and by the way, How do you have so much time this morning? Have all the kids played hooky today? We have been chatting here for quite some time now."

"I had a cancellation this morning, so I have some spare time," said Felicity.

"Oh, I see. You must be making quite a lot of money from your dental practice to afford to send all these messages. It's different for us. We are sharing the cost."

"Who are you? Who is there besides Johnny? It is unusual to chat with two people at once. Come on, who are you?"

"Now things are hotting up," said Tricia. *"Just as you don't know who we are, we don't really know who you are. We do know it was someone else chatting last night, so it's not that unusual? It's only unusual at this end. I imagine it's quite common at your end, though."*

Felicity became confused. *"This conversation is becoming very strange. Will you please tell me what is going on?"*

Tricia turned up the heat. *"Felicity, let's cut to the chase, shall we? If we were sitting together in a restaurant, none of this confusion would occur. But that's not possible. First, your name is not Felicity. It could be anything, Bob, Annie, Jack, who knows? Second, you don't live in Bilston. There are no Follies there. Johnny made up the name Folly Gardens; It doesn't exist. And we strongly doubt that you are even a dentist. And also, I am not Johnny. He is sitting next to me. My name is Tricia."*

"I bet that has got her thinking," said Johnny.

Felicity responded. *"Tricia, why are you chatting to me? Are you a lesbian? I don't mind if you are."*

"Bloody 'ell, she's trying to get off with you now," said Johnny. "I'll say this for her. She is bloody good at her job."

Tricia decided it was time to get to the nitty-gritty. This person, whoever they were, needed reigning in. She would first find out if they had any conscience regarding the possible distress they might cause those contacting them or the enormous wasted expense involved. She replied. *"No, Felicity, I am not a lesbian. I think it might be time for us to introduce ourselves properly. My friend and workmate is Constable Johnny*

Parsons, and I am Detective Constable Tricia Mason. We are both from the Ricton Police. Now, we are fully aware that you are not the person in your profile. We suspect you are not a robot because of the pigeon English we received yesterday. However, we are sure you are fake."

"I had to stop there, Johnny, because there is a limit to the number of characters you can type in one message. What nasty con artists these people are. You can't even write as much as you want without it costing you more."

The more Tricia discovered about this web site, the more disgusted she became. They seemed to have covered every avenue to get as much money as they could. Well, not for much longer.

"How will she respond to that message?" Johnny moved forward on his chair. "I bet that has given her something to think about."

"Yes, Johnny. While she is thinking about it, I'll Google 'Fraudulent Dating Sites' to see what I can find."

Tricia clicked on Google and searched for any information she could find. After a while, she found what she looked for.

"Here, Johnny, listen to this. This guy says that some of these dating sites have as many as three million women on them, and ninety-five percent of them can be fake profiles. Some sites use 'sexbots' to write messages. Those are computer robots. On those sites, you never get a response, so you go on to chat with someone else, and so it happens over and over again. The actual profile photos used can be from anyone who has put their photo up on the internet. They use the most beautiful women and enticing pictures. And he or she repeatedly promises to meet you in person but always seems to come up with an excuse to cancel."

"Damn it, Tricia," said Johnny, "what did I get myself into?"

"Yeah, good question. You're much better off chatting up someone at the pub than you are on here. Let's see if she has responded."

Tricia logged back into the dating site. Felicity had sent a message.

"What? Are you really both police officers? Look, I've been doing this now for a good few months without any problems. What now?"

Tricia answered. *"Felicity, do you honestly believe there are no problems? Not for you, maybe, but how about the thousands of men who are speaking to women they assume to be legitimate, like you, only to discover they will never, ever meet them. That's not a problem for you then?"*

Felicity replied, *"Not really."*

"Wrong answer," said Tricia. *"Felicity. Had you shown just a little remorse or empathy I might have let you off. As it is, I will be contacting the Police Online Fraud Office and do my absolute best to make you accountable for your fraudulent actions. So, I guess there's no more to say, except to wish you luck when this site gets closed down. We have all this conversation saved. That's probably more evidence than we'd need. If you can't sleep tonight - tough."*

"You used the right word, Tricia. You're one very tough cookie."

"No, Johnny, I'm only tough when I have to be. If she'd shown any concern, my attitude would have been different, but she couldn't care less. So, that's when my tough hat goes on."

"If you say so," said Johnny, in dismissal of Tricia's claim.

"To prove it to you, Johnny, I am going to do something that you'll not believe possible."

"And what's that?" Johnny moved even further to the edge of his chair.

"Johnny, my dear, would you like to take me out for dinner at the weekend?"

That was the moment Johnny fell off his chair, and the same moment Steve came in.

"What are you up to, Johnny?" he asked as Johnny struggled to his feet. "Fooling around again, I suppose."

"Sorry, sir," said Johnny.

Tricia smiled, picked up the telephone, and called the Online Fraud Office.

Story Fifteen – The Quizzing Sleuth
Part One

On Thursday morning at ten-thirty, the station received a call about a man's body found in a refuse container in Wardle Lane. There had not been a murder in Ricton for some time, and with such an event the entire village wondered if they knew the victim. In a small community, that was often the case.

Despite the nature of the crime, Detectives Inspector Stephen Kendall and Constable Tricia Mason were positive about the necessity to solve a substantial case. They both drove their vehicles to Wardle Lane, parked up, and walked to the scene of the crime. Although unusual, Doctor Handsworthy was already there.

"Hello, Richard," Stephen greeted him. "What have we here?"

"Bit of a mess," said the Doctor. "This guy has several stab wounds."

Stephen and Tricia looked around the area.

"Looks like it happened here," said Tricia, who followed the blood traces down the road. "Killed in that little recess, and then carried up to the container."

"Who found him?" asked Steve.

"Apparently, it was the man who lives in the house behind that gate," said Richard, "while he was putting out the rubbish."

"Where is he now?"

"I believe he's in his house."

"OK, I'll have a word with him later. Any idea how long the victim's been dead?" Steve asked, returning his attention to the man in the skip.

"I would say less than twelve hours," Richard estimated.

"Hmm. So, it could have been around midnight."

"Sounds about right," Richard confirmed.

Steve looked in the man's jacket and found a credit card.

"Looks like he might be a Robin West." Steve held the card up to Tricia.

"OK, Detective Constable, while I look around here, could you check the public house on the corner. See if they know the man. If so, ask if he was in the pub last night."

"Yes, sir. I'll get right onto it," said Tricia chirpily. She was in her element now with a murder to investigate. Tricia walked back up the lane to the corner and entered the pub, 'The Bricks and Mortar.'

"Good morning," she said to the bartender.

"Morning, Miss," he replied. "What's going on?"

"I'm Detective Constable Tricia Mason. I'm here with my superior, Detective Inspector Stephen Kendall. There's been an incident in the lane. Do you know a Robin West?"

"Yeah, know him well. He's a regular here. Why?"

"Was he in here last night?"

"Yeah, he pops in most nights. Quite friendly with my barmaid, Sandra," said the man.

"Oh, that's interesting. Is she here now?"

"Not yet," said the barman. "She's late today. Not like her to be late."

"Was Mr West alright last night? You know, anything out of the ordinary?"

"No, same old Robin," said the barman. "Well, I say old. Actually, he's in his twenties. What's this all about, Detective Constable?"

Tricia was quite pleased that he had remembered she was a Detective Constable. Often people merely called her constable. She was very proud of the fact she was a detective and a good one too.

"I'm sorry to say that your customer, Robin West is, dead, sir. Died in the lane last night."

"Crikey," exclaimed the barman. "Sandra is going to be very upset."

"Yes, is she very late?"

"No, not really. Oh, talk of the devil, here she is."

Sandra, an attractive young woman about twenty-two years old with long blond hair, came in. "Morning, Stan, sorry I'm late. Wasn't feeling too well last night. That's why I left early. Not too bad this morning though. Had a bit of a lie-in."

"Morning, Sandra," said Stan. "This is Detective Constable Mason. She'll want to chat with you."

Stan walked off, not wanting to be the one to tell Sandra the bad news. There were quite a few people in the bar now, and Tricia thought she had better get Steve in with her before she started talking to them.

"Just a moment, Sandra," she said. "I'll be back in a minute." Tricia went to look for Steve. She found him concluding his chat with the man who discovered the body.

"Excuse me, sir," Tricia interrupted. "When you have a minute could you come to the pub. Robin West was in there last night."

"Yes, I'll come now."

Johnny had turned up and was chatting with the doctor.

"Can I leave the two of you to get him away?" asked Steve. "I've taken some photos, so he's good to go."

"Yes, sir," said Johnny. "We'll sort it out. The ambulance is on its way."

"When you lift him out, make a thorough check for the murder weapon"

Steve addressed Tricia. "Right. Let's go, Detective Constable." They both went off to the pub.

"Seems he was very friendly with the barmaid, Sandra, sir. I haven't told her yet. Thought it would be better if you were there."

"Regrettably, I think you are right," says Steve as they entered the bar. Sandra and Stan were behind the bar serving. Clearly, Stan has said nothing. Tricia approached Sandra.

"Sandra, can we have a word in private, please?"

"Come with me," said Sandra, "we'll go in the back room."

Steve introduced himself.

"Sandra, I believe you are friendly with Mr Robin West. Is that correct?"

"Yes. He's not actually my boyfriend, but we are very friendly. What's the matter? Is he in trouble?"

"I'm afraid so, Sandra. I'm extremely sorry to have to tell you that he died last night just around the corner down the lane."

Sandra's face turned white, and she burst into tears.

"Oh, no, I should have met him after work, but I left early because I didn't feel well. Oh, no, no, no." Tricia put her arms around the girl and held her tightly as she sobbed on Tricia's shoulder.

"Poor Robin. Poor Robin." She repeated over and over. "Was it an accident or something?"

"No," Steve replied. "We have to go and speak with other people in the bar. Will you be alright if we leave you here?"

Sandra nodded.

They returned to the bar, and Tricia spoke to Stan. "Have you said anything to anyone?"

"No," said Stan.

"Were any of these people in here last night?" asked Steve.

"Yes, most of them."

"Do you know their names?"

"Again, yes, most of them," Stan confirmed.

"Would you do something for me?"

"Sure." Stan paid closer attention to Steve as he explained.

"Cast your mind back to last evening and make out a list of everyone you can remember who was here last night. If you think of any with whom you are not familiar, please jot it down with a brief description."

Stan found a notebook and pencil behind the bar and started scribbling a list.

Steve brought the customers to order. "Excuse me, everyone, I have to tell you something." The customers all looked toward him.

"I am Detective Inspector Kendall. I expect many of you know a man named Robin West."

Most of them nodded in affirmation. "I'm sorry to have to tell you that he died last night in the lane next door."

Everyone whispered to their friends.

"That means I'll need to speak with all of you. If you would be so helpful as to give your names and addresses to Detective Constable Mason, she will note them for future reference. Thank you."

Steve started chatting to the customers one by one. First, was a Frank Peters, who said he was only in for half an hour and left about eight o'clock. Then, Mrs Walters, who had sat with her husband all evening in the corner watching the darts match. Her husband was at home now. Terry Brown said he had been there most of the evening and left at around ten. Wally Worthington stayed until they threw him out around midnight.

Steve took down all their details until he came to a nervous-looking young man sitting alone in a corner. Steve asked him his name. The lad looked over at Stan but said nothing. Stan caught Steve's eye, came over and took Steve aside to speak with him.

"That's Trevor," he explained, "he's mute. He wasn't born dumb but stopped speaking when he was about four. No one ever found out why. People think he is an idiot, but he's very intelligent. He prepares all the questions on his computer for our quiz night."

"When is that?" asked Tricia who had just joined them.

"It's tonight," said Stan. "We have a quiz every Thursday evening. You should come along."

"Maybe I will," said Tricia.

"So," said Steve, "was he here last night?"

"Oh, yes. Trevor's a permanent fixture. He helps out around here, and we supply him with free drinks and a meal each day. He's always here until we lock up, last night too."

Steve spoke to all the customers, and Tricia took down their names, addresses, and telephone numbers.

"Well," said Steve, "there isn't a lot more we can do here now. We'll head off. We'll get more information from those who look interesting by calling them and inviting them to the station."

"They're not the kind of invitations most people find exciting," said Tricia. "Now that invite to the quiz night... that is something I don't mind. Is Susan into quizzes?"

"I wouldn't say she's into quizzes, but she knows more answers than I ever do," Steve replied. "Why, are you thinking of asking her to go along with you?"

"It would make a change from our usual night out," Tricia replied.

"For a night out, it will move you up from kidnappers to murderers. All very well if you like that kind of company," said Steve pointedly.

Tricia laughed. "Where will we go from there? Terrorists maybe."

Story Fifteen – The Quizzing Sleuth
Part Two

Steve and Tricia returned to the station and went through what they had established. Although the victim had been stabbed several times, no sign of the weapon showed up near Robin West or anywhere near the crime scene. Robin West had visited the Bricks and Mortar public house that evening. He attempted a relationship with Sandra, the barmaid, who had left early. Sandra, now too upset to question, would have to come into the station when she was more composed. Most of the others who'd been at the pub didn't seem likely for this murder. Terry Brown had not given them much to go on and so they might also call him in. They had nothing else.

The investigators needed the weapon, a motive, and a more reliable estimate of the time of the incident. The best estimate was that it occurred sometime between ten and about two a.m. They'd contacted Robin West's parents and arranged for them to identify the body. The Wests turned up at the mortuary, confirmed it was Robin, but provided no information to suggest he had specific enemies. So far, there was little to go on. Further interviews tomorrow might shed more light on the matter.

It was getting late, so they decided to quit until the interviews the next day. Steve sent Tricia home. She immediately called Susan and invited her to go to the pub quiz with her that evening.

"Yes, Tricia, why not," Susan agreed. "A quiz night will make a nice change from just eating and talking about the other diners and the waiters, great fun though it is."

"Susan, you are terrible," said Tricia. "I bet you will find just as many people to criticize at the pub as anywhere else."

"What do you mean, 'I will find them.' You are just as guilty. Now that you have brought it up, I really think it is you who is the bad influence."

"I hope so," said Tricia mischievously. "I like being a bad influence. No fun otherwise, is there?"

"Incorrigible, that's the only word for you," said Susan.

* * *

Susan collected Tricia and drove to the corner of Wardle Lane where she found somewhere to park. The pub was crowded, but they managed to find a table for two. Tricia brought their drinks across from the bar which they sipped while waiting for the quiz to begin. Young Trevor handed out envelopes bearing the words *'do not open until the quiz starts.'*

Eventually, Stan took to the microphone.

"For those who are new here and I can see at least two people, welcome Tricia, and friend. I should explain that we do the quiz in sections. It's not rocket science as there are no rocket scientists here. No, it's pretty straight forward and you will learn as we go."

"Right, you have six pieces of paper in your envelopes," Stan continued, "and on your table, a number. Write that number in the box at the top of each sheet of paper. Tonight, you don't have a name, just a number. Detective Constable Tricia will be familiar with this system if she has locked up many villains."

Laughter all around the room.

"OK, let's start with the paper for History answers. Write your answers in the space provided."

"Question one. What was the date of the Great Fire of London?"

Both Susan and Tricia wrote in 1666.

"Question two. What was the name of the last executioner?"

They both wrote in 'Pierrepoint'.

And so the questions continued through History, Art, Singers, Nursery Rhymes, Maths, Politics, Celebrities, and Comedians.

When the quiz was over and all papers collected, Trevor sat in his corner going through them.

"How do you think we did?" asked Tricia.

"Not so bad," said Susan. "There were a few I struggled with, but on the whole, I think we did well. Here, let me refresh the drinks. Do you want one of those lovely pies on the bar? They look really tasty."

"Go on then," said Tricia, "sod the waistline."

Susan went to the bar and waited for her turn

After a while, Stan returned to the mic and read out everyone's results as a percentage correct. Only one guy managed to get 100%. Susan got 96%, and Tricia managed a satisfactory 92%. They were both happy with their results.

As time pushed on, they had to leave. When they reached the exit, Trevor shoved an envelope into Tricia's hand. It surprised her as no-one else received anything from him.

"Thank you, Trevor," she said. "Very good quiz. We both enjoyed it."

Trevor nodded and indicated the envelope he had given her.

They went outside and got into the car.

"What's Trevor given us, I wonder?" said Tricia "Put the inside lights on for a minute, Susan."

They sat together looking at the paper they found inside the envelope. It was Tricia's results of the section on Nursery Rhymes. Tricia read out the answers she had given.

Where did the little boy cry?

'The Lane.'

This was a reference to Baa Baa Black Sheep. (One for the little boy who cries down the lane).

What did the sparrow do?

'Killed Cock Robin' as in 'Who killed Cock Robin? I said the sparrow with my bow and arrow.'

Who was being met in Banbury?

s 'A Fair Lady' as in 'Ride a cock horse to Banbury Cross.'

What cut the mice' tails?

'A Carving Knife' as in 'Three Blind Mice.'

In the song that starts Ha ha ha, He he he, what is the colour of the crockery?

Obviously 'Brown' as in the song 'Little Brown Jug.'

"I wonder why he gave me this sheet," said Tricia. "What about all the other sheets we did?"

"If he wrote all the questions, he is an intelligent lad," said Susan. "He wouldn't have given you that for no reason, I'm sure of that. Let me see it."

Susan looked at the paper and studied it. "I can't see anything special here, except for one thing."

"What special thing?" asked Tricia.

"If I remember rightly you told me earlier that the murdered man was Robin West. So I see a link between that and Cock Robin. Other than that, I'm baffled."

"Damn it, Susan, I think you are right. Let me have another look."

Tricia grabbed the paper and studied it again.

"Bloody 'Ell, Susan, I think this is the answer to the murder."

"How so?"

"Well, let's just take the answers. We have 'Lane', 'Robin', 'Fair Lady', 'Carving Knife' and 'Brown'. The murder took place in Wardle Lane, the victim's name was Robin West, he was there to meet a Lady, that would be Sandra, murdered with a Knife, and here is the main clue. The murderer's name was Brown. A man is coming in for questioning tomorrow. His name is Terry Brown."

"Tricia, that is the darndest thing I ever heard. A murder solved with a quiz."

"Yes, I reckon the lad Trevor witnessed the murder but is scared to say so. This way, no-one knows he has any involvement."

"He is one very clever lad," said Susan.

"He sure is. All we have to do now is piece it together and we've got him," Tricia said excitedly. "I can't wait to tell Steve."

"Why wait?" Tricia. "Come back with me now and you can tell him all about it."

"Thanks, Susan. That must be the easiest and quickest murder mystery ever solved. We should do quizzes more often."

They pulled into Susan's drive and got out. Tricia bounded out of the vehicle, so impatient to see Steve that she was inside the house before Susan had a chance to lock her car.

"OK, Tricia," said Steve, "calm down. Now, what is this all about?"

"We've solved the murder case," she blurted out.

"Not strictly 'we' though," Susan interjected.

"Well, no," Tricia had to agree, "but we did work out all the clues."

"Why don't you sit down, the pair of you, and quietly tell me what is going on," Steve suggested and so they did.

"That is extremely clever," Steve agreed when they had finished explaining. "However, the case is not strictly solved until we actually solve it."

"No," said Tricia, "now we have to find the evidence, the opportunity, and the motive. Maybe we were getting a bit too excited."

"But you have to agree that you do have the identity of the murderer," said Susan.

"On one person's say so," said Steve laconically.

The two women released a big sigh when they suddenly realised the reality of the matter.

"Never, mind," said Tricia with enthusiasm, "at least we can start an investigation tomorrow with a certain amount of confidence and direction."

"Direction, yes," Steve agreed, "but it will take some real evidence before I raise my confidence."

"Oh, dear," said Susan.

"Sir, tomorrow I suggest we concentrate on Brown. Get him in and interrogate him," said Tricia.

Steve smiled. Was there ever a detective constable with as much drive and enthusiasm as his girl Tricia? If there was, he had never met them.

"Yes Tricia, that is exactly what we will do," he said, "but tone down a little on the interrogation. Let's just call it questioning. I don't want you to get out the waterboarding kit and the electric cattle prods."

They all laughed, but still looked forward to the next day.

* * *

The following day the station set up for the questioning of suspects. Stephen and Tricia were in the questioning room, and Johnny prepared those people invited to the station. The prime suspect was Terry Brown, and Johnny took him into the room.

"Take a seat," said Steve, as he opened his notebook. Terry sat in the chair opposite Steve and Tricia.

"Now, Mr Brown, I have it here in my notes that you were at the Bricks and Mortar the night before last, and that you left at around ten. Is that correct?"

"Yes, Inspector. I rarely stay any later than that."

"OK. Did you know Robin West?"

"Yes, very well. He was almost like a brother to me."

"That is odd if you don't mind me saying so. When you learned that he was dead, I don't recollect you showing any great concern."

"No," said Brown abruptly.

"Why is that if he was like a brother to you?"

"It surprised and shocked me, but that doesn't mean I have to show concern."

"Not even if he was like a brother," said Steve pointedly.

"Not all brothers are close. Not emotionally," Brown replied.

"And do I read into that, you and Robin West were like brothers but not emotionally?" Steve queried.

"That's right," said Brown.

Tricia interrupted.

"I'm a little puzzled," she said. "If not emotionally, how can you say you were like brothers. In what way were you like brothers?"

Brown didn't answer.

288

"That's a logical question, Mr Brown," said Steve. "Would you give the Detective Constable an answer please?"

"We lived together when we were growing up," said a reluctant Terry Brown.

"What were the circumstances where you found yourselves living together?" asked Steve.

Again, Brown gave no reply. When it was clear he wasn't going to answer, Tricia said.

"Can I hazard a guess that maybe you were in care together? Or perhaps even adopted?"

Brown let out a sigh. He seemed resigned to the fact that he could not keep up his non-committal attitude any longer.

"They adopted Robin. Not me," he said.

"Were the family who had adopted Robin your carers?" Tricia suggested.

"Yes," Brown agreed.

Both Tricia and Steve mentally noted that here was the motive they required.

"It would have been much easier if you had simply told us this right away instead of us having to drag it out of you," said Steve. "What have you gained? Nothing. Is there anything else you should be telling us that you are holding back?"

Again, Brown was silent.

"Bloody 'Ell," chirped in Tricia, "It's like getting blood out of a stone with you. Come on, join in the conversation."

"Alright, alright," said Brown. "I'll tell you why I was not emotionally attached to Robin. I'm ashamed."

"And why are you ashamed?" asked Steve.

"I'm ashamed of what we did together, but it was Robin who always started it. I should have stopped him, but I didn't. That's why I am ashamed. But I had nothing to do with his death. Honestly, you have to believe me. I didn't."

"Come on, Mr Brown," said Tricia, "give us the full story. What did you do that made you ashamed of yourself?"

"We tortured the poor lad. Tied him up and pricked him with pins. I should have stopped him but he goaded me on and I got involved. I always felt sick afterward and despised myself. As I got older, the memory of what we did as kids gave me nightmares. No, I was never emotionally attached to Robin. I hated him. He was a bully."

A tear found its way to Terry's eye and he brushed it aside.

"OK, Terry," said Steve, "who was this boy you tortured."

"He was just a little kid. A lovely boy who didn't deserve it. He was being cared for by Mr and Mrs West. We ruined his life. But I didn't do this murder. I didn't."

Tricia looked at Steve.

"Sir," she said, "I don't think Mr Brown needs to tell us who the boy was. I think I know."

The tears were now running freely down Terry's face. He did not attempt to wipe them.

"Poor Trevor," he said. "We ruined his life."

For Tricia, everything now fell into place. Terry wasn't the murderer Trevor had implicated in his quiz. The murderer was Trevor who had devised an immaculate plan to get revenge on both of them by killing Robin and framing Terry for his murder. He had not counted on the fact that Terry was so full of guilt. If he hadn't been, Trevor might have got away with it.

Story Sixteen
The Invisible Thief

Most days at the Station kicked off much the same with a routine they all adhered to unless something unusual happened. Nothing very out of the ordinary happened this day. At least, not at the start.

Tricia reported to Steve, Mike did his usual round of phone calls, and Johnny went out into town to keep his eye on things. Often, the things he kept his eye on had two legs and wore a dress. And his eye focussed on more than one of them in town, especially at the supermarket.

Johnny called in the supermarket every day, as he did all the other business premises in the village. The supermarket always took up more of his time, not because it was the biggest store on the main street, but because it employed more females than any other. Unfortunately for Johnny, none of them were too interested in him since friendship with someone in the police produced mixed reactions. Some were positive, others not. Johnny took it all in his stride and continued with his daily visits.

He employed his usual chat up lines to little Rita in the checkout area until the Morning Manager, Samantha, called him over. Usually, he did his best to steer clear of Samantha. She had more than a passing interest in him, even though she had a husband and not the kind of guy Johnny wished to encounter. Johnny showed more interest in Rita and Mesha than the Morning Manager.

Out of nothing more than politeness, Johnny went to see what Samantha wanted.

"Good morning," he greeted her. "What can I do for you?"

"We've got a problem, Johnny," she said. Everyone called him Johnny since he was so well known in the village. Tricia, was always referred to by her title, Detective Constable. While Johnny loved the familiarity of people using his given name, Tricia revelled in hearing her title used with deference.

"What sort of problem?" Johnny asked her.

"Things are stolen every day and I have no idea how."

"That's a bit odd. What kind of things?"

"Well, that's what's strange. We know what items they are, and more or less, when. Just don't know how," Samantha was genuinely confused about it.

"What things are they?" Johnny asked again.

"Clothing," Samantha replied. "It's clothing, and every day too."

"I thought clothing was the thing most difficult to steal," said Johnny, remembering that every item of clothing had a security tag.

"Yes, it is," Samantha replied. "It's so damned odd though."

"What's odd? Explain to me," said Johnny, needing something tangible to work on.

"We hear the alarm bell but have never have a chance to stop the culprit."

"I reckon your security staff needs to get more on the ball then," said Johnny. "Haven't they had any training?"

"Of course. They are from a reputable company of security guards. That isn't the problem."

"So, what is? Can't they catch the buggers? Seems to me they need some athletic training to get more speed into their feet."

Samantha laughed. "Johnny, to catch someone, you have first to see them. It don't matter how fast you are if they aren't there."

"Now, you've lost me, Sam," said Johnny and immediately wished he hadn't. Calling her by the affectionately shortened name of Sam would undoubtedly give her the wrong impression, and he saw it in her eyes straight away.

"Sorry," he said, "I mean Samantha."

"That's alright, Johnny. Sorry, I've lost you. I wouldn't want that, would I?"

"Hm," Johnny grunted. "Explain to me why you can't see them."

"Cos they aren't bloody-well there, that's why," said Samantha irritably, having noticed Johnny's standoffish attitude.

Johnny let out a long audible sigh, mainly because he was getting no sense out of this conversation, but also partly because of Samantha's need for more than he could offer her.

"Right, Samantha, why don't you explain to me exactly what is happening here. I'll try to keep up," Johnny said sarcastically.

"Look, every day, some piece or pieces of clothing go missing. We only find out after we check the stock. But we know they usually disappear between ten and eleven in the morning."

"How can you be sure of the time?" asked Johnny, trying his best to keep up.

"Because that's when the alarm goes off," Samantha explained.

To Johnny, it didn't seem to be much of an explanation.

"It's five minutes to ten right now. If you can stay here for a little while, you will see what I mean."

"OK," Johnny agreed, "but after that, I'll have to move on. I have other premises to visit, you know."

"Alright, Johnny, that's fine. Just stay until the alarm goes off."

Rita sidled up to them and asked Johnny if he would like a cuppa.

"Thanks, Rita, I'll have a coffee, please," he said, and she went off to get it. Meanwhile, he chatted with Mesha until she had to deal with her customers. Rita returned with the coffee, and Johnny waited quietly to one side while they all got on with their jobs.

He finished his drink and sat on the low windowsill waiting. At about twenty past ten, the theft alert sounded all over the store broadcasting through several speakers. A flashing sign indicated that something left via the main front entrance. Johnny and Samantha dashed to the automatic doors where the security guard was operating.

"Did you see who it was?" asked Johnny.

"No," said the guard who was stopping a woman from leaving, "unless it's this lady. I don't think it is though, because she had gone through the door by about four feet before the alarm sounded. It usually goes off when they are in the doorway."

Samantha came forward.

"Sorry, love," she said to the woman. "As the alarm has gone off, it is simply a formality that we have to check."

"I don't have anything," said the woman.

"No, love, I'm sure you don't. We have this problem every day. Can I ask what you have in your bag?"

The woman carried a plastic supermarket bag. Inside were two containers of cream and a pack of strawberries - nothing else.

"OK, love," says Samantha. "I'm sorry about that, but we have to check."

"That's alright," says the woman. "Why has the alarm gone off, though?"

"Your guess is as good as mine," said Samantha. "Thank you and have a nice day."

She turned to Johnny. "See, that happens every day. We would put it down to a fault on the alarm system except that we always find a piece of clothing missing when we check."

"Always?" asks Johnny.

"Yes, we've lost more than a dozen items. This can't go on. We have to get to the bottom of it. Someone is stealing the clothes."

"Is there any means of tampering with the device on the clothing so that it delays before it goes off?"

"Johnny, that is an excellent question," said Samantha. "I've no idea. How about you, Reggie."

The security guard shook his head. "I don't think so. It's my impression that, even if it's possible, it would have to be the alarm that delays, not the clothes tag."

"Yes, I agree," said Johnny. "Well, clearly, we don't have a solution to this problem here and now. I'll go back to the station and check if anyone has heard of this.

* * *

Johnny returned to the station. It was a slow day, and Mike, Steve, and Tricia were all there. He explained the strange phenomenon. All were completely puzzled by it.

"That's an odd one, Johnny; I've never heard of that," Mike confirmed.

"Me neither," said Tricia.

"I've not heard of it," said Steve. "However, if this is happening, there has to be a reason for it. That will be your job for the day, Detective Constable. You'd better go down there with Johnny and use your magic methods to find the solution."

"Ha ha," Johnny laughed, "and a lot of luck she will have. I've looked at it, and so has Samantha and the Security Guard, and we haven't figured it out."

"In that case, it's unsolvable," said Tricia. "If all those masterminds couldn't find an answer, I guess the clothing disappeared by magic, and the warning triggered by the fairies. You didn't happen to catch sight of any, did you, Johnny?"

"Huh, come on, genius." Johnny nodded to Tricia. "Show me how the exorcist operates."

Johnny bowed, and Tricia reciprocated with a curtsy. "After you, Macbeth," she said and guided Johnny out the door."

* * *

Johnny took Tricia to Samantha's office at the supermarket.

"Back again, Samantha," said Johnny. "This is Detective Constable Tricia Mason," he introduced Tricia.

"Yes, we've met before," said Samantha. "It's obvious why he never reciprocates my advances with a pretty little thing like you around."

"Well, I'm pleased he doesn't," said Tricia, "we all know you are a married woman. So, what is going on here? Not haunted by ghosts, are you?"

"None that I've seen," said Samantha.

"You're not open during the night, are you?" asks Tricia.

"No, we close at eight every evening."

"Ah, that will be why you've never seen them," said Tricia. "You only see ghosts at night. There you are, Johnny, we are getting somewhere already."

They all laughed at the comic Tricia.

"Come on," said Tricia, "let's go and look at the system."

The three of them walked over to the checkouts.

"What controlled exits do you have?" asked Tricia.

"There is the main entrance/exit, and the rear exit, which is also the entrance for stock arrivals," Samantha explained.

"What about fire exits? Surely there must be some of those," Tricia asked.

"Oh, yes, I'd forgotten those," said Samantha. "There are two of them, one to the right that opens into the passage next door, and one at the rear that opens into the stockyard. They are both exits only and don't open from the outside. They have the usual bar control locking device."

"Right," said Tricia, taking control in the manner she always did on investigations. "Let's do this properly. Do you have a tag that I can use?"

Samantha went to one of the checkouts and removed a tag from a purchased item of clothing. She gave it to Tricia. Tricia led them to the main entrance/exit doors. With the tag in her hand, she walked through the doors setting off the alarm instantly. She came back in. Samantha indicated someone should turn off the alarm.

When all was quiet again, Tricia said, "That seems to be working OK. Let's go to the rear service area."

There, Tricia walked through the exit door with the tag in her hand. Again, the alarm activated.

"That one is fine. Let's check the fire exits," she said, leading the way.

Again, the alarms sounded when Tricia stepped through the doors.

"So, there is nothing wrong with the system," she said. "The solution has got to be something else. What is that door in the corner by the front entrance," she enquired.

"That's the staff toilets," Samantha explained.

"Can I take a look," asked Tricia, walking over to the door without waiting for an answer.

They looked around inside. There was nothing out of the ordinary in there. Tricia stood for a while, contemplating. Then she asked, "Do you have any plans for the building, Samantha."

"Yes. We keep them in the staff room," she replied. "Why do you need them? You can see everything there is."

"Not everything," said Tricia, mysteriously.

They all made their way to the staff room, and Samantha opened a large drawer in a plan chest. Tricia looked through the plans available until she found something that interested her.

"Ah, got it," she said. "Come with me."

Completely puzzled, Johnny and Samantha followed Tricia back to the staff toilets at the front of the building. They went inside. Tricia took the tag she had been carrying with her and tossed it into one of the toilet pans. Then she flushed it. When it had gone, they waited. Tricia had her finger to her lips to request silence.

Suddenly, the alarm went off, and they all rushed out to look at the alarm screen. It was indicating a theft at the front entrance doors.

"It's OK," said Tricia, "you don't need to go and check it out. Come with me."

Tricia led them back to the staff room and took out the plans of the drainage system.

"You see this," she said, pointing to the drainage from the staff toilets. "The drainage pipe runs to the right along the front of the building and right underneath the front exit doors."

"Well, bugger me," said Johnny, "this is why Tricia is a Detective Constable, and I'm not."

"So, what is happening here is that one of my staff steals the clothes. Probably puts them on in the toilet cubical under their overalls and flushes the tag down the loo."

"Exactly," said Tricia. "Every time that alarm goes off during the theft, you will find the thief in the staff toilets. Tomorrow morning, when the alarm goes off between ten and eleven, you need to check who is in the staff toilets, and you'll have your culprit."

"Damn it, Detective Constable, you are good," said Samantha.

"Well," said Tricia, "if that is it, we'll be off. Come on, Dr Watson, let's get back to the station, and you can make out the report."

"I've got to write it up, have I?" said a reluctant Johnny.

"You don't think I am gonna do it, do ya, Johnny. I've done my bit."

Johnny smiled.

"Yes, Sherlock," he said, "I guess you have too."

Story Seventeen
A Stitch Up

When Johnny called Tricia Sherlock, he was quite serious. He held her in very high regard, and rightly so. Tricia was one of those individuals who seemed to possess a sixth sense. She could always come up with solutions to problems that stumped others. It was all due to her very active mind. Tricia was a joker, a comedian, and that pushed her mind in more directions than most people.

Johnny had read an internet report which said that comedians scored higher on measures of verbal intelligence. And Tricia certainly was extremely funny, of that there was no doubt. She tripped Johnny up continually with her wit and humour. But Johnny loved it. While he did spend a lot of his time trying to chat up the supermarket girls, his real ambition in life was the conquest of the lovely, witty, delightful, Tricia. He knew he would never succeed, but boy, wasn't it fun trying?

"Not much on today, Trish," he said when he arrived at work that morning. "I think I'll take one of my days off owed to me. The weather is nice."

"What!" Tricia exclaimed. "You're taking another day off?"

He knew she was only baiting him with the insinuation that he was always taking days off when he was at work.

"Alright, I know you think I've already had eight days off this week," he responded, trying to beat her at her own comic game.

Tricia fired back, "Crikey, is that all? I thought it was more."

Johnny tried to keep up with her by responding, "It will be when I take today off."

"Yeah, getting on for a fortnight this week. Whatcha gonna do on this day off?"

"I've got something in mind. I won't waste it," said Johnny.

"Oh, good for you, Johnny," said Tricia. "You're gonna take a double shift off to get some time back. Good lad."

"No. I'm going to watch a local football match against Colston."

Mike, who had been quietly listening to the exchange between these two constables, interrupted.

"Speaking of Colston," he said, "since we cleared up that drug business where they were using Tricia's Dog, Tricky, Colston has been quite clean, I've heard. But just recently things have started going bad again. We will have to sort that one out soon."

"Yes, Sarge," said Johnny, "but not today. I'm taking one of my days off."

"So, I heard."

"Yeah, might take a double shift off, as Tricia suggested," said Johnny.

"Good boy," said Tricia, "you'll get brownie points for that."

"You had better be off," said Mike, "before Tricia talks you into staying. What sort of match is it?"

"They're using old equipment to teach the boys how football used to be years ago in the days of Stanley Matthews."

"How do you mean?" asked Mike.

"They're using old-style leather boots and a blow-up leather ball with the old inflatable."

"That should be interesting. I wouldn't want to head that ball with those laces in it."

"No, Sarge, me neither. But that's how it used to be."

"Yeah, well, I hope they have a good game."

"Me too," said Tricia, "and if they complain about the laces, tell them that's how I hold me tits up every day. Pussies"

The boys laughed and Johnny went off to the match.

* * *

At the Station, Mike chatted with Steve, and they agreed that maybe Tricia ought to go to Colston to see if she could make any headway with the drug investigation. Being Tricia, she was always up for a challenge and agreed to make some preliminary checks. She set off to Colston to talk to a young lad caught with a supply of drugs he was almost certainly selling. First, she called in to speak with Sergeant Peters in Colston.

"Hello, Detective Constable," he greeted her. "How is little Tricky? Has he uncovered any more drug pushers lately?" he joked.

"I don't think so," said Tricia. "At least he hasn't told me about it. That's the reason I'm here - to investigate your new crop of drug pushers. What can you tell me?"

"Not a lot. He isn't giving anything away. We caught him with a supply of drug packets, which we confiscated. Said he found them in a wheelie bin. Likely story. Kids like him don't find drugs. Professionals use these kids as pushers."

"What about his friends? Do they have any drugs to your knowledge?"

"Not that we've discovered. Of course, we don't have any grounds to search them or their homes, more's the pity," said Sargent Peters.

"What's the lad's name?"

"Jeremy, but they call him Jerry," said Peters.

"OK, shall we go and speak to him?"

"I'll take you round there. Or rather, you can take me. We'll go in your car, and I'll direct you."

They set off to see Jerry. His mother answered the door when they knocked.

"Hello, you back again?" said Jerry's mother. "He told you he found them in a wheelie bin. What more do you want him to say?"

"Well, for a start," said Tricia, "he could tell us where he actually got them. If you believe that story, he must have been getting away with murder his whole life. Is he in?"

"No," said his mother.

"Do you know where he is?"

"No, I don't."

"Well, that tells us a lot. Don't you take any responsibility for what he does?" said Tricia. "I know my mum told me always to tell her where I was going. It's safer that way. Keeps kids out of trouble."

"He ain't in trouble," Jerry's mother persisted, "unless you can get into trouble by finding things in wheelie bins."

"When you take them to well-known druggie sites and try to sell them, I imagine most sensible people would consider that 'trouble', wouldn't they? Or is that OK with you?"

Tricia was laying it on thick with Jerry's mum. More than Sargent Peters would ever have considered saying. But it seemed very acceptable from Tricia, and

Peters thought she might even be getting through to the exceptionally tolerant mother. The mother didn't answer. That wasn't good enough for Tricia.

"Well? Is selling drugs OK with you, Mrs…, didn't get your name."

"It's Mary. Mary Fullerton, and no, it isn't OK with me. Look I don't know where he is. He went out early, and some of his friends picked him up in a car."

"And you've no idea where he was going?"

"No. You could look down on the green where the football pitch is," said Mrs Fullerton.

"You think he's playing football," said the Sargent, speaking for the first time. "What makes you think that?"

"I don't need to be a detective to figure that out. Not when he takes a football with him," said Mrs Fullerton belligerently.

"Ah, yes," said the Sargent, "I did notice a football in his room when I searched the place."

"OK," said Tricia, "thank you for your time. Come on, Sarge, let's go and find this football pitch."

They got back into Tricia's car, and Peters directed her to the green. There was no football match played there and no group who looked as though they might play.

"Shit," exclaimed Tricia.

"Language, Detective Constable," Peters reprimanded her.

"Sorry, Sarge," said Tricia. "I didn't think it would sound as bad as bollocks."

"Oh, just as well you didn't use that word then," said Peters, but couldn't suppress the smile that came to his lips.

"Yeah, glad I didn't, Sarge. Are there any other football pitches around here?"

"Only the school pitch, but it's locked today. We passed it on the way here, so I do know it isn't open."

"So, where did he go to play football?" Tricia said to herself but out loud. "Perhaps we should go back to Mrs Fullerton and see if we can get more information."

"OK, Detective Constable, let's do that."

Mrs Fullerton, however, could give no more details of where he might have gone.

"I've no idea," she said. "All I know is that he went out with his mates and took that ridiculous football with him again."

"What d'you mean, ridiculous football?" said Tricia. "I'm thinking you don't like football very much."

"Football's alright. It's that old ball he has been using recently that I'm talking about."

"What old ball?" Tricia asked. The comment had pricked her detective mind, and it was already well ahead of the conversation.

"The old one what people don't use anymore," Mrs Fullerton explained.

"Are you saying it's an old leather ball with a bladder and laces?" Tricia asked.

"That's the one. Can't see why he wants to use it. It weighs a ton. You could break your foot kicking that."

"Thank you, Mrs Fullerton," said Tricia, "you have been most helpful. Come on Sarge, I know where he's gone."

They got back into Tricia's car.

"So, where has he gone, Mastermind?" asked Sargent Peters?

"He's gone to Ricton," said Tricia. "Look, I don't suppose you want to come all the way there with me, Sarge. Anyway, I'd have to drive you back again and my day would be all used up."

"No, you're right, I don't want to go to Ricton with you. But how do you know that he's gone there?"

Tricia explained the conversation she'd had with Johnny that morning and everything slotted into place.

"Never mind, Sarge. I'll catch up with him and keep you informed if I get anything to report."

* * *

Tricia dropped Sargent Peters off at his station and then made her return trip to Ricton. It was getting late, and she hoped Jerry Fullerton had not finished the game and gone back home to Colston. When she pulled into the Ricton Park and made her way down to the pitch, she found Johnny there chatting to some of the boys. The game was over, and most of them had gone home.

"Hi, Johnny," Tricia greeted him. "I guess the game has finished."

"Hello, Tricia, what are you doing here. I didn't think football was your game."

"What? Has it ended already? And there's me with me tits all laced up ready to go."

"Yeah, it finished about twenty minutes ago. A lot of lads have gone home."

"What about Jerry Fullerton from Colston? Has he gone home?" asked Tricia.

One of the lads overheard the conversation and interrupted.

"No," he said, "he's gone with two other Colston boys with Jim the trainer. I think they've gone to Jim's house."

"Bloody hell," said Tricia, "I'm going to spend all day at this rate before I meet up with him."

"I know where Jim lives if it's that important," Johnny said, trying to help. "Do you want me to take you there?"

"Would you mind, Johnny? I've been chasing around for him for the past two hours."

"Come on then," said Johnny. "What's this all about anyway?"

Tricia explained it to him when Johnny got into her car. Jim's house was quite a large detached property on the outskirts of Ricton.

"When we get there, Johnny, play it cool, will you?" Tricia asked. "You're not in uniform and neither am I and we've an unmarked car, so don't let on that I'm here on business."

"OK, Trish, you're the boss."

They pulled up outside of Jim's house where they saw an old banger parked at the kerb. Tricia pulled up behind it.

"That's the car Jerry came in with his mates," Johnny explained. "Come on, let's go around to the back."

Two Colston boys were sitting at a garden table. There was a tray of glasses and a large jug of orange juice on the table. The boys were cooling off with a drink.

"Hi, boys," Johnny greeted them, "Cooling off? That was a good game."

"Yeah," said one of the Colston boys, "it was OK. You and yer girlfriend want a drink?"

Johnny smiled and looked at Tricia, "Yeah, I'll have a glass. Want some orange juice, Trish?"

"Go on then," Tricia replied as she took a seat at the table.

"Where's Jim?" asked Johnny after he had poured the drinks.

"He's in the house with Jerry," one of the boys replied. "He'll be out in a minute."

"That was a tough game with that old leather football," said the other boy. "I wouldn't want to play with that every week. Don't know how they did it."

"No, I bet it's a bugger when you head it," said Johnny.

"Yeah, 'specially when the laces connect with your forehead."

"Where's the ball now?" asked Johnny.

"It's Jerry's ball. I 'spect he's got it with him."

"What's all this about a leather ball?" Tricia butted in. "What's a leather ball?"

The boys explained.

"So, it's laced up then," said Tricia showing interest. "What's inside of it?"

Again, the boys explained. All the while, Tricia's mind worked overtime. A picture of the drug operation was now clear in her mind. Just then, Jim and Jerry joined them. Jerry had the ball under his arm.

"Hello, Johnny," said Jim. "I didn't expect to see you here."

"Hi, Jim," Johnny responded. "This is Tricia."

"Hello, Tricia. I didn't know you had a girlfriend, Johnny. Very lovely she is too."

Johnny smiled.

"So, that's the funny ball everyone's talking about," said Tricia. "Can I have a look at it?"

Jerry looked at Jim nervously.

"It's just an old-style football," said Jim, "nothing special about it."

Jerry kept hold of the ball.

"I've never seen one," Tricia persisted. "Can I have a look?"

Tricia got up and went to Jerry, taking the ball out of his hands.

"It certainly is weird," Tricia remarked. "I didn't think it would be as heavy as this. It must hurt when you head that," she said and bounced the ball on the ground, except that it didn't bounce. Tricia picked it up and squeezed it. Then she turned to Jim.

"What's your surname, Jim," she asked.

"Fortune," said Jim

"That's an appropriate name, Jim Fortune." Tricia looked at Jim and smiled.

Johnny wasn't sure what was happening but put two and two together and more or less came up with the correct answer.

"Jim Fortune," said Tricia taking her ID out of her pocket, "I am arresting you and Jerry Fullerton on suspicion of dealing in drugs. You don't have to say anything..."

* * *

Back at the station, after locking the arrested pair in the holding room, Johnny said to Tricia, "I gradually worked out what you were up to, Trish. When did you know it's the football they use to transport drugs?"

"Oh, I knew that back in Colston when I heard Jerry was playing football in Ricton."

"I don't know how you do it, Tricia. I'm beginning to think this police station would close down if it wasn't for you."

"Really," says Tricia. "Oh, Johnny, you've just reminded me. I've got to bring Sargent Peters up to date in Colston. He's the only one there, so he will be happy to know we've arrested Jerry with all the evidence."

"Bloody hell, Tricia," said Johnny, "you're not keeping the Colston Station going as well, are you?"

Tricia laughed.

"Somebody's got to do it, Johnny. By the way, how is your day off going so far?"

"It was going fine until…"

Tricia broke in. "Until it got more exciting by solving a crime?"

"Yeah. I s'pose so."

"Now you know why I find work more fulfilling than odd days off."

"You've got me there," said Johnny. "What I can't figure out is how you always make your work more exciting than mine."

"When you find the answer, Johnny, you might start walking the road to promotion."

Tricia had never seen Johnny so deep in thought.

Story Eighteen - A Case of Identity
Part One

With Tricia's success rate rising, she became the toast of the Station. Steve decided to throw a party in her honour, and all at the Station agreed. Everyone chipped in to hold it at Mike's house as Mike's wife, Debbie, was eager to carry out the preparations, and they'd not have to worry about their two young children, Timmy and Lori.

The party got underway and Johnny used the opportunity to chat up Tricia.

"Well done, Trish," he said, "you'll soon be getting that promotion at this rate, and I hope you do."

"It's nice of you to say that, Johnny," Trish thanked him.

"The only downside will be, I'll have to make an appointment to talk to you, and God knows it's difficult enough already."

"Don't be silly, Johnny, you know I love talking to you. Making fun of you is one of the highlights of my day."

"Oh, Trish, you say the nicest things."

"What's she been saying now, Johnny?" asked Steve, who had overheard Johnny's comment.

"I'm over the moon. Trish has been making fun of me. You can't imagine how I'd feel if she ever paid me a compliment."

"Oh, Johnny," said Tricia, "you know I think you are the best police constable we have."

"Really," said Johnny, "I thought you said I was the worst."

"That too," Tricia replied, "considering you're the only one we have."

Just then, the telephone interrupted their silly banter.

Steve, took his phone from his pocket. "I'd better take this outside." He walked off into the garden. "Hello, Steve Kendall."

"Hi, Steve, it's Dave at the Met. Sorry, it's late, but we've got a case with a link to Ricton."

Steve replied, "What sort of case?"

"It's a murder. Don't suppose you get many of them down there, do you?"

"Not too many," Steve agreed. "So, how is it linked to Ricton?"

"We found this derelict dead in an alley. Right next to the body was a wallet. The details in the wallet indicate it belongs to someone in Ricton."

"Would that be the derelict, perhaps?"

"No. The dead guy had nothing, while this wallet contains credit cards and club membership, not to mention a couple of hundred pounds in notes."

"I see. It's a bit strange that the killer didn't take any of it, isn't it?"

"You're missing the point, Steve. We think it was the killer who dropped the wallet."

"And he lives in Ricton?" Steve asked.

"That's right. I thought that with you living there, you might want to follow up on it for us. You know, visit the guy, check him out, his movements, etcetera."

"OK, Dave. I guess it can wait until the morning, can it."

"Oh, yes, it's a bit late to get an investigation going tonight. Tomorrow will be fine."

"Right, Dave. Give me all the info you can now, and I'll get onto it first thing tomorrow with Detective Constable Mason."

Dave filled Steve in on all the details he could, and they rang off. Steve returned to the party and sought out Mike and Tricia. He relayed the points noted from Dave at the Met, and then took Tricia aside. "We need to visit this guy tomorrow early, so don't get carried away tonight. Sorry about that."

"That's alright, sir. You know me, I'd rather be on a murder case than at a party anytime." Tricia replied.

"Yes, I know. Anyway, this guy's name is Johnathon Stanley-Farthingale and he lives at the large mansion across the river."

"Bit of a poofy name, ain't it?" Tricia surmised.

"Yes, poor bugger, but it's not his fault. You can't choose your parents."

"No, I s'pose not, sir."

The party eventually came to an end, and they all went home, Steve with Susan, and Tricia dropped Johnny off.

"No goodnight kiss, then?" said Johnny, thinking it was worth a try.

"Sorry mate," said Tricia, "can't hang about. I gotta be up early."

* * *

The following morning, Tricia met Steve at the bottom of the long drive to Johnathon Stanley Farthingale's house.

"Morning, sir," said a spritely Tricia as she jumped out of her car to greet him.

"Good morning, Detective Constable. I'm glad to see you are awake this morning. Stay on your toes. This visit is going to be a surprise for Mr Johnathon, so keep your eye out for any little signs."

"Yes, sir. I'll be on the ball."

313

Steve smiled. Yes, he thought, that's my girl, Tricia. "OK, let's go. I'll lead the conversation but don't hold back if you think of anything relevant."

"Right, sir." Tricia got back in her car and followed Steve up to the house. It was a large property. The Stanley-Farthingales had made their money two generations ago from oil imports and were now an established upper-class family in the area.

Steve knocked on the large oak front door, and a butler answered.

"Good morning," said Steve. "I'm Detective Inspector Kendall, and this is Detective Constable Mason. We would like to speak with Mr Johnathon if he is available."

"It's a little early," said the butler. "I'll go to speak to him. Please come inside."

The butler led them into a hall so large that it had seating. Steve and Tricia made themselves comfortable. It was at least ten minutes before the butler ushered Mr Johnathon Stanley-Farthingale into the hallway. Steve introduced himself and Tricia.

"We would like to ask you a few questions, sir, if that is OK," said Steve in his usual polite manner.

"Yes, Detective. What is this all about?" asked Johnathon in a clear Eton accent.

"I am wondering whether or not you have been to London recently," asked Steve.

"Yes, Detective, I was there a few days ago."

"And what did you do there, sir?"

"I visited a friend in Knightsbridge," Johnathon explained.

"What was the purpose of that visit, sir. Could you explain it, please?"

"Of course. I arrived at about mid-day, we had a business meeting that lasted most of the afternoon, and then we went to the local pub in the evening for a meal and a drink. We got back to my friend's house at around ten. I stayed the night and returned early the next day."

"Thank you, sir," said Steve. "Did you visit Stratford while you were there?"

"Stratford? Why would I visit Stratford? I don't believe I have ever been to Stratford apart from a couple of days at the London Olympics," said Johnathon.

"You sound as though you don't like Stratford?" said Steve. "Any particular reason for that?"

"I neither like it nor dislike it," Johnathon replied. "It's in the East End. I tend to spend time in London elsewhere as I have no connections in the East End. Now, if you had asked about Stratford-upon-Avon, that might have been a different matter. What is all this about?"

Steve ignored the question.

"When you were in London, sir, did you lose your wallet?"

"Oh, so that is what this is. Yes, I did, but surely they haven't sent two detectives out to return it to me?"

"No, sir. In fact, I don't have your wallet. But London is where they found it," Steve stated.

"Don't tell me, Detective," said Johnathon. "They found it in Stratford."

"Yes, sir, that is exactly where it was. Unfortunately, they found it next to the body of a murdered homeless person."

"Oh, now, I see. And you think it was me who killed the person. That's quite ironic."

"Ironic? Why so?"

315

"Because only two weeks ago, my mother, and I donated five thousand pounds to the charity for the homeless in Ricton, something we do quite regularly."

"I didn't know that, sir. That is very commendable."

"We are not looking for commendation," said Johnathon quietly.

"One more question, sir, if you don't mind."

"I don't mind. Ask away."

"Do you own a knife?"

"Of course. What kind of knife?"

"I don't mean those that you keep in your cutlery drawer," said Steve pointedly. "Do you own a penknife?"

"I do. I keep it in my jacket pocket. I can't remember the last time I used it, though. Probably to sharpen a pencil." Johnathon looked towards the butler who was hovering in the background. "James," he said, "would you go and bring the jacket to my blue pin-striped suit?"

After a little while, James returned with the jacket over his arm. Johnathon searched through the pockets.

"That's strange," he said, "it isn't here. Are you going to tell me you have found my penknife also?" asks Johnathon.

"Does it look like this?" asked Steve, producing a photo of the knife he'd received by email.

"Yes, that is exactly it. You can see my father's name inscribed on it. He gave it to me when I was a boy."

"Is your father at home, sir?" asked Steve.

"No, Detective. My father died when I was nine years old."

"I'm sorry to hear that," said Steve sympathetically. "That knife, sir, cut the throat of the murdered derelict."

"Oh, my God," said Johnathon wearily. "Have you got any more gems you are going to drop on me?"

"I don't think so, sir. I'm sorry to be the bearer of this unwelcome news."

"Not your fault, Detective. You are just doing your job. I hope you get this bastard and keep me informed."

"I will do, sir. And we will get him; you can be sure of that."

"The wallet, Detective, was there anything in it?"

"There were several credit cards, a business card, a club card, and some money. How much money should there be in it?"

"Not very much. About two-fifty or three hundred pounds. I don't need the credit cards so long as they destroyed them because I have already cancelled them. How much money was there?"

"All of it, I think, sir. Bit odd that," said Steve. "It's unusual to find anything left in a stolen wallet."

"I'm sure it is," said Johnathon.

Tricia spoke for the first time.

"It is almost as if the perpetrator is trying to implicate you, making it look as though the murderer dropped the wallet unintentionally."

"Well, Detectives, I think if I were responsible, it would be a little remiss of me to leave my details to bring you here, don't you think?"

"Criminals have been wise enough to do that before, sir," said Tricia, "but rarely get away with it. Can I ask you a question? Do you know a man called Jensen Montek?"

"Jensen Montek? Now there's a name I doubt I would forget soon. No, Detective, I'm afraid I have never heard that name, to my knowledge, at any time in my life. Who is he?"

"He is the person who discovered the body," said Steve. "As far as I know, he is not under any suspicion."

"OK. If I can be of any further assistance, please feel free to call on me," Johnathon offered.

"Thank you, sir. We might need to speak to you again sometime. In the meantime, thank you for your help, and could you give the details of your friend in Knightsbridge to Detective Constable Mason," said Steve.

When she had recorded the details, he and Tricia walked back to their cars.

* * *

Back at the Station, the two of them compared notes. Tricia had put the recording device on her mobile phone for the interview.

"I'll get this all typed up for my report," she said, "and let you have it tomorrow."

"What are your feelings about the interview, Detective Constable," asked Steve.

"I don't think he's involved, sir. He seemed very surprised about everything, and when you told him his penknife had cut the guy's throat, his face went grey. No, sir, I don't think it was him."

"I agree with you," said Steve. "Let me have your report in duplicate. I'll take one with me when we go to the London Met tomorrow."

"Sir, am I going with you?" said a delighted Tricia.

"Yes, you can come along. It will be a new experience for you."

318

"Yeah, and I can check out the seating arrangements," said Tricia.

"Check out the seating arrangements?" Steve repeated. "What the devil are you talking about."

"Bit slow there, Steve," said Mike, who had been listening to their conversation. "She's booking her place at the Met. And if you don't think she will get there, then you don't know our Tricia as well as you should."

Steve laughed, "Yes, Mike. You got there ahead of me that time. Alright, Detective Constable of the Met, go and write up your report."

"It's Sergeant, sir," says Tricia. "They ain't gonna move me up there before my promotion takes effect."

Steve and Mike laughed.

"We're gonna miss you when you go," joked Mike.

"Really, Sarge. Better appreciate me while I'm still here then," said Tricia, getting in the last word, as she flicked her bottom into her chair and started writing up her report.

* * *

"That's a good report you wrote up yesterday," said Steve as he drove Tricia along the final stretch of the M4 into London.

"Thank you, sir."

Very soon, they entered Knightsbridge.

"We will call on Johnathon's friend, Percival, first," Steve informed Tricia, "seeing as we go through Knightsbridge."

"What is it with these people and their poofy names," Tricia mused. "There's Johnathon Stanley-Fotheringale; now we have Percival Ponsonby-Smythe. The only thing in his favour is that it's not his fault."

"You're right there," Steve replied, "we have to live with the name given us."

"Yeah, I suppose so. At least my name represents the trade my family was in, masons," said Tricia. "What the Ponsonby-Smythes did for a living is anyone's guess."

Steve laughed. It was always amusing to be out with Tricia. "I'm sure it was something respectable, so give him some respect when we meet him."

"I always do, sir, unless he's a bigger arse than he sounds."

The satnav told them they should turn left, with the property two hundred yards on. Then they would reach their destination. Steve pulled up outside, and they made their way to the house. Percival was expecting them and opened the door as soon as they knocked.

"Come in, Detectives," said Percival. "I'll get Dorrie to make you a drink. Tea or Coffee?"

They asked for coffee, and the cook and general housekeeper, went off to make it.

"Is anyone else at home?" asked Tricia.

"Just my mother," Percival informed her. "She is in the study reading a book."

"I imagine your friend Johnathon has been in communication with you since we saw him yesterday?" said Steve.

"Yes, Detective, he told me the gist of your meeting. It's dreadful. Simply dreadful. We could do without any of it."

"That is very true," Steve agreed. "Could I just check the details of Johnathon's visit with you? First, what was the purpose of the visit?"

"Johnathon came down for a business meeting. We needed to discuss some matters related to our mutual arrangements."

"How did that work out?"

"Johnathon arrived at around mid-day. We held our meeting during the afternoon and in the evening, we went to the Crown for a meal and a few drinks. We got back at around ten o'clock. Johnathon stayed the night and left early the next morning. That's about it. Nothing much more that I can tell you."

"I imagine Johnathon told you a man found murdered using his penknife had his wallet beside the body?"

"Yes."

"Did you see his penknife when he was here?" asks Steve.

"No, Detective, I did not."

"Would you have any idea how anyone stole his wallet and penknife? I mean, did you see anything suspicious while he was here?"

"No, nothing. I can't begin to imagine how they got hold of them. It's a damned mystery to both of us," said Percival."

"Sir," Tricia said, interrupting their conversation, "do you know a man called Jensen Montek?"

"No. Never heard of him. Who is he?"

"He is the man who found the body in Stratford," said Tricia. "Do you go to Stratford yourself, sir?"

"No, can't say that I do. It's on the other side of town."

"Well," said Steve, "you corroborate what Johnathon said, so I guess that is all we need at this time."

"Sir," said Tricia, "is it possible to have a quick word with your mother while we're here? It would be silly not to; otherwise, we might have to speak to her at some other time."

"That's no problem," said Percival. "She is in the drawing-room. I'll take you through."

"Thank you, sir," said Tricia, as Percival showed her into the room.

"Good morning, Mrs Ponsonby-Smythe," said Tricia breaking the ice. "This is a lovely house you have here. I am Tricia Mason, Detective Constable." Tricia always enjoyed introducing herself in that way. It made her feel professional.

"Good morning, Miss Mason," Mrs Ponsonby-Smythe responded, ignoring Tricia's title. "How can I be of help?"

"I just want to check the details Percival and Johnathon gave me. It's not that I don't believe them, you understand. It's simply that the more witnesses we have to corroborate events, the better it is for our investigation."

"Of course. Poor Johnathon. He is such a lovely young man."

"Have you known him very long?" asked Tricia.

"I've known him all his life," said Mrs Ponsonby-Smythe. His mother is my oldest friend."

"Oh, I see."

"Not really," said Mrs Ponsonby-Smythe. "No-one could understand our relationship. Poor Amelia. She's had such trauma in her life. I am possibly the only person who knows."

"Knows what?" asked Tricia, her curiosity piqued.

"I'm sorry, I shouldn't have said that."

"Why?" asks Tricia. "Is it a secret?"

"More than you realise," Mrs Ponsonby-Smythe responded. "Anyway, let's forget about that. What do you want to know?"

"Well, I'd like to know more about this secret," said Tricia mischievously, "but, no, could you please tell me about Johnathon's visit."

"Of course. Johnathon arrived at around mid-day, they attended to business all afternoon, and then went off to the Crown for dinner in the evening. They got back home somewhere around ten, and that's it. Johnathan stayed the night and left the next morning."

"Thank you, Mrs Ponsonby-Smythe," said Tricia, "and the secret had nothing to do with his visit, I guess?"

"You really are a detective," Mrs Ponsonby-Smythe said with a smile. "Nice try, but no, it has nothing to do with his visit. My goodness, it happened before either of them were born."

"What did?" Tricia tried a last-ditch attempt, without success.

"Good afternoon, Detective. It was nice meeting you... I think."

Tricia went back to join Steve and Percival. "All done, sir," she reported.

"Well, thank you for your time," said Steve. "We might need to speak to you again, but I think it unlikely."

"You are welcome any time," Percival replied.

When they had left, Tricia said, "This is a bit like a page out of Jeeves and Wooster. Stanley-Farthingales and Ponsonby-Smythes."

"I didn't put you down as a reader of Jeeves and Wooster," said Steve pointedly.

"Mrs Ponsonby-Smythe was reading one when I interviewed her. She's got a secret, but she wouldn't tell me what it was."

"What sort of secret?"

"Sir, if I knew that, it wouldn't still be a secret."

"I guess not." Steve smiled.

At the car, Steve said, "Before we leave Knightsbridge, I'd like to check out the Crown."

"We can walk down there," said Tricia. "It's at the bottom on the corner. I saw it when we arrived."

Story Eighteen - A Case of Identity
Part Two

It was quite empty in the Crown. The lounge was a salubrious modern affair with expensive tables and chairs all around. Looking through to the adjoining bar, they could see a darts corner and a pool table. A couple of young lads were playing pool and just one or two people were drinking. The bartender came over to them.

Steve made their introductions.

"What can I do for you, Detective? Is this about the street fight outside the other night?"

"No," Steve replied, "I am wondering if you know a man called Percival…"

"Ponsonby-Smythe," the barman finished. "Yes, Detective, I know him. He lives at the top of the street."

"That's the one," said Steve. "Was he in here about three nights ago?"

"Yes. He came in with a friend. They had dinner and a couple of drinks. Sat over there." The barman indicated a particular table.

"Any idea what time they came and went?" Steve enquired.

The barman finished drying a glass and placed it on the shelf. "Came in about six or six-thirty. Left around ten." he seemed quite precise in his timings.

"Did either or both of them have any reason to leave for a period during the evening?"

"Not to my knowledge. They were in deep conversation most of the time. "I can't believe they are in any trouble. Probably among the best and most respectable customers we have here."

"No, Barman, they are not in any trouble. We are just routinely checking out a few details."

Tricia spoke for the first time. "Quite apart from them, did anything special or different occur that evening?" she asked.

"Special? Different?" The barman mulled it over. "I can't say that it did. There was a fellow in the next bar though who seemed to be looking their way most of the evening, but that was probably just coincidence."

"Are you certain?" asked Tricia. "What exact coincidence?"

"When they departed, this fellow left at the same time. He bumped into them in the doorway. He apologised, and they all left."

"That's interesting,," said Steve. "What did this man look like?"

"Late twenties, quite scruffy, wearing jeans, a t-shirt, and a hooded jacket. To be honest, up until now, I never gave him much thought. I couldn't tell you what he looked like."

"Well, that is very helpful, thanks."

Steve and Tricia left the Crown and walked back to the car.

"Are we off to the Met now, sir," Tricia asked excitedly.

"We are," Steve confirmed. "We'll be there in about fifteen minutes."

* * *

"Hello, Dave," Steve greeted when they walked into the Detective Superintendent's office.

"Hi, Steve, it's good to have you working on this case with us."

"It's good to be of help," said Steve. "This is Detective Constable Tricia Mason. She is also assisting."

"I've heard good things about you, Constable," said the Super.

"Really?" said Tricia incredulously, the surprise showing by her expression. Then, in the style Steve was more used to, she added, "Who's been blabbing?"

"It's mostly, Steve," said the Super, "so I imagine you are doing something right."

"Whew! That's a relief," says Tricia.

"So, Steve, have you got anything more for me. I read the report. It looks like we might have to rule out Stanley-Fotheringale."

"I agree, Dave. I think we can eliminate his friend, Ponsonby-Smythe too. They might have names like idiots, but they are pretty straight guys, I think."

"I agree, sir," said Tricia. "Straight up, and handsome with it."

"I'm afraid handsome doesn't equate to honest," said the Super, "but maybe, in this case, it does. So, you were quite taken with these guys, were you Constable?"

"They're OK, Super, but I wouldn't want to take on their names. They'd have to change them to Mason-Stanley. That's got a better ring to it."

The Super laughed. "Bit of a comedian you have here, Steve," he commented.

"More than a bit," Steve agreed.

"Never mind, Constable," said the Super to Tricia. "I'll let you into a secret. It has been my experience in the force that the comedic officers are always the best ones. They have more imagination, and that is what you need in this job."

"That's good news, Super. I might make Commissioner after all."

"I don't think you'll require so much comedy at that level, Constable. Right, Steve, where do we go from here?"

"What do you think, Detective Constable?" Steve laid the responsibility on Tricia to decide.

"This guy Jensen Montek, Super, do you have a photo of him," Tricia asked.

The Super picked up the phone and asked the person on the other end to bring in the file. When delivered, he took out a photo and handed it to Tricia. Jensen looks scruffy but is not wearing either a t-shirt or hooded jacket.

"Don't know," said Tricia, "pity we didn't have this photo when we visited the Crown."

"True," said Steve, "he's scruffy but not exactly as described. Do we have an address, Super?"

"Yes, I've got it here on file. He lives in Stratford, the location of the homeless guy."

"He found him?" asked Tricia.

"Yes," the Super agreed, "but you realise we did thoroughly question him when he came in. There was nothing to suggest he did anything more than find the body. At this stage, he is on the list, but not a prime suspect."

"Well, I think we should go and have a chat with him, don't you, sir?"

"Yes, we will before we leave London," Steve agreed. "Dave, we'll push off and see this guy. I've got my psychic constable with me, so we might get somewhere."

"OK, Steve," said Dave, "check back with me if you have anything. Meanwhile, my guys are still working on it, and I'll keep you in the loop."

With that, they left and travelled on to the East End of London. As they drove into Stratford, they passed the Orbit Tower.

"Oh!" exclaimed Tricia. "Look at that monstrosity designed by Anish Kapoor. He's a Turner Prize winner. You can see why can't you? Piece of shit like all the other Turner prize pieces."

"I take it you don't like it, then," Steve observed.

"What's to like. Looks like something that survived an earthquake. I've seen more delightful shapes in a scrapyard."

Steve laughed. "I've got an uneasy feeling you are right," he said. "Gotta take the next left up here and then a right."

Steve found the address and parked up as best he could, seeing that no parking signs littered the place everywhere.

"Where do these poor buggers park their cars?" asked Tricia.

"With the rent on these premises," said Steve, "I doubt many of them can afford a car."

"Yeah, I reckon you're right. Still, there's plenty of transport to be had, so I doubt they even need a car. It's a different world here, ain't it?"

Approaching the house, Steve knocked on the front door. They got no response, so searched, without success, for a rear entrance.

"He's not in," said a voice behind them. It came from an elderly lady living next door.

"We are looking for Jensen Montek," said Steve.

"Yeah, he's the one who lives there, but he ain't in. I seen him go out this morning an' he ain't come back yet."

"Any idea when he might return?" asked Steve.

"Couldn't say."

"Just to be certain we are talking about the same guy," said Tricia, pulling out his photo. "Is this Jensen Montek?"

"Yeah, that's him. Everyone said he never looked like his mother. She died about three months ago, yer know."

"No," said Tricia, "we didn't know that. And he didn't look like his mother? Must have looked like his father then."

"Nope. Well, maybe. I never seen 'em."

"Never seen who?"

"His mother an' father. Adopted 'e was, when he was just a week or so old. Cute little bugger, too."

"So, you've known him all his life," said Steve.

"Yeah. 'E ain't bin the same since 'is mother died. 'E started looking fer his birth parents."

"Did he find them?" asked Tricia.

"No idea," said the neighbour. "Who shall I say called if I see him?"

"Never mind," said Steve. "We'll catch up with him another time."

"Yeah," Tricia replied, looking puzzled. It was a look Steve had seen on her before. Something was going through her mind, and usually, it meant she was onto something he had missed.

"What's up, Trish," he said, using her given name. "Something on your mind?"

"Yes, sir, something just occurred to me. Never mind, I'll sort it out."

"OK," said Steve. "Let's go."

* * *

Back at Ricton, Tricia typed up the day's report and gave it to Steve.

330

"I'll get this off to Dave in the morning," he said.

"Sir," said Tricia, "would it be OK if go to London tomorrow? I can drop this off, and then there are a couple of things I'd like to check into."

Steve realised that Tricia had something going. Something he hadn't considered and that, if left to her own devices, she would probably come up with the goods, as she usually did. Best to let her do her thing, he thought.

"OK, Detective Constable, I don't know what you have on your mind, but go ahead. I'll check with you when you return."

* * *

Two days later, Tricia marched into the office with the confidence of a conquering invader. Her dog, Tricky, left at the station, jumped up into her arms, stealing her limelight. But they couldn't mistake she had something important to tell them.

"Here we go again," said Johnny, "what have you been up to this time?"

"I guess she is about to tell us," said Sergeant Mike. "Look at her; she is about to explode."

"Come on," Steve invited, "take a seat and let us in on your solo visit to the London Met."

Tricia turned her chair around to face them and made herself comfortable.

"I did go to the Met Office, it's true, but only to drop off the report of the day before," she said, "I didn't spend any time there. No, I went on to Stratford. I was hoping to catch up with Jensen Montek, but unfortunately, he was not in again."

"That was a wasted journey then," Steve interrupted.

"Oh, no, sir, I wasn't too concerned about that. I spoke to his neighbour again. She was accommodating.

331

I asked her, since she has known Jensen all his life, how old he was, and she toldl me. It fitted with what I suspected."

Johnny groaned, and Tricia gave him such a withering look that he at once shut up and sat quietly.

"What did you suspect?" asked Steve.

"I'm coming to that, sir," said Tricia with some irritation, "if you would just have a little patience."

"OK, go on."

"When I left the neighbour - never did get her name - I was so excited, I went to the local records office. I wanted some details of Jensen's birth mother. Fortunately, they had them on hand because Jensen had been making inquiries there himself quite recently. As soon as I saw the name of his birth mother, I knew I was on the right track." Tricia paused for effect. It worked.

"Come on, Tricia," said Johnny, "don't keep us all in suspense."

"Jensen's birth mother's name was Miss Amelia Stanley."

Tricia pauses for effect.

"Not connected to the Stanley-Fotheringales," said Steve incredulously. "I don't believe it. And you suspected that, Tricia? How come?"

"It was the photograph, sir."

"What photograph?"

"The photo of Jensen, of course. I noticed a strong resemblance to Johnathon."

Steve opened the case file that lay on his desk and checked the photo.

"Well, you're damned right," he said, "I didn't notice that before, but they are like brothers."

"That's because they are brothers," Tricia pointed out unnecessarily. "The photo simply clinched it. Mrs

Ponsonby-Smythe told me that Amelia had a traumatic experience before either Johnathon or Percival was born. I put two and two together, and…"

"You're always doing that," Johnny interrupted. "How is it that when I do it, the arithmetic doesn't add up like yours?"

"Johnny, that's a whole separate subject. It would take too long to go into that right now," Tricia joked.

"So, what did you do next," asked Steve.

"I drove back to Ricton and located our records office. They were about to close, but fortunately, stayed open for me. I discovered that the date of the Stanley-Fotheringale's marriage was about two and a half years after Jensen's birth and that Johnathon was born about a year later. Everything was slotting into place."

"But what about the murder?" asks Johnny. "How does that get solved?"

"I have to be honest," said Tricia, "there's still a little work to do on it, but I'm sure the Met office will quickly sort that out. This is what I think. Jensen discovered his mother, or rather his brother is one of the wealthiest people in the country. Johnathon's father died in a mountaineering accident when he was nine years old, and all his wealth and business remained in trust by his mother until Johnathon was twenty-one.

Jensen must have thought if he just turned up, they might not accept him, but if he could discredit Johnathon, his mother would be more inclined to have him back. Perhaps he hoped the fortune and business would convert to him, so he set out to frame his birth brother for murder. When he left both the wallet and the penknife at the crime scene, I thought that was either a perfect tactic or extremely stupid. Turns out it was the latter."

"Well, Detective Constable, you have given the Met motive and opportunity. I'm sure it will be simple to tie Jensen into the incident at the Crown public house, and they will have their case sewn up. If you can make out your report for the Met, I'll get in touch with Dave and explain. They can arrest this Jensen guy while he isn't expecting it. Well done."

"You know, Steve, we were only joking when we said Tricia would soon be at the Met," said Mike. "Now, I'm not so sure."

"I like the sound of Detective Sergeant Mason," said Tricia. "Don't you think it's got a nice ring to it?"

Story Nineteen – The Gemini Murders
Part One

Tricia's great success with the recent case involving the Met and her promised promotion finally arriving, meant she was more than keen to engage in an important case in her new role as Detective Sergeant. But it wasn't happening. *'Sod's law,'* Tricia called it. But giving it names didn't help. Nevertheless, she always kept her smiling face and good nature. Tonight was quite exceptional, and Susan was not slow to notice.

"Tricia, you are positively glowing this evening. You haven't had another promotion, have you?" asked Susan.

"What, you mean, to Superintendent, or something?"

Susan laughed. "I don't think that will happen just yet."

"Wouldn't accept it, anyway," Tricia replied.

"Why is that?"

"I'm holding out for Commander. Got a better ring to it."

"Anything that has Tricia after it has a good ring. So, why are you glowing this evening?"

"I gotta nice letter today."

"Really. Who was it from and why was it so nice? You sure it wasn't another promotion?" Susan joked.

"I've never told you this," said Tricia. "Never told anyone. You remember that case a while back where a sniper was knocking off drug dealers?"

"Yes, I remember. You did a good job of solving it if I recall. Except you never caught up with the suspects."

"That's the one. The reason I never said anything, is because one of the homeless ex-soldiers accommodated by the killers was an old friend of mine."

"Well, you kept that quiet, Tricia," said Susan. "Who was he?"

"He was my childhood sweetheart." Tricia dropped the comment on Susan as though the guy was just someone she met in the street.

"Well, now I'm upset," said Susan. "You've never mentioned a sweetheart to me."

"Really?" said Tricia. "I thought I did."

"When was that?"

"A few seconds ago," Tricia joked.

"Come on. Now you've got to tell me all about it."

Tricia related the story while Susan sat, taking it all in.

"So, he went to Spain about six months ago, and now you've heard from him."

"Yes."

"Well, come on. Don't keep me in suspense," said Susan, filled with anticipation and excitement.

"He won some money on the European lottery. Not a lot, but enough for him to come home and get himself a place here."

"Damn, that was lucky."

"Yes, I hope it's just luck, and his army buddies in Spain aren't running some dodgy racket. He says he's going to buy a house here in Ricton."

"I don't know whether to be happy or sad," said Susan. "That probably means an end to our evenings out. You'll be wanting to spend time with him."

"Susan, nothing will ever interfere with our evenings out. These times we have together keep me sane after dealing with lowlifes most days."

Just then, Tricia's mobile rang. She saw the call was from Sergeant Mike who was on duty at the station.

"Sorry, Susan, it's Mike. Ain't no one able to cope when I'm not there."

Susan rolled her eyes.

"Hello, Sarge. What's up?"

"Sorry to interrupt your night out, but a body has turned up in the park, down by the river. Stephen is in London until tomorrow. I've sent the constable down there. Can you join him asap?"

"Sure, Sarge, right away." Turning to Susan, she explained the situation.

"You don't have your car here, Tricia," said Susan. "I'll take you and wait until you finish."

"Thanks. I don't know how long I'll be, so you don't have to wait if it takes some time."

"We'll play it by ear," said Susan. "Let's go."

* * *

Johnny was at the crime scene taping off the area when Tricia arrived. The doctor was also there with an ambulance. The body lay in the open grass about thirty feet from the riverbank.

"What have we got, Johnny?" Tricia asked as she ducked under the police tape.

"Young lad here. Can't be more than sixteen years old. Had his throat cut," said Johnny.

Tricia stooped down to look at him in the light of Johnny's torch.

"He wouldn't have lasted long," said the doctor as he approached Tricia.

"Oh, hello, Dr Handsworthy," Tricia greeted him as she shook his hand. "This is a nasty one."

"Very," the doctor agreed.

"I guess having my dinner interrupted is nothing compared to what his parents will endure. Anyone know the kid? He looks familiar." Tricia looked at Johnny questioningly.

"Yeah," said Johnny. "I've seen him about. I've got an idea I had dealings with him in Crickle Street. Hangs around with young Jimmy Carter."

"Is that the kid we grabbed for shoplifting?"

"Yeah, that's the one. I know where he lives."

Doctor Handsworthy interrupted them. "Detective Sergeant, have you noticed those odd cuts on his cheek," he asked.

"Yes, Doctor."

"Any idea what it is?"

"Yes. It's the symbol, pi, the Zodiac sign for Gemini."

"Crikey, how'd you know that?" asked Johnny, impressed with Tricia's knowledge.

"I know it, Constable, because it's my Zodiac sign. I'm a Gemini."

"Jesus, you don't think it was special for you to find it, do you?"

"Hadn't thought of that. Good point," said Tricia.

"Might get a lead if that's the case," said Johnny. "Must be a few people pissed with you. Not me, of course."

"But who knows my birthday? Don't think you even know it, do you?"

"Not 'til you just said, no."

"It's on the left cheek," Tricia commented. "Maybe that's significant. Are you taking notes, constable?"

"Er, no. Yes," said Johnny, taking his notebook out of his pocket and licking the end of his pencil for no good reason.

"We'll need to get the boys from the Colston Station out here," Tricia stated. "I'll give Mike a ring and get him onto it. We have to search for the weapon and anything else relevant."

"Can we take the body away now, Detective Sargent Mason?" the doctor inquired.

"I think so, Doctor. But let's be doubly careful not to disturb the ground too much."

Johnny sprayed marker paint around the outline, the doctor called the two medics over from the ambulance, and they took the body off on a stretcher.

"I'll check with you tomorrow, Doctor. Maybe when you get the body to the morgue, you'll see something not obvious here in the dark. Constable, can you organise some spotlights and a tent out here? I'll get Mike onto the Colston station to give you some help. Then I'll have to find this lad's parents. Where does his mate live?"

After Johnny gave Tricia the address of Jimmy Carter, she phoned Mike at the station.

* * *

Tricia walked across the park to the street and Susan's car.

"Sorry, Susan, this is going to take some time. Any chance of taking me home to get my car."

"Yes, sure," said Susan. "What's the story?"

Tricia wouldn't normally say anything about a new case, but Susan was Steve's partner, and she wouldn't tell her anything that wouldn't be in the paper tomorrow morning.

"Young lad with his throat cut. I expect Steve will be on it as soon as he gets back tomorrow. In the meantime, I have to get things moving."

Susan drove Tricia back to get her car. They said goodnight, and Tricia drove off to the station.

"Hi, Sarge, nasty business, this one."

"Yes, it sounds like it. I've been in touch with Colston, and they'll send three officers to come and help. Steve will be on the case tomorrow to give you a hand. Are you finished for the night?"

"I wish. Johnny recognised the lad, so I'm going to try to find his parents. Not the best job."

"No. Well, good luck with that. I guess I'll see you in the morning then."

Tricia drove off to Crickle Street, where she located the house, parked up outside and went to the door.

"Good evening. Mrs Carter, is it?"

"Yes, that's me."

"I'm Detective Sergeant Tricia Mason. No need for concern. I'm trying to get some details on your son's friend. Name, address, do you have them?"

"You mean Dicky? Dicky Sampson?"

"Maybe. Is that his best friend?"

"Yes. They practically live together. They're away right now, camping."

"Really. Can you get in touch with them? I mean, does Jimmy have his mobile phone with him?" asks Tricia.

"He usually does, but I found it on the side table this morning. So, no, he doesn't."

"Do you have Dicky's address, please?"

"Dicky lives down the street at number forty-four. What's this all about?"

"I can't say right now, Mrs Carter. If I need to speak with you again, I'll get in touch."

Tricia made her way to number forty-four. Usually, a visit of this nature required two people. But with Steve away in London, Mike holding the fort at the station, and Johnny on duty at the crime scene, they were very thin on the ground for a case of this severity. Steve would be back tomorrow, but Tricia had to get as much done as quickly as possible. She knocked on the door of number forty-four.

"Good evening, are you Mrs Sampson?" asked Tricia when the door opened to reveal a little woman wearing overalls and holding a spanner in her hand.

"Yeah. Watcha want? I'm busy."

"So, I see," said Tricia. "I'm sorry to bother you so late in the evening. I'm Detective Sergeant Tricia Mason. Can I have a word with you?"

"What's this about? Dicky ain't in trouble again, is he?"

"Do you know where Dicky is, Mrs Sampson?"

"He's in trouble, ain't he? He's gone camping with that Jimmy Carter. What they bin up to this time?"

"Mrs Sampson, I wonder, do you have a recent photo of Dicky?"

"Got loads of them on my phone."

"Are you in contact with him by phone?"

"Of course, who isn't these days?"

"Perhaps you might call him for me."

Mrs Sampson took her phone from her overalls pocket and selected Dicky's number.

"He's not answering, but it's ringing. That's odd. He always has his phone with him."

"Might I take a look at the photos of Dicky you say you have on your phone?"

Mrs Sampson brought them to the screen and showed Tricia. There was no doubt. The body in the park was definitely Dicky.

"Mrs Sampson, when is Dicky's birthday?" Tricia asked.

"It's December. Why? What are all these questions about?

December would be Sagittarius or Capricorn, not Gemini, which covered dates in June and July. So, no significance there. Now she had the sad chore of telling Mrs Sampson the bad news.

"Can I come inside?" Tricia asked.

"It's a mess in here. I'm trying to sort out the bloody boiler what ain't working. My brother is a useless twat. I tried to get him 'round here to look at it, but he ain't int'rested. Rather spend his time and money down the pub. Lazy bugger."

She led Tricia into the front room, which was a little tidier.

"Sit down, please, Mrs Sampson."

Mrs Sampson took a seat.

"You're frightening me now, Detective," she said. "What's going on?"

"There's no easy way to say this," Tricia started.

"Is he hurt? I knew camping out in the middle of nowhere was a bad idea."

Tricia took Mrs Sampson's hand and delivered the bad news. As expected, Dicky's mother broke down. Tricia took out her phone and contacted a support worker who agreed to come straight round to look after Mrs Sampson. When she arrived, Tricia decided she'd had enough for one day and drove home. The thought that occupied her mind was, *'Where was Jimmy?'*

* * *

Tricia was at the station early the next morning. There was a lot that needed doing to get a good start on this investigation. Mike had organised extra staff from local stations, and they were already arriving.

Three guys from Colston had been out all night searching the park for anything that might be relevant. Johnny had gone home to catch up on some sleep. Jenny Fisher arrived at the office to help, along with Seth Seymour, Gary Noble, and Shelly Leyton. All four were detective constables.

After introductions, Tricia started an investigation board. At the top was a photo with Dicky Sampson's name alongside. next to it, Jimmy Carter's name, but no image.

"I'll visit Mrs Carter this morning and get a photo of Jimmy," said Tricia. "Right. This is the situation so far. The body of Dicky Sampson turned up in the park last evening with his throat cut and a Gemini symbol cut into his cheek."

"What's a Gemini symbol?" asked DC Fisher.

"The Gemini symbol is the Greek letter pi. Of course, pi has other meanings as it's used frequently in mathematics. Right now, we've no idea why."

"Who's Jimmy Carter?" asked DC Noble.

Tricia moved to the board and wrote.

Jimmy Carter and Dicky Sampson are best friends. They had gone camping together.

"Mrs Carter told me last night when I visited her to get Dicky's address. Neither Mrs Sampson nor Mrs Carter knew their destination; only that they were going out into the countryside. We need to find that location. At this moment we don't know if Jimmy is safe."

343

"Is Jimmy a suspect," asked DC Seymour.

"Not at present," said Tricia. "Not until we find him and question him.

"Do we know what transport they had for their camping trip," asked DC Fisher.

"No. We'll need to get that information as soon as possible so we can check CCTV cameras," Tricia explained.

Just then, Mike came into the station.

"Good morning, Sarge," said Tricia. "This is Sergeant Mike Compton. He runs this station."

" 'Morning, Sarge," they greeted him in unison.

"When is DS Kendall due back?" asked Tricia.

"He's on his way. I don't think he'll be too long."

Tricia returned her attention to the constables.

"OK. Jimmy Carter left his phone at home, so we haven't been able to contact him. Dicky had his phone with him, but it hasn't shown up yet. There's a lot to do this morning. I'll be visiting Mrs Carter and Mrs Sampson first and then check with the doctor. DC Fisher, you can come with me."

"Yes, Sarge."

"We'll also look in on Mrs Carter since she is in the same street. DCs Noble and Leyton, when I have the mode of transport, I'll phone it in, and you can check out all the possible CCTV cameras that might have picked them up. We'll have an idea of the direction they were travelling, and perhaps Sergeant Compton could arrange helicopter surveillance of the area."

"OK, Trish, I'll do that."

"DC Seymour, you should go to the crime scene and check whether they have uncovered anything."

"Yes, Sarge."

"OK, Jenny, let's go."

Tricia led Jenny Fisher to her car, and they drove off to see Mrs Carter.

* * *

"Hello, Detective. Dicky's mum told me what happened. Now I'm worried about Jimmy. I haven't heard from him," said Mrs Carter.

"We're worried about him too," said Tricia. "We'll find him. Don't worry. We need to know what transport they were using."

"They went on their motorbikes. They're only little ones, but they've got panniers, and the boys took their backpacks."

"Thanks. Did they say how long they intended camping?"

"No. But knowing Jimmy, I doubt it would be more than a couple of days. He don't like sleeping rough," said Mrs Carter.

"Yeah," Tricia agreed, "neither do I. OK, thank you, Mrs Carter. I'll be in touch as soon as we know something."

"Thank you, Detective."

"What about a photo?" said Jenny.

"Oh, yes, I'd forgotten about that," Tricia admitted. "Do you have a recent photo of Jimmy, Mrs Carter?"

Mrs Carter took a framed photo from the bookshelf.

"Here, I took this about three months ago."

Tricia removed the photo and returned the frame.

"Thanks. There's just one other thing. When is Jimmy's birthday?"

"Jimmy's birthday? What has that got do with anything?"

345

"Sorry, Mrs Carter, it's just something we are investigating. Is it in June, maybe?"

"No, it's 20th February."

"Aquarius," said Tricia, "thanks."

Tricia phoned the boy's transport details through to the station and the two detectives went off to see Mrs Sampson. The support worker opened the door.

"How is she today," asked Tricia.

"Not so good," said the support worker. "I think she would like to see Dicky."

"Yes, I'll see what I can do. Hello, Mrs Sampson. I was just saying to your support that I'll see the doctor later, and we'll get you to identify Dicky."

The tearful Mrs Sampson just nodded her head.

"We haven't heard from Jimmy yet, but we are looking for him. We'll keep you up-to-date, and I'll see what I can do to get you to Doctor Handsworthy later today." Tricia put her arm around Mrs Sampson and gave her a comforting squeeze.

"Thank you," said Mrs Sampson.

"Mrs Sampson, was there ever any animosity between Dicky and Jimmy?"

"No, detective, they were like two peas in a pod. And they protected each other too."

"How do you mean? Have they needed to do so in the past?"

"Yes, there's a man called Stevie something or other who picked on Jimmy, and Dicky set about him. Had the police here too."

"Ah, yes, I remember Constable Johnny Parsons dealing with that. There were no charges made."

"That's right. They said he'd provoked them. Six of one, half dozen of other," Mrs Sampson recalled.

"OK, Mrs Sampson, I'll check the details back at the station, and maybe we'll visit him. Not much to go on, but it's a start. We'll get the perpetrator; you can be sure of that."

Tricia gathered up Jenny Fisher, and they left to go to the hospital.

* * *

"Hello, Doctor Handsworthy, this is Detective Constable Jenny Fisher," Tricia introduced her assistant. "How was the post-mortem? Find anything new?"

"No, Sergeant. Nothing much to go on. The lad died from the slash to his throat. Pretty quickly, too, I'd say. The killer cut the symbol on his face after he was dead. Apart from that, there's nothing."

"Pity," said Tricia. "It's always good to have something as a lead."

"You want to look at the body in the daylight?"

"Yes, Jenny can take a look too, so she knows what we're dealing with. Do you have any photos?"

"I took some and made copies for you."

"Got the symbol on them?" asked Jenny.

"Of course," said the doctor. "I guess that's the only clue you have." He picked up an envelope from his out tray and gave it to Tricia. The two detectives looked at them.

"Yes, it's definitely Dicky," said Tricia. "We obtained a photo of him yesterday."

"Right, follow me, ladies," said Doctor Handsworthy, leading them to the mortuary.

There were eight body containers in a row along the wall. The doctor went to number six and pulled it open. It was empty.

"Damn. I was certain it was number six," he said as he walked along the rows opening each one. Some were empty; some contained bodies. None were Dicky Sampson.

"What's going on," he said to himself. "I'll go check with the nurse, Felicity."

"Where's Dicky Sampson's body?" he asked her.

"I don't know, Doctor. It'll be wherever you put it."

"That's the point; it isn't. I put him in number six and it's empty. And he isn't in any of the others either. Who's been here this morning?"

"I got here at five-thirty, Doctor. No-one has been here. Been on my own most of the time."

"So, where the devil is the body. Get the senior executive here who was responsible from about two-thirty when I left here."

"Yes, Doctor."

The nurse rang the appropriate number; two minutes later the official arrived.

"Who's been here since two-thirty, either officially or unofficially?" asked Doctor Handsworthy.

"What do you mean Doctor?"

"Come on, man. I mean here in this department. Who's been in?"

"No one, Doctor. Only the nurse, and you people. No one else."

"How do you account for the disappearance of a body since two-thirty this morning, when I left?"

"I don't know, doctor. Although I'm responsible for who's allowed in, I'm not everywhere." The official was clearly annoyed. But not as much as Doctor Handsworthy.

"Get security to check every CCTV point. We need to get to the bottom of this."

"Yes, Doctor. I'll get onto it."

Tricia, who witnessed this, spoke up. "I'll send someone over here to work with your security. We need to find that body."

Story Nineteen – The Gemini Murders
Part Two

"With Dicky's body gone missing, I don't have a clue what I'll tell his mother," said Tricia. "I was going to bring her over to identify her son later, but there's not much point in that if you've lost the body."

"Oh, I see. Yes, we'd better work together on this. Strangest thing I ever come across."

"Look, doctor, we've got to get back to the station," said Tricia. With that, they left.

"Jenny, before we go back to the station, I want to look in at the crime scene. You need to see it too. I'll ring the station and get someone out to help security find that bloody body."

When Tricia, with Jenny tagging along, arrived at the park, Chief Inspector Steven Kendall was there. The two ducked under the police tape and into a tent erected over the crime scene. Steven was walking back from the riverbank.

"Morning, Chief Inspector, this is DC Jenny Fisher. We've been making a few calls. The last one was a problem though."

"Hello, DC Fisher, welcome to Ricton. So, what was the problem? Nothing serious, I hope. This case was somewhat clueless to start with."

"No, sir. Not a big problem if you can live without the corpse."

"What do you mean?"

"Bloody body's gone AWOL, sir. Could 'ave swore he was dead last night."

Jenny laughed. Tricia's banter was nothing new to Steve.

"Mind you; it was dark. I could have been mistaken," said Tricia.

"Where has the body gone?" asked Steve.

"That's the problem, sir. No bugger knows. Put in the drawer early this morning and now it's done a runner."

"Gone missing? How the hell can that happen?"

"Security's looking into it, and I've sent someone from the station to go help them."

Steve let out a deep sigh. "OK," he said, "come on, take a look in here." He led them into the tent and pointed to the outline of the body Johnny had marked.

"So, Sergeant, what do you find wrong here?"

"It's pretty obvious, sir. I didn't notice last night as we only had Johnny's torch. There ain't no blood. He had his throat cut, so there ought to be quite a lot."

"You've got it, Sergeant. He died elsewhere and the body was brought here. Not only that, it arrived here by boat up or down the river. There are definite signs of activity on the riverbank."

"Can we go take a look, sir," asked Jenny. Tricia nodded, encouraged thought it encouraging by the DC's initiative.

The three of them strode down to the riverbank, about thirty yards away.

"I'd say only one person brought the body here," said Tricia. "Look at that depression on the edge of the bank and the drag marks through the grass."

"Yes, I agree," said Jenny. "If there'd been two or more people, they'd have carried the body between them. They wouldn't have dragged it up the slope."

"OK, ladies, I think you've summed up the situation. I've taken a good look all around and can't see anything of value. Of course, three constables stomped around all night in the dark. I don't think they took anything away with them. Just left a lot of their footprints behind."

"Can't blame them for that, sir," said Tricia. "We ain't been issued with hoverboards yet."

Jenny covered her mouth and giggled at Tricia's wit.

Steve gave her Jenny an apprehensive glance. "Make good use of this visit to Ricton, Detective Constable. You pay heed to what the Sergeant says, and you'll be able to do a stand-up routine at the next police outing."

"You'll need to get a licence," said Tricia. "I don't do script-writing free."

They all chuckled.

They were still smiling when they arrived back at the station.

"Hello, Guys," said Mike, "why are you all smiling? This case hasn't got much to look happy about."

"Tricia's on the case. Do you want more info?" said Steve.

"Gotcha."

"Right," said Steve, "who do we have here?"

Mike introduced all the helping hands, and Steve looked to Tricia.

"Perhaps you could bring us up-to-date, Sergeant. What have you got?"

Tricia took the photo of Jimmy and pinned it to the board.

"That's Jimmy Carter, Dicky Sampson's friend. As you all know, they set off camping together two days ago, and Jimmy hasn't turned up yet. He doesn't have his phone with him. As far as I know, we haven't found

Dicky's phone either." She looked around for confirmation. No-one offered anything.

"Most of you probably know by now that they set off on lightweight motor-bikes. Has anyone discovered in what direction they went?"

DC Gary Noble spoke up.

"CCTV showed them heading out on the Springfield Road. That's due north. They showed up again near the Longbridge petrol station. That's about twenty-five minutes out of Ricton. After that, they were on the open road, and we've not found them."

Tricia was busy scribbling down the details on the board. Mike spoke up.

"I got in touch with the helicopter service. They sent someone out but haven't reported anything back yet. They're probably still out looking."

Tricia took the envelope Doctor Handsworthy had given her and removed the photos, which she pinned to the board.

"These are photos of the deceased. This one shows the Gemini symbol."

Steve added a comment. "Looking at the crime scene, it's quite clear they dumped the body in the park from the river after the lad was dead. It seems most likely there was only one person involved."

Tricia got everything down on the board.

"Now," she said, "I think most of you are aware that the body has gone walk-about. By that, I mean it is missing. That's under investigation as we speak." She walked over to the large-scale local map on the wall. "Look at this road." Tricia pointed it out on the map. "That's Springfield Road. As you can see, it heads due north from Ricton. Here is the petrol station, the last place anyone saw them. It's a good way out, and they were still travelling north when picked up by the cameras."

"Yes," Steve interrupted. "What's your point?"

"We know they brought the body to the crime-scene by the river. If you look at the river on the map you will see it flows in a generally east-west direction with a couple of bends east and west, which take it south."

"And your point is?" repeated Steve.

"Well, if the lads had driven a good way north – we don't know how far yet – the perpetrator would have to bring either Dicky, or his body, all the way back to Ricton and probably further since the river flows southerly. That seems a little odd when they could have left it out in the country due north."

"Yes, that's a good point. It's a lot of trouble to go to if you just wanted him dead," said Steve.

"So, there's more to it," said Tricia. "One, the perp wanted the body found. That's why he left it in the park. And two, he carved the Gemini symbol for a reason. We need to find out why".

"OK, Sergeant," said Steve. "Does anyone here have any ideas floating in their minds that might give us something to look at re the Gemini symbol?"

"It's not the birth month of either Dicky or Jimmy," said Tricia.

"I heard it was your birth sign," said Jenny. "Maybe that's significant."

"Could be," Tricia agreed, "but I can't see any reason. I didn't know the boy"

The station phone rang by the intake desk and Mike answered it. When he completed the call, he said, "Listen up. That was Morton police on the phone. They heard about this case and said they had a similar case about a month ago. A man's throat was cut, and he had a Gemini symbol on his cheek."

"Bloody 'Ell," said Tricia. "At least that takes me out of the equation."

The phone rang again.

"Getting popular today," said Tricia. "It's not another Gemini murder, is it?"

"It's for you, Tricia," said Mike. "Mrs Sampson."

"Hello, Mrs Sampson, sorry I haven't got back to you yet."

"That's alright, no need," said Mrs Sampson. "He's just come home."

"Who's just come home?"

"Dicky. Jimmy is with him. They got fed up with camping. You don't know how happy I am."

"I don't understand, Mrs Sampson. Can you run that by me again?"

"Dicky's come home. Here, have a word with him."

Dicky came onto the phone.

"Hello."

"Hello, you are Dicky Sampson?"

"Yeah. Why you tell my mum I'm dead?"

"And Jimmy is with you?"

"Yeah. Well, no, he's just gone home."

"OK, Dicky. We'll come around to see you. Don't go out, please."

* * *

"What's going on, Sergeant?" asked Steve.

"I don't know, sir. It's got me beat, and that don't happen often." Tricia went to her desk and sat down. "Dicky Sampson and Jimmy Carter have just arrived home."

"Then who have they got up at the mortuary?" asked Mike.

"Well, that just it. They don't have anyone up at the mortuary, do they? Perhaps we dreamed of this one. I've had some funny dreams before, but this one takes top gun."

"If you are going to the Sampsons now Sergeant, I think I'll come with you," said Steve. "Bring that doctor's photo with you. Come on, let's go."

Tricia took the photo from the board and the two of them set out to Tricia's car. Within ten minutes they were knocking on number forty-four Crickle Street. Mrs Sampson came to the door.

"Come in," she invited. Tricia introduced Detective Superintendent Kendall.

Dicky was in the living room. He was the image of the dead boy in the photo Tricia held. She showed Mrs Sampson. Dicky looked at it with her. They were both dumbfounded.

"Damn, he's the spitting image of you," said Mrs Sampson.

"Mrs Sampson. Do you have something you'd like to tell us?" asked Steve.

"What do you mean?" asked Dicky. "What can mum possibly tell you?"

"It's alright, Dicky," said Mrs Sampson moving to the armchair and sitting down. She put her head in her hands and started sobbing quietly.

"What up, mum?" asked Dicky, concerned.

"Take your time, Mrs Sampson," said Tricia. "I think we know what you are going to tell us."

"No, you don't," said Mrs Sampson, "at least, not all of it."

"Why don't you tell us," said Steve.

Everyone in the room found a seat, and Mrs Sampson started to explain.

"Dicky never knew his dad. I kicked him out two weeks before Dicky was born. He was getting paranoid about the birth."

"Didn't he want children," asked Tricia.

"No, it wasn't that. He had a stupid fear of look-alikes. No sense to it. When he found out about the babies, he went crazy. Said I'd have to kill them. If I didn't, he would. I reported it to my mid-wife. She was very alarmed and said I should report him to the police. Well, the man was sick, not a criminal. So, we had a discussion, and I decided to break off our relationship since we were not married."

"You said babies, Mrs Sampson. What did you mean by that?" asked Steve. "Were you expecting twins?"

"No, sir. I was expecting triplets."

"Strewth, where are the other two?" said Tricia.

"When I got shot of David, Dicky's dad, I was on my own. There was no way I could have managed to support three kids. I had two of them adopted. They were all boys."

"Crikey, Mum," said Dicky, who had been listening quietly to the explanation, "you mean I've got two brothers?"

"I'm afraid not," said Steve.

"Why? I must have them somewhere."

"This morning, we heard from another area that had a similar murder. I anticipate it could be the other brother," Steve explained. "We won't know for certain until we check it. Of course, we will keep you informed, but thanks for the information you've given us."

"Why do you think it might be the other brother?" asked Mrs Sampson.

"Because the victim had the same mark on his cheek."

"What is that mark?"

Tricia interrupted.

"It's the Zodiac sign for Gemini. We didn't know its significance until now. It's also the sign for twins."

"Do you know where this guy, David, is now?" asked Steve.

"No idea. I never wanted to see him again, so I've never bothered to keep tabs on him."

"What's his full name?"

"David Trenchard."

"OK, thanks, Mrs Sampson," said Steve. "I'm pleased your son is alright. I don't think he's in any danger now, but we'll get an officer out here just to be sure."

* * *

Steve and Tricia returned to the station and started taking steps to find Trenchard. Tricia was out front at the case board, the seconded assistants in front of her.

"Right, listen up. You'll see another photo on the board here. His name is Robert Bingham and he lived in Morton. His death was identical to the guy we found in the park. We still haven't identified him by name or address, but you will see a likeness between the two victims. That's because they are brothers, two of triplets. The lad we thought was Dicky Sampson is the third triplet.

"The number one suspect is this guy. No photo yet, just a name, David Trenchard. He used to live locally and worked at the hospital. He moved to London following the birth of the triplets, but some three months ago, he gave up his London hospital job and disappeared. No address established as yet.

"That's our priority, finding him. Although this looks similar to a serial killer case, I don't think it is. Not unless he comes across more identical twins or triplets. He has a phobia about look-alikes. I don't think it has a name yet. Perhaps we'll give it one when we've solved this case. I'd put my name to it, but they'd think I was one. The only phobia I have is not solving a case, so get out there and get to grips with it if you don't want me after you."

A little after midday, Steve spoke to Tricia. "You look tired. You've had a couple of late nights. I'll look after things here. You go home and get some rest, and I'll see you tomorrow."

"Are you sure, sir? I can manage 'til the end of the day."

"No, you get yourself off, and we'll see you tomorrow."

Tricia had something on her mind, so she stopped off at the library to check what was bothering her. She'd seen a book in the library's astrology section on a previous visit, in the area of books on the Zodiac. She found the section and went through the titles. There were dozens of them.

"Who believes all this crap?" she said to herself as she checked through them. Zodiac, by Robert Graysmith; The Zodiac Legacy, Stan Lee; Decode the Stars, Carolyne Faulkner; Modern Astrology, Louise Edington; The Zodiac Revealed, Mark Hewitt. And so, they went. Where the devil was that book she was looking for? Eventually, she found it - Rituals of the Zodiac, by Isaiah Trimble.

Tricia took the book from the shelf and thumbed through it. There it was, precisely what she was looking for. She took the book to the check-out, had it stamped, and made her way home.

Tricia made herself a sandwich, poured a drink, and sat down to look through the book. When she had read all she needed, Tricia picked up the directory and phoned several numbers. All of them were funeral directors. The last one bore fruit.

"Yes, detective, we did produce a coffin with that description. We delivered it yesterday."

"Can you give me the name and address, please? No? OK, I'll come over to you and bring my credentials. Thank you. I'll see you in about one hour; I'm thirty-five miles away."

* * *

Tricia turned up at the station early the next day. Steve was already there, and the team was beginning to arrive. After explaining to Steve what she had discovered, the two of them left in her car. They travelled some fifty miles or more before they arrived at a cottage in the country. It was relatively isolated with no neighbours nearby.

"Right, sir, I think this is Trenchard's home."

"I hope you are right. It's a long way to come on a fool's errand."

Tricia knocked on the door. There was no answer. A post office van pulled up at the gate and the postman emerged.

"What do you have there?" Steve asked, after identifying himself.

"It's just junk mail, detective. No names on it. Everyone gets one."

"Pity," said Tricia.

"Why?" asked the postman. "Do you want to know his name?"

"That's about the size of it," said Steve.

"It's Trenchard," said the postman. "He had a box delivered here yesterday. That's the name the delivery guy had."

"What sort of box?" asked Steve.

"I've an idea it was a huge box, about six foot by three foot and a foot deep," said Tricia.

"Yes, it was something like that," said the postman.

"How'd you know that?" asked Steve.

Tricia explained.

"According to rituals that I read in a book, if identical twins die before the age of eighteen, one must mark them with a Gemini sign, place them side by side in a coffin, and bury them in a remote location."

"Why?"

"I don't know, sir. It's in a stupid Zodiac book, so nothing makes sense."

"Are you suggesting they are here?" said Steve, with an incredulous look on his face.

"Maybe, I don't know. Perhaps they're not buried yet. Let's take a look."

They looked in the rear garden. There was a hole dug, the size of a burial grave. It was empty. They looked in the rear window. The box delivered was there on the table. It was the size of two coffins, highly polished with brass handles on the sides. It looked as though he'd screwed the lid down already.

"Damn it, Tricia, I think both bodies are already in that coffin. Let's make ourselves scarce, and I'll phone Mike."

Steve made arrangements for Mike and six others in three cars to drive out to Trenchard's home.

"When you get here, Mike, let me know and keep everyone out of sight. Hide their vehicles away from the main road and wait for my call. I'll give the signal to come to the property. No sirens."

"Right, Steve, will do."

"Oh, you'd better have a couple of firearms with you. That better be you and Johnny. I don't know much about our imported officers."

It was two hours before anything significant happened. Trenchard pulled up in a beaten-up Ford Escort and pulled off the road into the property. The man got out. He was about forty or forty-five years old and wore a white doctor's coat. Steve rang Mike, and everyone stood by.

Trenchard entered the property. Tricia had hidden her car from sight, and both she and Steve were in the back garden. Steve rang Mike's number and they sat back under the rear kitchen window, waiting. In less than two minutes, four cars pulled up at the cottage. Six officers plus Mike got out. Four went to the front door, two of them with a battering ram, and the others joined Steve and Tricia at the rear of the cottage.

As the officers broke down the front door, Trenchard ran out the back into the arms of the group of officers waiting for him. It was all over in a matter of seconds. After handcuffing Trenchard, Steve and Tricia entered the back door into the kitchen. One of the constables who'd come in through the front opened up the coffin. Inside were the wasted lives of the two murdered seventeen-year-old triplets.

* * *

Back at the station, Steve was addressing the officers before they returned to their local forces.

"Thank you, everyone, we've appreciated your help on this case. Glad we were able to tie it up in such a quick time. Particular thanks go to Detective Sergeant Mason. I guess her peculiar mind has its benefits after all. No-one else but Tricia would read a book called 'Rituals of the Zodiac' to solve a double murder."

"Careful, sir," said Tricia, "you've no idea what other dodgy stuff I picked up from that book. By the way, sir, what date is your birthday?"

Story 20 - Invasion
Part one

Everyone at the Ricton police station had arrived on time for a new day of work, except Tricia.

The street door opened, and in ran little Tricky, Tricia's dog, followed by Tricia. There came a gasp from everyone there. Tricia had donned her uniform, unusual for her since she was a plainclothes detective. The striking difference that made all catch their breath were the three stripes displayed on her arm.

"Tricia," said Steve. "Why are you in uniform?"

"Just keeping you guys up to date," Tricia replied.

"How have you managed to get your uniform adjusted so quickly?" asked Johnny.

"Silly boy, I've had it ready these past three months."

"Bloody hell. Talk about confidence," said Johnny. "I wouldn't have the nerve to do that."

"Well, Tricia has the nerve and the confidence," Mike spoke up. "I guess that's why she's so good at her job."

"Yes," Steve agreed, "and the Met has noted it, too." Turning to Mike, he asked, "Can you manage here without me and Tricia for a couple of days?"

"I managed before any of you came here, so I guess I'll manage again. Why? Are you two going somewhere?"

"Yes, sir," said Tricia showing a great deal of interest. "Where are we off to?"

"We have to report to the Met as soon as we can. I reckon that means today."

"What for, sir?"

"I've no idea, Detective Sergeant, but those are our orders."

"Crikey."

Steve looked Tricia over. "I think you had best go home and get back into civvies. Sorry, I realise you want to show off today. No chance of that, though."

"Right-o, sir. I'll go now." She paused at the door. "Bloody hell. Promotion and a Met job."

"Oh and prepare for a few overnight stays."

"Right, sir. Anything else?"

"Just one thing. The Met asked if you could bring Tricky."

"Bloody hell. They ain't promoting him too, are they?"

Steve went into his office. Johnny looked at Mike. "I wonder what that's all about, Sergeant. Any idea?"

"No, none. I guess if Steve doesn't know, then I'm hardly likely to produce anything of value."

"No, I s'pose not. Tricia looked happy, so I think this must be the best day of her life." Johnny looked downcast. "I wish I had half of her talent and confidence."

"Don't worry, Constable. The Force needs all kinds, including you. Just be thankful you have a job. Many don't."

"Yeah. I guess you're right."

Johnny picked up his hat and made his way to the door. "Better get on the beat. See you later, Sarge."

* * *

Steve drove Tricia to London in his vehicle. Tricky slept in his basket on the back seat.

"I wonder why they asked me to bring him," said Tricia. "That's bloody odd. It ain't as if he's a bloodhound."

"No," Steve laughed. "I have a little idea, but I don't want to presume anything. Let's wait for a proper briefing at the Met."

Tricia sighed. "Yeah, I s'pose so. Odd though, ain't it?"

Steve pulled in at The Yard shortly before eleven. With Tricky on his lead, they made their way to Superintendent David Forthright's office, Steve's friend.

"Morning, Dave," Steve greeted the Super. "You've met Detective Tricia Mason before."

"Yes, and I think congratulations are in order. How does it feel being a sergeant?"

"Haven't had time to get used to it yet, sir. Only 'ad me three stripes on fer 'alf an 'our before I 'ad ter take 'em off."

"Yes, she came in wearing her uniform this morning," Steve explained. "I couldn't believe she already had her stripes on the sleeve. Apparently, she's had them on for the past couple of months."

"Be Prepared. That's the old scout motto," said Tricia. "If it's good enough fer them, it's good enough fer me."

"Right," said the Super, "we'll have a coffee, and then I'll brief you on what this is about."

A young constable came in and prepared their coffee. They chinwagged a little before the Super got into his explanation.

"This is something quite different to anything you, or anyone else for that matter, has got involved in before."

"That sounds interesting," Steve interrupted.

"It might be. Then again, it might not. This is the situation. Steve will remember, and you, Sergeant, will probably have read about an incident that occurred in

366

1980. It is commonly known as the Rendlesham Forest Incident."

"Ah, yes. I've read about it," said Tricia. "A so-called UFO appeared in the forest. Lotta cobblers, I'd say."

"Yes, Sergeant, and you'd almost certainly be correct. The police didn't get involved much. They visited the site on the 26th of December and again the next day but found nothing to indicate it might be a UFO. Since the sighting occurred in the forest near the US Airforce base, it mainly interested Americans. They are always up for these kinds of events. The Brits here remained rational and either put it down to unusual weather conditions or a blip in the beams from the Orford Lighthouse, which is on the line of view of the incident."

"If I remember correctly," said Steve, "the American Airforce personnel exaggerated what had occurred and set the rumours off. The Base Commander, some guy named Halt, got excited about it, and then a sergeant – can't remember his name – made other unsubstantiated claims of an unknown craft in the forest."

"That's right. His name is Jim Penniston. Detective Sergeant Mason is spot on. Cobblers is a good word for Penniston's account." The Super scoffed at the idea.

"So, Dave, what has this to do with why they called us in?"

"Good question, Steve. Three people in the Rendlesham area have reported to the station at Martlesham, near Ipswich, another similar incident in much the same area. We have two guys at Martlesham, plus you and Sergeant Mason, who will set up a very secretive group to look into it. For someone to go to the amount of trouble they have for this event, there has to be something in it. You guys will find out."

"What's Tricky got to do with it?" asked Tricia. "You ain't setting him up for abduction by aliens, are you?"

"Ha ha. Don't worry, Sergeant. He won't need to make out any reports. Knowing you take your dog to the station and wouldn't want to leave him for long, I thought he might be useful in keeping your low profile. You'd be just another dog-walker to an observer." the Super explained.

"Ah, gotcha."

Steve asked, "What have these three people seen?"

"Two of them saw a bright blue light between the foliage, and the other one felt and saw a strong wind emanating from the same wooded area. He also heard strange music at the time. As he is a musician, he wrote down the notes he heard. Did you ever watch the film Close Encounters of the Third Kind? I heard a playback, and it's the same as that."

"Yes," said Steve. "That's an iconic sound. Richard Dreyfuss, wasn't it?"

"That's right. So, you know the sound. Good."

"I can't understand why we are here. It's obviously a hoax. What's so important?"

"Look. In the original incident, our police didn't get involved. The US military was all over it, and if they wanted to waste their time because of their infatuation with UFOs and the supernatural in all its variations, well, the police let them get on with it. But one police officer has a brilliant theory."

"Really?" said Tricia. "We leave the Yanks to it because they are superstitious, but we get involved because of a theory. Ain't a lot of difference, is there?"

"On the face of it," said the Super, "it might not seem so. You might change your mind when you hear the theory."

"Go on then. I'll buy it."

"Later, Sergeant. Let's take a break and go for some lunch. We'll discuss it this afternoon."

They all walked out to the car park. Tricia put Tricky back into Steve's vehicle.

"I'll have to give him a short walk after our break," Tricia said. "He'll need feeding too."

After Tricia settled Tricky in the car and made sure he had enough cool fresh air circulating, Steve locked the door, and the Super guided them to his eating place nearby.

* * *

After Lunch, and Tricky's feeding time, the three police officers resumed the briefing in the Super's office.

"Right, Sergeant Mason, you had some reservations about following a theory," the Super started. "Let me explain."

Steve and Tricia settled back in their seats and paid keen attention to what the Super told them.

"At the time of the first UFO incident in nineteen-eighty, a man had purchased a large country house in the area. The police in London knew him, a lifelong criminal. From the cost and quality of his country house, he'd amassed a considerable amount of money from his criminal activities. It was rumoured he kept most of his money in the house; this was backed up by his bank statements. Several weeks after the UFO incident, ironically, burglars targeted his home. Soon after, he sold up and moved to Spain."

"Ah, yes," said Tricia. "The criminal's country of choice."

"Now, this is the theory," the Super continued. "Those responsible for the UFO hoax had anticipated a massive police involvement. Seeing that we never became very much involved in it, we hadn't focused much on the hoaxers. If we had become embroiled in the UFO fiasco, most of our diminishing police personnel would have concentrated in and around the Rendlesham Forest. As that didn't happen, the instigators had to carry out their burglary later, as the opportunity presented itself.

"I know it's a flimsy theory, but it makes a certain amount of sense. If it's right, a group of criminals, possibly related to the original ones, could be planning something big in the area."

Steve spoke up. "If their plan didn't work the first time around, why would they repeat it?"

"That's a good question, Steve," said the Super. "Of course, there's nothing that proves the theory correct, but right now, there is a special exhibition in Woodbridge, where some extremely valuable objects are on loan for display."

"What objects are they?" asked Tricia.

"There's an art exhibition concentrated on the works of Constable. Not one of our constables, I might add. No, John Constable was born in Suffolk, and some of his most valuable paintings are of Suffolk scenes. The Haywain is probably the one you know most about."

"Yes, I studied Constable at college. There's Dedham Vale, Flatford Mill, Cottage in a Cornfield, Dedham Lock, Landscape with Boys Fishing, and many more. Too many to remember."

"Are police present at the exhibition?" Steve asked.

"Too right. Those paintings are worth millions. After learning of this theory, they've doubled the number of officers present."

"Right."

"Your involvement will concentrate on the UFO business. Hopefully, we might get a lead on those responsible."

"Just as well the Americans have left the area," said Tricia. "Otherwise, there'd be another internationally advertised UFO incident to keep the nutjobs engaged."

The Superintendent laughed. "So, that's it. You guys had best be on your way. Check-in at Martlesham and ask for Detective Inspector Robert Garfield and Detective Constable Shelly Turnbull. They are the two assigned to this case. They'll bring you up-to-date and direct you to your accommodation."

* * *

At the Martlesham Police Headquarters, a huge building set behind trees and off the main road, Steve located the two assigned to the Rendlesham UFO incident and introduced himself.

"Hi, Robert, I think you are expecting us. I'm Steve Kendall, and this is Tricia Mason."

"Hello, Steve, Tricia, this is Detective Constable Shelly Turnbull."

"I don't know how we can help, but we'll see. How are you progressing with this debacle?"

Robert Garfield smiled. "That's a good word to describe it. I can't understand how anyone takes these incidents seriously."

"Me neither. As for Tricia, well, I think you'll know soon enough what she thinks." Steve looked at Tricia.

"Don't get me started," she said, "except on the investigation. Can't wait to get onto that."

"I like your attitude, Sergeant. But don't get too excited. I don't think this one will take us far."

"We'll see about that," said Tricia. "Are we going to the site?"

"She's enthusiastic," said Robert Garfield. "One thing at a time, though. We'll take you to your accommodation first. It's on the way."

The house was a four-bedroomed property in Rendlesham. The police had rented it for the operation, and Steve and Tricia found a bedroom each and settled in their luggage. After that, they travelled with Robert and Shelly about a mile to the visitors parking area at the forest.

Tricia put Tricky on his lead, and they headed down a walkway between the trees. It was about eight feet wide, and off to each side were numerous smaller pathways, some almost too narrow to negotiate. Robert looked around to check for privacy and took them down one of the narrow paths. About fifty yards on, he went off-track into the shrubbery between the trees. Everyone followed.

"Try not to disturb the undergrowth too much," said Robert. "If we make it look like a beaten track, everyone will use it."

The growth was thick and included brambles so, Tricia carried Tricky. They reached a clearing between the trees. A circular area, burnt and depleted of all shrubbery, gave the impression that a UFO had settled there. It was about twenty feet in diameter.

"If this was a UFO," Tricia observed, "it either contained only one, perhaps two aliens, or they were all midgets. Still, I suppose they might be if they travelled from Mars."

"They'd have to travel from further away," said Shelly, "if they came from a distant planet."

"Yeah, then to get a bunch of them in this small craft, they'd have to be about two feet tall."

"Can't imagine that," said Shelly.

"Perhaps they are so advanced that their kids do all the space travel. More economic. Imagine a creche of three-year-olds spilling out here in the forest."

"Yes, alright, Tricia," said Steve. "I know you love your jokes, but we need to investigate this seriously."

"Sure, sir, but you gotta consider all possibilities."

"You have but excluding the ridiculous."

Steve and Tricia looked around the circular area. The groundcover showed definite burning. It was also exceptionally flat, as if a compactor had levelled the area. There were three indents about twelve inches in from the perimeter, forming a triangle. The repressions took on the shape of a plastic cup. Tricia paced between them and across them. They appeared accurately spaced. Suddenly, she dropped to her knees in the centre of the circle.

"Well, bugger me," she said. "Take a look at this."

Gathering around Tricia, she pointed out what could only be a hole produced by a stake or a rod.

"What do you think that is?" asked Robert. "I never noticed it when I visited before."

"It's the point from where they inscribed the circle," Tricia explained. "You can't create a circle this accurate without a measuring device."

"So, you're ruling out aliens," said Steve. "That's progress."

"Yeah, can't get hung up on those little buggers. They must have driven a stake into the ground here, and with a string, marked out the circle."

"Well done, Tricia," Shelly said, with admiration in her voice. "Aliens are well and truly dead. This was certainly planned to fool us."

Tricia moved from the centre and now drew their attention to something else.

"Here are some more marks. It's only a small depression, but I'd say something quite heavy stood here."

"Come on, genius," said Robert. "Tell us what stood there."

"OK," said Tricia with confidence. "Reports say a bright blue light shone from here. So, I'd say that is where they stood the light. It had to be extremely bright, so I reckon it was something like a searchlight."

"You're probably right," said Robert. "That would be quite a heavy piece of equipment. I wonder how the hoaxers got it in here."

Tricia moved off into the wooded area opposite the direction they had entered the clearing.

"Wow! Here's your answer."

They all followed to discover a clear path, broader than the entrance. Tricia put Tricky down, and followed the track. Eventually, it emerged onto a vehicle-width path on the edge of the forest. Following it back in the direction they started, it finally brought them to the clearing where they'd parked their cars.

"Well done," said Steve. "It looks like we've got to grips with this hoax pretty quickly. Now we should keep a surreptitious eye out for anyone suspicious. I don't think these hoaxers will have abandoned this masquerade yet."

"How long have you been on this case?" asked Tricia.

"We only got it today," Shelly replied.

"So, you haven't done anything much," Steve surmised. "That's good. We'll work as a team. We've already made a positive start by figuring out how they set this up. We need to look out for anyone here who looks a little out of place."

"How do you mean?" asked Shelly.

"Most people here are either taking exercise or walking their dogs. So, keep your eyes peeled for any who don't appear to fall into those categories."

"Like him over there," said Tricia, nodding her head in her direction of sight.

A man stood on the edge of the main path, speaking into his phone.

"Exactly," said Steve. "He's neither taking exercise nor dog-walking."

"I noticed him when we arrived," Tricia admitted. "He was on his phone then, too, so he's a prime example."

"Look," Steve interrupted, "the amount of travelling we've done today has eaten into our time. But we've made good progress, so we'll call it a day here soon. Robert and Shelley, go off to the car. I want to try something out with Tricia before we leave."

Steve turned to Tricia.

"We'll stroll down where that guy is. I don't smoke these days, but I keep a packet and lighter in my pocket for just such occasions as this."

"Crikey, sir, you ain't gonna make him talk using fag burns, are yer?" How did Tricia come up with these comic comments?

"No, Sergeant. This lighter doesn't work until you shake it. I'll try lighting a cigarette as we walk past him and stop to ask him for a light. Then we'll play it by ear. You're good at that."

"Right."

Steve had put a cigarette in his mouth and flicked his lighter constantly. The man watched as they approached.

"Damned thing," said Steve. "Excuse me. You don't have a light do you?"

The man dropped his phone arm and put his hand in his pocket. "Sure," he said. "You ain't got a spare cig, have you?"

Steve took the packet from his pocket and offered the man a cigarette, which he accepted while lighting Steve's. Then he lit his own.

"Thanks. I needed that," said Steve. "Haven't had one since we started our walk. We're on our way home now. Are you coming or going?"

"Oh, I'll be off soon," the man replied.

"Don't know why all the fuss. Do you?" Tricia butted in.

"What fuss?" the man looked puzzled.

"That repeat of the old UFO business." Said Tricia. "I think those people are on crack. Just seeing things."

"Oh, that. Why? Don't you believe it?"

"No. Lotta rubbish."

"Could be something in it," said the man. "I was here that evening and thought I saw something."

"What kind of something?" Steve inquired.

"Lights. I saw some lights."

"Really. Where?"

"Don't know exactly. Somewhere in the trees."

"Did you report it?"

"No. I don't want to get involved," said the man casually.

"Good point. Otherwise, the police would be all over it," said Tricia.

"Perhaps they should be," Steve added.

"Yeah, you're right," the man agreed. "I think they ought to be out here. Perhaps you should tell them."

"Maybe. Anyway, we gotta be off," said Steve.

They said goodbye and made their way to the car.

Story 20 - Invasion
Part Two

Steve and Tricia arrived at their vehicle and pulled out along the track a little before stopping in a small layby. There they waited.

"What do you think, Gov? He seemed anxious to get the police out here."

Tricia had summed up the situation expertly as Steve expected. "I have no doubts," he said. "That guy is way too keen on involving the police for someone who initially didn't know what I meant."

"Yeah. He jumped in as soon as I brought it up. He's involved; I'm sure."

Half an hour later, the stranger drove past. Tricia opened her notebook and took down his licence number.

"Are we going to follow him?" she asked.

"No. It's getting late, and we've had a long day. Let's get back to the house."

"Robert and Shelly will wonder where we are," said Tricia. "I expect Tricky is getting hungry, too." She patted the little dog sitting on her lap.

"Yes. I hope they are at the house and haven't gone home," Steve said. "We need to chat about tomorrow."

Steve pulled in behind Robert's car. Tricky ran up to the front door as if he'd always lived there. Shelly opened the door, picked up Tricky and took him inside.

"We saw you approaching a man as we left," said Robert. "What was that all about?".

"An interesting development," said Steve. "Tricia said she saw him there when we arrived, so we found an excuse to chat with him. He was inexplicably keen to get the police involved in the UFO incident, so we took down his vehicle registration as he drove away."

Tricia opened her notebook.

"Can you phone this nuber through to check it out?" asked Steve.

"We're just about to leave," said Robert. "I'll check it when we get back." He made a note of the number.

"OK. Tomorrow, we'll spend some time checking other possible leads. But today, we've only been on the case a couple of hours, and we've made a good start. If we are as fruitful tomorrow, we'll soon have this thing sorted. Let's hope that number reveals some useful information."

Robert and Shelly left, and Tricia checked the fridge. Plenty of fresh food provided them with a good meal, and Tricky cleaned his bowl before retiring in his basket.

* * *

The following morning at nine, Steve walked to the local shop and picked up a newspaper. He sat reading it over a breakfast of bacon and fried eggs Tricia had prepared.

"The Constable exhibition is drawing quite a crowd," said Steve. "It's held in a hotel off the A12 just outside Woodbridge."

"Anything else going on?" Tricia inquired.

"Not a lot. Here, take a look." Steve handed the paper to Tricia."

When the two detectives turned up, Shelly had her dog with her, a springer spaniel. After Tricky greeted the springer, Steve asked, "Any luck with that number?"

"Yes, I've got a name here, Micky Tunstall, better known as Tunny. He lives in London's East End and has a criminal record for burglary. Did a two-year stint

379

in Belmarsh Prison a couple of years ago. Nothing else."

"Ah, Tunny Mike. Yeah, I've heard the name. I don't think he's a major player in the London criminal community," said Steve. "Any links?"

"No, sorry."

"I'll ring Dave at the Met. He might know something."

Tricia sat up suddenly. Steve recognised the expression of inspiration on her face, something for which Tricia was well known.

"What is it, Sergeant? Something on your mind?" asked Steve.

"I have an idea, sir. I don't know if we can get them, but if these criminals are hoping for a big police presence here, perhaps we should give them what they want."

"I don't follow."

"If we could get six or eight uniformed cops to patrol the forest, it might give them the idea we are all over it."

"That's a damned good idea," said Robert. "They don't even have to be real policemen either. They just need to give that impression."

"That's all very well," said Steve, "but how are you going to arrange it? I don't think your local force will produce so many. They have a large presence at the Constable exhibition."

"That's why I suggested they don't need to be real cops."

Tricia interrupted. "Do you have a local amateur dramatics group?"

"There is," said Shelly, joining the conversation. "There's one based here in Rendlesham, on the old airbase."

"If they have people and costumes," Tricia explained, "they could stand in as cops."

"I'll get in touch with the office," Robert volunteered. "Maybe they can set something up."

After a lengthy discussion and a few calls, a group of amateur actors agreed to patrol the forest wearing police uniforms.

Meanwhile, Steve's call to the Met office revealed a possible connection between Tunny and Fingers Finnigan, an Irish leader of a criminal syndicate. That was one Steve did know. Although cropping up in numerous investigations, nothing could ever tie Fingers in with the various robberies in the East End. With any luck, this might be the one.

"That was a good idea, bringing your dog along," said Tricia to Shelly. "It takes the suspicion off us."

The group drove to Rendlesham Forest, where they separated and began their dog-walking vigil, while making observations. There showed no sign of the man they spoke to the day before. It was early, though. Perhaps too early for criminals to be up and about. Although they spoke to many other dog-walkers and joggers, no-one looked suspicious. In pairs, Steve with Tricia and Tricky, and Robert with Shelly and her springer, patrolled up and down the long main path between the woodland. They took opposite directions, passing each other at the central point.

After about an hour, two police cars pulled up in the parking lot, and eight uniformed officers stepped out. They distributed themselves down the main path at regular intervals.

Later in the day, the man identified as Tunny appeared. Steve saw him take one of the branch paths where another man met him.

"Ah, now we're getting somewhere," Steve said to Tricia. "See that guy. That's Fingers Finnigan. Perhaps we'll finally get something on him."

"Bloody 'ell," said Tricia. "Talk about looking the part. I've never seen anyone looking more like a villain than him."

"Yes, a nasty-looking character, isn't he?"

Fingers had the look that many might call chiselled, angular with prominent features. The problem was, those features showed aggression, cunning, and malice.

Steve and Tricia continued walking. When they passed Robert and Shelly, Steve, with a nod and whisper, indicated the criminals so they could all keep an eye on them. Eventually, Tunny and Fingers went to their cars and drove off.

"Tricia," said Steve, "it looks like your plan has borne fruit. A brilliant idea."

"Let's hope so," said Tricia. "I guess we should head back now."

Steve agreed, and after speaking with Robert and Shelly, they ushered their dogs into the vehicles and drove back to the house. With immense good fortune, they noticed Tunny's car parked at another house in the same street. Two other vehicles stood in the drive.

After the four entered the house, Steve said, "I think this could be the day. We'll need to get to the Constable exhibition."

"Won't these mobsters have firearms, sir?" Tricia asked.

"No doubt about it, Sergeant. Are any of you trained with weapons?" Steve looked around at the other three officers.

"Yes, sir. I've got a certificate at home," said Tricia. "It'll be online, anyway."

"Me, too," Robert and Shelly confirmed.

"Right, Robert. Would you organise some handguns? There will be others at the exhibition with firearms, so no need to get too excited. This isn't going to be the Battle of the Bulge."

"I'd prefer the OK Corral, if it's all the same to you, sir."

"Yes, Tricia. I'm sure you would. You ladies will have firearms purely for protection, you understand."

"Excuse me, sir," said Tricia, "but do men have the same firearms training as women?"

"Of course. Why?"

"Just asking, sir. I was wondering what we have to do if we see your life is in jeopardy."

Steve smiled. " Alright, Sergeant. I get your drift. Just act responsibly."

"We will, sir. Just like the men."

Steve kept his mouth shut. If he prolonged this line of conversation, he knew he wouldn't emerge from it well.

Robert drove to the Martlesham HQ to collect the firearms, and Tricia sat near the window, keeping an eye on the vehicles at the neighbouring property. When Robert returned, Steve drove with him to the exhibition location. Before leaving, he gave instructions to Tricia and Shelly.

"The exhibition doors close at ten. These lowlifes won't make a move before then. Keep your eye on them, and ring me when they leave. Follow them at a good distance. You won't need to keep too close since you know where they are heading. OK. See you both later."

This was the most exciting operation Tricia had ever been on, and she could hardly control herself.

"I wish these buggers would set off soon," she said as she watched tirelessly for any movement at the house the villains occupied.

Finally, at eleven-fifteen, she saw some development. Three men emerged from the property and got into one of the cars parked in the drive. They moved off.

"We can't follow them," said Tricia. "The others, Tunny and Fingers haven't left. I'll ring Steve."

After reporting to Steve that one car had left, Tricia and Shelly waited. A few minutes later, Tunny, Fingers, and another man got into the second vehicle on the driveway and pulled away.

"Right. Let's go." Tricia checked both she and Shelly had their firearms, got into their car, and followed down the road. Tricia let the Tunny group get ahead with plenty of space between them. She had no need to keep close since she knew where they headed. Joining the main road and on some three miles to the junction, Tunny's car turned right. Then on to a mini roundabout, another right down to the level crossing, and a hard left-hand bend. The next would be a crossroads with traffic lights.

"Better not get too close," Shelly advised. "Just in case the lights turn red."

As Tricia drew close, the lights did show red, but when they changed, Tunny turned left.

"Where's he going?" said Tricia. "The A12 is straight on."

"Yeah, he's going down toward Woodbridge village centre."

Tricia followed.

Driving through the main high street, Tunny's crew made a left turn down a cul-de-sac. Tricia pulled onto the pavement and parked just before the turning. They both alighted from the car and quietly approached the corner. The first car had stopped in front of a building. The two detectives watched and waited.

"That's an odd name on the building where they're parked," Shelly observed. "The Carrot Patch. What does that mean?"

"The Carrot Patch? Is that what it says?" asked Tricia.

"Yeah. That's what it looks like."

"Bloody 'Ell." Tricia used her favourite expletive. "It's a bloody smokescreen."

"Whatcha talking about?"

"I read the local rag this morning. There was a quarter page advertisement by The Carrot Patch. An' it weren't advertising carrots either."

"No. What was it, then?"

"That place deals in rough diamonds. These villains want us ter believe they're after John Constable paintings. I'd better let Steve know."

Tricia connected to Steve at the exhibition venue.

"Sir, you've gotta come over here. These jerks won't turn up at the hotel."

"What are you talking about, Sergeant? Where are you?"

"We followed them, sir, and they turned off to Woodbridge centre. Both of their cars are parked up outside a dealer in rough diamonds. Hang on," said Tricia, the excitement rising in her voice. "Four of the criminals have left their vehicles and are breaking into the diamond place."

As she watched, one of them, Tunny, she thought, produced a standard crowbar and levered the door open. An alarm bell went off, but Tunny burst through, and it stopped almost instantly.

"What's going on?" Steve asked.

"They're inside, sir. You'd better get down here now. Bring backup with you."

Tricia gave directions and rang off. The two detectives waited.

As time progressed, Shelly looked at her watch. "What's keeping Steve and the others" she asked. "They should have been here by now."

"True," Tricia agreed. "If they don't arrive soon, these jerks will be off, and the whole operation will end up as a car chase. That's the last thing we need."

"What are we gonna do?"

"Look," said Tricia, "opposite that business is a railing set on the kerb. It's sturdy and concreted into the ground."

"Yeah. So?"

"We'll go down there, yank open the car doors, stick our firearms in their faces and tell the drivers to get out. Then we'll handcuff them to those railings." Tricia had a plan along with more guts than most. She hoped Shelly would comply.

"You sure about this?" said Shelly nervously.

"Yup. You take the nearest car, and I'll dash to the one in front. Make sure you're assertive and waste no time."

Shelly took in a deep breath. Tricia grabbed her arm.

"Right. Come on and be quick."

The two officers dashed to the vehicles, Shelly to the first, and Tricia sprinted past to the second car. Simultaneously, they swung open the driver's doors, their guns to the fore, connecting to the driver's heads.

"Get out," said Tricia, "and don't do anything stupid."

Her victim quickly grabbed for a gun lying on the passenger seat. Tricia clipped him fiercely on the ear with her weapon.

"I said, don't do anything stupid," she shouted. "but then you're a dickhead. You wouldn't be here if you weren't."

Grabbing him tightly by the arm, she yanked him out of the car, turned the engine off, and snatched the gun from the passenger seat. With the two firearms pointed at him, she forced him across the street to the railing. Shelly already had her man there. They put the cuffs on the drivers and looped them through the railings.

"Where the hell is backup," Tricia exploded, but as if on cue, a vehicle stopped at the head of the cul-de-sac. Steve and Robert got out, and looking down the street, saw the ladies with their prisoners. As they drew close, Tricia put a finger to her lips and pointed to the door the villains had entered.

Six more officers followed.

"Tricia," said Steve. "What the hell have you been up to? You should have waited for us."

"Yeah, right, sir. Could 'ave sat an' 'ad me supper, too, while we waited."

"Cheeky bitch, this one," said one of the accompanying officers. "Get's the job done, though." He nodded toward the drivers handcuffed to the railings.

"That's my girl," said Steve.

Steve organised the officers, eight in total, along the front of The Carrot Patch; four on each side of the main entrance. Shelly and Tricia stayed with the handcuffed drivers. One started shouting before Tricia wacked him on the the back of his hand. He quickly stopped. They had waited three to four minutes before the felons appeared at the doorway. Unprepared for the police presence, they walked straight out. The officers quickly came up behind them, and with their guns in contact with the criminals' necks, they handcuffed and arrested them.

* * *

The time approached three-thirty before Steve and Tricia arrived back at the house and turned in. Even with the evening excitement still churning in her mind, Tricia eventually dropped off to sleep. Little Tricky, unaware of the past events, snuggled up to her in the bed. At midday, Tricky licked Tricia awake, demanding her attention.

After putting the dog into the rear garden, Tricia made breakfast. Steve chatted over the previous evenings' events with her.

"Tricia, you did a great job last night. I'll ring the Met shortly and tell Dave how the operation went."

"Be sure to tell 'em what a great asset I was," Tricia said, but Steve knew she had only tapped into her irrepressible humourous character.

"Sure," he replied. "I'll tell them if it wasn't for you, the whole case would have collapsed."

"Don't think yer need ter go that far, sir. I don't want ter come across as Superwoman. Just tell 'em I was irreplaceable."

"I think you are, Tricia. I've never come across anyone before with no comic off-button."

"Damn," Tricia retorted. "Even when I'm serious, yer think I'm joking."

"Well, jokes aside, we need to get on the road."

After loading their bags and Tricky into the car, they drove off to the Martlesham Police HQ. With reports in order and Steve's call to the Met completed, they got on the motorway back to Ricton.

"Yer know what, sir. I think I'll organise a meal for everyone at me an' Susan's favourite restaurant to celebrate properly. It will be on me."

"Are you sure about that?" Steve frowned. "It will set you back a great deal paying for everyone."

"Well, sir. It might be my only chance."

"Only chance?"

"Yeah, before they invite me to the Met."

Steve laughed.

"I didn't tell yer, did I?" said Tricia.

"Tell me what?"

"My boyfriend is moving into Ricton next week."

"I didn't know you had a boyfriend. You've kept that quiet."

"Yeah. I didn't know myself until a couple minutes ago."

Steve just shook his head. Where is she going with this now, he thought?

"On second thoughts, I'd best not accept that job at the Met yet. Boyfriend won't be 'appy if, as soon as 'e moves in, I bugger off ter London."

"You are aware that the Met haven't offered you a position, I suppose. Or have you been having realistic dreams."

"Nah. Wouldn't be much point if I only got ter be Superintendent by dreaming. You don't 'ave ter worry though, sir. I'll put a good word in for yer. After all, it were you what got me into this job. I'll miss Susan, though. Perhaps you can move up ter London with her. I'll miss our nights out. I'll tell yer what, sir...

Steve let out a long audible sigh. This was going to be a very long journey home.

Story Twenty-One
The Final Solution

The restaurant Susan and Tricia frequented each week seemed exceptionally busy. The two ladies had eaten their meals were relaxing with a final cocktail before calling it a night.

Susan took a sip and reclined in her comfortable chair. "That was a surprise, the management giving us our night out on-the-house," she mused.

"Very unexpected," Tricia replied. "If I'd known earlier, I'd 'ave starved meself for the past two days."

"Huh, that's a joke. If you hadn't eaten for a week, I doubt you could have tucked more away tonight."

"Are you saying I eat too much?"

"Obviously not, with a figure like yours."

The manager's kindness was his way of showing appreciation to Tricia and Susan for their part in the Frenchman's arrest.

They finished their cocktails and prepared to leave. Tricia visited the lady's room. Upon returning, the manager approached her.

"Hello, Detective. I hope you had a good evening and received satisfactory service."

"We did, and thank you for your kindness," said Tricia.

"That's good because we are short-staffed tonight."

"You know, I only did my job. It was Susan who went beyond the call."

"Yes. She was very brave."

"Why are you short-staffed? Is someone off sick?" Tricia asked.

"Our Italian waiter is away this evening."

"I like him and noticed he wasn't around tonight. I hope it's nothing serious."

"He isn't sick. It's his wife who has a problem."

"Oh, I see."

The manager took Tricia to one side and put on a serious expression. He looked around to check no one could hear him.

"Detective," he started in confidence, "may I speak to you off the record."

"That sounds ominous," said Tricia. "When people say that, they usually want to speak about criminal activity, hoping I will overlook it."

"I'm not asking that. Well, not exactly."

"So, what is it?

"Roberto has been with me a long time, and I don't like to see him in difficulty."

"What's he been up to?" asked Tricia, not expecting a proper answer.

"It isn't him. It's his wife."

"Really? I didn't know that. Its a good thing I never chatted him up then."

The manager smiled.

"Has she just come over from Italy?" Tricia asked.

"No. She isn't Italian. She's English," the manager informed her. "Roberto's wife is suffering from extreme anxiety and is seeing a psychiatrist. Roberto told me she committed a horrendous crime in the past, and it's eating away at her."

"This sounds serious. But why are you telling me?" asked Tricia.

"Roberto needs to know what she did. He says he can't help her while he doesn't know."

"Ah, I see. So you think I might find out."

"It's a longshot because Roberto isn't even aware if the authorities know about it. So, there might not be a record."

Tricia thought about it. "If it isn't on record, I won't find anything, will I? What's her name? I mean her maiden name."

"It's Marion Williamson," said the manager. "I appreciate your discretion, Detective. If you come up with something, I'll give you another night on the house."

"Blimey," Tricia exclaimed. "Better not try too hard then. I don't want to bugger up my figure with all this good free food."

The manager laughed. He was familiar with Tricia's sense of humour since she, along with Susan, kept his customers entertained every week.

"Thanks, Detective," he said as Tricia walked off to catch up with Susan.

"I saw you chatting with the manager. What did he want?" asked Susan.

"Oh, just thanking us for getting to grips with his French waiter. The last thing he wants working for him is criminals."

* * *

The following morning, Tricia entered Marion Williamson's name into her computer and checked every criminal programme. Many Williamsons and Marions popped up but no Marion Williamson.

"Hmm," she sighed. "It don't seem like we've arrested her for any crimes. Maybe she got away with something, and it's come back to bite her in the arse."

Tricia spent fifteen minutes more searching the various angles and double-checking others but found nothing. She phoned the restaurant manager.

"Good morning, Detective. Did you find anything?"

"Sorry to say, I found nothing. As far as I can tell, Marion has never been in trouble with the law," Tricia said. "But that's a good thing, isn't it?"

"I don't know. I know Roberto is so worried about his wife, he keeps taking time off work. She says she's done something terrible and needs psychiatric help to keep her settled. Anyway, Detective, thanks for your help. I'll pass it on to Roberto."

Tricia rang off. Why she wondered, would Marion be in such a state if she had done nothing? With real crimes to solve, she dismissed the non-problem from her mind. Later that day, while checking on something at the local registry office, a thought popped into her mind. What if Marion Williamson had changed her name? It was a longshot but worth checking while she was at the registry.

Tricia asked for details of people who had changed their names. The official directed her to the appropriate section. He left her to it. Unaccustomed to the procedures, Tricia spent longer than she would have liked on this potential waste of time. Eventually, she found the list of those who had become Williamsons after the name change. Luckily, there were only a few, and even better, only one Marion.

Marion's former name showed up as Mary Whittingshaw. So, she kept the same initials. Tricia wrote the name in her notebook and returned to the station. She did nothing with it that day due to other work commitments.

The first thing the next morning, Tricia entered Mary Whittingshaw into the criminal records programme. Nothing. Oh, well, she had done as much as possible with it; time to let it go. She crossed to the coffee machine to make herself a drink.

"Want a cup, Johnny?" she asked as she passed his chair. "It might wake you up so you can go out on your rounds."

"Don't worry, I'm wide awake," Johnny responded. "Enough to know you're wasting your time checking people we're no longer investigating."

"Whatcha talking about, Johnny?"

"That one on your computer. We gave up on her a few years ago. Feeling guilty 'cause you couldn't arrest her?"

"Johnny, what on earth are you going on about?"

"Whittingshaw. The one that got away."

Suddenly, it hit her like a thunderbolt. She knew she'd seen the name somewhere before but had dismissed it. Now it came back to her.

"Bloody hell, Johnny, I thought the name rang a bell. Must be getting forgetful in me old age."

"I don't see how you could forget that one," said Johnny, probably feeling important that he had got one over on the incredibly efficient Tricia.

"Johnny, I must be getting senile. I know the name but still can't place it."

"Well, it was a long time ago. Your first case connected to Ricton."

"My God, yes. Jake Whittingshaw. The eight-year-old boy that was killed with a longbow arrow. How could I ever forget that?"

"That's right. And the boy's mother is Mary Whittingshaw, the number one suspect for all five of the revenge murders."

"Yeah. That's right."

"Come on, Tricia. I know you're having me on." Johnny suddenly realised he wasn't as important as he thought. "Why else would you have that name on your computer?"

"Good question, Johnny. Excuse me; I've got to see the boss."

Tricia hurried to Steve's office, but he wasn't there.

"Do you know where Inspector Kendall is, Mike?" she asked.

"They're keeping him at the Met 'til tomorrow. Need him on some investigation."

"Bugger," Tricia exclaimed. "OK, thanks."

Tricia rang the restaurant manager.

"Hello, Detective," he answered.

"Hi. What's your name? I can't keep calling you sir or manager. I'm Tricia."

"Oh, hello, Tricia. I'm Jason. Jason Fuller. Do you have some information?"

"Are you free for me to come to see you, Jason?"

"What, now?"

"If that's alright."

"Yes, sure. I'm going nowhere."

Tricia shot out the door and leaped into her car. Why, she wondered, did Roberto need to take time off work? Just how bad was his wife, Marion? And why did he involve his employer, Jason Fuller? These thoughts floated through her mind along with another point. Even if Marion proved to be Jake Whittingshaw's mother, no absolute evidence determined she was the longbow murderer.

Within a few minutes, Tricia arrived at the restaurant. It was outside of business hours, so Jason let her in.

"Hello, Tricia."

"I need to clarify one or two things, and I'm hoping you might help me."

"Sure, if I can."

"Reet, I'd fust li' ta kna if Marion speyts li' dis," said Tricia in her broadest Yorkshire dialect.

Jason laughed. "If you are asking if she has a Yorkshire accent, the answer is yes. But I can tell you; it's not as Yorkshire as that. Just enough to detect she comes from the North."

"Thanks, Jason. That is my most important question. I thought as much."

"I don't understand. How did you guess she's a Northerner?"

"I can't tell you that at the moment." Tricia paused a second before asking, "Do you know if she changed her name; if it wasn't always Marion Williamson?"

"No," Jason replied. "Why do you ask? Has she?"

"Can't tell you that either. Does she have any unusual hobbies or interests?"

"None I'm aware of. Even if I did, you wouldn't tell me why you're asking," said Jason, in recognition of the one-sided nature of the questions.

"Huh. That one, in particular, is a definite no-no," said Tricia. "Now, can you tell me how long Roberto has known Marion?"

Jason breathed a deep sigh. "No, Tricia. I can't."

"You can't, or you won't?"

"You see. One can play this game two ways," said a frustrated Jason. "But no, I have no idea. Is that it?"

"Just one other thing, Jason. That extra free meal. I don't think that's going to happen, even if I do solve the matter of Marion's problem."

Tricia left Jason scratching his head in confusion as to what the conversation had meant.

On the other hand, Tricia found satisfaction in the knowledge that her suspicions were right.

* * *

Later that afternoon at the station, Johnny walked in from his village patrol duties. The phone rang, and he picked it up. "Hello, Ricton police station. – Oh, just a minute." He placed his hand over the mouthpiece. "Tricia, it's your boyfriend," he joked.

"Whatcha fekking talking about? I don't have a boyfriend."

"Thought perhaps you might have. You're always going on about the handsome Italian at the restaurant. This guy sounds Italian."

"Ah, Roberto," said Tricia. "I didn't expect him to ring me."

Johnny handed the phone to Tricia, "So he is your boyfriend."

"No, you dope," Tricia said. "Hello, Detective Constable Mason speaking."

"El-o, Detective. Tis eez-a Roberto from de restaurant-a. I tink you ave information 'bout my wife. Marion."

"No, Roberto. Why do you think that?"

"De managoi tinks you ave found somting."

"Roberto, you must know we cannot talk about police business with the public," Tricia said.

"I tink you ave somting-a you no say," Roberto replied.

How should Tricia handle this? If her suspicions were correct, then Roberto and his wife would be getting a visit very soon. She must handle this both with care and sensitivity.

"Roberto, we might have something we need to speak to your wife about, but we can only discuss it with her, not you. Do you understand?"

"Boot she eez-a my wife." Roberto had a point.

"Yes, that's correct. I'll tell you one thing that should take you out of the picture. The matter we might discuss relates to a time before Marion was your wife. In that respect, we cannot speak to you about it." Tricia hoped that would deter Roberto from asking further questions.

It was sufficient. "I see," said Roberto and put down the phone.

"Damn, Steve chooses the most awkward times to be away," thought Tricia. At least he would be back tomorrow.

* * *

The following day, Tricia desperately tried to conceal her excitement. Steve came in a little late, having arrived home after midnight. Tricia gave him ten minutes to settle in but would have exploded if she waited any longer.

"Good morning, sir," she gave him her belated greeting. "Was your trip to the Met interesting?"

"Hello, Tricia. Interesting? Yes, I'd say that would describe it accurately," Steve responded.

Blimey, Tricia thought. Better steer him off that subject.

"That's good, sir. Bet it don't come anywhere near mine, though."

Masterful.

"Really? What have you been doing? Don't tell me. You've been crime quizzing again with Susan."

"That would be good. I'd enjoy that. But no, it's much more interesting than that."

399

"Well, are you going to tell me or keep me guessing?"

Good. She'd got him hooked.

"Sir, even if you took all week, you'd never guess this one."

"Bloody hell, Tricia. Spit it out. I know you're dying to tell me something. One thing is certain; I'm not going on a fishing trip. So, what is it?"

"I might have a lead on the Longbow Murder case." Tricia was a little disappointed Steve didn't fall off his chair.

"This better be good," said Steve drily. "I don't fancy another wild goose chase. It took me a few hundred miles the first time around."

"It won't even take you three miles this time, sir. This is local."

"What is?"

"The probable suspect. She lives here in Ricton."

Steve furrowed his brow andlooked at Tricia, his eyes squinting. "Now that's the most unlikely statement I've heard in a long while. Your detective skills, or detectiving as you call it, are good, but not that good."

"Sir, it's true. Whether she done it or not, I don't know, but she is definitely here."

"Go on."

"If you remember, her name is Mary Whittingshaw, the mother of the kid, Jake. She changed her name to Marion Williamson and married Roberto, the waiter." Tricia looked triumphant.

"And you have proof of this?" asked Steve with some scepticism.

"Yes, sir. It's on record at the local registry office. I checked. It's almost definitely her. I've not met her yet, but I understand she speaks with a northern accent. That can't be a coincidence."

"Anything else?"

"Yes, sir. I understand she is receiving psychiatric help due to a crime she committed that's driving her crazy."

Steve seemed hooked and showed more interest.

"OK, Tricia. You've uncovered all this yet, you haven't yet met with her. "Why not?"

"Sir, it's your case. I didn't want to go further with it without you involved."

"That's very considerate of you, Detective. I think you had better fill me in with all the details."

Tricia and Steve spent the next hour together while she laid out everything that had transpired. They put Mike and Johnny in the picture. Both were amazed that Tricia had come up with goods yet again. Then Tricia and Steve left to visit Marion Williamson.

The two detectives pulled up outside Roberto's house and parked their vehicles. Tricia knocked on the door. Roberto answered.

"El-lo. I did no expec to see you 'ere."

"We are here to speak with your wife, Marion," Tricia replied. "May we come inside?"

Roberto ushered them into the lounge where his wife sat on a settee. The two introduced themselves, and Tricia began the conversation.

"I was at the Registry Office a couple of days ago, Marion, and discovered you had changed your name."

Roberto looked surprised; it was obvious he knew nothing of this. Marion said nothing.

"I wondered why you did that," Tricia continued. "There is nothing wrong with your previous name, Mary Whittingshaw."

"I didn't need the constant reminder," Marion explained.

"Reminder of what?"

"I'm sure you know archers killed my son, Jake."

"Yes, Marion, we do."

"Jake's father was into archery. Since I'd taken his name, it reminded me of Jake's death."

"I see," said Tricia. "I understand how that might cause you some stress."

"Tell me, Marion, why did you move here to Ricton?" Steve jumped in. "You must know that one of the men involved in your son's death met his end here –murdered."

Marrion remained quiet for a moment before saying, "Yes. That is why I came here."

"That sounds odd," Tricia interrupted. "I mean, for someone who didn't want reminding about her son's death."

"Yes. Please explain that," Steve said. "I'd have thought this was the last place you'd want to visit."

"I don't know. It seemed right at the time. You know – confront it."

Steve grunted. "Hmm. Were you here when the second culprit in Ricton died?"

"You mean the one who murdered my son?" said Marion, anger rising in her voice. When her bristling manner subsided, she started shaking and crying. Roberto brought her some medicine.

"You moost no oopset er-a. She eez-a aving medicine for er stress-a."

"I understand," said Steve, "but we have to ask these questions." He directed his following words to Marion. "Have you ever used a longbow, Marion?"

That question seemed to send Marion into a fit. Roberto gave her more medicine, and she gradually calmed down.

"I tink you should go now-a. She eez-a voiy sick-a." Roberto put his arm around Marion and held her tightly.

"Alright," Steve agreed, "but we will probably need to see her again." He made his way to the door. Tricia and Roberto followed.

While Steve walked to his car, Tricia lingered with Roberto in the large brick-paved vehicle area in the front garden. There were no vehicles parked there, and the garage door remained shut.

"How do you get to work, Roberto?" asked Tricia. "Do you have a car?"

"No, I do no drive. I ave leeft with neighbour."

"Does your wife drive?"

"Yes-a, boot er car no ave repair-a. It eez-a in de garage."

An improbable thought popped into Tricia's head, an outside chance vaguely worth investigating. "May I see it?" she asked.

Roberto looked puzzled by Tricia's interest but took a keyring from his pocket and unlocked the garage door. Taking hold of the handle at the bottom, he swung the door up and open. Inside stood a red hatch-back covered in dust. The front bonnet was a caved-in mess and displayed wide scratch marks, the paint removed from the distressed surface. The bare scratches extended from above the bumper back to the windscreen area. The badge in front of the radiator indicated it was a Peugeot.

Recovering from her astonishment, Tricia looked over at Steve, who stood next to his car in the street. She called out to him.

"Sir, there's a vehicle here you might want to look at."

The End

Other work by Chris Randall

Incognito
Mist of Time – Trilogy
Stephen Kendall Mysteries
Growing Up With Stitch
Growing Up |With Stitch - Screenplay
The Dilmun Contract
The New Beginning
The Truth Will Set You Free
The Case for Uncommon Sense
Twenty-Twenty Vision